THE
OBSIDIAN
MIRROR

K.D. KEENAN

DIVERSIONBOOKS

ALSO BY K.D. KEENAN

Fire in the Ocean

Diversion Books
A Division of Diversion Publishing Corp.
443 Park Avenue South, Suite 1008
New York, New York 10016
www.DiversionBooks.com

For more information, email info@diversionbooks.com

Second Diversion Books edition February 2018.
Paperback ISBN: 978-1-63576-263-1
eBook ISBN: 978-1-62681-813-2

LSIDB/1801

Dedicated to my husband, Tom,
who has always believed in my dreams
(even when I didn't).

I am deeply grateful to the people who took the time to read and comment on my manuscript: Cynthia Bournellis, Linda Duyanovich, Kerry Gil, Tom Keenan, HiC Luttmers, Susan Monroe, Abbe Seitzman, Pamela Sundell, and Steve Farnsworth. I would also like to gratefully acknowledge Gail Z. Martin, a wonderful fantasy writer whose advice was invaluable in helping me to craft this story, and Randy Peyser, of Author OneStop, for her assistance in finding a great editor.

CHAPTER 1

With a sigh, Sierra set down a cardboard box filled with a meager collection of personal belongings and fumbled in her purse for a house key. A movement in the bright evening sky caught her eye as something floated gently down toward her, twisting and turning in the faint currents of air. She watched it as it danced on the wind, flashing color as it spun. It was a brilliant blue-green feather, perhaps six or eight inches long—but a feather from what kind of bird? Surely there were no large birds in Northern California with plumage that bright.

She gazed at it, momentarily distracted from her gloomy thoughts. Then she tossed her black braid over her shoulder and opened the lock. She stooped to pick up the open box. As she straightened, the feather spun and came to rest on the contents of the box, nestling comfortably between a coffee mug and a name plate that read "Sierra Carter, Public Relations Manager." *Well*, she thought bitterly, *I won't be needing* that *anymore*. As the feather settled, seeming to sparkle slightly in the evening light, Sierra heard a single chime, like a crystal bell. She looked around, but certainly no one was out on the street ringing bells. She looked down again at the feather. Despite her miserable mood, she was drawn to it. *It really is beautiful,* Sierra thought. *Maybe it's from an escaped parrot or something.*

She shouldered the door open and walked down the short hall to her kitchen, setting the box on her kitchen table. She sighed heavily and poured herself a glass of wine, its fragrance redolent of wild berries. She tilted her wine glass to her lips but before she could take a sip, her phone rang. She heaved another sigh and answered it. It was Kaylee, who worked at Black Diamond Semiconductor Corporation as a marketing manager.

"What's going on?" Kaylee asked. "I saw you walking out to your car with Clancy Forrester." Kaylee's voice was always warm, as rich and dark as chocolate mousse, but now she also sounded a bit mischievous. "Something going on there that I should know about?"

Squelching an impulse to sigh again, Sierra replied, "Yep. I was with Clancy all right. He was perp-walking me out of the building. I got laid off. Fired. Whatever."

There was a stunned silence at the other end of the phone.

"Laid *off? Fired?* Is this a joke?"

Sierra emitted what she hoped was a bitter laugh.

"No joke. Mark called me in today and said there was a ten-percent layoff across the board. I just happened to be ten percent of Marketing, I guess."

Another silence greeted this statement.

Kaylee said carefully, "I haven't heard of anyone else being let go. That doesn't sound right."

"He said it was a layoff. And they're giving me a severance package," Sierra said. "It's actually a really nice package. Mark specifically said it wasn't a performance issue and it wasn't personal." Her voice held the slight upward swing of a question.

Kaylee was quiet for another moment.

"You know, I did hear something, but I didn't think too much about it at the time. I wonder if it's connected somehow."

"What?" Sierra asked impatiently. "What did you hear?"

"About BDSC hiring an outside agency. Is that something you knew about? I assumed you did, being in PR. I didn't pay too much attention at the time."

"Agency? You mean, a public relations agency?" Sierra asked incredulously.

"Uh-huh."

Sierra went on, "I haven't heard a word about it. Why would

they hire an outside agency? It'll cost them a ton of money—way more than they were paying me. That just doesn't make sense!"

Kaylee's voice was a verbal shrug. "Sorry, doll. That's what I heard."

"You don't happen to remember the name of the agency, do you?"

"Nope. I can find out, though."

Sierra slumped into one of the chairs surrounding her small kitchen table. She closed her brown eyes, feeling almost too weary to care.

"Yeah. I don't suppose it matters, but I'd like to find out," she said. "I worked for an agency before I came to BDSC, you know. I know most of the agencies that handle high tech."

"You've mentioned that before. Called Rapper, or something? I gathered you didn't like it much."

"It was called Clapper & Associates. And yeah, you're right I didn't like it. Long story. But I liked my job at BDSC. Oh well—easy come, easy go."

"I'll miss you girl," said Kaylee. "We'll need to get together more, now that we won't be seeing each other every day."

"I'll miss you too," Sierra said, feeling a bit awkward. "We can still stay in touch."

But she didn't quite believe it. In Sierra's experience, people in Silicon Valley were too busy to make friends outside of work. She knew people with spouses and children, but because they were always working, she wondered how much family life they could possibly be enjoying.

"So, have you thought about what you're going to do now?"

"Erm, no. Not really. I'm still in a state of shock over the whole thing. Find another job, I suppose."

"Well, I'll give you a great reference," Kaylee said. "I thought you did a wonderful job on the XLP-1099 launch. And I enjoy working with you, too. You're a great team player."

"Thank you," said Sierra gratefully. "You have no idea how much that means to me right now."

"Do you want company? I could bring a bottle of wine and…"

"No. Thanks, Kaylee, I really appreciate it, but I'd be lousy company right now. I'll be better in the morning, but right now I'm just kind of beat."

"I'll call you tomorrow, then. In the meantime, I'll nose around here and see if I can find anything out."

Kaylee hesitated for a second and then asked, "So, what about Clancy? I thought maybe…"

"No, Kaylee. Nothing happened. He said he was sorry to see me go and was really polite and carried my box of personal stuff to the car. Do you really think he's interested in dating someone who was just fired?"

"Laid off. That's different."

"No, it's not. Anyway, I'm getting a headache. I'll see you tomorrow, okay?"

"Okay, doll. Take care." And then Sierra was alone with her worries.

Sierra slumped at the kitchen table and looked around her. The tidy kitchen with its granite counters and cobalt blue accents, usually a source of quiet pleasure, only reminded her that she needed to find another source of income to be able to pay the mortgage. The severance package from BDSC would last for perhaps four months, but only if she were careful. She sat quietly in the darkening room. Her mind, like a stubborn moth against a windowpane, repeatedly battered itself against the question of "Why?" Surely there had to be employees at BDSC who were less valuable and less productive than Sierra Carter. And how had they hired a PR agency without her hearing even a whisper? Nervously, she flexed her long-fingered hands, pale from winter and working indoors, but still a light caramel. In the summertime, her hikes and rambles in the hills baked her skin to coffee with merely a dash of cream.

Maybe it really *was* something personal. She had always wondered where she stood with Jenna Simmons, BDSC's president and CEO. Sierra had been careful to get as much personal publicity for

Jenna as she possibly could, knowing the woman's appetite for the limelight. Sierra had been responsible for getting some of Jenna's coverage in the newspapers and on television. Jenna's ubiquitous presence on the Internet was largely due to Jenna herself; she was a relentless social media user, and she never allowed her staff to "front" for her online presence.

Jenna displayed a beautiful grin and sparkling charm in front of a reporter and a camera. Her Snow White looks—creamy skin, ebony hair cut in a sleek bob and sweet, rosebud mouth—belied her enigmatic personality when the world wasn't watching. As outgoing and personable as Jenna seemed to the world, her eyes were always cold. They were odd eyes; most people with blue eyes had depth to them, with rings of darker color and tiny lines radiating out from the pupil like miniature sun flares. Jenna's irises were a flat, cornflower blue, like the painted eyes of an antique doll. They conveyed no emotion, and Sierra—who was good at reading people—found Jenna impenetrable. Sierra had never known if Jenna was pleased with her performance or not—but as no one else seemed to know what Jenna was thinking, she had refused to fret about it.

Maybe this was all Jenna's idea, Sierra thought. Jenna took advantage of this layoff to get rid of me. Personally. Does that even make sense?

Eventually, her mind wandered and Sierra found herself thinking about dinner. Her stomach rumbled, and she regretted not stopping for take-out on the way home. Foraging in the refrigerator, she found leftovers that weren't discernibly moldy, heated the food in her microwave, and ate without tasting a thing.

After dinner, she sat down again at the kitchen table, enveloped in gloom. The blue-green feather, still perched atop the box, caught her eye. Eagerly grasping at something unconnected with BDSC, being fired, or finding another job, Sierra plucked it from the cardboard box and began rolling the shaft between her fingers, idly wondering what kind of bird had shed such a beautiful feather, and speculating on why it seemed to sparkle as it caught the light. *It looks as though it were frosted with silver dust,* she thought.

She located a magnifying glass in her odds and ends drawer and looked closely at the fine barbs. Even under magnification, she couldn't see what made it sparkle. She really didn't know what to do with it, but it was too pretty to throw away. Finally, she took it upstairs to her bedroom and tucked the feather into a carved wooden box where she kept an assortment of random things she liked—colored rocks, a green glass frog, a ruby crystal drop from a chandelier that she had found in an junk shop.

Then she went to her garage workshop. The garage was full of storage boxes, tools and equipment, leaving no room for the car, which took its chances on the driveway outside. Sierra's secret passion and ambition was to design and make jewelry for a living. As it was, she sold enough at art fairs and the occasional gallery to pay for tools and materials, but it was her public relations work that paid the mortgage. She had never mentioned this particular ambition to anyone at BDSC (except to Kaylee, of course). Anything less than the appearance of complete devotion to BDSC and all its works was decidedly career-limiting. *At least I'm doing something about my dream,* she often told herself. *It's not just wishful thinking.*

Overnight, a colony of wispy little spiders had constructed a web between her workbench and a bookcase where she kept her design journals and reference books. Sierra shooed the spiders away from the web and ruthlessly destroyed it with a rag. She was sure the spiders were glaring at her from the sidelines as she destroyed their handiwork, but she told them firmly that they were lucky she didn't squoosh them as well. She tried to avoid killing them, although she drew the line when it came to black widows in her house. Even the most dedicated arachnophile would kill a poisonous spider lurking in one's lace unmentionables or the pantry.

Sierra pulled out a package of silver clay and opened it. Inside was a small gray lump that looked exactly like something dropped from a potter's wheel. Sierra knew that when it was shaped and fired in her kiln, the gray clay would be transformed into pure, shining silver. It was easy and fun to work with, but she used it in her designs sparingly, as it was expensive. She rolled out a flat sheet of the clay. When she had a smooth, even surface, she pressed a small leaf firmly into the clay. Removing the leaf, she examined the impression critically. It was a clear, crisply textured copy of the original.

Humming to herself, she carefully removed the excess clay. She smoothed tiny flaws from its surface with a rubber tool and put the leaf aside to dry. She planned to fire the leaf in her kiln and set it with garnets to look like berries. It would make an attractive pendant.

Sierra abruptly realized she had not thought about being fired once during the past hour or so. In fact, she was feeling distinctly better, for no good reason. It was getting close to her usual bedtime, but she certainly didn't have to get up early, and she wasn't tired anymore. She cleaned up her workshop and returned to the kitchen. Feeling somewhat at loose ends, she poured a glass of wine and went to the living room to watch television.

"…against recycling, Mr. Fanshaw?" a sleekly groomed man was asking, peering earnestly into the camera and not at his interview subject. The scene shifted to a round-faced man with a disgruntled expression. With his pursed little lips and frowning brow, Sierra thought he looked like a giant baby about to throw a tantrum. A tag at the bottom of the screen read "Charles G. Fanshaw, Citizens Against Recycling."

"It's an outrage!" the round-faced man whined in an aggrieved tone. "I'm not going to separate my glass from my plastic and my paper from my metal. I'm not a garbage man! The whole idea is an imposition on a free people!"

The camera shifted back to the reporter.

"But what about the landfill problem, Mr. Fanshaw? Or the masses of waste twice the size of the Continental United States floating in the middle of the Pacific Ocean?"

Fanshaw sneered.

"Have you ever *seen* this mass of waste in the Pacific Ocean?" He didn't wait for an answer.

"Of course you haven't. You haven't ever seen a unicorn or Santa Claus, either! Urban myth, that's what it is…"

Sierra switched channels, shaking her head. She found another news program and sat back to watch, but this story was about the building of new nuclear power plants. Realizing that watching the news was just upping her anxiety level, she switched it off and went upstairs to bed. Lying awake in the dark, she tried not to think about getting fired. She tried not to think about looking for a new job. She tried not to think about continents of floating plastic, or about nuclear waste. She tried not to wonder why so many people didn't seem to see what was happening right in front of their eyes, as the wild places of the Earth vanished. She was not entirely successful, but eventually sleep claimed her.

Sierra dreamed about her mother, who had died eight years previously. They were walking together on the beach, and she could smell the salt spray and hear the roar of the waves. Instead of shells and dried-up kelp bladders strewn on the sand, there were treasures—carved stone boxes, mirrors set with jewels, swords with runes etched on their blades. Her mother said, "He sent you an invitation. Did you get it?"

"Invitation?" Sierra was puzzled. "No, I don't think so. Who sent me an invitation?"

"You must respond to the invitation," her mother said, patting her on the shoulder as she used to do and kissing Sierra's cheek. "It's the polite thing to do."

"What invitation?" Sierra asked, confused. "Who…?"

But her mother had vanished. Sierra looked down at a green and blue feather in her hand and began to cry. But then she was typing at her computer in her cubicle at BDSC, and she received an email. The email said, "*Everything is not what it seems. Or nothing is what it seems. Take your pick.*"

When she woke up, all Sierra remembered was the dream of walking with her mother on the beach, something they had done many times together, and she felt sad. Missing her mother made her think about her father, who lived nearly five hundred miles away in Los Angeles. She thought she should call him soon. They didn't see each other as often as she would like. Yes, she must call him soon—but not to tell him she had been fired. She knew it would only cause him anxiety, and there was nothing he could do.

Sierra washed her face and went through the rest of her morning ritual, which had the benefit of bringing her to full awareness, as she was not a morning person. She went downstairs and stuck bread into the toaster. She shuffled to the front door in her slippers to fetch the newspaper. Opening the door, she was startled to find herself confronting a man who had just raised his hand to knock at her door. This left him with his fist raised at about Sierra-nose-level, and she ducked instinctively. This maneuver brought her face to face with an extremely furry face with a long nose and bright, yellow-amber eyes. Sierra jumped back and moved the door defensively between her and the invaders.

"Oh, sorry, Ma'am," said the man on her doorstep. "Are you Sierra Carter?"

Sierra nodded, noting that he had called her "Ma'am" and not "Miss." Men had shifted to calling her "Ma'am" a few years ago, and it never failed to annoy her. He was wearing Silicon Valley's standard bright-young-engineer-going-to-work uniform: jeans, running shoes and polo shirt emblazoned with the graphics from his company's latest product introduction. What made him distinctive was the fact that he was standing on her normally man-free doorstep, and that he had a largish coyote at the end of a stout rope.

"I found your dog a couple of blocks away and thought I'd better bring him back to you."

"I don't have a dog," Sierra said ungraciously. "And anyway, that's a coyote. I'm surprised he hasn't bitten your fingers off." Amazingly, the coyote was sitting quite peacefully by the man's side. It looked at her with bright eyes and wagged its tail. The wag looked a bit stiff, as though it had been practicing in a mirror.

"Arf," said the coyote. It didn't bark. It said, "Arf." The man didn't seem to notice this oddity.

"Look, lady, I don't know what your deal is, but it has a tag with your name on it," the man said. As he bent to pull the tag forward, Sierra saw that the coyote—*was* it a dog?—wore a beaded collar, woven with geometric patterns of red, black, yellow and blue that reminded her of Southwestern Indian work. She cautiously bent to inspect the engraving on the silver tag:

"Chaco"
Sierra Carter
111 E. Belinda St., Sunnyvale, CA
408-555-7171

Stunned, she didn't resist as the man thrust the rope into her hand.

"OK, I gotta go to work now. You shouldn't let your dog run loose like that. You're welcome," he added bitterly. He turned and strode away.

Sierra looked at the animal, which stared back with interest. It was a coyote, no doubt about it—she had seen many of them when she went hiking in the hills. It was the size of a Border Collie, but with a wild, sharp, un-doggie face. Its fur was thick, buff and gray with long, dark guard hairs and a slight ruff around the neck. It was slender, with pricked ears and those amazing bright amber eyes, so different from the warm brown eyes of most dogs.

The coyote stood up and walked calmly through Sierra's open front door. Sierra followed it and shut the door behind her. Part of her mind was screaming that she had just allowed a large and probably dangerous animal into her house, while another part was explaining in a reasonable tone of voice that the coyote was clearly not vicious, it had a collar on—a very nice collar—and seemed well behaved.

Upon which, her brain screamed, "Why does it have a tag with my name on it?"

No reasonable answer immediately occurred to her, so Sierra walked into the kitchen and rummaged in a cupboard to find a suitable water bowl, reasoning that if the coyote had been running around Sunnyvale, it was probably looking for food or water. The coyote followed close behind, which did not relieve her misgivings. As she looked for a bowl, it sat on its furry haunches and watched her attentively. She found a heavy stainless steel mixing bowl, filled it with water and set it on the floor, near the sliding door that led into her back yard. She stepped back and eyed the animal. The coyote rose and walked over to the bowl, claws clicking on her tiled floor. It bent to lap up the water once or twice, then lifted its head and stared at her again, drops of water falling from its muzzle.

Maybe it was a dog. It didn't look like a dog, but it was acting like one. Perhaps it was some kind of exotic new breed. People in Silicon Valley went in for that kind of thing, she knew, having seen her share of briards, Bedlington terriers and catahoolie hounds in the area. Sierra went to her home office and sat in front of her computer. The coyote followed her, pacing calmly behind.

"Let's see what Google can find on coyotes," she said aloud to the animal. She wished it would stop staring at her with those strange eyes, eyes that followed her every move.

Several minutes into her search, she hadn't learned anything new about coyotes. The photographs confirmed that the beast sitting next to her was, beyond any shadow of doubt, a coyote. She did find a site dedicated to coyotes with an interesting question from one of the site's visitors:

"My sister was driving near her home in Utah, and she found what she thought was a dog that had been hit by a car. She put it in the back seat and took it to a vet. The vet said it was a coyote, not a dog, but he fixed it up and she took it home. It seems very gentle and friendly, but I'm worried. Is it dangerous to keep a coyote as a pet?"

The answer was worrisome:

"It is not only dangerous, but illegal to keep a wild animal as a pet. Your sister should not have taken the coyote home. Coyotes are wild animals, and they are not safe to keep as pets. I strongly advise your sister to contact the local animal rescue people and have them relocate the coyote away from human habitation.

Coyotes who become used to humans are the most dangerous, as they lose their natural fear of humans, and are likely to attack if they are threatened or think the person has food."

Sierra did not share this observation with the coyote. It sat there, panting gently, eyes never straying from her. She pushed her chair back from the desk, and the animal leaped to its feet, giving her an adrenaline rush. Sweat broke out on her forehead.

Aloud, she said, "What on earth am I going to do with you?"

"Well," said the coyote, displaying rows of white teeth that seemed sharper than they should be. "You could start by giving me breakfast."

CHAPTER 2

Sierra opened her eyes. She was confused. Surely, she shouldn't be staring at the ceiling? She was looking up at the ceiling without bending her neck backwards, so that meant...she was lying down. With her head in someone's warm lap. A person's face swam into her field of vision, upside down and out of focus, and she pulled her head hastily out of the lap and scrambled to her knees.

The lap belonged to a slender yet well-muscled young man who looked as though he might be Latino, with ruddy brown skin and black hair falling into his face. He wore a bright, beaded necklace. His mouth seemed too wide for his rather long face, and his full lips turned up at the corners, making him look as though he were smiling when he was not. Although his features were all slightly odd, like a character sketch where the artist exaggerates for effect, they melded together into an offbeat beauty. He did not have the dark eyes of a Latino, though; his eyes were a bright, feral amber.

He looked at Sierra with concern, frowning slightly. "Are you all right?" he asked. "How do you feel?"

Sierra stared at him, feeling as though she had wandered into some alternate universe. Apparently, she had fainted—a first for her. And just before she had fainted, what had she been doing? Oh, yes. She had been talking to a coyote...

Sierra scrambled hastily to her feet. She stared at the young man kneeling on the floor. He unfolded his long legs and rose to his feet with an effortless grace that would have taken her breath away under more normal circumstances. The events of the morning came rushing back, rudely dispelling the fog of confusion, and her heart raced.

"What the hell are you doing in my house?" she demanded, trying to sound menacing, though she could feel the sweat of fear beading on her upper lip.

"I'm sorry I scared you," he said. And he really did look sorry.

A sense of suffocating panic seized her and she had trouble thinking. Only one explanation for what was happening occurred to her; she had cracked from the strain of losing her job. She was crazy. A crazy woman who heard animals talk. She glanced around for the coyote, but there was no sign of it. With an effort, she took three deep breaths and calmed the pounding of her heart.

"What are you doing here? In my house? Who are you?" she asked. She was proud of her ability to craft such a complex question, given that she was now a raving lunatic.

He wrinkled his brow.

"I'm Chaco," he said simply, and gave her a charming smile. His wide mouth became even wider, showing strong, white teeth. The smile warmed his strange golden eyes, and he seemed to radiate good will.

Chaco? Wasn't that the name on the coyote's collar? Sierra took several more deep breaths. "Chaco," she began carefully. "Chaco, I'd like to know why you are trespassing in my house. Did you have anything to do with that…coyote? The one that was just here?" Her eyes darted around again, searching for the animal.

"That's me," he said cheerfully. "It's a nickname. My real name is Coyotl." He pronounced it with a distinctive tongue click at the "tl." "Do you have anything to eat? I'm starving. I rooted through some trashcans on the way here, but there wasn't anything good. Maybe a stale bagel or two, but that's it."

Sierra felt she really did not have time to be insane. She had to find a job. She did not need any coyotes, talking or otherwise, and she did not need this young man, who was not only illegally intruding in her house, but was also apparently completely around the bend in his own right. "Get out! Now. I don't know what you think you're up to, but get the hell out. And take your coyote with you!"

Chaco looked slightly hurt.

"Well, okay, I'll just put something together myself. Go on. I know my way around a garb—uh, kitchen."

Sierra studied him.

"No," she said evenly, "I mean you have to leave. Now!"

Chaco got up from the floor, dusted the knees of his tight jeans, and sauntered down the hallway toward her kitchen. He had clearly elevated sauntering to an art form.

"Sorry," Chaco said over his shoulder. "No can do. We've got business."

Several movies played themselves out behind Sierra's eyes as she watched his progress into her kitchen. The scenes ranged from *Psycho* to *Cape Fear*. As Chaco disappeared into the kitchen, she sidled into the living room and picked up the phone. There was no dial tone, and she went cold all over. She crept quietly into her front hall. Chaco was standing in the kitchen doorway, arms folded, looking at her with a serene expression and those wild eyes.

"I'm not going to hurt you," he said, amiably. "Why don't you come and sit down? We need to talk."

"Did you cut my phone line?" asked Sierra, voice quavering slightly. He didn't look particularly menacing, but what kind of person cuts your phone line and sneaks into your house? The answer to that question had to be seriously bad news.

"Nope," Chaco said cheerily. "Just put it on hold for a while. While we talk, I mean. It'll be good as new when we've had our little discussion. Why don't you come and sit down?"

"Right," Sierra said brightly. "I just need to get the newspaper. Be there in a moment." *If I can get to the door, I can jump in the car before he can stop me.*

She turned her back resolutely on Chaco and started toward the door. Behind her, she heard rapid scrabbling. Before she could turn to see what was making the noise, the coyote bounded ahead of her and sat, blocking the door. It panted a little, long tongue lolling. Sierra turned furiously, to tell Chaco to call off his coyote, but Chaco was gone. Sierra, one eye nervously on the animal, walked to the kitchen and cautiously peered around. No Chaco. She returned to her front door, and reached for the handle, making tentative shooing motions with her hand. She intended to make the coyote move away from the door, and then to run like hell for her car in the driveway. But the coyote didn't move. It just sat there, staring at her.

Sierra turned the handle and pulled it toward her, hard. But the coyote, instead of scrambling out of the way, seemed to Sierra's horrified eyes to be melting. But if he was melting, he was massing into something larger, instead of getting smaller. The sharp muzzle softened and shrank back into a hairless face; the body stretched out grotesquely and rearranged itself. Sierra found herself staring into the same wild amber eyes, but they were the eyes of the dark young man. He blocked the door firmly and made an apologetic gesture as Sierra abruptly slumped to the floor again, her trembling knees unable to support her.

"Sorry," he said, in a kindly tone of voice. "We really do need to talk."

He held out one brown hand to her, and Sierra, whose brain appeared to have taken a leave of absence, put her hand in his. His hand was strong and warm as he pulled her to her feet. Without letting go, he urged her toward the kitchen. Sierra's brain was still replaying the scene in her mind: coyote became man. This would imply, given the coyote-free state of the kitchen, that man became coyote. Then her rational mind called a halt to the proceedings and she started all over, seeking for a shred of sense in the chaos.

In a state of numbed confusion, Sierra followed Chaco into the kitchen. He gestured toward one of the chairs at the kitchen table, but she hovered uncertainly.

"You want coffee?" she asked, striving for normalcy. Chaco's eyes brightened, and if he had not been a young man at the moment, he might have wagged his tail.

"That'd be great," he said. Sierra began preparing the brew.

"So you're Chaco?" she said, scooping the beans into the grinder just as if she weren't entertaining a figment of her imagination.

"Yup."

"And Chaco is you? I mean, you are the coyote? And the coyote—that's you, too?"

Best to be absolutely clear about the matter. She buttered the toast that she had put in the toaster earlier—this was during what she now thought of as her pre-Chaco existence—and put it on a plate, which she set down in front of him.

"Yup."

"One thing I'd really like to know," she said, pouring ground beans into her coffee maker.

"Yeah?" He cocked his head.

"Can I trust you?"

She expected Chaco to quickly affirm this, but he didn't. He sat at her small kitchen table and regarded her seriously. It seemed like the wrong response. Her heart began to pound again as adrenalin surged through her body and he watched her with those scary eyes.

"Well," he said slowly. "Yes and no."

Sierra began to back away.

"I don't mean that I would *try* to hurt you, Sierra," he said earnestly. "I just mean that it's in my nature."

"*What's* in your nature?"

"It's in my nature to be untrustworthy. Sort of. I mean, you can always trust me to *try* to do the right thing, but sometimes I don't do it the way you think I'm going to. And," he admitted with a sigh, "Things don't always turn out the way I mean them to." He picked up a piece of toast and crunched it.

"What the hell do you mean by that?" Sierra asked wildly, wishing for the first time in her life that she had a gun in the house.

"I mean, you've *heard* of me, right?" asked the young man, peering at her anxiously.

"No. Why would I have heard of Chaco the Coyote?" Sounds like a Saturday morning cartoon, she thought. Now all we need is a roadrunner.

"Oh." Chaco seemed slightly depressed by this. "I suppose not many people have heard of me these days. I'm an Avatar. You know, Coyotl. The Trickster? The one who brought fire to The People?"

Sierra stared at him.

"But, that's just a myth. A legend. There's no such thing."

Chaco's lean length blurred suddenly, his form shrinking and changing proportion. His thin brown face was suddenly sharp and furry. A coyote sat on her kitchen chair with toast crumbs on its black lips. It hopped down, shook itself and stretched, forelegs straight, butt in the air, plumy tail arched over its back. It yawned, showing teeth like the ends of knitting needles and a long, pink tongue.

"What*ever*," said the coyote.

"Here's your coffee," said Sierra.

It seemed the only sane thing to say at the moment. She set a full mug down on the table, wondering if perhaps she should pour some into a bowl and put it on the floor.

"Milk? Sugar?"

Did coyotes drink café-au-lait? Or did they take it black?

"Black, thanks," Chaco said, waving his tail lazily in the air. "You got the invitation, I believe?"

Sierra felt as though she should know what he was talking about, but she didn't.

"What invitation?"

"He sent you the invitation. I know you got it because he told me so," explained Chaco, speaking as though to a small and dimwitted child.

"Look," said Sierra, "I didn't get any invitation. Go through my mail. Go through my garbage. No invitation."

"Oh, may I?" asked the coyote, brightening.

Then he shook himself back into the shape of a brown young man again.

"I mean, no, thank you. The invitation is unmistakable. Somewhere, I know you have a bright green and blue feather. And this feather makes a noise, kind of a chime. Right?"

Chaco began to sit on his haunches, remembered he was not in coyote form and sat with dignity at the kitchen table.

"Oh," she said. "Wait here a moment."

Chaco started up with an alert expression, but she waved him back.

"I won't try to leave. I promise."

She went upstairs, found the feather in her carved box and returned to the kitchen. She showed the feather to Chaco.

"Is this what you're talking about?"

"That's it," Chaco said with satisfaction. "So now we have to go see him. He sent me to guide you. It's not the easiest trip, if you're human."

Sierra stared at him blankly.

"I'm not going anywhere. I just got fired. I have to find a job. I have bills to pay. I don't even know what—or who—you're talking about."

Her voice rose sharply.

"I can't *believe* I'm talking to a coyote anyway. I have a ton of stuff to do."

"We really do have to go see him," said Chaco seriously. "When he sends an invitation, you can't refuse. He really needs to see you."

This left Sierra more confused than ever—if that was possible.

"Who he?" she asked ungrammatically.

"Quetzalcoatl," he replied, again giving the final "tl" that strange tongue click. "The Big Q."

Sierra poured herself a cup of coffee and sat down.

"This sounds familiar. There's a sculpture in a park in downtown San Jose that's supposed to be Quetzalcoatl. A giant snake, coiled up, but if you don't look too closely, it looks just like, well, just like giant dog poop."

She had no idea how to make that strange click at the end of "Quetzalcoatl."

Chaco looked horrified. "You're kidding? I hope he doesn't

know about that! He'd be…unhappy, I think. He's awfully, um, dignified."

"Wasn't he supposed to be some kind of god?"

"Well, the Aztecs worshipped him, but he's really an Avatar, like me. Very powerful, though. Kind of a super Avatar."

Sierra restrained herself from asking if he had a red cape, and said, "I thought he was one of those gods they sacrificed people to, in the old days."

"I'm not saying no one *ever* sacrificed people to the Big Q," Chaco said carefully, "But he never approved. People got him mixed up with his twin brother. *That* one is always out for blood."

"Quetzalcoatl's evil twin," Sierra said, feeling giggles begin to foam up inside, a precursor to hysteria. She could *not* be having this conversation. "So you're telling me that Quetzalcoatl has an *evil twin?*"

Chaco looked at her in surprise. "Yes. Is there something funny about that?"

"It's kind of a cliché, don't you think?"

"It's true. Look it up. Where do you think clichés come from, anyway?"

"OK, point taken. I *will* look it up," she said.

"Fine. You do that," Chaco said. "You'll find that Q is the creator; his brother is the destroyer. Q is the light; his brother is the dark. Q brings fertility and prosperity; his brother…"

Sierra no longer felt like giggling. "This twin," she interrupted, "What is *his* name?"

"It's not a good idea to speak his name," said Chaco, shaking his dark head. "Speaking his name gives him power. He has too much power in the world already, because he goes by many names, and people call on him every day. Anyway, Quetzalcoatl has called *you*. *You* must answer."

"Why? What does he want?"

"He thinks you can help. There are dangerous forces at work, things called into being by his brother. He thinks you can help push back the darkness."

"I think he has the wrong lady," said Sierra, sipping at her mug of coffee. "I'm just a lowly, out-of-work public relations manager. I don't have any special powers, I can't use a sword, I can't fly, and I'm afraid of violence. Not a good candidate at all. There must be hundreds of people who would be better at battling the forces of darkness than me."

Chaco regarded her levelly. "He thinks you're the right one. Why don't you ask him about it? I'm just the messenger."

"Even if I am the right one, I can't do it," Sierra replied. "I need to find another job. It's been interesting meeting you, Chaco, but I can't go."

"But look on the bright side," he urged. "Now there's nothing to keep you from going with me to see the Big Q. You're free."

"*Free?*" retorted Sierra. "Free? There's no such thing. How'm I gonna pay for this place? Buy gas? Pay for food?"

"Oh, don't worry about me," murmured Chaco, "I can find food just about anywhere."

"I'm NOT worried about you, you moron," snapped Sierra. "What about *me*? What am *I* going to eat? Stale bagels? Rats? What?"

Chaco drew himself up proudly. "No one has ever accused me of not providing well for my people. If it's rats you want, rats you shall have."

"Yuck," said Sierra wearily. "No, Chaco, I don't want rats. I have some savings. Actually, the company gave me a nice severance package. I can eat for a while. But now I have to explain to a bunch of bozos in other companies why I suddenly decided to leave a good job at BDSC without first finding another job."

Sierra realized that she wasn't feeling frightened anymore. Chaco seemed harmless enough. Then she recalled that she was having a conversation with someone who was a part-time coyote, and her anxiety that she was losing her mind returned in full force.

"Look," she said, resisting the urge to put her face into her hands. "This is crazy. I think I'm going crazy. I think you're just a hallucination, if you want the truth. And I am not going anywhere with a hallucination. I'm not *that* crazy!"

"I can wait until you're ready," he said, stirring his coffee calmly. He sipped it, watching her over the rim of his mug.

"You're gonna wait a long time, then," said Sierra. "Goodbye, Chaco."

CHAPTER 3

Sierra discovered that Chaco was easier to acquire than to lose. She tried asking him nicely to leave. She tried ignoring him, settling herself down in front of her computer for several hours to scan the job sites. While she was busy, he helped himself liberally to the contents of her refrigerator and cupboards. While roaming restlessly around her apartment, he happened upon a photo album and came to her computer to show her a picture of Sierra and Kaylee at a Black Diamond Christmas party. Their arms were entwined, they were raising champagne flutes, and both were grinning broadly in those happier times. Kaylee looked resplendent in an African-print dress that draped over one shoulder, and she wore her red-orange heart and amber bead necklace.

"Who's this?" he asked with interest.

"That's Kaylee Shore," replied Sierra. "I worked with her at Black Diamond, and we got to know each other. She's turning out to be a real friend."

Chaco said nothing more, but leafed through the rest of the album quietly.

By nightfall, Chaco's poking into her private possessions, nosy questions, and relentless foraging for food had driven Sierra to the screaming stage.

"I'm going to call the police right now!" she threatened, reaching for the handset. "See how you like it in jail!"

But Chaco just glanced up from the book he had taken—without asking—from her shelves. He was sprawled comfortably on her couch, his athletic-shoe-clad feet resting on her sequined throw cushions.

"You're not going to call the police," he commented, returning to the pages of *Hiking Trails of the South San Francisco Bay*.

"That's all you know," Sierra hissed, punching three numbers into the phone.

"Please say the city and state," said a digitized voice at the other end of the line.

"Yes, there's an intruder in my home," said Sierra.

"I didn't hear you," the voice said patiently. "Please say the city and state."

"I'm at 111 East Belinda Street in Sunnyvale," Sierra stated, frowning at Chaco. "Yes, that's right. Please hurry—I think he's dangerous!"

Chaco yawned and turned the page as the voice insisted, "I didn't hear you. Please say..."

Sierra put the phone back in its cradle. "You'd better get going. The police are on their way right now, and the police station isn't that far from here."

Chaco looked up at her as she loomed over him. "You didn't call the police," he said, putting the book down. He swung his long legs around, sitting upright.

"Yes, I did."

"There's no point in lying to me," Chaco replied calmly. "You can't lie to a born liar, you know."

"If you're a liar, why should I believe anything you say?"

Chaco considered this seriously.

"Well, you've got a point," he conceded. "You'll just have to trust me, I guess."

Sierra stared at him, speechless. The situation reminded her of the riddle about the two doors, each with a guard. Behind one door lay untold riches and behind the other was certain death. One guard always lied and the other always told the truth. You had to figure out how to choose the right door by questioning the guards. Sierra had always become terminally confused, inevitably choosing certain death. This reflection did not comfort her. She fumed silently, frowning at Chaco. He looked at her mildly for a little while, then stood and faced her. He spoke in a formal and serious tone he hadn't used before.

"Sierra. I swear upon the Ancestors. I swear upon all that is sacred. This is important. It's more important than me. It's more important than you. Please come with me. Quetzalcoatl does not call upon mankind lightly, and he has called *you*."

"But *why*?" she burst out. "Why me? I'm not..."

But whatever she intended to say remained unsaid, for at that moment, the lights flickered, dimmed, and died, leaving them in darkness.

"Damn!" exclaimed Sierra, annoyed. "The circuit breakers are in the garage. I have a flashlight somewhere..."

But the rest of her sentence was cut off by Chaco's hand over her mouth. His arms wrapped roughly around her shoulders, but before she could react with a fierce instinctive kick, he whispered urgently in her ear.

"Quiet! Don't make a sound. It's not the circuit breaker. We're in trouble."

Sierra stopped resisting and his palm dropped from her mouth. She stood quietly, straining to hear, but the house was quiet. She could hear the traffic noises from the street. Light from the streetlamps created a dim illumination through the curtained windows. Gradually, her eyes adjusted, but she could see nothing but the dark outlines of her familiar furnishings.

Something suddenly moved past one of the living room windows, briefly blocking the light. Sierra saw that the light outside the kitchen windows was flickering, as though several objects were moving rapidly outside the house and obscuring the streetlights for a second as they passed. She felt an atavistic tension grip her throat, and the hair on her head prickled. She reached out a shaking hand to Chaco.

"What is it?" she whispered. More things flickered past the windows.

"Later," he breathed. "Stay here, and don't move." He grasped her hand, squeezed it as though to comfort her. By the faint light from the windows, she saw him shift. The coyote laid its belly close to the floor and began to crawl toward the kitchen. As fear ran cold fingers down her spine, Sierra realized she had left a kitchen window open, letting in the warm spring air. She could hear noises now, like people muttering softly. From the tones, Sierra didn't want to know what they were saying.

Slowly, she sank to the floor, hoping to hide in the shadows. She pressed her back against a bookshelf. *Now they can't come at me from behind,* she thought. She watched the living room windows fearfully. There were shapes flitting about outside, moving in a way that made no sense to her. They were the size and shape of the large red rubber balls that elementary schoolchildren play with at recess—and they were flying in the dark air like obese bats, but with no visible wings. None of this made any sense to her, adding to her fright.

A sudden crash came from the kitchen, accompanied by snarls and shrieks. Sierra jerked back hard against the bookcase and if it hadn't been bolted to the wall because of the earthquakes so common in the Bay Area, she might have sent it toppling. As it was, volumes from the top shelves fell, one striking her shoulder painfully.

There was a flurry of activity outside. The shapes knocked against the windows in their haste, and then they were gone. The house lights flared abruptly, blinding her for a moment. When she regained her sight—still with a large purple spot swimming in her field of vision—she ran to the kitchen to see if Chaco was hurt. The din had been enough to bring her neighbors running, she thought.

Chaco, now a young man again, stood in the middle of the kitchen, broken glass strewn about him like glittering confetti. He had smears of blood on his face and hands. "You're hurt!" she cried, but he shook his head.

"Not my blood," he replied gruffly, and pointed at the floor.

Sierra saw that there was more than glass on the floor. A large round object, also covered in blood, lay at his feet. Sierra stared down at something birthed by a nightmare. It was a *head*, a head larger and rounder than a man's. It had bulging, staring black eyes with no whites, and a mouth like a jack o' lantern with the snaggled sharp teeth of a mako shark. Even nastier, instead of hair it had long, gnarled fingers, each tipped with a cruel claw. The face had been slashed and gashed as though by razors—from Chaco's fangs, Sierra knew. Her stomach heaved and she rushed out of the kitchen to the downstairs bathroom.

She emerged a while later, wiping her mouth and still trembling, to find the kitchen restored to normal—except for the plywood nailed across the broken window. The glass and blood were gone, and Chaco was rinsing a rag at the sink. The ghastly head had vanished.

"You okay?" he asked, wringing the rag out and turning to face her. Sierra nodded, but her eyes were darting around the room, searching for the hideous visitor.

"It's gone," said Chaco, firmly. "The others are gone, too. But I'm afraid they'll be back. Or he'll send something else. He knows where you are, now."

Sierra gazed at him numbly, "*Who* knows where I am?" she asked, wondering when she would wake from this horrible dream. "And what was that…thing?"

"Big Head," Chaco answered, tossing the rag into the trash. "You don't see them much anymore. He must've called them up especially for you. Very dangerous, as you saw."

"Who called them up?" Sierra asked again, a small spark of indignation igniting amidst her fear and confusion.

"Is this your Mr. Q, your Kets-all-whatever? Because if he thinks he's going to push me around like that, he's…"

But Chaco was shaking his head. "No. Not Quetzalcoatl. He doesn't operate that way. His brother. You can call him—let's see, he has a lot of names. You don't want to speak his real name; it's too toxic. But in English, it means 'The Obsidian Mirror.'"

"The Obsidian Mirror? What kind of name is that?"

"I'll explain later. Right now, we have to leave. Before something else comes along. Trust me, you don't want to wait around for whatever it is," Chaco said.

Sierra thought about the Big Head lying in its blood on her kitchen floor and shuddered. "Yes, all right, I'll go. Where are we going?"

Chaco sighed. He stopped short of rolling his eyes, but nonetheless effectively communicated exasperation. "I *told* you," he said, with exaggerated patience. "We're going to see Quetzalcoatl."

Well, Sierra thought, *someone needs me. It doesn't sound like paid work, but someone needs me.* "Okay," she said. "But do you promise me he won't sacrifice me? Or eat me?" She peered anxiously at Chaco.

"I don't usually promise anybody anything," said Chaco. As Sierra's face went even whiter, he said hastily, "But I do promise he won't hurt you."

Sierra relaxed slightly.

Chaco continued, "But I *can't* promise you that what he asks you to do will be safe. Or easy."

"What is he going to ask me to do?" Sierra asked suspiciously. "Why me?"

But Chaco wouldn't say. He shook his head.

"Just come with me. It's important. And we need to get out of here *now*."

It didn't take long to load up her car, as Sierra kept her camping equipment ready to go at all times. She packed some food and located her road maps. She sent an email to her father in Los Angeles to let him know she was taking a brief vacation. She didn't mention that she'd been fired, because he'd probably offer to send her money. She told him she was taking a Magical Mystery Tour. Magical Mystery Tour had been her mother's expression for a spontaneous outing. She'd bundle everyone in the car and they'd take off, not knowing where they'd end up.

She looked up Kaylee's work number, scribbling it down on the notepad she kept by the side of the phone. She didn't call Kaylee's house, even though it was a Saturday and Kaylee was probably home, because she didn't want to get into a conversation about what she was doing or why she was doing it—Sierra herself had no idea. She wrote Kaylee's name next to the number, shading it in and doodling looping swirls around it as she left a voicemail.

"Hey, Kaylee, I'm going camping for a little while to think things over. I'll call you when I get back. Don't worry about me, OK? I'm doing fine here."

Well, maybe not fine, she reflected as she returned the phone to its cradle. But I can't tell her I've been attacked by big, flying, flesh-eating heads. That might create a little anxiety.

Then she watered the plants and suspended her mail and newspaper deliveries.

"I'm ready now, Chaco," she said, hefting a backpack. "I only have one sleeping bag. Maybe we should go get another one for you."

"No need," said Chaco. "I've got a fur coat."

Sierra stared at him and then remembered. "Right. Well, let's go. Um, where are we going?"

"East."

"East? I thought we'd be going to Mexico. Isn't that where Quetzalcoatl hangs out?"

"He's an Avatar. He can be anywhere. Do you know how to get to Sacramento?"

"Of course I do."

Sierra considered asking Chaco what the Plumed Serpent God of the Aztecs was doing in Sacramento, but decided against it. She consulted her maps and planned a route.

"OK, Chaco. Let's get going."

As they walked out her front door and she locked it behind her, a thought flitted through her mind that she might never see her home again. She had a hollow, light feeling at her core. It was a free feeling, but it was the freedom of no attachments, of not belonging. Somewhere under the free feeling, panic was beginning to bubble up like black tar. She shook herself, trying to bring back a sense of normalcy. As though anything would ever be normal again; she was, after all, setting out to meet a god or Avatar, accompanied by a shape-changing coyote, with monsters apparently hard on their heels. She got into the driver's seat, and Chaco sat beside her.

"Seat belt," said Sierra, noticing that Chaco had neglected to fasten this item.

"I don't need one. It's impossible to kill an Avatar."

"Good for you," she replied, "But if we get stopped by a cop, I still get a ticket."

Chaco fumbled with the strap, and Sierra had to show him how it worked. At last, she backed out of her driveway and headed for the freeway.

CHAPTER 4

It was well after midnight on Sunday morning and the roads were eerily deserted. Neither of them felt like talking, so after an hour of quiet driving, Sierra switched on the radio, tuned to a National Public Radio channel. The news was on.

"The president announced today that he is launching an initiative called the 'Clean Air for Americans Act.' Under the president's proposed plan, funds will be earmarked for the construction of twenty-five new nuclear power plants in twenty states, including Alaska and Hawaii," the announcer said. An audio clip of President Harmon's voice followed.

"Nuclear power is clean power," he said in the reverberating bass voice that was recognized around the globe. "Bringing twenty-five new nuclear plants online will cut America's dependence on foreign oil by nearly twenty percent. Drilling for new oil resources in Alaska and along the coasts of California and Florida will reduce that dependence even more, giving Americans control over their energy destiny."

The announcer continued, "President Harmon dismissed the issue of nuclear waste disposal, noting that subterranean storage has been proven safe by his Commission on Nuclear Waste Safety, which released its report simultaneously with his announcement. Given his party's majority in both the House and Senate, it is unlikely that this initiative will meet with much resistance in Congress..."

Sierra changed the station. Chaco cocked an eye at her.

"Don't get me started," she said. They had cleared the San

Francisco Bay area and were heading for the Altamont Pass. The sky ahead was pink with a hint of the rising sun.

"He said he was a 'green' candidate, but everything he's done has been the exact opposite of green," Sierra complained.

"How do you suppose that he can get away with it?" Chaco asked quietly. He kept his eyes on the countryside rolling past them.

"I don't know. I don't understand how he can lie like that, saying that nuclear waste can be stored safely underground. I just don't get it."

"Well," Chaco, said, plucking uncomfortably at the seat belt strap across his chest, "Why don't you ask Q when we get there? He's a very wise being, and he's been around a long time. Ask him."

Sierra tuned the radio to a music station. By the time they reached Altamont Pass, the suburbs and industrial parks had petered out. The morning sun showed that the grassy hills, bright green a few weeks earlier, had begun to turn the straw-gold of a California summer. Hawks soared above the fields of wind turbines that rose out of the grass like giant white pinwheels, while cattle grazed peacefully below, casting long black shadows down the hillsides. Then they started down the grade into the Central Valley. The land flattened out and the freeway ran straight as far as the eye could see.

"How about breakfast?" Chaco asked.

As far as Sierra could tell, he was always hungry. They stopped in Tracy, a town that apparently had competed for the largest number of chain restaurants and businesses—and won. Sierra pulled into the parking lot of Chik-Be-We, a national chain restaurant renowned for its iron adherence to blandness. She had a salad and Chaco ate two hamburgers with a side of French fries, then ordered more fries.

"How can you stay so skinny?" she demanded. "If I ate like that, I'd be completely circular."

Chaco just grinned.

"Avatars don't gain weight," he said smugly. "Anyway, sometimes the pickings are slim when I'm Coyotl. Ever try gaining weight on a diet of mice and salmon berries?"

"Um, no. I'll pass. Can we talk about where we're going, now?"

They pushed the dishes aside and spread out a map. Chaco pointed to a spot south and east of Sacramento. "We're going there," he said. Sierra peered at the spot at his fingertip.

"Where is that? It looks like the middle of nowhere."

"It's kind of in the boonies," Chaco agreed. "But there are little gold rush towns and wineries. It's the gold country—where they came and dug everything up, hoping to get rich. That was a bad time," he said gloomily. "The Miwok people were my people, and they were about wiped out by the miners. And the gold diggers poisoned the land with mercury, too."

"Mercury? Why did they do that?" asked Sierra.

"I'm not clear on the details. All I know is they used it to separate the gold from the ore, then dumped it. How do you think all that mercury wound up in the San Francisco Bay and in the Sacramento River Delta? But they don't use mercury any more."

"Oh. That's good."

"They use cyanide."

Sierra felt they were wandering from the subject at hand. She had enough on her plate without taking on mining industry practices.

"So where do we end up today?" she asked.

"There's a state park near Volcano." Chaco pointed at the park on the map. "It's called Indian Grinding Rock. It was sacred ground to the Miwoks. We can camp there."

"Is it a real volcano?"

"Naw. The white settlers thought it was, but there's no volcano. Anyway, all the volcanoes around here are dead. Or sleeping."

"Well, there's a bit of good news," said Sierra. "I can get us there. Ready?"

As they were getting into the car, Sierra asked, "If you were around in eighteen-forty-nine for the California Gold Rush, just how old are you, Chaco?"

Chaco looked thoughtful.

"I don't know. Thousands of years, anyway. Maybe hundreds of thousands? I don't keep track."

"You don't look very old. In fact, you don't look a day over twenty-five."

Chaco twinkled at her. "The Trickster is perennially young. It wouldn't do to go around playing pranks on people if you're too old to run fast!"

"Yeah, well just don't play any tricks on *me*, fella," warned Sierra.

As they turned off the freeway onto Highway 88, the gray-green-brown flatness of the Central Valley began to disappear as the land began its long, slow rise to the Sierra Nevada mountain range. They drove through miles of orchards on either side: walnut, almonds, and cherry trees. The orchards eventually gave way to vineyards, heralding the approach of Amador County's wine region.

The land hunched into low, rolling hills, growing higher with every mile. They began to see live oaks dotting the open grassland, spreading their heavy branches low to the ground. They skipped to the east of Sutter Creek, where the original gold strike had been made in 1849, drove directly into Jackson, then made an abrupt left turn in the center of town onto Highway 49. By the time they arrived at Pine Grove, the last town before reaching Indian Grinding Rock State Historical Park, they were in the Sierra Nevada foothills. The scenery alternated between rolling hills dotted with live oaks, scrublands, and forests thick with pines, black oak, and red-skinned madrone.

It was not long before they reached the entrance to the state park. They paid the overnight camping fee and in return received a small map. The ranger showed them where their site was.

"It's a fair distance from the parking lot," he said, marking their route in pencil with an X on their site. "You have to haul any water or wood into the site, but it's worth it."

Fortunately, the ranger station sold firewood, as it was not among Sierra's camping provisions. Having completed that purchase, they headed to their site. As in most state park campgrounds in California, the campsites were located right next to each other, like tract houses. During the high season for camping, these enclaves became extensions of suburbia, with tots on trikes, teenagers playing hip-hop, and martini-drinking adults who apparently had tried to bring their living rooms with them in their bulging RVs. But in mid-May, the campground had only a few other campers, located far enough from their site to provide a pretense of privacy.

Setting up the tent and arranging the campsite took an hour or so. Sierra and Chaco worked well together, chatting as they set up camp. Finally, the tent was pitched and the site arranged to Sierra's satisfaction. They snacked on cheese and crackers while they worked, washing it down with iced tea that Sierra had brought in a large thermos jug.

"Now what?" she asked Chaco.

Chaco scrutinized the afternoon sky.

"It's too late to go see Q. We'd be walking in the dark coming back. Doesn't bother me," he said with a grin, "but you humans can't see worth beans when the sun goes down. Let's just relax tonight and go in the morning."

This suited Sierra, and she and Chaco went to see the park's main attraction, a broad expanse of flattish rock located near the visitors' center. Smoothly rounded holes in the rock showed where the Miwoks had once sat and ground acorns. There were pictograms scratched in the rock as well, but it took a sharp eye to pick them out. Sierra imagined the women sitting on the warm rock in the sun, grinding acorns and gossiping among themselves. She wondered if each woman had her own grinding hole, worn gradually deeper by her mother and her grandmother and her great-grandmother before her. Then she realized that she could ask Chaco—and did.

"Well, I don't think it was all that formal," he replied, leaning on the zigzag log fence that prevented visitors from walking across the rock. "They had their favorites, I guess, but mostly, one would pick a hole and start working, then the others would settle down around her so they could talk."

Sierra and Chaco spent a lazy afternoon walking around the park and talking. Chaco was a wealth of information, and he told her several funny stories about members of the Miwok tribe he had known. Finally, they headed back to their camp.

Dusk was falling, and the air began to chill. Back in Sunnyvale, the evenings would be mild, but in the Sierra Nevada foothills there was still a breath of winter.

"What's for dinner?" Chaco asked.

"How can you be hungry again? We just had snacks," Sierra grumbled, but she competently built a fire and began preparations for cooking as bats flew overhead and the moon rose in a cobalt sky. The other campers were quietly going about their own business, and as it became fully dark, it was almost possible to believe they were alone in the wilderness. A wilderness with hot showers down the road and toilets, of course.

Sierra and Chaco sat by the fire, eating the simple canned hash and salad she had fixed. Sierra relaxed, enjoying the crackle of the flames, making her front rather hot while the night breeze cooled her back. She scrambled up to find her windbreaker and to get a bottle of wine from her food locker, which sat to one side. It was unlikely there would be bears in this area, so she hadn't bothered to secure it up in the trees. She'd stow it in the car before they went to sleep.

Settling back down by the fire, she poured wine into a blue-enameled coffee cup and passed it to Chaco, then took a cup herself.

"You said the Miwok were your people. What did you mean by that? I thought the Coyote stories were from the Navajo and the other Indians that lived in the desert in Arizona and New Mexico."

She thought she remembered that from studying Native Americans in elementary school.

"I figure in The People's stories from all over," said Chaco. "The Miwok say I created them. Do you want to hear the story?"

"Yes." Sierra hadn't had anyone tell her a bedtime story in ages. She leaned toward him attentively.

Chaco spoke in his formal voice, telling the story in the third person, as though he were not a participant in it. "The world was peopled six times. The fifth people were the bird and mammal people, and Coyote was one of them. Coyote was very clever," Chaco said, and not one muscle twitched in irony or self-deprecation.

"Coyote was very clever, and he created the land. Then he created the foods to grow upon the land. But he needed people to eat the foods. He gathered many wise men together and asked them what he should do and they said he should create a new People immediately so that the foods would be eaten. But Coyote wasn't sure what kind of People he should create.

"He looked at his foot and asked, 'Do you see my foot? Is that the kind of foot the new people should have?'

"'No,' said Otter. 'Make a foot like mine.'

"Coyote looked at Otter's foot. 'Your foot is round, like mine,' he said. 'The new People can't use round feet.'

"Then Lizard spoke up. 'You are right. The new People won't be able to pick up the food with round feet like yours. Look at my foot. I have five toes so that I can pick things up and use the bow and arrow and do all kinds of things that are useful.'

"Coyote said, 'You are right, Lizard. Your feet are the proper kind.' So Coyote made the new People with lizard feet, and arranged it so that their villages would be close together, and each man had a wife so they could have a child every year. And Coyote said this was to be the last creation of people on the earth, and he sent them off to live in every direction. He also spoke to every creature and told each what kind of life he would live from that day forward: frogs in the water and birds in the air and bears in the forest. And that is the way it has been from that day to this."

Sierra got a bit confused between "people" and "People," and she thought the story didn't make much sense. She was about to ask about the preceding four peoples of the earth, but Chaco spoke first, as the fire sent a spray of red sparks into the air.

"There's another one about how Coyote loses his penis," said Chaco. "That one's a *lot* funnier."

"What…!" Sierra started to say, but before she could collect her wits, Chaco's fire-lit figure suddenly shifted into coyote form and launched into the scrub at the periphery of their campsite.

Sierra sprang to her feet, heart pounding wildly, as she heard crashing and snarls in the bushes. Before long, the coyote came back, lugging a struggling figure in his jaws. He brought it to the fire and placed his forepaws firmly on a squirming creature like nothing Sierra had ever seen before.

As Chaco morphed back into human form, the firelight limned something the size of a pygmy goat, with thin arms and legs and fat, splayed toes like a salamander's—except there were six toes on each paw. The creature's huge orange eyes glowed in the light of the flames. Its skin was gray-green and hairless, and its watermelon-shaped head bore a tiny lipless mouth with slits where a nose should be. Its mouth was open, emitting piercing squeals.

"What the hell is that?" she yelped.

CHAPTER 5

Chaco grinned down at the creature.

"Mannegishi," he said, looking wolfish even in human form.

"Man-a-whatee?"

"Mannegishi," Chaco repeated. "Kind of like leprechauns, but uglier."

The mannegishi stopped squealing as Chaco shifted his grip to one of its legs.

"We are *not* uglier than leprechauns," it said with dignity. "It's all a matter of taste. We happen to think leprechauns are fantastically grotesque. Only humans are nastier-looking."

Overlooking the insult to her species, Sierra asked, "What in the name of…of whatever is a mannegishi? And how do you know about leprechauns? There aren't any leprechauns in America. I mean, there aren't any leprechauns."

Chaco looked at her with one dark eyebrow cocked.

"You're sitting here with an Avatar and a mannegishi, and you still think there aren't any leprechauns?"

"The horrible little things are all over the place," said the mannegishi primly. "We have a terrible immigration problem in this country."

"Never mind that," growled Chaco. "What were you doing skulking around our campsite? What're you up to?"

"Nothing!" protested the mannegishi. "I mean, nothing bad. I was sent to tell you something. Something important!"

"OK," Chaco said. "Tell us."

Like a chameleon, the mannegishi rolled one huge orange eye at Sierra, as the other eye remained fixed on Chaco.

"I'm not sure I should tell her. Can we speak in private?" asked the mannegishi.

"No, we can not," Chaco said, tightening his grip on the creature's thin leg.

"All right, all right!" the creature said, shrinking from Chaco. "The Big Q sent me. He said to tell you that Mahaha is on your trail."

Chaco released the mannegishi's leg.

"Mahaha!" he exclaimed. "Why is Mahaha after us?"

The mannegishi rubbed its leg where Chaco's hand had gripped it. "You *know*. Tezcatlipoca sent it to stop you."

Chaco went pale, discernible even by firelight.

"Don't say that name!" he hissed at the mannegishi. "You give him power when you say his name. Call him Necocyaotl if you must speak of him."

The mannegishi squatted lower to the ground.

"Sorry. Wasn't thinking." It stuck a stubby digit in its mouth and sucked it nervously.

"What is going on here?" demanded Sierra. "Who's Mahaha?"

"Do you have any food?" asked the mannegishi. "I'm hungry."

What is it with these things, thought Sierra. *All they think about is food.* Aloud she snapped, "Not until I get some answers!"

Chaco turned to her.

"Mahaha is a sort of ice demon. It tickles you."

Sierra raised her eyebrows.

"*Tickles* you? Forgive me if I don't swoon with terror. That doesn't sound very scary."

"When you were a kid, did anyone ever hold you down and tickle you until you peed in your pants?" asked Chaco.

"Well, yes. That was unpleasant, but it still doesn't sound very frightening," replied Sierra.

"Okay. Now imagine that the someone who's holding you down is as cold as ice and as strong as steel. He has long, sharp fingers that reach into your body, then he tickles you until you go insane, and then he freezes you solid. Mahaha isn't from around here. He's an ice demon from the Arctic."

"Oh," said Sierra, who had an excellent imagination.

"This is bad news. We need to see Q as soon as possible, but I don't think we can get started until dawn. You can't hike up there in the dark."

"I don't want to stay here and wait for Mahaha!" Sierra protested.

At that moment, she heard footsteps crunching on the gravel road, coming towards their campfire. She turned in terror, looking for the hatchet she had used earlier to splinter kindling for the fire. Before she could locate it, a man stepped into the firelight. Just an ordinary man, clearly not an icy-clawed monster. He was wearing a plaid flannel shirt with a padded khaki vest over it, jeans and hiking boots. Another camper, obviously. Sierra's heart began clambering its way down from overdrive.

"Hi," said the man, looking around. "I came to see if everything was OK over here. I heard some really strange noises."

Sierra recalled the crashing, snarling and squealing of a few minutes previously. She also remembered the mannegishi and whipped her head around to locate it. Whatever would this person think of the melon-headed, saucer-eyed thing at her campfire?

But there was no mannegishi. There was only a coyote wearing a beaded collar, sitting on its haunches and wagging its tail in a friendly manner.

"Oh," she said weakly. "I think you must have heard, um, Chaco, here. He heard something in the bushes and went after it. But everything is fine here. Really."

She smiled up at him and caught her breath at the wide, white grin that responded.

"Nice-looking dog you've got there," said the camper. "You say his name is Chaco? What breed is he?"

"Yes," said Sierra, wondering why everyone thought Chaco was a dog. "He's um, he's a Navajo sheepdog." Chaco gave her a cool yellow stare.

"I thought they didn't allow dogs in the park?" he asked.

"Oh? Well they didn't say anything when I came in," she responded, truthfully.

"Maybe I'm mistaken," he said cheerfully. "Well, now that I'm here, mind if I sit down for a few minutes? I'm camping on my own, but it's nice to have a little company, too."

"Be my guest," Sierra said. He really *was* nice looking. He was tall, with gray-sprinkled sandy hair and a nice build. He had kind-looking blue eyes with deep laugh lines at the corners.

"Would you like a glass, uh, cup of wine?"

"Sure. Thanks."

Sierra poured wine into another enameled cup and passed it to him. He sat cross-legged near her. Chaco heaved an exaggerated sigh and flopped over, belly nearest the warmth.

"My name is Aiden," he said, sipping. "What's yours?"

"Sierra. Aiden sounds Irish."

"It's Irish all right, but I've got as much Irish in me as anything else—you name it. Italian, German, Serbian, a little bit of Spanish. I'm a real mutt, very American. Sierra is an unusual name."

"My parents were nature lovers," she said fondly. "They loved hiking and the mountains. It actually means 'serrated' in Spanish, but they named me after the Sierra Nevada Mountains, of course. I'm a mutt, too. A little bit of everything, even some American Indian, so goes the family lore."

They talked for nearly an hour as the campfire waned. Sierra learned that Aiden lived in the area, he had recently been in a long-term relationship that had broken up (he didn't blame the woman or complain, Sierra noticed, which was good), and he was out in the woods to think things over. Aiden learned nothing about Sierra except that she was in high-tech public relations and liked camping and hiking. Sierra enjoyed the conversation but found it hard going. She was afraid she would blurt out something like, "And tomorrow, I'm going to go see Quetzalcoatl with my friend the coyote and find out what he wants."

Sierra finally got up to add more wood to the fire as the chill of the night began to creep through her windbreaker and the sweater beneath. Aiden pulled himself to his feet and set down the enameled cup.

"Well, better get back. It's bed time," he said reluctantly. "I guess whatever was crashing around in the bushes is gone. Anyway," he added with a smile, "You've got Chaco here to keep guard."

Aiden leaned down to ruffle Chaco's fur—which, Sierra was relieved to see, Chaco accepted with a doglike thump of his tail. Sierra watched Aiden's tall form disappear into the night until she could no longer see the bobbing circle of his flashlight.

She turned to find Chaco in his human form. The mannegishi was sitting on its fat bottom nearby, its orange eyes glowing like traffic reflectors in the firelight.

"Oh, Aiden, tell me more about yourself," Chaco mocked in a falsely sweet voice. "Where did you say you were from, Aiden? Oooooh, Aiden…"

"Shut up!" Sierra said in a menacing voice. Hanging out with Chaco was like having a pesky little brother sometimes.

"Where did the mannegishi go while Aiden was here?"

"He just disappeared," said Chaco. "They're good at making things disappear. Have you seen your wallet lately?"

Sierra lunged for her backpack and rummaged through the side pocket where she stowed her wallet. The pocket was empty. She turned to the mannegishi, who cowered and produced her wallet from nowhere.

"See what I mean?" said Chaco.

"Uh-huh. Does it have a name?"

Chaco looked at the mannegishi, which rolled its eyes madly in different directions and squeaked, "Fred."

"Fred? That's ridiculous. He can't possibly be named Fred," said Sierra.

"My real name is Shoemowetochawcawewahcatoe. It means 'High-backed Wolf.' You can call me that if you like."

"Right. Fred it is," Sierra said. "Listen, Fred. If you ever steal another thing from me—even a scrap of paper—I'll see to it that your name is Dances-with-Speeding-Cars. Got it?"

Fred nodded vigorously, eyes wheeling.

"Here's a granola bar."

Fred grabbed the bar and had it unwrapped and in his slit of a mouth in a split second.

"Now," said Sierra, "Let's talk about this Mahaha. It sounds nasty and extremely scary. I vote for a nice motel."

"I will protect you from Mahaha," Chaco said, his voice assuming tones of nobility. "I'm going to sleep with you. He won't dare come near."

"Oh, no you aren't."

"Yes I am."

"No, you…"

Chaco transformed back into coyote form.

"How's this?" he asked, showing two rows of sharp, white teeth in the firelight.

"Sounds good," Sierra said, and headed for the tent.

She zipped herself into her sleeping bag. Chaco's furry form came through the tent flap and curled up beside her. She saw the side of the tent sag slightly as Fred leaned against the exterior. Chaco's warmth and presence did make her feel safe, and she dropped off quickly. Although she was aroused once or twice by vigorous, behind-the-ear scratching, her dreams were pleasant and free of nightmares.

Chaco—now on two legs—woke her before dawn with a steaming cup of coffee, poured into one of the same blue-enameled cups they had used for wine the night before. She propped herself blearily on one elbow to sip the brew. It was barely light outside and the birds were still asleep. Not even the wind stirred the pre-dawn stillness.

"Do we have to get up in the middle of the night?" she complained to Chaco.

"I thought you wanted to move quickly—remember Mahaha?"

Oh, right. Stay ahead of the ice-clawed demon, she recalled. She unzipped her sleeping bag and crawled out, groping for her shoes.

When she emerged from the tent, rumpled, her dark hair braided askew, Chaco had scrambled eggs and bacon ready. The mannegishi was busily stuffing itself, using the twelve digits on its two front paws to shovel food into its little mouth.

Chaco handed her a plate.

"Eat up," he said. "We've got a ways to go today."

After breakfast, Sierra hoisted her backpack over her shoulders.

"Lay on, MacDuff," she said.

Chaco morphed back into coyote and plunged into the brush, quickly disappearing from sight.

"Chaco!" she called. "I can't see you!"

He trotted back.

"OK, I'll walk like a turtle. Humans!" He began walking with exaggerated slowness, still heading into the undergrowth. The mannegishi was resting by the campfire, its six-fingered paws in the air, belly comfortably distended.

"Are you coming, Fred?" asked Sierra.

"Nope," said Fred. "It's a long walk. See you when you get back."

When Sierra looked again, there was nothing to be seen.

Swearing under her breath, Sierra followed Chaco into the brush. She had studied a map of the park the previous day, and Chaco was heading away from the marked trails. She hoped they didn't run into a ranger, who would be bound to cite her for hiking off-trail. A ranger would be unlikely to cite a coyote, she thought, bitterly, so Chaco was safe enough. *From rangers, anyway.*

Two hours later, having clawed her way uphill through manzanita, scattering its waxy pink bells, through deer brush and coffee berry bushes, and across rough and broken rock, she called a halt. Sitting on a semi-flat boulder, Sierra pulled a water bottle out of her pack and drank deeply. She was hot and sticky, and strands of hair stuck to her neck.

Chaco's form melted and flowed. A young man again, he sat beside her. She saw with annoyance that he hadn't even broken a sweat. Her hair was full of twigs and if she didn't have ticks, it was just sheer good luck. She was certain that at one point, she had brushed an arm against a young poison oak vine, shiny with pustule-inducing oil.

"How much farther?" she asked, trying not to pant too obviously, as sweat trickled down her face.

Chaco took her water bottle without asking and took a generous swig.

"It's just up this next rise. We're almost there."

He handed the bottle back to Sierra, and she didn't bother to be discreet about wiping the opening before drinking again. He just grinned.

"You can't catch cooties from an Avatar, you know," he said. "We never get sick."

"How nice for you," she replied tartly.

Her feet ached, and ever since the idea of poison oak had occurred to her, she felt itchy all over.

Chaco let her rest for a few more minutes, then pulled her to her feet.

"Off we go. That's my girl."

He morphed and began to climb up a particularly nasty scree. On four legs, he maneuvered it easily.

Groaning, Sierra hefted her backpack and followed. She slipped several times on the treacherous, shifting gravel of the scree and skinned her palms. Sweating and bleeding, she finally made it to more solid ground, where Chaco was waiting. He rose to his four feet and, like a shadow, glided between two enormous granite boulders.

Sierra followed. Concealed by the boulders was the mouth of a cave. She felt a stream of cool air from the opening, like a long sigh. Chaco had already disappeared into the darkness. Sierra really didn't want to go into a cave. She had never been a spelunker and preferred her cave visits complete with pre-wired lighting and a guide with a two-way radio. There could be anything in an unexplored cave, including drop-offs of hundreds of feet waiting in the darkness for the unwary wanderer and mazes of little twisty passages leading nowhere. She slid her pack to the ground and rummaged around for her flashlight.

"Are you coming?" asked Chaco, reappearing in the cave mouth. "Is there a problem?"

"I'm just getting my flashlight. I can't see in the dark, as you have already pointed out."

"You won't need a flashlight. Come on, he's waiting for you."

Sierra's groping hand closed around the cool barrel of the flashlight and she drew it out. She felt safer with it in her hand.

"Coming."

She walked slowly into the dark of the cave, pausing to let her eyes adjust. The roof of the cave was a few feet over her head. The walls were just rough rock, easy to see in the light still visible from the outside, but the cave extended before her into the darkness. It ran straight for a few yards, and then appeared to turn. A faint light shone from around that turn in the passage.

"What is this place?"

Chaco trotted back to where she was standing.

"It's part of a cave complex that runs through this whole area. The part that's open to the public is called Black Chasm, but the complex is much, much bigger. This part is actually more beautiful, so it's a good thing the entrance is so well hidden. People would've been all over this cave, breaking off stalactites for souvenirs. Come on."

Sierra followed him down the rough rock corridor. As she went around the bend, the ceiling began to rise and the mysterious light became stronger. Finally, she emerged into a huge chamber that seemed to glow softly with its own light. Far overhead, great draperies of caramel-striped rock flowed, and stalactites hung like sparkling crystal spears. The walls seemed covered with frost, but a closer look revealed curlicues, shoots, and squiggles of white crystals everywhere. They grew out of the rock wall in all directions, like crystalline roots, or spurts of water frozen into ice in mid-air.

Sierra gawked for several minutes, then registered that there was another presence in the great chamber besides herself and

Chaco. Seated cross-legged on a flat outcropping of rock was an old man. His face was brown and deeply lined. He had the great, high-bridged nose of the Mayan Indian; large, almond-shaped eyes and a firm, narrow-lipped mouth. His cheekbones were high and prominent. His long, silvery hair was braided down his back like Sierra's (but more neatly). Around his corded neck he wore a heavy necklace of carved green stones.

But strangest of all was the sense Sierra experienced that this was not a man at all. His presence seemed to fill the great cavern with massive, shadowy coils that she could not quite see. He breathed quietly, and yet, it seemed the breathing of a giant creature, its unseen bulk receding into the depths of the mountain.

The old man raised his dark eyes to Sierra, and he smiled at her. His face crinkled into hundreds of tiny wrinkles, like the surface of a cooling lava flow.

"You have come," he said. His voice was soft, but it seemed to Sierra it filled her up entirely, her and the vast cavern in which she stood. "Thank you for coming."

Sierra stood awkwardly before him.

"You're Quetzalcoatl?" she asked, her tongue forming the final click of the "tl" as though she had always known how to do it. Once out of her mouth, it seemed a stupid question, but the old man nodded without irritation.

"I didn't understand your…invitation. If Chaco hadn't come to get me, I wouldn't have made it here."

Quetzalcoatl glanced at Chaco, who had flopped to the floor to one side of the flat rock where the other Avatar sat.

"Coyotl is a good boy," said Quetzalcoatl fondly. "Now, my child, we must discuss something of great importance. I need your help."

Sierra sensed the shifting of great coils in the dark and shuddered. She felt as safe in the presence of the great Avatar as she had ever felt in her life, and yet she felt danger waiting beyond the circle of power present in the cave. She sat on the cave floor, at the old man's feet.

"Tell me," she said.

CHAPTER 6

"There are times when the balance between light and dark, between good and evil, is overturned," said the old man. "This is such a time.

"I have seen times like this before. The Maya people lived hundreds of years ago in a paradise. They had everything they needed: rich soil, abundance of food, clean water. They built a great civilization. Now all their temples lie empty and abandoned, and the people are scattered and without power. How could this happen? The Maya were the greatest power in all the lands they occupied. What could bring them down so completely?"

"Maybe they sacrificed too many people to the gods," Sierra suggested, but even as she spoke, the hair at the nape of her neck stirred with fright. Quetzalcoatl had *been* one of those gods.

"I think you are partly right," he responded gravely. "In the midst of plenty, they worshipped pain and blood. This I never demanded of them, though my brother has always delighted in slaughter and suffering.

"It was my brother who led the Maya to destroy the earth that fed them. They drained the soil of its nutrients and would not replenish it nor allow it to recover. As the crops began to fail and the people were hungry, they shed more blood and still more blood, hoping to appease the gods. In the end, the people just abandoned the cities, letting the jungle reclaim their houses and temples. And my brother moved on to other peoples, still hungry for blood and ruin.

"But now is a time of peril not just for one tribe of people, but for all people. And not just people, but for every living thing on the earth." His voice was tired and sad.

"Are you talking about climate change?"

"That is a great danger. But there are other dangers, too. There is poison in the air and in the waters and in the soil itself. In the past, when people have destroyed their own land, the damage was confined to a small area. Eventually, the earth was able to repair itself. But now you have spread to every corner of the earth, and it is the earth itself that is dying."

"Are you saying it's too late?" Sierra asked fearfully.

"No. It is not too late. But I fear that my brother may triumph this time. Do you know his name?"

"Mmm, not really. Fred said it, and Chaco shut him up. Chaco said to call him Neco-something."

"Necocyaotl," said Quetzalcoatl. "Necocyaotl means 'Enemy of Both Sides.' His real name—which I will not speak here—means Obsidian Mirror. It is a fitting name for him. When people follow him, it is as though they are all gazing into an obsidian mirror, dark and distorted. All they can see clearly reflected are their own beings. Their actions and their thoughts are all for themselves, their comfort, their pleasure, their wealth. They cannot see beyond themselves at all, and once they gaze into the mirror, they are helpless to look elsewhere—such is his power. These are the followers of Necocyaotl. He does not need blood rituals now. Much blood will be shed in the end. All the blood of all the creatures of earth."

"How can we stop it?" she asked, her throat constricted with dread.

"You must ask instead, how can *you* stop *him*?"

"Me? I'm nobody. I have no magical powers. But you're an Avatar. You're powerful."

The old man shook his head, causing the green carved stones to sway heavily on his chest.

"I cannot. In a direct battle, we are too evenly matched. Neither will win, but great damage will be done in the struggle—perhaps as many innocent lives would be lost in war between us as would be lost if Necocyaotl continues unchecked. I must work against him by thwarting his works, by winning his people to my side. You know of one such person yourself. She was your overseer."

Sierra sat up straighter, startled.

"You mean Jenna Simmons? The head of Black Diamond Semiconductor?"

Quetzalcoatl nodded.

"I never exactly liked the woman, but I didn't think she was evil."

"She is my brother's creature," returned the Avatar. "But I think you can stop her."

"What is Jenna Simmons doing that's so bad? I've never seen her do anything destructive. She runs a corporation, and as far as I can see, she runs it well. She isn't even breaking any laws—not that I know of, anyway."

"Let me ask you a few questions," said Quetzalcoatl. "These things of crystal and gold that the company makes, what do people use them for?"

Sierra spread her hands wide.

"If you mean semiconductors, lots of things," she replied. "The ones we make go into all kinds of things—computers, mobile phones, cars, all kinds of electronic equipment."

"And where would you find this equipment that has the crystals inside?"

Again, Sierra spread her hands.

"Just about everywhere. Most people have some sort of electronic equipment, even if it's just a mobile phone. Or a TV. Lots of people have computers. And computers are everywhere—stores, office buildings, factories. Everywhere."

Quetzalcoatl regarded her somberly.

"Do you see it yet? What she's doing?"

Sierra gazed back in complete perplexity. Chaco sighed, a small sound that echoed in the vastness of the cave.

"I see you do not," the old man said. "Yours is not a suspicious nature, child. That speaks well of you. But you must learn to be more wary."

Sierra heard this with impatience.

"So what is Jenna Simmons doing that is so evil?" she asked again. "So what if there are semiconductors in everything? Is the electromagnetic radiation frying people's brains, or giving them cancer, or something?"

Quetzalcoatl smiled unexpectedly, his wrinkles deepening across his weathered face. He shook his head.

"No. If it were that easy to detect, it wouldn't be so danger-ous. The threat cannot be detected by any of your instruments or machines because it isn't of the human realm. Only a being with the powers of a great Avatar could have concocted such an evil. Here is what happens: a tiny bit of Necocyaotl is added to every crystal that leaves your making-place. These go into the machines you mentioned. The machines are shipped out to homes and busi-nesses all across this earth. And when these machines are given food, and the crystals come to life, Necocyaotl is there. Everywhere those crystals go."

Sierra stared at him in disbelief.

"What do you mean 'given food,' and 'brought to life'?"

The ancient Avatar looked uncertain for the first time.

"I don't have the words," he admitted. "I see that the crystals eat the same ethereal substance that also animates living creatures, and they grow warm and do things as though they were alive. But they are not alive."

"Oh. Semiconductors work on electricity. You're right—they aren't alive. But what you're saying is crazy," she protested. "What do you mean? How can Simmons put a little bit of Neco, Neco—whatever—into every semiconductor? She wouldn't have *time* to do all that. She's not even at the company half the time—she's out meeting people and talking to Wall Street people or the press. It's just not possible!"

Quetzalcoatl smiled, but sadly, and patted her hand in a grandfatherly manner.

"I didn't mean that she does it herself," he said. "People are so clever, so amazingly creative. It's no wonder they don't believe in us anymore. Why should they, with such wonders as they have created?"

"Do all the semiconductors in the world have a little bit of Neco—your brother—in them?"

"No, only the ones from Black Diamond," returned the Avatar. "If you think about it, I'm sure you can see how it is done. Why are the Black Diamond crystals different from all the others?"

"The silicon," breathed Sierra. "That's why it's called Black Diamond. The silicon is formulated differently. It comes out darker, somehow—more like gunmetal than silver. It's a proprietary process, and the silicon runs way cooler than other semiconductors, so it's used anywhere heat is a problem. Is the silicon doped with something from your brother?"

The old man merely nodded.

"What does it do?"

She thought of all the electronics upon which her Silicon Valley life relied, wondered how many of them had Black Diamond products inside, and thought uneasily about being poisoned.

"The Obsidian Mirror has discovered a way to spread his essence across the world inside these tiny crystals," answered Quetzalcoatl. "When a vulnerable person comes into contact with his essence, he begins to gaze into that dark mirror, and his vision is forever clouded while he is under its influence. Have you ever wondered," he continued, "why people pour filth into the rivers and oceans, even though they know that they themselves drink from the rivers' waters and eat from the seas? That their own children likewise are poisoned by this?"

"Yes," Sierra said. "I don't understand it at all. I really don't."

"Now you do. They have breathed Necocyaotl's evil being. They see nothing but their immediate personal gain, comfort, or convenience. They are gazing into the Obsidian Mirror, and they can see nothing but their own gain."

Well, that's the first time I've heard an explanation that made any sense, thought Sierra, and then realized that in the rational light of day, the explanation made less "sense" than ever. Still, she was inclined to believe him. *If you can't believe a thousands-of-years-old Avatar, whom can you believe?* Then she reflected that Neco-whatever was just as old and just as much an Avatar as the ancient creature in front of her.

Why trust this one? she asked herself. Then she thought, *because I trust Chaco.* Before she had a chance to challenge this thought, Quetzalcoatl spoke again.

"You have told me that you can't help me. But you haven't asked me why I believe you can help."

Sierra gave him her full attention but did not speak.

"You have two very important assets," said Quetzalcoatl. "First, you have worked where these things are made. You know the people. You know how things are done. You know where everything is."

Sierra nodded.

"Yes, but you're overlooking one important fact. I don't work there anymore. They have strict security. I won't be allowed anywhere near the place, because I was fired."

The old man waved this away.

"The other important asset is that you can't be seduced by the Obsidian Mirror. You have been amply exposed to its influence, but you haven't succumbed. You see clearly what happens when the natural world is destroyed. You are not one who would put poison in her own mouth.

"And you," he said, leaning toward her so that the carved green stones around his neck clacked together, "you are the one who can stop this woman. Stop her forever from spreading ruin across the earth."

Sierra stared at him, chilled. She hastily began to rise to her feet. Chaco opened his amber eyes and raised his head alertly, ears pricked.

"You've got the wrong person." Her heart slammed against her chest again. "I'm not going to kill her. Not for you. Not for anyone!"

"You misunderstand me," said the old man sadly. "I am not asking you to murder her."

Sierra sat down again.

"What *are* you asking, then?"

"Necocyaotl cannot inhabit the soul of any creature who has contact with me or my essence," explained Quetzalcoatl. "Take some of my feathers. If you find a way to bring them into contact with her skin, my brother's influence will vanish. He will never be able to touch her again."

"I'm sorry. Things have changed. I've been fired. The company wouldn't even let me back in the building—at least not past the front desk. There's no way I could get close enough to her now. I'm sorry you wasted your time on me."

Quetzalcoatl studied her face for a long while and then his brown face crinkled in a smile.

"I don't think I have wasted my time, Sierra Carter. I think you will do what I ask. I think you *can* do what I ask. You have powers you have never suspected. They sleep inside you for now, but they will awaken when you most have need of them."

Sierra was dismayed. Why didn't he ask her to do something easy, like spin straw into gold, or count every grain of sand on the shore? "What powers?" she asked. "I'm just ordinary. I've never had a paranormal experience, or seen a ghost, or…"

The ancient Avatar shifted slightly, commanding her attention, and she stopped speaking. He leaned forward and placed his dark brown, wrinkled hand on her forehead. It felt dry and warm. She closed her eyes. Behind her lids, her brain suddenly lit with colored fire: flames of purple, gold, green, red, and blue. Her eyes popped open in surprise and she stared at Quetzalcoatl. "What did you just do?"

"I only showed you a glimpse of the power you possess, child. It's there, inside you. But only you can call it into action, only you can use it. Find a way to use your power to fight Necocyaotl and his servants."

She felt extremely tired suddenly. Things were happening

too fast, and they were happening way too weirdly. She wished with all her heart that the past few days had never happened, and thought longingly of her once-despised cubicle with its cozy, familiar computer.

Quetzalcoatl did not seem impatient as she sat silently before him. He neither spoke nor moved while her mind spun like a gerbil on a wheel.

"How do I use the power you say I have?"

Quetzalcoatl smiled tenderly at Sierra. "That, too, is something you must find for yourself. But you will find it. And you will use it to touch Jenna with my feathers and dispel the evil that lives inside her."

She asked, "Does it have to be the actual feathers? Touching her skin, I mean?"

"It must be the feathers, or something imbued with the essence of the feathers," he replied. "Something of me must come into direct contact with her."

"OK," Sierra said, resignedly. She didn't see what she was supposed to do, exactly, or how she would do it. But if the Avatar was telling her the truth, she might actually be able to help. She was tired of watching the world being paved over with concrete. Better to trust this old god and his wild coyote than continue to do nothing. Having special power sounded like it might even be possible. Assuming she could figure out how to use it.

"I thank you."

As he spoke, his voice became a deep, resonant susurrus, and the cavern was suddenly extremely full of snake. But this was a snake like none other since the world began. Its massive loops and coils would have dwarfed even a dragon, if such had ever existed, and instead of scales, the skin was covered with glowing blue-green feathers. Sierra found herself staring into eyes like vast green moons.

"Take these," hissed the great snake, and a shower of feathers fell at her feet, ringing like wind chimes in a gale.

Sierra grabbed the gleaming feathers, stuffed them in her

backpack, and fled. As an old man, Quetzalcoatl had seemed almost grandfatherly, but the Presence back in the cavern did not feel anything like family. This was an ancient power, and no matter how well inclined, it was terrifying.

Sierra shot out of the cave into the sunlight. She leaned against one of the boulders guarding the cave mouth. Her heart hammered in her chest, and she bent over, panting. Presently, Chaco trotted out of the cave and sat next to her, tail curled neatly around his feet.

"That went well, don't you think?" Chaco asked, grinning in a doggy sort of way.

Sierra glared at him.

"No. I do not. The fate of the world apparently rests on me, Sierra Carter, out-of-work public relations professional. I can't think of a worse scenario, can you?"

"Oh, I think you're selling yourself short," Chaco said encouragingly. "If the Big Q thinks you can do it, trust me, you can do it."

"You don't call him that to his *face*, do you?"

She would never again think of that vast and ancient presence by Chaco's flippant sobriquet.

"The Big Q? No. Who would dare?"

He stretched and yawned, showing a great deal of long, pink tongue and sharp teeth.

"Well, better get back to camp. We've got work to do, I hear."

The way back was easier only because it was largely downhill. She slid down the scree leading up to the cave mouth mostly on her rear end, sending up prayers of thankfulness to the inventor of heavy denim. Chaco had disturbed nothing in his passage through the scrub, but Sierra was able to take advantage of the trail of broken branches and crushed grasses she herself had left behind. They arrived back at their campsite after hiking no more than an hour and a half. When Sierra pushed through the bushes into the cleared area, she stopped short in utter dismay.

The camp had been ravaged. The tent was collapsed over the ruin of her sleeping bag, which was leaking stuffing from long slashes. The duffle bags had been ripped open, and her gear was strewn everywhere, broken, snapped and ripped. The cooler had been dumped out and the food ground into the dirt. Standing in the middle of this wreckage was Aiden, looking worried, then relieved, as he saw her.

"There you are! What happened here? I walked down here to say hello, and when I saw what had happened, and you were nowhere around—well, I was about to call the sheriff's department."

Mahaha, she thought. *It was looking for us. Or something was.* She walked over to Aiden. When he wrapped his long arms around her and hugged her, she relaxed into his embrace gratefully. Even though he was virtually a stranger, after the shock of seeing the camp, the hug was welcome. For a few seconds, she felt warm, safe and protected. Then she pulled gently away.

"It must have happened while we were out hiking. Kids, probably. Damn it."

Aiden gazed down at her, his blue eyes worried.

"Kids?" he said. "I don't know. This is beyond petty vandalism. Whoever did this was vicious. Malicious."

"Yeah. Well, we were going home, anyway," she responded.

Sierra felt a pang of regret; she would have liked to spend more time with him, but now was not the moment.

"We?" inquired Aiden, in a carefully neutral tone of voice.

"Yes, me and Chaco, of course," she replied ungrammatically, slightly cheered by his interest.

On cue, Chaco sauntered out of the bushes. He began sniffing around the site, as though looking for something.

"I guess I'd better get this mess cleaned up," she sighed.

Replacing all this equipment was going to cost her, and she couldn't afford it without a steady salary.

"I'll help," said Aiden, and he began to pick up the bits and pieces of her camping gear.

Sierra located some plastic garbage bags that had escaped destruction, and for the next hour, they worked side by side, chatting about places they had camped, about music and movies. They seemed to like the same things, Sierra thought. Once in a while, when she found an item she particularly regretted, like the shreds of her expensive, waterproof windbreaker, she sighed again. Chaco sniffed diligently around the campsite as they worked.

They finished cleaning up the camp, dumping as much as possible of the ruined things into a nearby trash can, but most of it had to go into the trunk of her car.

"Well, that's that," she said. "Thanks so much for helping me, Aiden. It was really nice of you."

He flashed her a smile that made her knees a little wobbly.

"I didn't mind at all," he said. "I'd like to get together again some time. Under happier circumstances."

Sierra's heart leaped, but she merely smiled and wrote down her phone number and email address on a scrap of paper for him. He gave her another heartwarming hug, so welcome in its humanity after what she had seen and learned. Then she opened the car door for Chaco and climbed in herself. Aiden stood waving after her as she drove off. She watched him in the rear view mirror until Chaco yelped, "Watchwhereyou'regoing!" in time for her to miss a pine tree inconveniently located at a turn in the road.

She swerved, corrected, and noticed that Chaco was in human form again, glowering at her.

"Put your seat belt on," Sierra said automatically, and Chaco strapped himself in.

"Why did you spend so much time with that guy?" growled Chaco. His black brows lowered over snapping amber eyes.

"Why not? He was very kind to spend all that time helping me clean up. Good thing, too. *You* were no help at all."

"I couldn't very well change shape in front of him, or just appear. That would raise a few questions. There *are* protocols for this sort of thing, you know," he protested, then said, "I don't want you to see him again."

"Why not?"

"Just don't."

"Listen. You and your boss have roped me into this thing,

but that doesn't mean you get to decide who my friends are," Sierra snapped.

Chaco subsided and sulked for at least a hundred miles. Sierra barely noticed. She was thinking hard about the task she had taken on, its impossibility, and—to be honest—its improbability.

Finally, Chaco broke the silence.

"I'm hungry."

Naturally, thought Sierra.

Aloud, she said, "OK. Let's stop in Pleasanton and get a bite." She pulled off the freeway and found a coffee shop. As she opened the door, she heard a squeaky voice from the back seat.

"Get me a BLT and a side of fries and a cola to go," it said.

Startled, she peered into the back to find Fred curled up on the floor of the car.

"Please," Fred added, staring up at her with gleaming orange eyes.

"What are you doing there? How did you get in my car?"

"I'm not doing anything," said Fred, sucking placidly on a digit. "I just climbed in while you and Chaco were away."

"How? The car was locked."

Chaco said, "Fred's a mannegishi. It's what they do."

"So, are you gonna get me a BLT?" Fred asked again, peering hopefully into Sierra's face. "And a cola and…"

"Yes, all right," interrupted Sierra.

"And fries?"

"Yes!" Sierra snarled, and slammed the door.

She steamed into the restaurant, Chaco close behind.

"Fred may come in handy," Chaco observed after they were seated.

Sierra was unconvinced.

"I don't see how. I'm going to go bankrupt, feeding the two of you," she said ungraciously, scanning the predictable menu.

The server came over to their table. Ignoring Sierra, she blinked in disbelief at the sight of Chaco. He lowered his thick black lashes slightly and gave her a lazy grin. The server smiled back and leaned forward slightly, affording him a glimpse down the front of her well-packed blouse.

"What can I get for you today, sir?" she asked sweetly.

"*I* will have a chef's salad. Please also get me a BLT, cola, and fries to go," Sierra said pointedly.

The server—her name tag, pinned to the ample swell of her left breast, read, "Bettina"—noted something in her order book without looking at Sierra and smiled brightly at Chaco.

"Two Beluga Burgers and a double order of fries," Chaco said. "And a milkshake. Chocolate, please."

"I love to see a man with an appetite," Bettina said and swayed away, but not without another peek at Chaco.

He smiled to himself.

Sierra was annoyed. And she was annoyed at herself for being annoyed. It was nothing to her if Chaco wanted to flirt with Bettina. And vice versa. Nothing. She chewed her way through a tasteless chef's salad, then flagged Bettina down to remind her about the BLT, fries, and cola to go. Bettina shot a meaningful glance at Sierra's thighs, made a note in her pad, and strode away, leaving Sierra fuming again.

Chaco wolfed down his burgers, fries, and milkshake with a chaser of mud pie and coffee. Finally Fred's order arrived, and Sierra paid the bill. When they got back to the car, she handed down the food to Fred in the back and said, "Don't you dare spill that soft drink all over my carpet, Fred. You hear me?"

The mannegishi nodded and began slurping at the plastic straw, sounding like a clogged kitchen drain.

Sierra made sure Chaco was in his seatbelt, every minute feeling more like someone's mom, which annoyed her still further. As she pulled onto the freeway, she had a sudden realization.

"Fred?" she said, unable to see him in the back. "Fred, what happened at our camp? Who tore it up while we were gone?"

"I dunno," came the answer from the back seat, somewhat muffled by BLT.

Chaco leaned over the back of his seat.

"What do you mean, you don't know?" he asked crossly. "You were at camp when we left. You were obviously there when we got back. How could you not know?"

There was a moment of silence.

Then, sheepishly, "I wasn't there when it happened. I kind of went over to someone else's camp to see if they had any chocolate. They did, and they were gone, so I stayed a while. When I got back, Whatsisname was at our camp, so I disappeared, and then you came. I'm sorry, but I didn't see anything."

Chaco twisted back around, sighing with frustration.

"I just don't like it," he said. "Something isn't right."

"I'll say something isn't right!" Sierra snapped. "I just lost a couple thousand dollars' worth of camping gear. Personally, I think it was that Mahaha thing."

"Naw," Chaco said. "I would've smelled it. Mahaha was never anywhere near us."

"Then maybe it was just kids."

"Mmmmph," Chaco grunted, and that's all he said for the rest of the drive back to Sierra's home. Fred took up the conversational slack by singing in a chirpy voice all the camp songs he had ever heard hanging around the state park, including "One Hundred Bottles of Beer on the Wall."

By the time Sierra parked in front of her house in the falling dark, she had a tension headache from gritting her teeth. This was not helped by discovering that Fred had gone to sleep, spilling the remnants of his sticky brown drink on the car's carpet. She poked him sharply to wake him up, causing him to disappear.

"C'mon, Fred, we're home. You stay disappeared, OK? And I want you to come back out here and clean up this mess."

She didn't wait to see if Chaco and Fred were following. As she had carried her backpack with her on the hike to the cave, it was the only piece of camping gear that hadn't been spoiled by the vandal or vandals, so she hefted it over one shoulder and left the ruins of the rest of her gear in the trunk. She unlocked the front door. Chaco stood motionless in the middle of the sidewalk, nose twitching and staring around in an unnerving manner, but she ignored him. The inside of her house was dark, and she groped with her hand for the light switch near the door and flipped it on. Nothing happened.

"Darn it!" she said to herself. "Another power outage."

She stepped into her front hallway and set her backpack down to retrieve her flashlight. As she bent to rummage in the depths of the pack, her front door slammed violently shut and locked, cutting off the dim evening light from outside. She became aware of a sharp, cold odor—the odor of impending snow— at the same instant that a heavy, bony body hit her hard, and sent her sprawling on the floor.

Then, inches from her face, she saw the thing. Red, glowing eyes, slit like a goat's. Ice-blue skin with a few coarse white hairs straggling from cheeks and chin. Yellow tusks in a lipless, grinning maw. Slotted nostrils in a flattened face. And long, long, bony fingers ending in gleaming, scythe-like claws.

In the few coherent thoughts she could summon, she was pretty sure she was looking at Mahaha.

CHAPTER 7

Sierra screamed, lashing out with her booted feet. The ice demon laughed a high laugh, "Mahaha!" as her boots slammed into its bony chest, and it raked her shins with taloned fingers, sending lightening-bolts of pain along her nerve ends. Moving faster than Sierra could believe possible, the hideous thing leaped at her again, trying to pin her under its body.

All the while, the thing kept laughing like a stage villain, "Mahaha! Mahaha!"

Sierra rolled to one side as fast as she could, still gripping her backpack, but not quite fast enough. The creature jabbed its clawed hands at her, and Sierra gasped with pain as an icy pang slid toward her heart. It felt as though a frozen knife were sliding into a space between two ribs, turning her warm flesh to ice in its path.

• • •

Sierra found herself near a corner formed by the wall and the rise of the stairs. She heaved to a sitting position, gasping with pain, and wedged herself into the corner, protecting her back. She began frantically grubbing inside the pack's main compartment with one hand, fending off the monster with her feet. She was dimly aware that someone was pounding on the front door and yelling, but the door had locked again when it slammed shut. The pain in her side grew more intense every moment, and she could barely breathe from the agony.

Sierra's back was now protected and she could brace herself against the wall for more powerful kicks, but she was literally cornered, with no way to retreat. After taking the first surprise blow from her feet, Mahaha evaded her kicks easily, but could not get past the barrier of her furiously jabbing feet. It finally caught both her ankles with its bony fingers and yanked, hard. As she felt herself slip down, she brought her right hand up out of her pack, gripping what she had sought so desperately and shoved her hand toward the demon's fanged face. Then she slid helplessly down, head banging sharply on the hardwood floor, and abruptly lost all interest in what was happening.

• • •

Sierra found herself in a long stone hall, standing at one end. The blocks of stone composing the structure were the size of small cars, massive and cleanly squared. The air was hot and humid, with the musty closeness of a confined space. The long chamber was lit with torches, burning in sconces fixed to the stone walls. Stone bas-relief friezes, brightly painted in rusty red, blue, yellow, black and brown, decorated the length of the hall on both sides. She slowly turned all the way around, looking for a door, but there was no entryway or exit. At the end farthest from her, she could see a huge black oblong, flanked by stone sculptures and shining darkly in the torchlight.

There was no one else present, but she could hear drums and chanting, as though from a great distance. She began to walk slowly down the length of the hall, as there was really no other way to go and nothing else to do. She drew closer to the painted friezes on the left-hand side of the hall, trying to make out what they represented.

At first, the bright paint made the friezes appear attractive and cheerful. She associated the style with the art of the Aztecs or the Maya: highly stylized, blocky figures accompanied by strange shapes and ornaments she did not recognize. As she stared at them, she began to discern what the figures were doing. There was a chief—she thought it was a chief because he was larger than the other figures—cutting the tongues from the mouths of bound captives. There was another figure, prone on a stone altar, his heart, in the grip of a priest, pumping blood into the air. Each scene was a depiction of torture, human sacrifice, pain, and gore.

Sierra continued walking, each step bringing her to a new scene, each one more terrible than the last. The parade of cruelty increasingly oppressed her as she walked, but she seemed to have no choice but to go on.

At last, she stood before the shining object at the end of the hall. It was a sheet of black stone, obsidian, nearly twice as tall as she and as wide as her workbench was long. It had been hewn from a single, impossible sheet of volcanic glass; its opaque, gleaming surface reflected her image, distorted by the flaking cuts used to smooth the stone. She stared into the black mirror, fascinated by the way her reflection constantly distorted with even her smallest movement.

"Sierra." Her name was whispered, echoing in the stone chamber.

She whirled around, but no one was there.

"Sierra," said the voice again.

It was a deep voice that reverberated inside her chest, like a drum.

"You are in my house. This is my mirror. See yourself."

Sierra turned back to her dark reflection.

"See what I will do for you," the voice said in caressing, almost seductive tones.

For a fleeting moment, she remembered the "power" that Quetzalcoatl told her she possessed. But the memory of those bright flames misted away as her reflection took on a life of its own in the black mirror. She was wealthy. She had become a renowned designer of fine jewelry, her work sought by the rich and powerful throughout the globe. She had a sleek, high-powered car. She traveled around the world. She knew many powerful people and men dreamed of her. She was known and welcomed everywhere in the finest restaurants, the most luxurious hotels, the most exclusive society.

"See what you will become, as my beloved," the voice said. "Everything you have ever dreamed of. Everything. All you need do is come to me."

Sierra stared dreamily into the depths of the obsidian mirror. How lovely everything would be. No more bosses. Lots of money, enough money to play with. Fame and recognition for her work. She raised her hands and rested her palms on the cool, black surface. All she had to do was go through the mirror, like Alice, and this would be her life. The surface of the stone seemed to shimmer around her hands like black water. No more worries, no more problems. Sierra sighed, yearning toward this vision that the voice had promised.

Then she frowned. *Wait a minute*, she thought, *I don't think this is* my *dream*. She looked again. She wanted to use her creativity to design jewelry and earn a living doing it. But sleek, fast cars? Fame and fortune? Yearning men? One yearning man would be enough for her. Now that she really thought about it, this wasn't her vision at all. She didn't see any hiking or camping in there. She didn't see true friendships or true love. No, not her dream at all. She pushed away hard from the stone, and whirled, half expecting to see the speaker behind her.

Instead, she saw a massive stone altar where none had been before. Lying on the altar, chest empty and bleeding, eyes lifeless, she saw herself. She screamed in terror, and the scream seemed to build until the vast hall rumbled and shifted, and the ceiling stones dropped as the structure began to collapse around her. Still she screamed, and the obsidian mirror shivered, exploding into fragments and deadly black dust, sending a barrage of razor-edged shards flying at her.

• • •

Sierra gradually became aware that time had passed. She felt a cold trickle down her neck. *Blood?* She opened her eyes, but couldn't see.

Am I dead? she wondered. She lay quite still, hoping that more information would be revealed about her current status. Then she realized that someone nearby was snuffling loudly.

"Oooooooh!" someone wailed. "I'll never forgive myself if she dies. Oooooooh!"

Why, that's Fred, she thought in amazement. *I can't be dead, because Fred can't die. Can he?* Then she realized that she couldn't see because someone had placed a very wet towel over her eyes and forehead, causing the cold trickle down her neck. She also became aware that she was lying in bed, probably her own bed, which was undoubtedly getting wet from the sopping towel. Groggily, she swept the towel off her face and tried to sit up. Pain stabbed her side as if an icicle had speared her. Her throbbing head persuaded her to lie back down again, but the cold, wet pillows sent her right back up. Fred stopped wailing and began a joyous, if earsplitting, squeal.

"Chaco! She's alive!"

Chaco leaned over her anxiously from the other side of the bed, where he was sitting in an armchair.

"Are you all right?"

His amber eyes were soft with concern as he peered into her wet face. He was holding a bundle of burning herbs over an abalone shell that had most recently decorated her downstairs bathroom. A thin veil of sweet-smelling smoke arose from it as he set it down carefully on her bureau.

"I'm not sure," she responded, holding her side.

She felt the oddest sort of pain in her ribs on the right side, not a hot, throbbing pain like an infection, but a deep cold, as though there were ice embedded in her flesh.

"What happened? No—first, could someone get me some ibuprofen? Please? It's in the kitchen. Cupboard next to the sink."

Chaco loped downstairs to the kitchen and returned with the bottle of ibuprofen and a glass of water. Sierra moved carefully away from the wet pillows and took the glass in a shaky hand. Chaco sat down beside her on the bed, shook out two tablets and put them in her hand, then took the glass and held it to her lips. She sipped and swallowed the tablets. He put a strong arm around her and hugged her gently. Fred grasped one of her hands in twelve of his fingers and squeezed.

My goodness, she thought. *This is sort of nice.*

Then she asked again, "What happened?"

"You remember Mahaha?" Chaco asked.

Sierra shuddered. She remembered the thing's icy claws and her stomach clenched.

"I see you do. Anyway, it was waiting for you inside. It slammed the door shut when it attacked you. The door locked again, and we could hear you screaming and Mahaha laughing and a lot of thrashing around. Then Fred opened the door…"

"How did Fred open the door? You said it was locked."

Chaco grinned at the mannegishi, who was—unusually, for Fred—staring at Sierra with *both* his huge eyes. "That's just another thing that mannegishis are good at. They can get into anything. Especially if there's food involved, of course."

"So it was Fred and Chaco to the rescue?"

"Oh, no," responded Chaco. "The door locked behind you. We didn't realize at first that anything was wrong—not until we heard the demon laughing." He shuddered slightly. "By the time we got into the house, you'd already killed Mahaha. You were out like a light, and Mahaha was dead."

"Um," said Sierra. "I'm afraid I'm a little vague on that part. How did I kill it? I thought *it* was killing *me*."

Chaco managed to look proud and worried simultaneously.

"You must have remembered that the feathers were in your backpack. You grabbed them and stuffed them down its throat. No creature of Necocyaotl can survive contact with Quetzalcoatl. It died."

"Oh, no," moaned Sierra. "How are we going to get rid of that thing? I can't exactly call the county coroner or put it out with the trash. It's too big to bury in the back yard…"

"Oh, don't worry about it," Chaco said. "It vaporized. It left kind of a nasty stain on your floor, but we got most of it out."

"Vaporized?" Sierra said, feeling more dazed than before.

"Um, yes. And the feathers, too," Chaco said ruefully.

"*All* of the feathers? Every last one?" cried Sierra in horror.

"Yes. But you saved your life. That was quick thinking."

Sierra cradled her throbbing head gently in her hands. She recalled grabbing the feathers, although she had not been so much thinking rationally as grasping at straws. She couldn't remember anything after shoving the feathers at the creature.

"We'll have to go back to the cave, then," she said. "We'll have to get more feathers from Quetzalcoatl."

"I don't think we can do that," said Chaco. "He wouldn't be there anymore."

"Why not?"

"It's not like he lives there," Chaco replied. "He's gone back."

"Gone back where? Can't you call him?"

"He's gone back to wherever he is when he's not somewhere else," responded Chaco, with the maddening air of pointing out the obvious. "And no, I can't call him. Did he seem like somebody you can ring up on a cell phone?"

"No," Sierra muttered. Her thoughts were muddled, her side and head hurt, and she wondered if she had a concussion. "What are we going to do, Chaco?"

"Nothing for tonight. You've been unconscious for days, you know, and you're in no shape to do anything until you've healed a bit."

"*Days?*" asked Sierra. "I've been out for *days*? Why?"

She was wearing pajamas, and not the jeans and camp shirt she had been wearing when Mahaha attacked her. That meant Chaco had carried her up the stairs, undressed her and put her to bed. Her face suddenly felt warm.

"Mahaha wounded you pretty badly, in your side. You're lucky he didn't get to your heart—that's where he was aiming. You were horribly cold, like a corpse. Does your side still hurt? You kept crying out about your side hurting."

"Yes," said Fred, solemnly. "It was awful, especially when you screamed and screamed."

Sierra felt her right side, which still ached with cold. There was a thick bandage covering her ribs beneath her pajama top.

"It hurts," she said. "But not too badly. Thanks for taking care of me."

She didn't want to think about days spent writhing unconscious in a fever. She hoped she didn't say anything embarrassing.

Fred said, "And you said Chaco was *muy guapo,* and so were Aiden and Clancy. Who's Clancy? I didn't know you spoke Spanish."

Helplessly, Sierra felt her face flame.

"Never mind that," she said, crossly. "When my grandmother was coming out of anesthesia she said she wanted spider juice to drink. It doesn't mean anything."

Fred looked thoughtful. "Sounds kind of tasty," he said, "Depending on the type of spider."

Sierra tossed the covers aside and said, "I'll let you do the experimenting, Fred. Now, both of you—out. I need some privacy."

"Wait!" cried Chaco, but she was already on her feet.

"C'mon, guys. Out you go."

"I'll go get you something to eat," said Chaco. "You must be starving."

She was still shaky and weak, but she stood steadily on her feet until Chaco and Fred left. She closed the door and grabbed the soaking pillows from her bed. Thankfully, the bed itself seemed fairly dry. She rummaged in the closet and found an old, rather flat pillow which would have to do for now.

Then she collapsed breathlessly on the bed and began peeling the bandages away from her side. Beneath the bandages, her skin was covered with a pungent, greenish paste. There was just one ragged cut, but it seemed very deep. She touched the scored skin gently and winced. It felt like a shard of ice was lodged between her ribs. But the cut was scabbed over and apparently healing cleanly, from what she could see in the mirror. She got into the shower to wash off the stinky paste. Afterwards, she dried the wound carefully and applied antibiotic ointment and new bandages.

Chaco brought her soup and toast in bed, and sat in the armchair while she ate.

"I almost forgot," he said. "You had a few phone calls. I took messages."

He ran lightly downstairs and then returned with a slip of paper. Sierra was faintly surprised to see that his handwriting was delicate, with swooping flourishes, like Victorian script.

Sierra deciphered the notes. There was a call from her dentist reminding her of a cleaning appointment.

"What day is it?" she asked Chaco. He told her. "Damn," she said. "I'll have to reschedule."

Her father had called, asking her to phone when she was back from her trip. Kaylee had left an almost identical message. And there was a message from Clancy Forrester, asking her to call him at work. Sierra groaned.

Chaco looked at her.

"Are you in pain?"

"No," Sierra sighed. "At least, I'm not in any more pain than I was. It's this guy Forrester. Why on earth would he call me? He's the head of security at Black Diamond, so it can't be good news. Maybe he thinks I stole the secret formula for Black Diamond silicon," she finished bitterly—and then recalled that she did, indeed, know the secret.

"Probably just routine," said Chaco in a comforting tone, scooping up the soup bowl. "You should be resting."

He turned off the light and left the room, leaving Sierra to reflect on how little Avatars understood what was routine in the high-tech business environment. It certainly was not routine to get a call from the head of security of the company that had just fired you—not unless you were in some sort of trouble.

Sierra lay in bed, worrying about Clancy's call. Did he think she had taken something proprietary? He had watched her clear out her things, so he knew she hadn't had time to copy anything from the computer. What did the man want? Couldn't they just leave her alone, after booting her out?

As Sierra fretted over Clancy's call, she began to drift off. Just as she sank into true sleep, she saw Mahaha leaping at her out of the darkness, and she jerked herself awake, causing another lance of icy pain in her side. This happened again and again, but each time it became harder to rouse herself from the nightmare. Finally, she lay on her bed, muttering and jerking, skin cooling despite the warm spring night.

CHAPTER 8

The next morning Chaco prepared a tray with oatmeal, orange juice, and toast. He ascended the stairs, humming tunelessly, and knocked on Sierra's closed door. There was no response. He knocked again and waited. Finally, he opened the door a crack and peered in. In the darkened room, he could see the covers humped over Sierra's motionless body.

"Rise and shine!" he called, switching the light on and stepping into the room.

As soon as he saw her pale and sweating face, he knew something was terribly wrong. She was cold to the touch, breathing shallowly. He shook her. Her eyes opened a bit, but showed only half-moons of white under the lids. She did not awaken.

Chaco dropped the tray on the nightstand and ran downstairs.

"Fred! Sierra's worse. I'm going to get help," he called. He found the number Sierra had scrawled on the pad of paper next to the phone and had a brief, urgent conversation with someone on the other end.

Fred pattered upstairs to check on Sierra. He clambered onto the chair next to her bed and felt her forehead.

"Oh, this is bad," he muttered to himself.

He climbed back down and went to the bathroom, where he had to scale the toilet to reach the sink. He put a towel in the sink and flooded it with warm water. Climbing back down, he returned to her bed, tenderly placing the wet towel on Sierra's clammy forehead and soaking her one remaining dry pillow. Then he settled down to worry and wait.

A half an hour passed, and Sierra twitched and mumbled unintelligibly but did not wake. Fred had just completed his third trip to the bathroom and back to soak the towel with warm water when the doorbell rang. Fred instantly disappeared. He heard Chaco answer, and footsteps came quickly up the stairs. Chaco entered the room accompanied by a tall, dark-skinned woman wearing an orange, black, and brown African-print dress and a chunky stone necklace. She had large brown eyes—currently shadowed by a tense frown—and a generous mouth to go with her generously endowed hips. She rushed to Sierra's bedside and felt her face.

"She's all wet and cold!" Kaylee turned accusing eyes on Chaco. "What happened to her? Who are you, anyway? What are you doing here? Why didn't you take her to the hospital?"

She seemed likely to continue with her questions without waiting for an answer, but Chaco held up a hand.

"Sierra has been...wounded badly."

He held up his hand again as Kaylee drew breath for another barrage.

"Hear me out. Please. I need to find someone who can heal this kind of injury."

Kaylee narrowed her eyes dangerously.

"What do you mean by that? I know a doctor. And Sierra needs medical care..."

"No, she doesn't," interrupted Chaco. "Sierra's wound can't be healed by a doctor."

Kaylee blinked at him, long, curly lashes flickering over her dark eyes.

"Just who *are* you?"

"I'm Chaco. A friend. It's a really long story, Kaylee, and we don't have that kind of time. Later, I promise. Sierra needs help, *now*. She needs someone who—I can't think of any other way to say it—who deals with the supernatural. Someone who can heal a supernatural injury."

"Show me."

Chaco gestured at the bandage under Sierra's pajama top. Kaylee eased the fabric up and gently peeled back the bandage.

She hissed between her teeth at the side of the puffy, white flesh ridged around the wound.

"She's so cold," Kaylee whispered. "Why is she so damn *cold*?"

"The creature that attacked her uses cold as a poison. I don't really know how it works, but I'm afraid she's freezing to death from the inside."

Chaco twisted his long fingers together nervously. Kaylee stared at him for a beat, then made up her mind.

"I need to make a phone call," she said, and whipped out her mobile phone and punched in a number. She had a brief conversation, giving directions to Sierra's house, and put the phone away.

"We've got a few minutes now," she said. "I think you'd better tell me exactly what's going on while we wait." Kaylee sat, settling herself in a chair with a determined thump.

"Suppose you tell me how you know about me for a start," Kaylee said, her dark eyes boring into Chaco's amber ones. "I never told Sierra about me. Thought she'd freak, I guess. But somehow you know that I practice Vodún, don't you?"

"Easy. It was your necklace," Chaco said. He gestured at the carved piece that Kaylee wore around her neck. "Sierra showed me a picture of you, and you were wearing it. I recognized it right away."

She touched the stone absently, her slender fingers exploring its surface as though trying to remember what it was. Carved from red-orange stone, the pendant was heart-shaped. Lines were incised across it, making squares, which were pierced, forming a kind of filigree. A snake wrapped around the heart, its head resting across the widest part.

"You recognized the vévé of Madame Ézilee?" she asked, one eyebrow cocked.

Chaco nodded. "I did," he acknowledged. "Of all your loa, she is my personal favorite."

"So she's your favorite, eh? Our goddess of love, our black Aphrodite?"

Chaco nodded earnestly again, but smiled this time. "I look forward to my next encounter with her—more than I can say!"

Kaylee eyed him with amazement. "You *know* Madame Ézilee?" she asked, incredulously. "Who *are* you?"

Chaco's rather self-satisfied grin faded and he shifted uneasily. "I'm—well, I'm sort of like Ézilee," he responded. "I'm Coyotl the Trickster. An Avatar."

Kaylee regarded him for another moment in silence, apparently turning this information over in her mind. "What do you mean by an Avatar?" she asked finally. "I know what the dictionary says, but how do *you* define it?"

Chaco looked cornered. "There are so many names," he replied. "Gods. Spirits. Sidhe. Loa. Deities. Some are called demons. Or angels. We aren't physical, but we can take physical form. We aren't mortal, but we can be destroyed under certain circumstances. We have great powers—but we aren't all-powerful. I can do many things that humans can't, but I can't heal Sierra. I have no influence over the evil that hurt her. That's why I called you."

"I see," said Kaylee. "Well, then, Mr. Coyotl. What *are* your special powers?"

She smiled slightly, as though not expecting much. The smile vanished abruptly, replaced by a look of wide-eyed alarm, as Chaco's body began to melt and flow into his coyote form. He sat on the floor, looking up at her with yellow eyes and panting a bit, but definitely grinning.

Kaylee recovered from her astonishment quickly.

"OK," she said. "That's enough. I believe you. And don't think I haven't seen stranger things, because I have!"

She sat back, arms folded across her chest, as Chaco returned to human form.

"And who's that other person? The one who's been sneaking around the room while we've been talking?"

Kaylee smiled again, knowing she was scoring a point.

Chaco, now completely anthropomorphic, brushed a few coyote hairs off his jeans.

"Oh, you probably mean Fred," he replied. "He's not exactly a person. How'd you figure out that he was here?"

Fred exploded into view, his orange eyes wheeling madly in several different directions. Kaylee started violently, but maintained her composure.

"And just what the hell are you supposed to be?" she inquired sweetly.

Two or three digits popped wetly out of Fred's mouth as he answered, "Mannegishi."

As Fred didn't seem inclined to elaborate, Chaco said, "Mannegishi are sort of like leprechauns…"

"Not!" exclaimed Fred. "That's insulting. Take it back!"

"Well, let's see," snapped Chaco. "You can disappear, you trick people, you steal stuff, and you're green. The only difference is…"

Fred swelled ominously, making little spluttering sounds of indignation, but Kaylee intervened.

"It doesn't matter, Fred, Chaco. We have a desperately ill woman here. This is no time to get into a spat."

Chaco and Fred subsided, glaring at each other, and that was the last of the conversation until the doorbell rang. Chaco jumped up, but Kaylee rose with more dignity and said, "Better let me."

She walked downstairs. Fred and Chaco could hear the door open and the murmur of women's voices, followed by the sound of footsteps on the stairs.

Kaylee re-entered the room, followed by a second woman. The newcomer was tall and very dark-skinned, with the graceful bearing of a dancer. She was swathed in a white robe, a white turban was wrapped around her head, and she held a battered leather satchel. She turned her large eyes, slightly almond-shaped and thickly fringed with dark lashes, on Fred.

"Long time since I see one of those," she commented in an accented voice as deep and rich as coffee liqueur.

"Fred, this is Mama Labadie. She's a Vodún mambo from my hounfour—my temple," Kaylee said. "She said she might be able to heal Sierra."

Mama Labadie strode to Sierra's bedside with an air of authority and twitched back the covers. She peeled the bandages back and gave a sharp hissing intake of breath.

"Look at this, coyote, you. No wonder."

Without pausing to wonder how Mama Labadie knew what—or who—he was, Chaco looked at the gash in Sierra's side. The skin was as white as bleached coral. The scab was black and oozing.

"It was OK last night," he protested. "We put a shegoi poultice on her, but she must have washed it off."

"That maybe help, but that ice demon, his poison too strong. She got ice in her *ti bon ange* now, her body too cold. She need heat."

Mama Labadie set down her satchel and began fishing out various objects. She gave Fred several candles and instructed him where they should be placed in the room.

To Chaco, "Go get me banana, melon, rice, eggs, cornmeal, grapes. Any of that. And a basin of clean water."

Chaco hurried out and came back with everything except bananas. She set the food in front of an improvised altar she had decorated with shells, beads and silk flowers.

"What are you going to do?" asked Chaco.

She glared at him. "You, coyote, you play drum for me. You, mannegishi, you take this rattle. Kaylee, you know how to chant. Make music for me. Don't stop for anything 'til it's all over. I ask you to stop, don't stop. You hear?"

Everyone nodded wordlessly.

"I call Damballah-Wedo. He is the wise serpent, and he have the power to heal this woman. He will be me for a while and I go away. When I come back, you stop. Only then. Do not talk. Just play and chant. You comprehend?"

Chaco, Kaylee, and Fred nodded silently again. Chaco began a rhythmic and hypnotic drumming; Fred's rattle was erratic at first, but in time it melded with the drumming. Kaylee began a chant and Fred squeakily joined in. Mama Labadie began to dance gracefully on her bare feet. She swayed and spun, arms over her head. This continued for some minutes, and then she suddenly stiffened.

Her eyes rolled back in her head, showing only the whites against her espresso skin. Sweat dripped down her face, and she smiled, a wide, gleaming, tender smile quite unlike her somber mien of a few minutes before.

Still showing only the whites of her eyes, she swayed toward the altar. First she plunged her hands into the basin of water, then bathed her face. She ate the food, smiling all the while but never speaking. Then she glided to the bed where Sierra lay. The mambo bent over and spread her arms above Sierra's still figure, rocking back and forth to the rhythm of the instruments. Then, without touching the unconscious woman, she passed her hands over Sierra's body, muttering softly. She kept this up a long time, Chaco doggedly drumming, Kaylee chanting, and Fred shaking his rattle all the while.

Finally, Sierra gave a long sigh. Black tendrils of cold mist issued from her lips, dissipating reluctantly like oil spreading across water. Mama Labadie passed her hands through the dark mist until it disappeared, then suddenly folded in on herself and sank quietly to the floor in a heap of white cloth. The others continued their chanting and playing until Mama Labadie raised her head, eyes now dark and very tired.

"You can stop now," she said. "Ugliest damn music I ever hear."

The drumming and rattling subsided raggedly. Kaylee went to Sierra's side and inspected her wound. The skin was clean and smooth, the deep, fishbelly-white slash gone as though it had never been. She pulled the covers over Sierra and noted she was sleeping naturally and her skin was comfortably warm. Her face was rosy. Kaylee turned to the others with a smile.

"She's fine! She's healed," Kaylee reported.

"Thank you, Mama Labadie," Chaco said. "I owe you. I won't forget."

"No you won't, coyote, you," she rejoined, starting to pack her things. "Sometime I call you, you come. Lotsa times I need a tricky one like you." She smiled briefly, a quick tightening of the lips completely unlike the wide and generous smile of her dancing.

"Is Damballah-Wedo the same as Quetzalcoatl? They both assume the form of great snakes," Chaco asked.

The mambo spared him a glance and shrugged.

"I dunno. Damballah-Wedo is the greatest of the loa, the kindest, most generous. He have any other name, I don't know."

She packed the silk flowers in her satchel, gave the room a glance all around and turned again to Chaco.

"She fine now. But you playin' with some evil things here. Dangerous. Next time," she shrugged again. "I dunno. Maybe she dead next time. You be careful." She hefted her old satchel and left, Kaylee following behind.

CHAPTER 9

Kaylee returned to Sierra's bedroom alone. "You might not have realized it," she said to Chaco, "But that woman has a Ph.D. in electrical engineering. She kind of scares me, to tell the truth." Kaylee checked on Sierra again.

"She seems fine, now. Can I trust you two to take care of her? I don't want to find out that she's been attacked by another demon, or something."

Chaco looked uncomfortable and Fred stuffed a paw into his mouth and began to hum.

"Well, there's a problem," Chaco admitted. "You see..." And he told her the whole story. Kaylee's brown eyes went wide with dismay.

"Are you telling me that this, this Neco-something is sending monsters after her? That this is the *second* attack? That there will be more? We've got to get her out of here! She can't stay here. What are..." Again, Kaylee seemed likely to go on for quite a while, so Chaco interrupted.

"It doesn't matter," he said simply.

"What do you mean, 'It doesn't matter'?" she asked on a rising note. "Of course it matters. We can't let Sierra stay here and be attacked and possibly killed by..."

"I mean," said Chaco patiently, "That it doesn't matter if she stays here or goes somewhere else. Necocyaotl will find her no matter where she is."

"Why? What's Sierra done to deserve this?"

"It isn't what she's done. It's what she's *going* to do that he wants to prevent. But she'll be all right for now. Fred and I will be here, and I think that Damballah-Wedo left his protection on the house. Don't you feel it?"

Kaylee shook her head doubtfully.

"Well, I do," Chaco said. "Go home, Kaylee. We'll take care of Sierra."

"Why doesn't this Quetzalcoatl take care of her?" Kaylee demanded. "Damn, that sounds familiar, where have I heard of Quetzalcoatl before?"

Chaco looked embarrassed. "Well," he said tentatively, "Sierra told me there's a statue in a park..."

"Yes!" Kaylee exclaimed triumphantly. "That's it. But it doesn't look like a plumed serpent to me. It looks like a giant..."

"Yes, yes, I know," interjected Chaco. "And Quetzalcoatl is doing what he can, but his brother is just as powerful as he is. Anyway, I believe she's safe for now. I promise I'll look after her."

Sierra slept on through the night as Chaco and Fred took turns watching her. As the birds began to fuss outside in the gray morning light, Sierra turned in bed and stretched. Then she saw Chaco sitting in the chair beside her bed, and she choked in the middle of a yawn.

"What are you doing here?" she asked, clutching the covers to her chest. She noted with annoyance that the pillow beneath her head was unpleasantly wet and cold. She was sure she had gotten a dry pillow. She sat up and threw the pillow off her bed.

"We almost lost you," said Chaco, swallowing hard. His eyes were suspiciously bright, and he turned away from her for a moment.

"Lost me? I'm right here. Just where I was the last time I woke up. Why are my pillows always wet?"

"You were really sick. Mahaha's poison was worse than I thought. And you washed off the shegoi poultice, so the poison had a chance to take hold of your soul. The last time you woke up was a day and a half ago."

Sierra sat up. She didn't feel sick. Her headache was gone. She pushed down the covers and felt her ribs for the bandage, which was gone. "What did you do? It's like nothing ever happened," she said, running her fingers over her side in amazement. Apparently, she had once again been sidelined during an important play, and she was getting tired of it. Although, come to think of it, she was pleased that the deep, lancing pain had disappeared along with the bandage.

"It's a long story," said Chaco. "First, breakfast. Then I'll tell you all about it."

Chaco brought her an enormous tray of food—eggs, bacon, toast, juice, oatmeal, and coffee—and Sierra found she was ravenous.

"Honefftly," she protested through a mouthful of toast, "I don' uffually eat iff mush."

"Oh, I love to see a woman with an appetite," Chaco said. His face was impassive, but she thought he was definitely repressing a grin. While she polished off the food, he told her about finding her unconscious and icy cold and how he asked Kaylee to find a mambo to heal her.

"What's a mambo?"

"A priestess of Vodún."

"Vodún? Is that like Voodoo?" she asked, her skin crawling.

"Oh, Voodoo is just Hollywood nonsense," Chaco scoffed. "Vodún is real, and it's a healing practice. At least, most of the time, it's for healing. There's always a few bad apples, but Mama Labadie is a good woman, and powerful."

"Where did you find a Voodoo priestess in Sunnyvale, California?" wondered Sierra. Voodoo and high technology seemed unlikely neighbors.

"Vodún," Chaco corrected. "There are Vodún practitioners everywhere. You just have to know where to look. I knew that Kaylee had connections with Vodún, and I knew you had written her number down on the note pad next to the phone, so I called her."

"No kidding?" Sierra said slowly. "Kaylee is a Voodoo worshipper? I never would've thought it. How did you know?"

"Vodún," Chaco said again, a bit crossly this time. "Kaylee wears a vévé, a symbol of the loa Madame Ézilee. She's wearing it in that picture of you two in your photo album. No one could mistake it."

"You mean that necklace she always wears? I just thought it was because she likes to wear African-print dresses and things." She shook her head. "You think you know someone…"

But her mind had returned to the task she had been given. Suddenly, she wondered how much time she had lost since her encounter with Mahaha. The day she had been attacked had been May fifteenth.

"Chaco, what day is it today?" she asked in a panic.

"May twenty-second."

That long? She had lost an entire week of her life, with nothing to show for it. She sank her head into her hands. Then she sat up straight and took a deep breath.

"OK. I'd better get on with it. Could I have some privacy, Chaco?"

Chaco left the room, closing the door behind him. Sierra showered and brushed her furry-feeling teeth. The morning ritual was soothing, making her feel as though everything were normal. She had almost forgotten what normal felt like.

She brushed out her damp hair, braided it, and marched downstairs to look for her backpack. She found it still in the front hall, where it had been tossed the day she was attacked by Mahaha. She took it into the living room, sat on the couch, and began methodically searching through the pack. She lifted out waterproof matches, a flashlight, and a small tool kit and set them aside. She found a small towel, a plastic bag full of trail mix, and a water bottle. She dug a little deeper and discovered insect repellant, sunscreen, and a squashed canvas hat. Reaching the bottom of the pack, she discovered what she had been hoping to find, stuck between the pages of a dog-eared paperback novel: two glittering blue-green feathers that had made their way into the book's pages and escaped being used as her weapon against Mahaha. She pulled them out, stroked them flat against the palm of her hand, and sighed with relief as they chimed sweetly at her touch.

Holding the delicate feathers in her hand, she went upstairs to her bedroom and located Quetzalcoatl's "invitation" in her little carved box. Back downstairs, she went into the kitchen and showed the feathers to Chaco and Fred.

"Three whole feathers," she said. "I hope that will do it."

Fred regarded the feathers anxiously, orange eyes swiveling. "Now what?" he asked.

Sierra gazed at the brilliant feathers, her expression blank. She had no idea what came next.

"I wish I had just a little more information here," she said plaintively.

"What kind of information?" asked Chaco.

"Like what the feathers are all about, and what they're supposed to do. Little things like that."

Chaco settled back in his chair, wearing what Sierra had come to recognize as his storytelling face. "Have a seat, Sierra, and I'll tell you." Sierra sat. Fred plopped his fat bottom down on the floor, stuck a toe in his mouth, and watched Chaco with enormous orange eyes.

"Feathers can be magical," Chaco began, but Sierra interrupted him.

"All feathers?" she asked. "How about pigeon feathers? They're all over, and you don't see anything special happening."

Chaco looked patient. "Not all feathers, not all the time," he explained. "But feathers can be filled with power. You know why the Native Americans used eagle feathers in their headdresses and ceremonies?"

Sierra shook her head.

"The eagle is the greatest of birds. It flies close to the gods, and can be a messenger from the gods. Its feathers carry their power, and that power can be tapped by a shaman, someone who has learned to commune with the gods through nature."

"But," continued Chaco, warming to his subject, "the eagle is not the only sacred bird. In fact, all birds are sacred…"

"Even pigeons?" Sierra interrupted skeptically.

Chaco regarded her with some annoyance. "Just because you think they look or sound funny doesn't mean they aren't sacred," he said severely.

"Okay," she said meekly. "Just asking."

"Have you ever really looked at a pigeon?" Chaco asked.

Sierra shook her head.

"No. I think of them as rats with wings."

"Next time you see one, look at the feathers around its neck. They are as glorious as the feathers of a bird of paradise. Anyway, back to Quetzalcoatl's feathers. If even ordinary bird feathers are magical, how much more magical are the feathers of an Avatar of such great power? Each feather springs from his pure essence, which is creativity, communion with all natural things, nurturing, love. That's very powerful stuff. You could change the world with just a few of Quetzalcoatl's feathers. What do you plan to do with them?"

"I don't know," Sierra admitted. "There are two problems here. I mean, there are more than two problems, but there are two overall issues." Chaco's golden eyes were fixed on her face with an intensity that made her nervous. Fred clambered into another chair and sat up alertly to listen, like a meerkat guarding its den.

"First, I have to figure out how to get the feathers in contact with Simmons. I can't just walk up and say, 'Ms. Simmons, take a look at these feathers, willya?' I need to find a way that won't seem weird or suspicious. Maybe as a gift that's supposedly from someone she knows, or something."

"Feathered cape," suggested Chaco. "They used to be *very* popular."

"That was a long time ago, and I can't make a feathered cape out of three feathers," replied Sierra. "Second issue: I need to make sure she receives it, whatever it is. If I try to get in to see her, I'm sure she'll refuse. She must have had something to do with firing me, even if I can't figure out why. I don't know anyone who knows her on a personal level, so I can't deliver it through a friend. To be honest, I don't even know where to start."

Chaco got up and stretched, causing interesting things to happen down the length of his lean body. "One thing at a time," he said. "I know we need to solve the problem quickly, because you're in real danger. But when I get stuck on a problem, I go and do something else for a while. Eventually, the answer comes to me."

"What do you like to do?" asked Sierra, immediately regretting it as Chaco rewarded her with an evil grin. Blushing, she weighted down the feathers with a saltshaker to keep them from being blown about and lost, and retreated to her workshop. She would work on jewelry for a while. It was always relaxing to lose herself working with the metal and stones.

She picked up a half-finished setting from her workbench and held it to the light. The pieces always looked like junk at this stage. The silver was discolored from the heat of the torch, and the metal was still crusted with flux, used to make the solder run properly under the torch flame. She scrubbed the setting with a toothbrush and warm water to remove the flux. She had textured the metal in a pattern reminiscent of seaweed or water, and she planned to add a tiny starfish molded from silver clay. The stone would be a lovely, irregular cabochon of turquoise from Arizona's Sleeping Beauty Mine, a clear, robin's egg blue with no matrix inclusions or veins in its perfect surface.

Sierra picked up her packet of fresh clay, intending to start on the starfish. As she did so, she saw the unfired silver clay pendant she had made from a leaf. It seemed like a lifetime ago. She stared at it for a long moment, then ran back to the kitchen for the feathers. Back at her workbench, she put the feathers in front of her and began to draw in her idea sketchbook. Several times she ran to her office and used her computer to search for images, then sketched some more in her book.

By evening, her neck was kinked and her hands tired, but she felt she had made real progress. She set the results of her work in her small kiln, and programmed it for the amount of time and heat required to transform the fragile, gray objects into pure silver. The kiln would shut itself off after the prescribed time, so she tidied her workspace, washed up, and went into the kitchen. Chaco was busy at the stove and Fred was watching him intently, drooling slightly.

"Smells great, Chaco. I didn't know you could cook," Sierra said as she uncorked a bottle of wine. "Care for any?"

Chaco nodded. Fred squeaked, "Can I have some, too?"

"Don't give him any," Chaco advised. "Mannegishis can't hold their liquor."

"Can too!" protested Fred.

"How old are you, Fred?" asked Sierra.

"Mmmm, maybe a thousand? More? I don't remember."

"Well, you're all grown up, then," Sierra said, and poured a small glass of wine for him.

"You'll be s-o-o-r-r-y," Chaco said in a singsong voice, stirring something fragrant in a pot.

"Give him a break," Sierra said, handing Chaco his own glass. She sat down at the kitchen table. Before long, Chaco had served bowls of soup, redolent with sausage and herbs and full of vegetables. Slices of warm sourdough bread with garlic and herb butter complemented the soup. Nothing was said for a while as they enjoyed the food, though it was far from silent, as the mannegishi tended to slurp.

After dinner, Chaco piled the dishes in the sink. "You ought to be getting some rest," he told Sierra. "You've been through the wringer, and you need to take care of yourself. Fred, make yourself useful and wash the dishes."

Chaco half-pulled Sierra up the stairs to the background accompaniment of Fred protesting that he couldn't reach the sink and didn't know how to wash dishes anyway. In her bedroom, Chaco pulled back the covers and fluffed the pillows (now mercifully dry). "There," he said, sitting her on the side of the bed. "How are you feeling?"

"I feel pretty good," Sierra said. And she did. Nothing seemed to remain of the attack—except for her memories. She was afraid she'd be reliving that in nightmares for a long time to come.

"I think you could feel even better," he said fondly, putting his lean, brown hands on her shoulders and drawing closer. His mouth closed over hers, and in her surprise, she only knew that the closeness of him was sweet. For a moment, she melted into the embrace like warm chocolate. It had been a long time since a man had kissed her like that. And Chaco was, by even a conservative estimate, the most gorgeous man she had ever seen. Heat ran like lightning across her skin where he caressed her, and her rational resistance (*"He's not even human!"*) drowned in a flood of sensation and desire. *He is so beautiful,* she thought. *So long, so strong, so...*

This line of thought was interrupted by the sound of crockery and glass shattering downstairs, accompanied by a raucous chorus of "Love the One You're With."

"Fred!" roared Chaco, leaping to his feet and running downstairs. Sierra followed him, nerves jangling with the abrupt transition from sensual delight to noisy chaos. Fred had dragged a chair over to the sink, which was now overflowing with sudsy water. Sitting in the midst of the suds, the mannegishi belted out the song, singing off-key but with enthusiasm. A bowl and three wineglasses were on the floor in shards. The bottle of zinfandel, which had held at least another glass of wine in it, lay empty on the table.

"I *told* you not to give him any wine," Chaco said crossly. He turned off the tap and began picking up the bits and pieces on the floor. Sierra extracted Fred from the sink and wiped him down with a dishtowel. It was like trying to dry an enormous and slippery baby. By the time she had him dried off, he was snoring loudly, his great orange eyes hidden behind heavy lids. She deposited him on her living room couch under a throw rug, and went back to help Chaco clean up.

"You were right, Chaco," she said, humbly. "No more wine for Fred."

Chaco gave her a wry grin. "His timing was bad, that's for sure."

Sierra twisted a lock of her dark hair and looked at the floor. "Chaco, about that…"

"Let me guess. It would be a mistake, you're going to say."

"That is what I was going to say."

"Why? I like you. I know you like me."

"I do, Chaco," said Sierra, looking into his amber eyes. "But can you tell me that you won't break my heart?"

He washed a bowl and set it in the dish drainer. "No. I can't tell you that. I wouldn't mean to hurt you, of course, but, well, I never stay in one place for very long. Or with one person. It's in my nature," he concluded, looking at her apologetically, but with a wry grin. Evidently, he didn't feel too bad about his nature.

"Right. I guess I'd be snorting in disgust if you were human. But you, I believe. Good night, Chaco." Sierra went back upstairs, alone, and climbed into bed. If she had any regrets, they soon succumbed to a deep and dreamless sleep.

CHAPTER 10

The next morning, Sierra woke feeling full of energy. True, she didn't exactly have a plan yet, but she had a solid objective, which was an improvement. Before breakfast, even before her first cup of coffee, she hurried into the garage and opened the now-cool kiln. She gave a sigh of relief. The silver clay pieces had turned out beautifully.

She held three perfect replicas of Quetzalcoatl's feathers in her palm. She had pressed the feathers into the clay, then placed them in her kiln. The feathers had burned away, leaving the exquisite detail of their shafts and barbs imprinted into the metal. Unpolished, they looked as though they had been spray-painted white. She took up a wire brush from her workbench and scuffed the surface of one of the feathers. Instantly, the surface shone silver as it began to reflect the light. Sierra brushed the feathers until they gleamed. She laid them on the bench and began to look through her collection of gems. She picked out several gemstones, referencing them against her design, rejecting some and keeping others. She worked until Fred poked his head into the garage and told her that breakfast was ready. She looked up in surprise.

"Breakfast? Who made breakfast?" she asked. "Chaco, of course," said the mannegishi. "I can't reach the stove. And I don't know how to cook." He gulped a bit and looked away. Fred looked a bit pinkish this morning, Sierra thought.

"How are you feeling today, Fred?"

Fred looked at her dolefully. "Not so good. I have a headache," he replied. "I only want coffee."

"Bit too much to drink last night?" Sierra inquired, with an air of innocence. "You're looking kind of, well, *pink* today."

Fred rolled his eyes at her, then winced. "Hmph," was all he said. He went back inside the house. Sierra, her stomach rumbling, followed him.

"So," Chaco said, ladling scrambled eggs with chorizo onto her plate, "What are you up to today?" Fred, sitting on a phone book on one of the kitchen chairs, averted his eyes from her plate and sipped from a mug of coffee. When he wasn't sipping, he held the mug in his hind paws.

"I think I'm going to call Clancy back," Sierra said, crunching her toast. "Might as well get it over with."

After breakfast, Chaco decided to teach Fred how to wash the dishes, with the aid of a chair so that the mannegishi could reach the sink. Sierra left them bickering over the suds and called Kaylee at work.

"Good to hear your voice," said Kaylee, but she sounded a bit wary.

"I hear I have you to thank for being alive and well today," Sierra said. "So thank you! I don't know what would have happened if Chaco hadn't called you. And if you hadn't called Mama Labadie."

"Hmm, yes. So I guess we both have a secret life that we haven't been exactly open about," said Kaylee. "I'm sorry, but I just don't share that with a lot of people. You can see why."

"Yes," said Sierra. "I think I do. But I have to tell you, all this started very recently. For me, I mean. I guess Chaco told you everything?"

"I don't know about everything," replied her friend. "But he gave me an earful, for sure. And he says you're still in danger, Sierra. I'm worried about you."

"Um, yeah, that seems to be true, but I have Chaco and Fred here to help me."

"Fred!" Kaylee snorted. "I don't know how much help *he'll* be. Chaco, maybe. Anyway, what do you plan to do next?"

"Well, Chaco says I got a call from Clancy Forrester while I was sick. Before I call him back, is there anything you may have heard about why he's calling me?"

"No idea. Did he leave a message?"

"Just to call him back. It has me kind of worried."

"I think you've got a lot more worrisome things going on than Clancy Forrester, girl. What I really wanted to know is what you're going to do about…this Neco-character that Chaco was going on about."

"I don't know, yet," replied Sierra. "I have the beginnings of a plan, but I haven't figured everything out. Anyway, you're sure you haven't heard anything at Black Diamond that might be a clue as to why Forrester is calling?"

"No. Sorry, Sierra. By the way, that PR guy from New York is all over the place. You can spot him a mile away around here. Silk suits and Hermès ties, and everyone else is in jeans. What's the story on that dude?"

"Well, I worked for him when he had an agency in Palo Alto. He was pretty successful but decided that to play with the big boys, he had to move the agency to New York. Silicon Valley wasn't good enough."

"But you didn't go?"

"No. I was really uncomfortable with Clapper's business dealings. I thought he was sleazy, and I know he charged clients for more than they were getting. I didn't like a lot of the clients, for that matter—I was working on some pretty innocent things like disk drives and semiconductors, but a few of the other clients looked like fronts to me. I didn't want to move to New York anyway."

"What do you mean by 'fronts'?" Kaylee asked. "Like, money laundering?"

"Maybe. I never found out. Clapper fired me. That's two for two. I'm beginning to feel like an albatross," Sierra concluded glumly.

"Why'd he fire you? I've seen you in action, and that just doesn't make sense to me," Kaylee said.

Sierra sat and thought. Finally, she said, "You know, I'm not really sure. He told me that I just wasn't needed in New York, but he took several other people with him who were willing to move. He's a secretive kind of guy. I asked a lot of questions, and he clearly didn't like it. If he really *was* up to something—if some of the clients weren't legit—maybe he thought I'd expose him or report him. I wasn't actually sorry to leave the agency."

"Sounds like kind of a creep, Sierra."

"Yeah, that about describes him," she agreed. "Kaylee, I need to talk to you about something. Can you come over here for lunch today?"

"Sure. I don't have any meetings, for once."

They agreed to meet at noon. Then she told Chaco and Fred that Kaylee was coming for lunch.

Chaco nodded his dark head. "And I suppose you expect me to cook for the two of you."

"No, Chaco. You've been very sweet to do so much for me, and I love your cooking. But I don't expect you to cook lunch for us," she said. Chaco looked pleased.

"Actually, I don't mind. How about *chalupas poblanas* and *nopalitos*?" asked Chaco. "I saw some prickly pear cactus in a vacant lot near here."

"Prickly pear cactus? Well, I guess you know what you're doing. It sounds wonderful," she said insincerely.

Chaco went out to get his cactus, and Sierra sat down at the phone. After staring at it apprehensively for a few minutes, she took a deep breath and dialed the Black Diamond main number, asking for Clancy Forrester. He picked up on the first ring.

"Clancy Forrester, Security," she heard him say.

"Clancy, this is Sierra Carter," she said. "I got your message to call." There was a brief silence at the other end of the phone.

"Look," she heard him say. "I need to talk to you. But this isn't the time or place. Can you meet me for lunch?"

"Oh, sorry. I already have a lunch appointment. Can you tell me what this is about? Maybe I can just settle it over the phone," Sierra said, puzzled by the turn the conversation had taken.

"I can't talk now. How about tomorrow?"

"For lunch? I guess so."

They arranged a time and place to meet, and Sierra hung up the phone, burning with curiosity. Going to lunch seemed to imply that whatever it was that Clancy wanted, she was probably not in trouble.

Chaco returned in an hour or so with a bag of groceries and another bag full of flattened "paddles" of cactus, the kind Sierra had always called "beavertail." She watched with interest as Chaco held the paddles in the flame of the stove burners, using tongs to protect his hands.

"Why are you doing that?" she asked.

"Burning the needles off," he replied. "You don't want cactus spines in your salad, do you?"

"No," she said. *So that's how you eat cactus.* She went into her workshop and spent the rest of the morning working on jewelry. A few minutes before noon, she turned off her torch, cleaned up, and went into the kitchen, where Chaco's cooking filled the house with delicious fragrances. Fred, looking somewhat greener than he had earlier in the day, was in rapt attendance.

"What have we got here?" asked Sierra. "It smells wonderful!"

"Chalupes poblanas with homemade tortillas," Chaco said, stirring a pot. "You put two tortillas on a plate. Then put salsa verde over one and salsa roja over the other. Then top with chicken, onions and cheese. The nopalitos go on the side." He gestured toward a bowl full of light green chunks.

Chaco offered her some of the sauce in a wooden spoon. As she was savoring its fresh spiciness, the doorbell rang.

Kaylee stood on her doorstep, and Sierra was abruptly grateful for the sight of her cheerful face and sheared black curls. She looked so…normal. She reached out and the two women hugged each other.

"Come on in," Sierra said. Kaylee walked into her front hall.

"What is that wonderful smell?" Kaylee asked, sniffing appreciatively.

"Chaco made lunch," Sierra said, and Kaylee raised her brows.

"All that, and he cooks *too*?" she asked, shaking her head.

The women made their way into the kitchen, where Chaco made a low, sweeping bow, one arm gesturing toward the table, which had been set for four. Fred was already perched on his phone book, and Sierra was relieved to see that he had his knife and fork clutched eagerly in his paws. Fred's table manners had improved since arriving, as Sierra had adamantly refused to allow him to shove his face into his plate and gobble.

"What's this?" Kaylee asked, poking the nopales with her fork.

"Oh, that's nopales—just a little salad made out of, um, prickly pear cactus."

"Wow," said Kaylee and took a bite. "This is great. I never had this before."

Neither had Sierra, but she didn't say so. Kaylee was right. The nopales were tart and slightly crunchy in a dressing of lime juice and olive oil. Chaco had added tomatoes, peppers, and cilantro as well. And the chalupes were heavenly.

The meal was consumed in companionable silence except for an occasional burp from Fred. Finally, Kaylee set her fork down and sighed.

"That was wonderful, Chaco. Thanks." Chaco acknowledged this with a nod of his dark head and a grin.

CHAPTER 11

As Fred polished off the last of the chalupes, Sierra recounted the entire story, leaving nothing out.

"So I'm meeting Clancy for lunch tomorrow," she concluded. "I still have no idea why he wants to talk to me. But if we're going to lunch, I'm probably not in trouble with Black Diamond. What do you think?"

Kaylee frowned slightly, her eyes troubled. "Why did he ask you to lunch? Doesn't that seem kind of odd?"

Before Sierra could reply, Chaco spoke up. "Because he likes her, that's why." He didn't look pleased.

Kaylee's brows rose and her lips quirked a little. "That makes sense," she said.

"I don't know," Sierra responded. "He doesn't really know me. We used to flirt, sort of, but it never went anywhere. Since then he has seen me for all of ten sub-optimal minutes while he was marching me out of the company that just fired me." She got up and went to the cupboard, "Want some tea?"

Fred did, but Kaylee and Chaco declined. Sierra fixed tea for the mannegishi and herself, then sat down. Fred poured a couple of ounces of sugar into his mug and slurped this revolting concoction with every sign of enjoyment. Kaylee patted him on his melon-shaped head. Fred winced slightly, and his eyes spun dizzily until she stopped.

"He's a bit under the weather," Sierra explained. "He's usually a kind of nice sage green."

"Oh, sorry, but you're such a cutie, Fred," said Kaylee. Sierra rolled her own eyes to the ceiling.

"That's just because you don't know him yet," she said. "Kaylee, could you find out something about Clancy? What he's like, what people know about him?"

"Whether or not he's married," Kaylee added.

"Well, he doesn't wear a ring," said Sierra.

"Doesn't mean anything," said her friend. "Sure. I'll find out what I can. What are you going to do in the meantime?"

"Come and look," said Sierra, and showed the way to her garage. Kaylee followed, and the two disappeared into Sierra's workshop. They emerged two hours later, grimy but happy.

"That's fantastic," said Kaylee. "I knew you made jewelry, but I had no idea how hard it is. You're great at it, Sierra." She held out a hand, now adorned with a silver ring set with a turquoise cabochon. "I love it! How much do I owe you?"

Sierra stopped and faced her friend. "Nothing," she said. "You helped me. You listened to Chaco, and you listened to me. I didn't think anyone, ever, would believe what's happened to me in the last few days."

Kaylee looked at her, smiling. "I believed Chaco," she said. "He's the most convincing coyote I ever met. He's also the only coyote I ever met, but nonetheless, extremely convincing."

You have no idea, thought Sierra, then aloud, "Anyway, the ring is yours. I'm delighted for you to have it."

"Well, thank you!" Kaylee said, extending her fingers to admire the ring again. "I'd better be going. I have to catch up on a few things for work tomorrow, and I have some research to do for you. Where are Chaco and Fred? I'll just say goodbye."

They found Chaco and the mannegishi playing checkers on the living room floor. Chaco looked slightly annoyed, and Fred was obviously winning. Sierra wondered if this was because Fred could make the checkers disappear, but decided the tubby little creature wasn't cheating—he had the right number of pieces stacked on the floor next to him. When the two women entered the room, Chaco stood up in one lithe movement and pushed his dark hair out of his eyes. Kaylee's eyes swept up and down, appreciatively. She held her hand out.

"Thanks for a great lunch, Chaco," she said, smiling. They shook, both standing quite close, Sierra noted, and then tried not to note.

"Come back soon, Kaylee," said Chaco, and leaned forward to kiss Kaylee's smooth cheek as he held her hand. Kaylee dropped her purse, which Chaco picked up and handed to her with a bow. Sierra thought Kaylee's cheeks flushed under her *café au lait* skin.

"Thanks," Kaylee said, a bit gruffly. "Well, gotta run. Bye, Fred."

Fred waved six fingers at her, but didn't take either of his enormous eyes off the checkerboard. Sierra walked her to the door. "Thanks again, Kaylee," she said. "I couldn't do this without you."

"Oh, trust me, it's the most exciting thing that's happened to me since Jimmy Johnston kissed me behind the gym in seventh grade," said Kaylee as she went out the front door. Sierra closed the door, walked back into the living room and sat on the couch with a sigh. She closed her eyes for a moment, feeling more tired than she could remember. She wondered if this was a lingering after-effect of Mahaha's attack. Surely, she hadn't felt so tired in years...

Coffee. She needed coffee. But she didn't want to make an entire pot. "Chaco, Fred, I'm going out for a bit," she said, stifling a yawn. She grabbed her wallet from her purse. Her favorite coffee shop was a few blocks away on Castro Street, and she intended to walk.

The fresh air felt good and perked her up a bit. She walked briskly and soon entered the front door of The Daily Grind. The barista recognized her, waved, and began to prepare a latte for her without taking her order. He served it in a thick, brown mug. She wrapped her fingers around the mug, enjoying the warmth and breathing in the milky fragrance of the latte.

"Well, hi. It's Sierra, isn't it?" The voice was familiar. Sierra looked up into a man's face. For a split second, she thought he was a complete stranger, but then she recognized him. Aiden. The man she had met at Indian Grinding Rock. She stared up at him in astonishment.

"What are you doing here?" she asked. *Whoops—that sounded kind of hostile.*

But Aiden didn't take offense. "Can I join you?" he asked, smiling and pulling back a chair. Then, "Hang on. I'll get some coffee first." He strode off toward the bar. Sierra watched him with mixed emotions. He was extremely attractive, true. And she had wanted to get to know him better, true. But wasn't this a bit too much of a coincidence?

Aiden rejoined her with his own gently steaming mug. He sat down, stirred his coffee and smiled at her. "This is great," he said. "I thought about calling you when I came to town, but I was afraid it was too sort of…stalkerish, if you know what I mean."

"Why *did* you come to town?" Sierra asked mildly. She *had* given him her phone number, after all. Most people would view that as an invitation.

"Business," he responded, taking a sip of coffee.

"Oh? What kind of business are you in?" Sierra asked. Neither had discussed their professional lives at the campground.

"Oh, I'm just another civil service employee," Aiden replied. "I work for the Feds—you know, government work. I'm not supposed to chat about it, so maybe you'll forgive me if I don't go into details. But I had to come down today to the field office for a meeting. Boring." He rolled his blue eyes and grinned at her.

Government work? Well, that could mean anything. But Sierra relaxed a bit, and they began to discuss the best camping sites and hiking trails.

"…and then he reached around to get a marshmallow out of the bag," said Aiden an hour later. "And he put his hand right on the skunk's back!" Aiden shook his head, grinning. "We all piled in my SUV and made Jim drive home by himself. None of us could stand being anywhere near him."

Sierra asked, "Did the skunk get the rest of the marshmallows?"

"Every one. Say," Aiden looked at his wristwatch. "I've got

a few things I need to take care of, but would you like to go to dinner later?"

Sierra hesitated for a moment. Aiden noticed and quickly said, "I understand perfectly if you can't. I just showed up unexpectedly, and I'm sure you have plans."

"Noooo," she said slowly, thinking. "No, I don't have plans. I'd love to go to dinner with you."

Aiden grinned again, pleased. "That's great! Would you make reservations? I don't know the local eateries. Where should I pick you up?"

"Meet me at CasCal. It's a restaurant on the corner of Castro and California Streets. See? It's just down the block." Sierra pointed through the window. "You'll like it. It's sort of a Spanish tapas place."

"Okay, thanks. How about seven o'clock?" Aiden stood.

"Sounds good."

"See you there at seven," Aiden said, smiling at her. Then he turned and left the coffee shop. Sierra watched him go, fingering her long-empty cup absently. She consulted her inner watchdog. Seems nice, but won't or can't talk about work. Odd that he shows up here, but stranger things, she mused, had happened to her recently. This seemed like a garden-variety coincidence. And he said all the right things; friendly, but not too friendly. Didn't try to push things. Her inner watchdog concluded that having dinner with him was probably going to be fine. She hadn't given him her address, after all.

At home, Sierra explained her evening plans to Fred and Chaco. Fred just sucked his toe and went on watching a soap opera on TV. Chaco growled, "I don't like that guy. Don't do it, Sierra."

"Why *don't* you like him?" Chaco just shook his head.

"I'm just having dinner with him, so if you can't give me a real reason, that's what I'm doing." Chaco gave her a dark look and retreated behind a book. "If I should happen to bring Aiden back here," Sierra continued, "the two of you just stay out of the way,

OK?" Fred nodded without looking up, but Chaco's stony silence spoke for him.

CasCal was trendy in the extreme, with blown-glass lamps, towering glass walls, and splashes of bright primary colors. It was packed with well-to-do young Silicon Valley types—all talking at the tops of their voices.

The food was wonderful, but conversation was difficult. "Great restaurant," shouted Aiden across the small table. Sierra cupped her ear.

"What?" she yelled back. He shook his head, looking amused. Despite the noise, they managed to carry on a conversation. Sierra found herself sharing her bewilderment at being laid off from Black Diamond, and the odd way she had been dismissed.

"The weird thing is," she added, "even if they hired my old boss to take over the company's PR, there are a million things that have to be done—more than the new agency would even want to take on, because it's so routine. They specialize in the big, splashy events, really. So I don't understand why BDSC wanted to get rid of me."

"I don't know," Aiden responded gravely. "Were there any other issues? Did you get a negative performance review?"

"No!" Sierra said, emphatically. "No. I always received great reviews. I got raises every year. Mark always said he was happy with my work. I just don't get it."

"I suppose you could sue them for wrongful dismissal..." Aiden started to say.

"Nope. If I sue them, I won't get hired anywhere else. Besides, I'd rather just find another job and move on," she said with a sigh.

"Makes sense," he said.

Afterwards, they emerged into the warm and quiet night with some relief. Aiden took Sierra's hand in a gesture that felt natural, and they strolled down the sidewalk, watching the people coming and going from restaurants and stores.

"I loved the food," Aiden said after a bit. "But it was hard to to talk."

"Right," Sierra agreed. Aiden's surprise appearance had thrown her off balance. But for the first time in many days, she was feeling relaxed. True, she had a daunting task ahead. But there wasn't a thing she could do about it at this particular moment, so she chose to enjoy it. She hadn't had a "date" in months. At least, she was beginning to suspect it was a date. Yes, the world might be coming to an end, she might consort with Avatars and mannegishis, but Sierra was on a date. *Carpe diem*, she thought. *Might as well enjoy.*

"How long have you worked in public relations?" asked Aiden. "I don't even know what that is. Is it like advertising?"

"No," Sierra said. "We have a saying: in advertising you pay, and in public relations, you pray." Aiden looked at her with one eyebrow cocked quizzically.

"What that means is, in advertising you pay for space in a magazine, or for air time. You get to say where the ad will run and how often, and you control what the ad says and what it looks like." He nodded. Most people knew this.

"With public relations, you're trying to convince journalists and editors in the media that you have a good story—one that their particular readers or listeners will want to know about. So you 'pray,' because you have no control over the process, really. You have to understand what each and every magazine or newspaper wants, and what their journalists and editors consider to be news, and what the individual journalists are covering. They don't particularly trust or like PR people, so it's not easy."

"Oh," said Aiden. "I always thought public relations meant telling lies, or covering up the truth. Sorry, but that's how people use the term. You know, they say, 'That's just PR' when they think someone is glossing over the truth."

This was familiar, if depressing, territory to Sierra. "Yeah. I know that's what they say. And sometimes it happens that way—especially in politics, if you ask me. But mostly, we're just trying to get the word out about companies or widgets or people. And if I lie to a reporter and the reporter finds out, that journalist won't ever deal with me again, so lying is definitely a bad career move in public relations."

Aiden took this in. After a few moments he said, "So, were you happy with the job? Did you like it?"

Sierra thought this over. "I loved it at first," she admitted. "It was fun, and I felt good about the products I was promoting. I was asked to lie about a few things when I used to work for an agency, but I just wouldn't do it." She felt Aiden's hand tense as she spoke, and squeezed back. "So I've always been able to sleep at night. But lately—I don't know. I'm bored with it, I guess. The thought of going back to the same old routine? I'm not too excited about that."

"What would you do if you didn't do PR?" he asked, his voice easy and warm.

She hesitated. She was very shy about mentioning her jewelry work. She knew it sounded unrealistic—a pipedream. *Everyone wants to be an artist or write The Great American Novel*, she thought. *But very few people ever make a living that way.*

"You're awfully quiet," said Aiden. "What are you thinking?" They were standing outside a brightly lit bookstore, full of people browsing through books and drinking coffee in cardboard cups. She turned and looked up at him. She thought he had a kind face, made more so by the laugh lines around his eyes.

Finally, she spoke. "I design jewelry," she said. "That's what I'd like to do." To her relief, he didn't get that skeptical look that said, "*And I'd like to make money skiing, but that don't pay the rent.*" Instead he asked, "What kind of jewelry?"

"Sterling silver," she replied. "One-of-a-kind pieces with really interesting stones and original designs. I learned how to silversmith a few years ago, and I make pieces in my garage and sell them at craft fairs. But I can't make enough money that way, and it's a lot of work. Sometimes I don't make enough at a fair to cover my costs."

"Would you show me? I'd like to see what you do," he said. She felt a surge of gratified excitement. She hadn't expected him to show much interest. Most men weren't very interested in jewelry. At the fairs, she always had a crowd of women, but men usually scanned her table briefly, and then moved on. *Unless Valentine's Day or the anniversary is coming up,* she thought.

"I'd love to," Sierra said. "Let's go back to my place and I'll show you."

To her relief, there was no sign of Chaco or Fred when they came in. Chaco, she assumed, was out and about, and she hoped Aiden wouldn't ask about him because she could hardly explain why she allowed her "dog" to take himself out at night. Fred, she hoped, was invisible and staying that way. She went into her garage and turned on the light. She opened her storage cases and began laying out necklaces, earrings and bracelets, an array that shone and sparkled under her bright work lights.

Aiden picked up several pieces and asked questions. He seemed genuinely interested as she explained what the stones were and how the pieces were constructed. "You have a lot of tools for a girl-type person," he observed. "What's that thing?" He was pointing at her tank of acetylene gas, which was firmly strapped to the leg of her workbench to prevent it from falling over—a necessary precaution in earthquake-prone California. If it fell and damaged the gas regulator, it might explode or cause a fire.

"That's a tank of acetylene gas," she answered. "It's attached to the torch tip, there. It's used to solder the pieces together or to melt metal." He picked up and examined some of her specialized jewelry-making tools and asked more questions.

"It takes a lot of tools and equipment to do this," Sierra said. "But I've really gotten into it—I get more of a thrill from a new tool catalogue than I do out of shopping for shoes, so I guess that makes me a bit…eccentric."

"I like eccentric," he said with a smile, and then caught sight of her current project. "What's this?" He picked up one of the silver feathers, which trembled and gleamed on his palm. Sierra took it from him and swept all the unassembled components into a drawer. As she did so, she reflected that Quetzalcoatl's feathers seemed to have no effect on him. *I guess that's a good thing,* she thought.

"Nothing. Just something I'm working on. Would you like a glass of wine?"

"Sure," Aiden replied, but he looked curiously at her, and at the closed drawer. They went into the kitchen. Aiden took off his jacket and sat at the table, resting his elbows on the table. He had nicely muscled forearms, she noticed. She pulled the cork from a bottle and poured two glasses. As she did so, she heard a distinct squeak. Aiden looked around. "Is that Chaco?" he asked. "Here, Chaco, good dog."

Chaco trotted in from the living room. "What kind of dog did you say he was?" asked Aiden.

Sierra paused, trying to remember her spur-of-the-moment fib. "Navajo sheepdog. I think. I got him from the shelter."

"He looks like a coyote," Aiden said. "I see a lot of them when I'm out hiking and camping. He's got those yellow eyes, and he's the right size and color, too."

Sierra thought for a moment. "Well, that could be, couldn't it? Dogs and coyotes can interbreed. Maybe he's a coyote-shepherd mix, or something."

"Maybe," Aiden said, eyeing Chaco again. "I think coyotes are fonder of *eating* dogs than mating with them, though."

Chaco rolled over on his back and waved his paws in the air, looking as doggy as possible. Aiden rubbed his belly. "Well, it's an interesting thought, but I suppose we'll never know," he said.

"No," said Sierra, anxious to move the conversation away from Chaco. "I guess we'll never know. Have you ever been camping around this area?" Aiden said he hadn't, and the subject of Chaco's species was dropped as they moved back to the topic of great camping spots. Sierra enjoyed the discussion, but Aiden's next conversational opening stopped her in her tracks.

Aiden stretched his long legs out in front of him and took a sip of wine. "So, why don't you tell me what it was like working for Jack Clapper?"

CHAPTER 12

Sierra gaped at Aiden, her mind racing. Had she mentioned Jack? Even if she had, why would Aiden care what it had been like working for Jack Clapper? Her hand trembled slightly as she carefully put her glass of wine down on the table.

"How do you know about Jack?" she asked. "How do you know that I worked for him?"

Aiden looked surprised. "You mentioned him when you were telling me about getting fired. You said that Black Diamond hired Jack Clapper's agency, and he was someone you had worked for."

"I didn't," said Sierra, firmly. "I think you'd better explain yourself, Aiden. You didn't show up here to take me out to dinner and admire my jewelry. What are you up to?"

Aiden looked across the table at her with eyes the clear and guileless blue of a summer day in the mountains. "I just stopped by because I wanted to see you, Sierra. I like you. And you did mention Jack Clapper and his agency to me. You've just forgotten. Don't go all paranoid on me."

Sierra stood up. "It's late. You'd better go." Aiden stayed seated, smiling up at her with an undeniably charming smile.

"Oh, come on, Sierra. I haven't finished my wine. And it's early, still—only eight-thirty." A low growl greeted this pronouncement. Chaco stood stiff-legged in the door, fur bristling, baring his fangs at Aiden.

"No, Aiden," Sierra said. "It's really time to go. Please."

Aiden stopped smiling and rose carefully to his feet, keeping the table between him and the bristling Chaco. He shrugged on his jacket. "OK. You and Chaco win, Sierra. I'm really sorry it turned out this way, though."

Me too, Sierra thought, but she just nodded. She followed Aiden out to the front door and stood aside as he went through. Then he turned and quickly kissed her full on the mouth before she realized what he was doing. "Goodbye, Sierra," he said, then left.

Sierra banged the door shut and locked it, fuming. *How dare he?* She scrubbed at her mouth with the back of one hand. *What the hell was Aiden playing at? How did he know about Clapper, and why did he care?*

She turned, and Chaco, now on two long legs, stood behind her, glowering. "What was he doing, Sierra? Why were you throwing him out? What did he do to you?"

"He didn't do anything to me, Chaco. I take it you didn't hear the whole conversation?"

"No. I was staying out of the way—like a good dog." Chaco growled a more human growl this time. "But I heard you tell him to leave. He wasn't taking the hint."

Sierra led the way back to the kitchen and caught Fred about to stick his snout into Aiden's abandoned wine glass. "Fred! Bad mannegishi!" She swept the glass away from him and poured it into the sink. Then she pulled a soda for Fred out of the refrigerator and poured a fresh glass of wine for Chaco. They sat around the table and Sierra recounted her evening out with Aiden.

"Then he asked what it had been like to work for Jack Clapper," she concluded. "But I never mentioned Clapper's name to him. I just said that Black Diamond had hired my old boss to take over my project. That's all I said. So how does he know?"

Chaco pondered this, tilting his glass this way and that to watch the dark, garnet-colored wine roll around his glass. "I have no idea," he said finally. "If you never mentioned Clapper, then he knows something he shouldn't have known. It's hard to think he's just an innocent bystander. And now it doesn't seem like a coincidence that he was at the same campground as us."

Sierra stared at Chaco with fresh horror. "You think *Aiden* was the one who trashed our camp? Why? What possible reason?"

Chaco shook his head. "I don't know. But I don't like this one bit. Sierra, please be careful. You've had some experience with what...Necocyaotl...can send against us. We don't know who this man is, or what he wants. For all we know, he's a servant of Necocyaotl."

Sierra considered Aiden, remembering that she had thought him kind. "I don't think so," she said uncertainly, and explained that the silver feathers hadn't affected Aiden at all, so far as she could tell. "Unless firing them in the kiln destroyed their power," she said, with sudden anxiety. "Do you think I ruined them?"

Chaco looked worried. "I don't know. Q's feathers are extremely powerful, but I never heard of anyone putting them in a kiln before. They're all we've got, so I guess we have to try to use them."

Chaco and Fred went back to their checkers game. Sierra sipped her wine and watched. She felt tired and rather depressed. It had been a disappointing end to the evening. Fred trounced Chaco, who lost with reasonably good grace. Sierra said goodnight and went upstairs to bed. She was asleep moments after her head hit the pillow.

• • •

It was so dark she couldn't see her hand in front of her face. She fumbled in her pockets for matches or a flashlight, but her pockets were empty. Then she heard it.

"*Mahaha! Mahaha!*" The manic laughter echoed, as though in a vast chamber. "*Mahaha!*"

No! she thought, You're dead. No!

She stood, frozen, listening. She heard a steady drip, like water dripping down stone. Nothing else. The pounding of her heart was so loud she was sure the creature in the dark could hear it, too. She was cold, too cold, but willed herself not to shiver. She strained to hear, but aside from the dripping, she could hear nothing but the rush of blood in her ears.

She remembered the colored flames that Quetzalcoatl had awoken in her mind. *Where is my power? I need it now!* She strained to feel some sort of strength to resist this terror, but there was nothing. Nothing at all.

For long moments she stood motionless, barely breathing for fear Mahaha would locate her by the sound of air hissing in and out of her lungs. Still she heard nothing. Finally, she put out a cautious hand, feeling for a wall or a familiar piece of bedroom furniture. Her hand encountered damp, cold rock, and as she touched it, several bits flaked away and clattered to the ground. In the deathly silence, their fall sounded like a small avalanche.

Light flared abruptly, and she saw the ice demon spring at her, fanged mouth open, claws outstretched. She shrieked and threw up her hands to defend herself and Mahaha hit her hard, knocking her to the stone floor. The icy cold of its breath rolled over her.

Then there was nothing. As she cowered on the ground, eyes squeezed shut in terror, nothing attacked. There was no sound, and the icy cold diminished to mere coolness. She opened her eyes cautiously, taking in the torches ensconced on the rock walls of the all-too-familiar stone hall. A voice whispered, "You thought there was only one Mahaha? Only one messenger? I have many servants, they are everywhere. There's a part of *me* in you now, Sierra. I'll always be a part of you. Always. Always…"

The voice came from the other end of the great hall, where the great black mirror stood. Running along either side of the hall were the loathsome murals, just as before. And she saw with despair, but no surprise, a stone altar standing before the mirror.

"Come, Sierra," said the voice, seeming to beckon her closer to the altar and to the mirror. "Come serve me. I can give you anything. Everything."

She saw there was a knife resting on the altar, a large leaf-shaped blade fashioned from obsidian, dark and shining in the torchlight. The knife was meant for her, she thought. All had been prepared for her. She had only to take a few steps to the altar and it would all be over...

"No," said the voice. "This is not for you. I have a purpose for you, and I will reward you for fulfilling that purpose. The knife is for the one who must be sacrificed. Bring him to me, Sierra, and you shall have everything you want—this I promise! Everything."

Sierra found her voice. "I'm not bringing anybody to be sacrificed," she said. "And whatever you've got to give, I don't want it."

"Then die!" hissed the voice, inhuman in its rage and intensity. She felt herself impelled toward the grim altar and its wicked blade, as though sucked into a riptide. She flung herself to the rough stone floor and scrabbled with her fingernails to find a grip, but there was nothing to hang on to as she was dragged sobbing across the rough stone.

In some corner of her terrified mind, a rational voice spoke. *This isn't happening. It's a nightmare. Wake up!*

• • •

Sierra woke shivering in the gray dawn. She was soaked with sweat and breathing hard. It had seemed so real, but it was a nightmare. Wasn't it? What was it the voice had demanded? A sacrifice? It never said who was to be sacrificed. But dreams never made sense, and this was only a dream. Sierra shuddered and decided that the idea of going back to sleep was impossible and even repugnant. She showered, dressed in jeans and a T-shirt, and went quietly downstairs to make coffee. By the time Chaco and Fred were up, the birds were singing, it was a fine spring day with a blue-washed sky and wispy clouds, and Sierra had all but forgotten her nightmare.

She waited until ten o'clock to call Kaylee, hoping this was enough time for Kaylee to have made some discreet inquiries about Clancy. At ten sharp, she dialed Kaylee's number at work.

"Kaylee Shore," said a crisp and professional voice.

"Kaylee, it's Sierra."

"Yes, hello. May I call you back? I'm in a meeting at the moment."

"Sure," said Sierra. She hung up and waited another long, long hour. Finally, the phone rang.

"Sierra? It's Kaylee. Sorry I couldn't talk earlier."

"No problem. Were you able find out anything about Clancy?"

"Yes, indeed. Let's see. He's not married, but I couldn't find out if he ever has been..."

"Not that! Come on, Kaylee. I mean what kind of person is he? Do you think he's safe?"

"Safe? What do you mean? D'you think he's a homicidal maniac or something?" Kaylee sounded taken aback, and Sierra reflected on how many things had happened just since saying goodbye to Kaylee the previous day. No wonder she sounded odd to her friend. Paranoid, Aiden had said.

"No, that's not what I mean. I just want to know if you think he's...working for the opposition."

"The opposition? Oh. Right. Um, it's not that easy to tell, Sierra. I mean, I don't know if he donates to Greenpeace, you know? Here's what I've been able to find out..."

Kaylee told Sierra that Clancy had worked for BDSC for five years. He was the chief of security for the company. He had a lot of access and authority throughout the company.

"People generally think he's a nice guy, but tough. Not someone to mess around with. But he's not a jerk; he's reasonable and easy to deal with as long as you don't start bashing heads with him. Sort of a cop mentality, but a good cop."

"I suppose the cop mentality goes with the job," commented Sierra. "What did he do before he joined BDSC?"

"Don't know. He's been here longer than most folks. You know how people move around here in the Valley." Kaylee was right. Five years was a long time in the restless, upwardly mobile environment of Silicon Valley.

"Did you get his email or phone extension?"

"Yes." Kaylee gave Sierra the information. "Sorry I didn't get more on him personally. The people who work for him probably know more, but I didn't want to seem like I was snooping. Even though I was."

"That's all right. Thanks for finding out as much as you did. So, people generally think he's OK?"

"Yes. Professionally, anyway."

Sierra thanked Kaylee and hung up. She sat for a moment, thinking. What on earth did he want with her? Well, she'd find out soon enough. In an couple of hours, she'd be meeting him for lunch. She shook herself briskly and went to her computer, where she spent a productive hour checking the job boards.

When she had finished putting her resume online at various job sites, and sent off a few applications, Sierra went to Google News to check the news headlines.

"President Pulls Teeth of Endangered Species Act," read one headline. "Nuclear Power Plan Sails through Congress," read another. Sierra sighed. So much to do. Was she supposed to turn this tide of destruction?

CHAPTER 13

Sierra had arranged to meet Clancy at an unpretentious lunch spot in Santa Clara. The food was unremarkable but the surroundings were gorgeous. The café was located in an older industrial park. Land had been cheaper in the good old days, and the developers had planted a grove of towering redwoods amid the glass-walled office buildings. In the midst of the grove there was an artificial waterfall that ran over real-enough rocks into a large pond. The surrounding gentle slopes were bursting with flowers, and there was a large, flat lawn that enjoyed both sun and shade during the day.

Sierra arrived early and sat on the outside patio at a table under a green umbrella, with a perfect view of the little oasis tucked away amid the halls of industry. She sipped an iced tea and watched the ducks paddle around the pond. She wondered if they made any distinction between this tiny, perfectly groomed imitation of nature and some scummy, but genuine pond out in the woods. Then she wondered if *she* could tell the difference between reality and illusion. Given the latest events in her life, this was a valid question, she thought. Maybe she was just like the ducks, blissfully paddling around, unaware that beyond the flowery borders of her vision, there was another, quite different, reality.

As she was pondering this, lost in thought, Clancy placed a hand on her shoulder. She startled, spilling her drink into her lap.

"Oh, shit!" she yelped, then blushed and clapped her hand over her mouth. "Oh, sorry, Clancy. I didn't mean to say that. I was startled."

Clancy handed her a wad of paper napkins from a dispenser

on the table, and then sat down opposite her. "I think I've heard that word before," he said, amiably. "Checking...checking. No, I don't think you shocked me."

Sierra, who was fortunately wearing jeans and not white linen trousers, mopped up the tea. "Well, sorry anyway. I'm trying to cut back on the profanities, but they pop out sometimes."

"No problem," returned Clancy. "That was quite a leap you made when I touched you. Is something wrong?"

"Oh. No. Nothing wrong!" said Sierra, who disliked lying. "Let's order, shall we?"

They ordered their sandwiches and drinks (Sierra opting for plain water this time around) and sat for a few minutes in silence. Finally, Clancy broke the awkward silence.

"Some people take...termination...rather hard, you know. Your boyfriend said you were indisposed when I called," he said, carefully.

"Chaco isn't my boyfriend," Sierra hastily interjected, then regretted it because she had no other explanation ready. "He's, ah, a friend of, eh, a friend." Clancy was quiet for a heartbeat.

"How nice of him to take care of you while you were ill," he said carefully.

"It was nothing," Sierra said. "Just a cold or something. Chaco stopped by to, to return a book."

"I see. I got the wrong idea, then. Your friend gave me the impression you were really quite sick."

"Well, yes. A very *bad* cold," said Sierra, wishing desperately that Clancy would move on to something else. "But I'm fine, now."

"Well, I'm very glad to hear it," said Clancy, and he really did sound pleased. His tone had lightened, and he had a smile in his voice. Sierra reflected for an instant how odd it is that you could tell someone was smiling even when you couldn't see that person. Something about the timbre of the voice changed, she thought.

There was another moment of silence, then Sierra said, "So you called to see if I was slitting my wrists because I got fired?" *Too bristly. Too in-your-face.* "Sorry, Clancy. That came out wrong.

I mean, it was nice of you to call and check to see if I was OK. Really. Very nice." *Shut up now.*

"I didn't think you would slit your wrists," he replied, apparently not offended. "You didn't seem like the type."

"Good call. I'm not. I'm taking a little time off before I start looking for another job. To think things over. You know," she said abruptly, "I did *not* get canned because I was doing a bad job or because I was stealing paper clips."

"I know," said Clancy in his pleasant tenor voice.

"You do?"

"Yes. You had a good record at BDSC. And people liked you. I heard a lot of muttering from people who thought it was a shame you were terminated. They don't understand it."

"Should you be telling me this?" asked Sierra, genuinely surprised.

"Probably not," he admitted cheerfully. "And I probably shouldn't have checked your employment record, either, but I did."

"Why did you?"

"I was interested. Usually, when someone is terminated, I know the reason. Nobody said a word about why you were let go. And when I first met you, I liked the way you handled yourself. So when you were laid off, I asked around a little bit and looked through your files. Couldn't find a thing wrong. So I thought that was odd. In my line of work, I don't like mysteries."

Sierra smiled to herself. "You mean you didn't become a private cop because you read *The Hardy Boys* when you were a kid?"

"No. I never read mysteries. The police procedure ones annoy me, and the cozies annoy me even more. I'm more of a non-fiction kind of guy."

"Really?" Sierra said. "Me too! What do you like to read? I'd guess history. Or world politics."

"You're all wrong about me," he said, looking straight into her eyes. In the light of the midday sun, his eyes were a clear, jade green. She stared back, momentarily at a loss for words.

"I mean," he said, taking his eyes from hers to concentrate on making inroads into his sandwich, "About my taste in literature."

"Oh, that," said Sierra, relieved at finally having something to say. "Well what do you like to read, then?"

"Byawphugee," he said, seriously impeded by a mouthful of chicken breast with goat cheese.

Sierra leaned closer, as though that would somehow make him more intelligible. "What?"

Clancy chewed hard and swallowed. "Biology. Natural history. Earth studies. That kind of thing."

Sierra sat up straighter. "Really? And why do you like reading about natural history and so forth?"

"Hmm. I don't really have a reason for liking it. But I could make one up, if you like."

Sierra smiled, tickled by his reply. "OK. Make one up."

"It seems to me that the more we know about the way things work in this world, the more likely we are to make better decisions about things. Take BDSC, for example."

"Yes," Sierra said, dryly. "Take BDSC. Please."

Clancy acknowledged her little joke with a quirk of his mouth. "Well, at BDSC, we use a lot of dangerous chemicals in processing. The ground underneath Silicon Valley is riddled with aquifers, which is where we get a lot of our drinking water. Chemicals that spill or leak sink into the ground and pollute the groundwater. We've seen that in the south of the county—there are plumes of jet propellant contaminating the aquifers from a manufacturing plant that's no longer there. The people down there can't drink the tap water."

"OK," Sierra said. "So how does that relate to anything that BDSC is doing?"

"Well, the company discovered that one of the chemicals it was using, which starts with an 'N' and I can't remember the name now, was a toxin that caused reproductive harm to humans. So the company immediately tried to find an alternative, which they did. They started using diluted oxalic acid in the same equipment," which meant they didn't have to replace all the etching machinery, and it's far less toxic. It was a win-win."

"Oxalic acid," said Sierra suspiciously. "That sounds toxic, too."

Clancy took a drink of water. "You know that weed that comes up in the spring with bright yellow flowers and tastes sour?"

Sierra nodded. "We used to chew on it when I was a kid. We called it lemon grass. I found out it's really not lemon grass, though."

Clancy nodded. "It's called oxalis. Because it contains oxalic acid."

"Oh." Sierra regarded him thoughtfully. "So BDSC substituted something that I actually ingested as a child to replace a real poison."

"That's it," said Clancy. "But unless we understand these things, we can't make good choices."

"Right," said Sierra, and gazed at him, thinking. *Could she trust him?* He was saying the right things. But what could she tell him that he would believe? What a quandary.

"So, why didn't I ever hear about the oxalic acid change?" she asked. "You'd think it would make a good story for the press. You know, 'Black Diamond Semiconductor Switches to Green Process.'"

"I suppose the company didn't want the press to point a finger at the other side of that story," Clancy said. "You know, 'Black Diamond Semiconductor Admits Use of Birth Defect Chemical.'"

"Hmmmm. Yes, the news media probably *would* take that angle," she admitted, and subsided into a thoughtful silence.

"So," said Clancy, trying to keep the conversation rolling. "What do you like to read?"

"Pretty much the same things," Sierra responded, still distracted. "I also read about camping and hiking and wildflowers. When I go hiking in the spring, I like to identify flowers. I also read a lot about metallurgy and minerals."

"Metallurgy and minerals? Why?"

Sierra came back to the present with a start. "Oh. I design and make jewelry. Silver jewelry. So I read about jewelry making, and techniques for working with metals, especially silver. And I guess I really got into making jewelry because I like the stones, so I read about them all the time. It helps me to develop new ideas for designs, and encourages me to try new techniques. Does that sound, um, odd?"

Clancy looked surprised. "No. Everyone needs interests, hobbies, whatever. I have an old friend that collects air sickness bags."

Sierra looked at him skeptically. "Air sickness bags? You've *got* to be kidding."

"No," protested Clancy. "Most of them are from the airlines. But he's got a really rare one that was produced in honor of the nineteen-seventy-two Republican National Convention by something called the Neo-American Church of Florida. Jim's very proud of that one."

"I bet," Sierra said. "And you say this guy is a friend of yours?"

"Well, someone I went to school with, anyway," replied Clancy, looking a trifle sheepish.

"Whew. You had me worried there. And I thought pounding on metal in my garage was nerdy."

"Well, *I* don't think so," responded Clancy, and they looked at each other for a few moments. Sierra noticed that his dark hair was threaded with silver, and his long-fingered hands looked strong. She flashed for a moment on what it would be like to have those strong hands running over her body…She shook her head, and her long braid bounced vigorously.

"What is it?" asked Clancy. The sunlight turned his eyes to translucent jade.

"You do not want to know," she said, feeling the heat in her cheeks. He gazed at her intently.

"Oh, but I do."

"Nope," she said, with a tone of finality.

"Well, then," Clancy said, "How did you learn how to make jewelry? It's not like you can pick it up on your own, is it?"

"No," Sierra replied, happy to move into neutral territory

again. "I thought about it for years. Then one day, I just decided to do it, so I signed up for a class."

"So it was something that you liked right away?"

"Actually, no," she admitted. "I wasn't sure I was going to succeed at it. First of all, during the class I realized just how many tools and how much equipment I would need. I was going to have to spend a lot of money if I wanted to continue on my own. Secondly, it seemed like kind of a guy thing."

"A guy thing? Making jewelry? Sounds like a girl thing to me."

"No, really, it's like blacksmithing, only in miniature. You heat the metal with a torch, hit it with hammers, bend it, twist it, and throw it in acid. There's a very male kind of energy involved, at least that's the way it felt to me. And there's a certain amount of risk of getting cut or burned, of course."

"So what made you decide to continue?"

Sierra grinned. "I started to get good at it."

Clancy reached across the table and took both her hands in his. Reflexively, she began to pull back, then relaxed. He examined her hands. She knew he was seeing the rough skin, the short, unpolished nails and the healing cuts caused by her jewelry work. He pressed her fingers gently, then returned her hands to her. She placed them self-consciously under the table.

"They say you can tell a lot about a person from their hands," remarked Clancy, smiling as he noticed her hands disappear.

"So what do they tell you, Sherlock?" responded Sierra, trying to keep things on the light side for a few minutes longer.

"I guess if I didn't know about your...hobby doesn't seem quite the right word. If I didn't know about your jewelry making, I would have guessed you were a craftsperson of some sort. A lot of the women in the office have false nails. You don't. Most of them have soft hands. You have calluses and cuts. Even a few old burns. So you obviously work with your hands, but I know for a fact you earn your living with a computer."

"Earned. Past tense," said Sierra, trying not to sound bitter.

"I can't wear acrylic nails or even polish because the metal work ruins them."

"It's OK with me," said Clancy. "And you'll find another job." He leaned back, smiling gently at her.

"So what do you do when you're not at work? Any hobbies?" she asked.

"I like photography. Mostly nature photography. I hike in the Open Spaces around here with my camera. I've got some great wildlife shots. And I pick locks."

This was surprising. "You pick locks? Isn't that kind of an odd hobby for a law-and-order guy?"

Clancy smiled. "You'd be surprised how many legitimate uses there are for lock-picking. And there are all sorts of locks. It's always fun to get a new one and learn how to pick it. There's even an organization that promotes it as a hobby."

"You have got to be kidding," Sierra said in disbelief.

"Nope. Honest."

Another moment of silence followed. She paused to gather her courage and then plunged in. "Listen, Clancy. What did you want to see me about? Why are we meeting? I thought I was in trouble when I heard you had called."

Clancy leaned back, considering her. Then he seemed to make a decision and leaned forward, forearms resting on the table. "I like you, Sierra. I wanted to get to know you better." He kept his green gaze steady, looking into her eyes.

Chaco was right! was her first thought. And her second thought was, *This is not a good time, not a good time at all.* Sierra sat still, torn between her liking of the man and the mission she had been given. She could not see a reasonable way to combine them. She had no way to explain her current friends and activities to a potential boyfriend—at least, no way that wouldn't send him screaming in the opposite direction. On the other hand, telling him the truth was probably the only way to go forward with a relationship. If this didn't scare him off, nothing would.

Reading her hesitation as a lack of mutual interest, Clancy's face took on a slightly self-mocking expression. "I suppose you have someone?"

"No," she said hastily. "No, I don't. It's just that…" Words failed her.

"It's just that there's…what was his name? The guy who answered your phone. Chaco?"

"It isn't what you think," she said. "He's just a friend of sorts." This triggered a cocked and cynical eyebrow. "No, not that kind of friend. Just. A. Friend. And there are things you need to know about him and about me." Again, she saw that world-weary look. "No! Not about Chaco and me. About Chaco. And then about me. Separately. Can you keep an open mind?"

Clancy sighed. "The last time a woman asked me to keep an open mind, she told me that she was into role-playing bunny rabbits during love-making."

"Ack! No. It's nothing of the sort," Sierra protested, feeling the heat rise into her cheeks again. "Nothing at all to do with sex, I promise."

"Then what?"

"Come to my house tonight, and I'll let Chaco tell you all about it," Sierra said, hoping she could persuade Chaco to cooperate.

Clancy looked at her carefully, considering. She saw the cop in him, analyzing, warning, telling him that something was amiss here. As though reading his mind, she saw the man struggling with the cop. One wanted to trust her; the other definitely did not. Finally, he said, "Sierra, I don't know what's going on here. Experience tells me that when I don't know what's going on, something is off. This just smells wrong. You seem like a nice lady, but something is just not right here."

"You're correct," she said, unsmiling. "There is something terribly wrong. And I need your help. I would never do anything to harm you or get you into trouble. But I need help, and Chaco needs help. Please. Come to my house tonight. I'll explain everything then."

"Why not tell me now?"

"I can't," she said desperately. "You wouldn't believe me. You need to speak to Chaco." No one would ever believe what I have to say. You have to see Chaco the man transform into Chaco the coyote.

Clancy rose to his feet, looming above her. "Sierra, trust goes both ways. You don't trust me enough to tell me what's going on. I don't trust *you* enough to come to your house and listen to Chaco. It's too bad. I'm really sorry, but I don't think this is going to go anywhere that I want to go." He tossed some bills onto the table, turned, and walked away without a backward glance. Sierra put her face into her hands and fought back tears that were as much from frustration as disappointment.

After a few minutes, she sniffed, blew her nose into a rough and too-small paper napkin, and pulled herself together. She dug her cell phone out of her purse and called Kaylee.

"Kaylee Shore." This was Kaylee's professional, at-work voice.

"Hi, Kaylee. It's me," Sierra said in a small voice.

"Sierra? What's the matter, sweetie?" Now it was Kaylee's warm-and-comforting-friend voice.

"Oh, Kaylee, what *isn't* the matter? I just got shut down by Mr. Forrester, is what's the matter." Sierra sniffed again.

"What? He wouldn't go out with you?"

"Kaylee, for heaven's sake! Yes, he seemed interested. But how could I even imagine having a relationship with someone who doesn't know what's going on, or what I'm trying to do? I actually thought for a second that he might be able to help me with this, this thing. But I can't just come out and *tell* him. Think about it. He's a skeptical, hard-headed cop-type guy, and the dingbat broad babbles on about men that change into animals—not that it doesn't ever happen—and about feathered serpents and evil twins. He'd try to have me committed in a hot New York minute. And that would be the *good* part." She paused to sniff again and wipe her nose with a crinkly paper napkin. "What a disaster. First he obviously thought that Chaco was my boyfriend…"

"You could do worse," muttered Kaylee.

Ignoring this, Sierra plunged on. "Then he decided that the whole thing was fishy and backed off faster than a cat meeting a rattlesnake. Said it was a matter of trust being a two-way street or something. All because I wouldn't explain the whole, damn, crazy, bizarre, unbelievable, delusional, idiotic mess right here at lunch." The dam burst, and Sierra dissolved into sobs.

Kaylee tried a soothing approach. "Oh, honey, it's OK. It will be all right. Really. Please don't cry."

Sierra cried.

Kaylee tried the tough approach. "Sierra. Snap out of it. This isn't doing any good. We just have to think of another way."

"Oh, yeah?" Sierra snapped. "Like what? What's the next move, Kaylee?"

There was a moment of silence at the other end of the connection. "Listen, Sierra. I know you're upset. But don't take it out on me. I believed you—and Chaco. I'm on your side."

Sierra, already feeling guilty, sighed, and wiped her eyes. "I'm sorry, Kaylee. I really, really am. I just don't know where to go from here. I thought maybe Clancy could find a way to get access to Jenna, so that I could get Q's feathers to her. Now I don't know what to do. I just don't know what to do."

"Listen. I'll meet you at your place after work. I'll try to leave early, if I can."

Sierra sniffed again. "Thanks, Kaylee. I don't know what I'd do without you at this point."

"No problem. See you later." And the line went dead. Sierra, feeling emotionally washed out, sat for a few minutes. After a bit, the lunchtime mob began to clear out, leaving her to the peace of the little pond and its redwood grove. She wished she were in the mountains, hiking or camping, and thought about some of the places she had hiked in the area. That led to thoughts about her ruined camping gear. She decided to go window shopping at the CampOut Superstore. She could start making a list of replacement items, even if she couldn't afford to buy them yet. Then, she decided, she'd go home and send out a few more resumes. There really was a normal life somewhere waiting for her, and sending out resumes seemed like a way to get back to it.

Three hours later, Sierra awoke from a dream of ultra-light, multi-fuel camp stoves in the middle of CampOut Superstore's backpacking aisle. She glanced at her watch; it was four-thirty! If Kaylee had left work early, she might already be at Sierra's house, fuming on the doorstep.

No, Sierra remembered, Chaco would let Kaylee in. She heaved a sigh of relief, and hustled out of the mammoth store. She had a long wish list of items she wanted, too. The technology was improving all the time, and she wasn't entirely displeased that she would be forced to replace some very old pieces of equipment with new, lightweight, and better-performing gear.

As she pulled up outside her house, she saw with surprise that Kaylee was, indeed, on her doorstep. Kaylee stood up as Sierra got out of her car.

"*There* you are," she remarked mildly. "I thought you were so upset you'd be in bed, wailing."

"I'm sorry," said Sierra. "I feel better now. I still don't know what I'm going to do, but I'm not upset anymore. Thanks for coming over. Didn't Chaco answer the door?" Kaylee shook her head. "He must be out shopping or something. And Fred is under strict orders not to come to the door. He tends to disappear whenever someone rings the doorbell, anyway." Sierra turned the key in the lock and opened the door. The two women stepped into the front hall. The house seemed deserted, and there was a nasty burning smell.

"Chaco?" called Sierra, walking into the kitchen. There was a small pot smoking on the stove, but no sign of Chaco or Fred. Sierra grabbed a potholder and thrust the pot into the sink, turning on the water. As steam hissed up from the sink, she turned off the burner.

"Sierra. Over here," said Kaylee. Sierra turned. Kaylee was at the door that led into the garage from the kitchen. The door was open. Sierra hurried over and switched on the garage light.

The first thing she saw was a drawer lying on the floor. It was the drawer where she stored her design with Quetzalcoatl's silvered feathers. It had been wrenched out of her workbench, and was lying on the floor. It was empty.

Then she saw the sprawled form of Chaco, in human form, lying motionless on the concrete floor.

"Sierra," said Kaylee in a choked voice, "I don't think he's breathing!"

CHAPTER 14

Sierra rushed over to Chaco's body, followed closely by Kaylee. "Oh no, no, no," Sierra heard Kaylee say under her breath as they knelt next to him.

Chaco lay on the floor like an angrily discarded doll, legs and arms flung out at awkward angles. His eyes were closed, and his lashes cast shadows on his lean cheeks under the harsh florescent lights. He was lying on his stomach with his head turned, his left cheek resting on the cement. His long, black hair hung in his face. He was unresponsive and eerily still, but they could see no blood or any sign of a wound. Sierra bent down so that her cheek was next to his slightly open mouth.

"Can you tell if he's..." started Kaylee, but Sierra hushed her. She waited, feeling grit scrape her cheek as her knees protested against the hard concrete. Finally, she felt a tiny stirring of air from his mouth against her face. His breath was sweet, like a puff of breeze across a meadow. She straightened up.

"He's breathing, but barely," she said. She gingerly felt his neck, which seemed normal. No sharp angles under the too-cool skin; everything appeared to be in the right place. "Help me to roll him over so we can check for wounds."

Kaylee and Sierra, one on either side of the prone Chaco, rolled him gently to his back, carefully placing his right arm back down on the concrete and cushioning his head. He neither stirred nor made any noise during this operation. Once they had him on his back, they surveyed him carefully, running gentle fingers over his skin.

"I don't see anything," said Kaylee. "There's not a scratch on him." She smoothed his hair back from his face, then ran her fingers over his skull. "No bumps. No bruises. No soft spots. What's the matter with him?"

Sierra lifted Chaco's T-shirt. She put her ear to his chest where she hoped his heart would be. *If Avatars even have hearts*, she thought, but she was rewarded with a faint, rhythmic thumping.

"I can hear his heart beating," she reported with relief. "It sounds kind of faint, though. And he feels cold, too cold." She pulled down his shirt. "I don't know what's wrong," she told Kaylee. "I thought Avatars couldn't be harmed. Chaco himself told me that they can't be killed." *Power,* she thought bitterly. *I could use some sort of power right now.* No flames of gold, green, red, purple, or blue. Only a growing feeling of dread and helplessness.

"Well, let's get him off this cold floor," Kaylee said. They checked his arms and legs to make sure there were no broken bones. Then Kaylee put her hands under his shoulders and Sierra lifted his knees. Chaco, a dead weight hanging between the two women, was no light burden, but they managed to maneuver him onto the couch in the living room. They collapsed, panting on the floor for a few minutes.

"Let's get him warmed up. Do you have an electric blanket?" asked Kaylee. Sierra did, and went to get it as Kaylee pulled off his shoes. They spread the blanket over Chaco's still form and switched it on. Then they turned and looked at each other.

"What on earth do we do now?" Kaylee said, speaking for both of them. They stared down at the unconscious Avatar. Something about him seemed diminished. Some force that had always been present, but invisible, was gone. His body was like an empty house, Sierra thought. It looked the same on the outside, but the life within had traveled elsewhere.

"Could Mama Labadie help him?" mused Sierra, aloud.

"I'm not sure. We don't know what happened to him. Maybe Fred can tell us," Kaylee said.

"We'd have to find Fred, first," Sierra noted dryly. "Could you call your mambo, anyway? Maybe she can do something. She did a great job on me."

Kaylee pulled her cell phone out of her purse and dialed a number. She waited for a bit, frowned, then dialed another number. Finally, she put the phone away. "No answer at work or at home. We're going to have to find another healer, I guess. I don't think we should wait—he looks too sick."

They checked Chaco again. He lay as still as ever. They couldn't see his chest move, and in alarm, Sierra held a pocket mirror over his mouth. To their relief, a faint mist appeared on the silvered surface.

"I've always read about people doing that," commented Kaylee. She felt Chaco's face, which seemed paler than before. His normally warm brown skin seemed to have acquired a gray tinge. "He's so cold," she said, frowning. "I'm not sure the electric blanket is doing any good."

"You know, neither one of us has suggested calling 911," Sierra said. "Do you think we ought to get him to the hospital?"

"How about a vet?" suggested Kaylee, who then burst into tears instead of laughter.

"No," said a small voice from the door. They wheeled around, startled, and there was Fred. He was muddy, and his melon-shaped head hung dejectedly.

Sierra was the first to speak. "Where have you *been*, Fred?" she demanded. "What happened here? What's wrong with Chaco? And where are Quetzalcoatl's feathers?"

"I'm sorry," said the mannegishi, and now tears began to fall from his huge orange eyes. "I ran away. I am a coward. Me— Shoemowetochawcawewahcatoe. High-Backed Wolf, my father called me. Oh, he should have called me Ogumwhowurst—Yellow Wolf." Fred began to wail in earnest, slumping to the floor and rocking back and forth.

"Fred, never mind that. What happened to Chaco?" demanded Sierra. "What's wrong with him?"

"When she came to the door, Chaco went to answer it. I don't know why he didn't recognize her for what she was. Oh, why did I run? Now he'll be destroyed." Fred gasped this out and then began to wail again.

"Fred, SHUT UP!" Sierra roared. Fred froze, one eye fixed on Sierra, the other on Kaylee. His face, normally a healthy green-gray, was yellowish and shiny with tears, and his stubby digits were clenching and unclenching in agitation. Sierra knelt next to him and offered a box of tissues, which he took. She patted his smooth head soothingly.

"Now, Fred, you have to start making sense, or Chaco may be in real trouble here," she said quietly.

Kaylee put in, "Who came to the door, Fred? Let's start there."

Fred sniffed loudly. "Tzintzimitl," he gulped. "I saw right away who she was and ran out of the house. So I didn't see what happened to Chaco."

Kaylee and Sierra looked at each other, then back at Fred. "Who or what is Tzintzimitl?" asked Kaylee.

Fred loudly blew what passed for his nose. "She's an Avatar. But she's an evil Avatar. She wields dark stars that suck the life out of things. She murdered Quetzalcoatl's wife, Mayahuel, that way. Necocyaotl sent her. He knows you need Chaco to help you."

"But I thought that Chaco couldn't be injured, that he couldn't die!" protested Sierra.

"But he *can* be destroyed," said the mannegishi miserably. "The darkness of Tzintzimitl overpowers light, snuffs it out. And Chaco is of the light, so he couldn't fight her off. Not by himself. And no one was here to help him!" Huge, hot tears welled up again and ran down the little creature's face. "Why didn't he recognize her?"

Sierra rocked back on her heels. "Now what?" she said, mostly to herself. "Now what do we do?" She thought about Chaco's wide, cheerful grin and amber eyes, so often filled with laughter. She remembered all the meals he had prepared for her with true affection, hoping to please her. He had fetched Kaylee to help her and stayed by her side until she was safely through that crisis. She thought about the way he'd come to her defense when he thought

Aiden was threatening her. She remembered his lips on hers, and the stirring of something hot and dangerous that had caused.

"Sierra," said Kaylee, breaking into her painful reverie, "We don't need a doctor here, that's obvious. What we need is a shaman."

"A shaman?" said Sierra. "Is that a priest or something?"

"A shaman is someone who mediates between the spiritual and the physical world to heal. Like Mama Labadie. Chaco's human form is physical. He's been injured by something not of the physical world. So we need a shaman," she said firmly.

"How the heck are we going to find a shaman?" Sierra asked. "Do you know a shaman, Fred? You spent all that time hanging out at Indian Grinding Rock. There's a roundhouse there, where the Native Americans hold ceremonies. Shamans must come there all the time. Did you get to know any of them?"

Fred looked uncomfortable and popped a digit into his pursed mouth, thought for a moment, then popped it out. "Well, not exactly," he admitted. "Mostly I was, um, you know…"

"No, Fred. I don't know," said Sierra, barely containing her impatience. "Tell me."

"Well, there were shamans, but I didn't exactly *meet* any of them," said Fred, looking up at Sierra with an expression she took to be disingenuous innocence.

"Go on."

"I was sort of, that is, I didn't…"

This time it was Kaylee who exploded. "For God's sake, Fred, just tell us! Chaco is dying!"

Fred gaped at Kaylee, then squeaked, "I was stealing their medicine bags and hiding them. That's what I do, OK? If any of those shamans ever caught up with me, they'd stake me out for the ants. I don't know any shamans! I ran away, I'm a coward, and now I don't even know how to save Chaco's life!" Fresh floods of tears followed.

Sierra got to her feet, feeling completely beaten. How could she carry out her task without Chaco? Not only was Chaco out of the game, her one hope for reaching and changing Jenna Simmons was gone, too, with no hope of recovery.

Kaylee went to check on Chaco. "He looks worse," she reported. He's not the right color, and he's very cold. I'm going to call Mama Labadie." She pulled out her cell phone and dialed. Vertical creases appeared between her brows as she listened, then ended the call. "She's not there. And this is an emergency—Chaco looks terrible. What on earth are we going to do?"

"We can't look in the Yellow Pages under 'shaman,' can we?" asked Sierra. They looked at each other, hope dawning. But a quick dash for the Yellow Pages yielded nothing between "Sharpening Service" and "Shavers."

"How about Google?" Kaylee suggested. This yielded more than twelve million links. Poring through the top links resulted in very little of practical value. There were some shamanic healers listed, but hopeful clicks usually resulted in either "404: Requested Page Not Found" or healers located in places too far away to be helpful.

"OK," Sierra said, finally. "Let's wrap him up and get him in the car. I have one, last, desperate idea." The two women bundled Chaco's limp form in blankets and lugged him to the back seat of Sierra's car, Fred fussing and getting underfoot. He insisted on coming with them, perching on Chaco's chest and peering soulfully into the Avatar's vacant face. Now and then, he patted Chaco's cheek gently with his six-fingered paws.

As the women settled Chaco under the blankets and backed out of the car's rear seat, a police car rounded the corner at speed, lights flashing, and came to a halt beside them. A quick glance assured Sierra that Fred had vanished. Under the blankets, Chaco's still form was indiscernible—but of course, if they decided to search the car...

Sierra straightened up and closed the car door as an officer stepped out of the squad car. She smiled brightly. "Evening, Officer. How can we help you?"

The policeman, unsmiling, shone his flashlight first in Kaylee's face, who squinted in the glare, then in Sierra's. "Miss Sierra Carter?" he asked. Sierra nodded.

"May I see some identification, please?" the cop asked, now shining his flashlight into the car. "Certainly, Officer," Sierra responded, turning his attention on her again. She began to rummage in her purse. "May I ask what this is about?" She glanced across the roof of the car at Kaylee, who looked frightened.

The cop did not respond, but scrutinized her driver's license and her face. "I'm afraid you'll have to come with me, Miss," he said, finally. "You have the right to remain silent…"

Sierra listened to the prescribed ritual with a sense of numb disbelief. This could not be happening now—not when Chaco was so ill. He needed her! She had to help him, or…or she didn't know what. Once the policeman finished his spiel, she said, "I'll come with you with no problem, sir. Just give me a second to talk to my friend." He nodded curtly and she turned to Kaylee.

"Well, I don't know what this is about, but I guess I'll have to take a rain check on that dinner at Quetzalcoatl's Corner. Here are your keys." And she tossed her car keys to Kaylee, who caught them and stared at her, eyes huge. "Tell Chaco I'm sorry, but I know you'll take care of things." With that, she allowed the policeman to march her to the squad car, where his partner sat observing the scene, and to sequester her in the back seat. As the squad car pulled away from the curb and down the street, she looked back at Kaylee, standing alone beside Sierra's car. Her car, with Chaco lying helpless and unconscious in the back.

CHAPTER 15

Sierra spent the ride to the Sunnyvale police station obsessively worrying about Chaco. Did Kaylee understand what she had meant by "Quetzalcoatl's Corner"? Even if she did understand, what good would it do Chaco to go there? Maybe it was a stupid idea in the first place. There were so many things that could go wrong, and Chaco's existence hung by a slender thread.

She barely gave her own quandary a thought until she was ushered into the station, booked, fingerprinted, and photographed. To her bewilderment and horror, she discovered that she was being arrested for theft but couldn't get any more detail from the police, who told her to talk to her lawyer. *My nonexistent lawyer*, she thought, numbly.

"Don't I get a phone call?" she demanded, as she was herded towards the cells. The policewoman who had taken charge of her shrugged, halted with a resigned expression on her doughy face and changed direction, pointing at a wall phone.

"Feel free," she said, and crossed her arms above her gun belt, waiting. *A woman of few words,* Sierra thought, digging in her pocket for change, which she fed into the phone and punched in a number. As she expected, she got voice mail.

"Clancy, it's Sierra Carter. I know you're kind of unhappy with me, but I don't know who else to call. I'm down at the Sunnyvale police station, and they've booked me for theft, but I don't know why. Anyway, I need a lawyer, and I figured you must know one or two. *Please* help me out here. Please. Thank you."

She hung up the phone with a sense of defeat. She had left the message at the only phone number she had for Clancy, which was his work phone, so he wouldn't even get it until he got to his desk the next morning. She was in for a night in the cells, with no hope of helping Kaylee with Chaco. She was in some sort of serious legal trouble, but rack her brain as she might, she couldn't think what she had done that would cause her to wind up in jail. She had never stolen anything in her life—unless you counted taking a purple crayon from Celeste Buerger's desk in second grade.

The policewoman escorted her to a large cell. Several of the bunks were already occupied by snoring, blanket-shrouded figures. By the reek of stale alcohol on the air, it was unlikely that any of the ladies present were going to wake up and make trouble. Sierra, clutching a blanket given to her by the bored policewoman, picked a bunk and lay down gingerly on its stained surface.

Although she was certain that her worries would prevent her from sleeping, it was with surprise that she was awakened from a deep slumber after a few hours. The policewoman was standing over her.

"Your lawyer is here," she said gruffly. "Bailed you out. You can go. Don't even think about leaving town."

Sierra, groggy and unkempt, shuffled down the corridor behind the cop. Waiting for her in the foyer was a slender, dark young man dressed in casual clothes—jeans, a T-shirt, windbreaker, and loafers—but carrying a highly polished black leather briefcase. He smiled at her and held out a tanned hand.

"Hi, Sierra," he said, shaking her hand. "I'm Chris Jumlin. Clancy sent me along to straighten this thing out for you."

"*What* thing?" Sierra asked. "They said it was theft, but that was all I got from them."

Jumlin looked annoyed, a frown creasing his brow. He shook his well-groomed head. "Incompetents," he growled. "Don't worry, Sierra! This whole thing is just going to go away. Trust me."

"Anyway," he continued, gently guiding her to the door with a hand on her back, "Let's talk about it in the car. I'll fill you in on the details, but I'm telling you, it's a very flimsy case. In fact, you may have grounds for harassment here, if you want to pursue it…"

He continued talking as they walked into the parking lot and located his car, a sleek, black Mercedes. It chirped as he unlocked it. It was early in the morning, by the look of things. The sky was still black, but the air had the pre-dawn chill typical of a spring morning in the Bay Area. There was no traffic on the street and no one was around.

"...so Black Diamond filed a complaint against you this morning for stealing their patented process with intent to sell it to the competition," he said, and as she tried to protest, he continued, "Yes, I know that's ridiculous. There's no evidence against you." He stopped and faced her, looking serious. "There *is no evidence* against you, is there, Sierra?"

She shook her head. "No, of course not. But how could I steal the process? The process isn't something you can..."

Jumlin cut her off smoothly, opening the door to the back seat. "Come on, Sierra, let's get you home now." Sierra thought it was odd to seat her in the back, but she complied, settling herself on the leather bench seat. He closed the door after her, climbed into the driver's seat and started the car.

• • •

After Sierra and Jumlin drove away, the parking lot was a quiet and untroubled place for several hours. The eastern sky turned a lighter shade of gray, and birds began to rustle and sing in the trees. Dawn began to turn the clouds rose and gold. Cops left the building and greeted their fellows just coming to work. Around seven o'clock in the morning, a Jeep turned into the lot and parked. Clancy got out, followed by a rumpled man in a sweatsuit and running shoes who was carrying a worn brown briefcase. Clancy and the man walked quickly into the police station. After several minutes, Clancy bounded back down the front steps, running, followed at a trot by the rumpled man. They jumped into Clancy's Jeep, and it took off with a screech of tires that was most unwise, given that they were in the police station parking lot. The Jeep disappeared down the street.

CHAPTER 16

Kaylee stood for several long moments, still staring after the squad car. By now, it was the middle of the night, and the streets were quiet and deserted. She jumped nervously as a squeaky voice said, "What are we going to do now?"

Fred had reappeared, still perched atop Chaco's motionless body. He was wringing all twelve of his digits together in a distraught manner, and his eyes were wheeling around in a way that made Kaylee slightly seasick.

"What did she mean by 'Quetzalcoatl's Corner'?" she asked the mannegishi. "She had something specific in mind. What was it?"

Fred's eyes stopped wheeling and focused on Kaylee. "She must have thought there was somewhere she could contact Q, I guess," he said, looking anxious. "But Q can't be found unless he wants to be found. You can't just drop in on him."

Kaylee opened the driver's side door and sat heavily in the seat. "Well, think hard," she said, "Because Chaco's life depends on it. How's he doing?"

Fred checked on Chaco. "Not good," he reported. "Still feels cold. Still not moving."

Kaylee sighed, and rested her forehead on the steering wheel. What on earth had Sierra meant? She felt as though she ought to know. Something nagged at her; she was sure that Sierra had provided an easily guessed clue.

Suddenly, Kaylee sat bolt upright. Her eyes gleamed with triumph. "I've got it," she crowed, "Fred, I know where to go now." She started the car and drove, answering Fred's excited questions as they went.

"Stop asking questions," Kaylee ordered. "You keep an eye out for the cops. We don't want to get stopped with an unconscious body in the back." Fred disappeared, but Kaylee heard him as he moved to peer out to the left, right and behind as she drove.

Kaylee pulled onto the 101 Freeway and headed south. Before very long, she exited at Guadalupe Parkway, and exited again in downtown San Jose. She drove down Market Street, which eventually parted around a small park in the center of the street, like a stream around an island, and Kaylee pulled to the left side of the street in a "No Parking" zone, right next to the park.

"Watch for the police," she hissed at Fred, who hopped down from Chaco's chest and clambered out of the car. "The last thing we need now is a curious cop." Fred sat on the grass, upright and vigilant like a meerkat, eyes swiveling and scanning. The small park was deserted, illuminated in patches by streetlamps. Even the posh Fairmont Hotel, located across the street on the other side of the tiny park, seemed deserted at this time of night—no guests were walking in and out, and there was no valet or doorman on the sidewalk outside.

Kaylee half-carried and half-dragged Chaco's slack body across the grass toward a large, dark form humped on the grass and dimly visible in the streetlights. Fred moved along with her, occasionally attempting to help, but mostly scanning their surroundings for danger. They laid Chaco on the grass near the base of a statue. Even in the gloom, the shape was unmistakable.

"It looks exactly like a huge dog dootie!" whispered Kaylee. "This is hopeless." But she placed her hands palm down on the rough surface of the statue and closed her eyes, trying to summon Quetzalcoatl just as she tried to summon the loa during a Vodún ceremony. She made herself open and humble, asking for help.

"Quetzalcoatl," she whispered. "Help us. Please. Chaco is being destroyed. By...what was the name, Fred?"

"Tzintzimitl."

"Tzintzimitl. The one who killed your wife. She came and

145

did something to Chaco, and her darkness is destroying all his beautiful light. Please, please help us."

The night remained silent, the statue inert. She let the tears pour down her face. This was desperate and ridiculous, she thought. How could this ugly thing help Chaco? What made Sierra think that the great Avatar would be found anywhere near this stupid, man-made artifact? She felt despair wash through her at the thought of Chaco's warmth and beauty snuffed out with such casual cruelty. Kaylee's tears dripped from her cheeks onto the rough surface of the statue.

Then she felt the cold, dark concrete grow warm under her hands. Not daring to hope, she opened her eyes. In the gloom beneath the trees, she thought the statue was beginning to glow. Surely, there was a coppery sheen around the head—which really did look like the head of a Plumed Serpent. But as she peered at it eagerly, if there had been a glow, it faded. *The thing was nothing but an eight-foot-high, cement turd after all,* she thought. She bent down to Fred and they hugged each other wordlessly, then stretched down to touch Chaco where he lay, lifeless in the short grass.

"Someone's coming!" Fred chirped urgently. Kaylee looked beyond the statue, toward the hotel. Someone was walking briskly toward them, outlined by the light from the streetlamps. She bent and tried to pick Chaco up, but she was weary, Chaco was dead weight, and he slipped from her grasp. She sat down abruptly as Fred disappeared and the figure strode up to them.

"Looks like you've got some trouble here," said the figure, in gentle, female tones. "What's going on?"

"Are you a cop?" asked Kaylee, nervously.

"No. What's wrong with your friend?" The woman kneeled next to Chaco and put a slender hand on his forehead. She started violently and turned to Kaylee.

"What the hell are you doing with Coyotl, the Trickster, the Creator, in César Chavez Park in the middle of the night?" she snapped.

CHAPTER 17

Sierra awoke to a darkness so profound that she couldn't tell if her eyes were open or closed. At first she feared it was another vision of the terrifying stone hall, but after a moment of panic, she realized she was lying on a soft surface, not stone. She sat up, straining to see, and groped cautiously around in the dark for something—anything—familiar.

Her hand collided with a small table, which rocked slightly. Judging by the crash and liquid splash, she had knocked a glass off the table. She felt more cautiously across the surface of the table and encountered a lamp. After a bit of fumbling, she found the switch and the room flooded with light.

Sierra was lying in a wooden four-poster bed furnished with a wonderfully comfortable mattress and a lacy canopy. Down pillows covered in real linen cases embroidered with tiny flowers were tumbled about the silky coverlet. The bed stood in a large room with a high ceiling and crown molding. A few elegant tables and chairs were tastefully scattered about, and opposite the bed stood a large, ornately carved antique wardrobe, its dark wood gleaming softly in the light. Once Sierra's eyes adjusted to the light, she could see her reflection, wavery and dusty-looking in the aged mirrors set in the wardrobe doors. And as the fog of sleep cleared, Sierra remembered.

She had been ushered into the back seat of the black Mercedes by Chris Jumlin, the lawyer Clancy had sent. As they drove away from the police station, Jumlin continued to talk. He seemed articulate, confident that Black Diamond had no case against her. Worried and more than a little puzzled, she listened intently, asking occasional questions, and didn't notice for quite a while that he was not driving her home.

"Wait a minute," she had said, suspicion lending a sharp edge to her voice. "You're not taking me home. What are you doing?"

Jumlin glanced back at her briefly and smiled. "I'm sorry," he said apologetically. "I'm actually taking you to *my* home. You'll be safer there."

"Safe from what?" she had asked, trying to keep the anxiety from her voice. "You think Black Diamond's going to have me assassinated or something?"

"Well, stranger things have happened, Sierra," Jumlin said seriously. "I've had a client or two go missing before they came to trial, you know. I just want to make sure that sort of thing doesn't happen in your case."

"That's awfully kind of you," Sierra said, letting the sarcasm creep into her tone. "I suppose it's all part of the service? Do you bring all your clients home with you?"

He laughed easily. "By no means! But I just have a feeling about your case. I've learned to trust my hunches in this business." His tone was light, but sincere. "I understand your concerns, Sierra." Now his voice was warm and soothing. Sierra suddenly felt sleepy, like a small child past her bedtime.

"You don't know me, but I'm your *lawyer*. You can trust me. I will take care of you," Jumlin assured her. That sounded nice. It would be lovely to have someone take care of her. There had been too many dangers in her life lately, too many overwhelming responsibilities. Too many threats. But Jumlin's soft, warm voice felt like a security blanket warding off the nightmares of her recent life. Sierra felt comfortable and safe. Nothing could touch her now that Chris Jumlin was there to protect her. Sierra slumped bonelessly against the seatback, reveling in a sensation of utter relaxation and freedom from fear.

Somewhere inside, a small voice was screaming, beating itself against her obliviousness like a moth at a lighted windowpane.

Sierra, wrapped in the cozy blanket of Jumlin's hypnotic voice, was deaf to all else.

Eventually, Jumlin pulled off the road and into a gated drive. The tall, wrought iron gates swept open smoothly as he approached them and continued down the wooded drive. Soon, the car emerged from a screen of trees and shrubs, and Jumlin pulled to the right around a circular drive fronting what Sierra could only think of as a mansion. It had been constructed in the 1920s or 30s. It was a Spanish-style house, shining white in the moonlight, with a red tile roof and many arched windows and doors. A short flight of stone steps led to a stone terrace flanked by French doors. Light shone golden and welcoming from several of the windows. Sierra pulled at the door handle. It was locked. She tried to unlock the door, but couldn't.

Jumlin climbed out of the front seat and opened Sierra's door. *He has no trouble opening it from the outside,* she thought. *But I couldn't open it from the inside.* It didn't seem important. He held out his hand to help her out of the car.

"You must be very tired," he said, smiling. "I'll show you to your room." Sierra suddenly realized she was exhausted. The evening had been one shock after another—first Chaco, then the arrest. She was drained. She wanted to go home, she wanted to find Kaylee and Chaco and Fred—but she had no more resources. She would stay for tonight, and in the morning, she'd go look for them—Jumlin or no Jumlin. So she had followed him meekly into the great house, accepted a bag containing a thoughtful selection of personal care items, and was finally left alone in this pretty room to sleep.

Sierra had no idea how long she had been asleep, but it was time to find a bathroom. There were three doors in the room, and she reasoned that one led to the hall outside, one to a bathroom, and one to a closet. Taking a guess, she headed to the door on the left and cautiously opened it, shielding her bare body behind the door in case she was wrong. It was the hallway. She shut the door hastily and tried the door on the right. This one led to a large bathroom. She used the facilities, drank a glass of water from the tap—and remembered that she had spilled a glass on her host's plush wool carpet.

She grabbed one of the thick towels from the rack and ran back to the bed. On the floor beside the bed, an empty wine glass, unbroken, kept company with a dark, well-absorbed pool of red liquid. She recalled that her host had pressed a glass of wine on her as she headed off to bed. Using an obviously expensive and beautifully fluffy towel on this mess wouldn't do. She'd have to ask Chris Jumlin for a rag and some soda water. And confess her clumsiness.

Sierra found her clothes where she had left them, thrown in an untidy pile on one of the chairs. Grimacing slightly at dressing in the grimy outfit in which she had been arrested—how long ago? It seemed like days—she pulled on her clothes. An investigation into the small bag of toiletries revealed a new toothbrush, but no paste. She returned to the bathroom and began opening drawers. Her search was quickly rewarded by the discovery of a tube of toothpaste. Sierra reached into the drawer for it—and swiftly withdrew her hand. A large, black spider sat suspended in a web, motionless in the rear of the drawer.

Sierra was tempted to brush without using the toothpaste, but her teeth felt furry, and she craved the freshness of the paste. The second notion that occurred to her was to smash the spider with a wad of toilet paper and flush the victim down the toilet. Sierra sighed as her conscience kicked into gear, and she began searching around the bedroom. She located what she was looking for and returned to the bathroom. The spider still crouched in the drawer, apparently aware it was the focus of her attention, as it hunched down slightly at her reappearance. Sierra quickly lowered the empty water glass over the spider, slid a sheet of paper under it, and lifted the paper and glass simultaneously, the spider neatly trapped. She opened the bathroom window and dropped the spider onto the ledge outside, where it scuttled away as she hastily shut the window. She brushed her teeth briskly, felt distinctly better, and decided to venture out of her room.

The house was quiet. Her room was on the second floor, one of several lining a long hallway. A long runner, which looked like an antique Persian rug, lay on the shining hardwood floor, cushioning her footsteps. She found the stairs, which curved sinuously down to the foyer of the house. The foyer was bright with sunlight streaming through tall windows, and more Persian carpets were strewn across its parquet marble floors. Sierra still heard no signs of life in the house. Cautiously, she said, "Hello?"

After a short interval, Chris Jumlin appeared in a doorway off the foyer. Moving with the easy grace of a cat, he looked slim and wiry in form-fitting jeans and sports jacket over a dark T-shirt. He smiled at her. "Good morning. Ready for some breakfast?"

Sierra's stomach emitted a loud rumble at this suggestion.

"I guess it's obvious that I am," she said, "But I'm afraid I've made a mess. I knocked over my glass of wine when I was trying to turn on the lamp, and it's made a nasty stain on the carpet. I need something to clean it up."

Jumlin seemed unperturbed at this news. He gestured for her to follow him into the next room, which proved to be a large dining room overlooking a patio with a sparkling swimming pool. Flowering shrubs and palms in gaily painted pots were massed on the patio's flagstones, and there was a selection of tables, chairs, and umbrellas to accommodate poolside loungers. But the patio was empty of other people.

"Don't worry about it," Jumlin said, holding a chair out from the table for Sierra to sit. She did so, feeling grubby and out of place amid this elegance. "I'll send Theresa up to take care of it." He sat down and rang a silver bell that sat on the table. Almost immediately, a short, dark-haired woman appeared through a door at the end of the room. Although she did not wear a uniform, from her bearing, it was clear she was a servant of some kind. She stood respectfully by Jumlin's chair and said, "Yes, sir?"

Chris Jumlin told Theresa about the spilled wine and politely asked her to attend to the cleanup. Sierra could have sworn that

Theresa nearly bobbed a curtsey, but, catching her boss' eye, she merely nodded and left the room.

Sierra helped herself to eggs scrambled with crab and dill, sausages, toast, and coffee. Everything was served on fine china, an elegant and dainty floral pattern with a narrow rim of gold. The silverware was definitely silver. Even the juice glass was crystal, if she was any judge. Jumlin must be a very high-priced lawyer, she decided, and experienced a pang of worry.

"So, how do you know Clancy?" she asked after an interval of reflective chewing. Jumlin looked up from *The Wall Street Journal.*

"Who?" he said, looking puzzled for second. Then his brow cleared. "Oh, Clancy Forrester? I've, that is to say, we've been acquaintances for a long time." Leaving Sierra none the wiser, he returned to his paper.

She attacked a piece of toast and tried again. "I suppose Clancy told you that I don't have a job right now, Mr. Jumlin. I'm not sure I can afford your services."

"Oh, don't worry about that," was his reply, delivered from behind the newspaper. His tones were comforting, reassuring. Sierra remembered how reassuring this had been the previous night. She remembered last night's sensation of total relaxation and safety and suddenly wondered at her easy acquiescence.

She waited for a few more minutes. "Well, it was really nice of you to put me up for the night, but I really have to get going. There's a few things that I urgently need to attend to. Um, could you call me a cab or something?"

The newspaper went down. Jumlin folded it deliberately and laid it to one side. "Well, Sierra," he said, leaning forward and fixing her with his dark eyes. "I don't think that's a very good idea. It would be best if you stayed here for a while. Remember, you need a safe place to stay until we can settle this bit of trouble with Black Diamond." Again, his words surrounded her like a warm cloud, promising security and freedom from fear. For an instant, Sierra teetered toward that alluring sense of safety. Then her hackles went up, and she pushed temptation away.

What she *needed* was to find Kaylee and Chaco and Fred, and assure herself that Chaco was going to survive. *Well, Jumlin didn't know about Chaco,* she thought, so she gave it another try.

"Mr. Jumlin..."

"Call me Chris," he said, smiling amiably and setting the newspaper aside with no sign of impatience. His teeth were very white, like a movie star's, against his smooth, tanned skin.

"Chris, then. I have a friend who's in bigger trouble than I am, and I need to find out what's happened to him. So I need to go home and start tracking him down and talk to some people, and..."

"Oh," said Jumlin, looking surprised. "I didn't realize that. Well, I see that there are other priorities here. Certainly, you must help your friend! I'll drive you home." He stood up and courteously pulled out her chair for her as she stood.

Surprised but relieved at how readily he had agreed, Sierra walked back into the foyer. Jumlin opened the door for her, and she could see the sleek Mercedes waiting for them.

"Hang on, Sierra," he said, reaching behind the door. "Tell me, do you think the rear tire looks a little flat?

Sierra peered at the car, which seemed to have four perfectly inflated tires.

She started to turn back to him, saying, "No, Chris. They all look..."

But she never completed the sentence. Chris Jumlin looked down dispassionately at her crumpled body on the marble floor and replaced the heavy oak walking stick behind the door.

"Theresa," he called. "Can you come down here for a minute, please?"

CHAPTER 18

There was a long moment of silence as Kaylee stared at the newcomer. Then she said, "How did you know?"

"It's my business to know," returned the woman. "Now answer my question; why are you here with Coyotl? What did you do to him? Quickly, now. He's going fast."

Kaylee, abandoning any hope of sounding normal or rational, said, "We didn't do anything to him; he's our friend. We found him like this, and ah, another friend said he had been attacked by…dammit! What's that name?"

"Tzintzimitl," squeaked Fred, suddenly reappearing by her side. "It was Tzintzimitl, Wise One." He looked at the newcomer with adoration. "Thank you for coming, Wise One! Coyotl needs you."

"And a mannegishi, too," said the woman, shaking her head. "Well, we'd better get the Trickster away from here. And fast." She bent and put her arms beneath Chaco's shoulders. "You take his legs. Where's your car—that must be it, over there. The one that's parked illegally, right?"

Kaylee nodded, and she took Chaco's legs. Fred scuttled alongside. With two working together, Chaco was easier to carry. They put him in the back seat again, tucked him under the blankets, and Fred climbed on top of him.

"I'm driving the white van over there," the woman said, pointing down the street. "Follow me." Without another word, she strode away. Kaylee pulled out as she saw the van move and began to follow.

After several minutes, Kaylee asked, "Do you suppose Quetzalcoatl sent her?"

"I don't know. I thought I saw the statue glow, but just for a second. Then she showed up," said Fred.

"It doesn't seem like a coincidence to me," remarked Kaylee. "How does she know Chaco?"

Fred piped up from the back seat. "She is a Wise One, of course."

"A Wise One? Do you know her?" Kaylee asked.

"Nope. Never saw her before. But she is a Wise One. You can tell," said Fred.

"Well, I can't tell," retorted Kaylee. "*I* thought she was a cop. What's a Wise One?"

"One who knows. One who heals."

"Sounds like the right kind of person, then," Kaylee said. "I'm glad you saw the statue glow, too, Fred. I thought it was my imagination."

Fred began to chant softly in the back seat, a tune with what sounded like nonsense words, and Kaylee listened in silence as she drove.

The white van sped down the freeway, exited on Highway 17 south and headed toward the coast. They followed as the highway began to climb into the Santa Cruz Mountains and became curvy and steep. There were few other cars on the road. Soon they were into redwood country, the trees towering on either side of the highway. Before long, they passed the summit and the highway began to wind down the other side of the mountains. A thick, gray fog began to obscure the tree tops as they descended. Suddenly, the white van signaled a right turn, and Kaylee turned close behind it.

They drove down a narrow road that snaked its way deeper into the mountains, away from the more populated areas. The night became darker as fog closed in under the redwood trees. Finally, the van turned into a gravel driveway, even narrower than the paved road they had been traveling. Kaylee glanced at the clock in the dashboard. It was now three-forty-five in the morning. She felt weariness descend on her like a lead blanket. She rubbed her gritty eyes and yawned. She heard an answering chirpy yawn from Fred in the back.

The gravel drive ended at a cabin. The windows were dark, and there was no exterior light on. The woman parked her van and, leaving the headlights on, walked to the front door and unlocked it. She disappeared through the door for a moment, and warm yellow light burst from the cabin's windows, creating a welcoming glow. Then she went back to her van, killed the headlights, and walked to Sierra's car. The two women picked up Chaco and lugged him through the cabin door, blankets trailing. Fred scurried in behind them.

"Let's put him on the couch for the moment," said the woman. "I have some preparations to make, and then we need to take him outside." Without paying any more attention to Kaylee or Fred, she began bustling around the cabin, opening boxes and baskets and collecting objects from their depths.

With Chaco safely ensconced on the couch, Kaylee looked around. The cabin's main room was fairly spacious, with a high, raftered ceiling. A small kitchen area was partitioned off from the main room by a bar. The rafters were hung with bunches of dried plants, and on the walls hung objects that seemed to be of Native American origin: blankets woven in a Mayan pattern, reed baskets decorated with grasses or feathers, a flint axe, a carved and painted totem, a shield, and a bow with arrows in a buckskin quiver. Pueblo pottery rested on shelves that were bursting with books. Kaylee noted in particular a plaque representing Quetzalcoatl on the wall. The rear wall of the room was mostly glass, and the faintest early light beyond the windows revealed a small patio outside, with a fire pit and several chairs apparently crafted from small logs and branches.

Kaylee listened to Chaco's heart and breathing and felt his face, but there seemed to be little change, and certainly none for the better. Having nothing to do for the moment, she sat down on the floor next to Chaco's couch and watched the woman as she went about her preparations. Fred snuggled into Kaylee's side, like a dog seeking comfort, and she patted him. A chorus of small, bubbling snores soon issued from his mouth.

The woman was tall, with a round, brown face. Her black hair, streaked with silver, was caught in a clip, and streamed down her back in a straight fall. Although she seemed to be in her fifties, her face was not deeply lined. She had strong, high cheekbones and a high-bridged nose over full lips. She was wearing a pragmatic ensemble of jeans, running shoes, a T-shirt, and a gray fleece hoodie. Making an odd contrast to her very down-to-earth clothes, she wore a heavy silver necklace set with turquoise and red coral.

Finally, curiosity won. "Did Quetzalcoatl send you?" Kaylee asked. The woman set a bundle of dried plants bound with twine in a basket and looked at her.

"I don't know," she replied. "I was driving home from a healing, and something told me to stop at the park. I never ignore those messages, even if they seem crazy, so I stopped, and there you were. And Coyotl, dying. Even though he can't die, exactly. As an Avatar, Coyotl can't be killed, but his spirit can be destroyed, changed into something evil. So *someone* sent me, yes."

"I asked Queztalcoatl for help just before you arrived," said Kaylee, daring the women to laugh at her.

"And he heard you? Well, stranger things have happened since the world began," said the woman, and put a few small implements into the basket. "I'm Rose Ramirez. I'm a shaman, a traditional healer. Tell me more about this attack on Coyotl."

Kaylee nudged Fred, who awoke with a snort. "Rose wants to know about the bad Avatar, whatshername," she told him. Fred rubbed his eyes.

"Tzintzimitl. She's an evil Avatar," he told Rose. "She called dark stars from the Otherworld, and they are sucking the light from him."

"Stars," said Rose. "This Tzintzimitl is a sky power." It was a statement, not a question, but Fred nodded. "She is the same one who killed Mayahuel?" The mannegishi nodded again. "Yes, Wise

One," he said in a respectful tone that was beginning to grate on Kaylee's nerves just a tiny bit.

"Ah. Now I know what to do," Rose said, and, going into the kitchen area, opened a cupboard and removed a bottle of amber liquid. "I'm ready," she said, adding the bottle to her collection. "Let's get him outside." She nodded to the patio, now bathed in the pearly gray light of pre-dawn. Carrying her basket, she went through French doors to the patio, and returned to help Kaylee with Chaco. Fred brought up the rear, dragging seat cushions from the couch.

The patio was roughly paved with flagstones, and Fred arranged the cushions on these. "What are those for?" asked Rose, panting a bit with the exertion of carrying Chaco's inert body.

"For Chaco," Fred explained, in surprise. "He's very cold, and he shouldn't be lying on the cold stone out here."

"No," said Rose, regretfully. "I'm sorry, but he must be in contact with the stones, or with the earth. I need him to be near the fire, so you must let him lie on the stones."

"But he's freezing," protested Kaylee. "And the stones are wet. Won't that be bad for him?"

"He must lie on the earth," Rose said firmly. "Please." Kaylee, shivering with empathy, helped to place him flat on the flagstones, which were damp with the heavy fog from the nearby Pacific. His long legs sprawled, and though Kaylee tried to position his head comfortably, it lolled to one side, cheek against the stone.

As Rose went about her preparations, she began to tell them the story of Mayahuel and Quetzalcoatl. "Mayahuel was Tzintzimitl's granddaughter, and she lived with her grandmother in the sky. Tzintzimitl was evil, and she stole the light from the people. She forced them to worship her with human sacrifices so that they could have a tiny bit of light to live by."

"One day, Quetzalcoatl wearied of this, and went to the sky to find Tzintzimitl to kill her and put an end to the everlasting darkness and the human sacrifices. Because Quetzalcoatl has always opposed human sacrifice. He is a creator of life, not death, and a lover of light, not the dark. But when he came to the sky, he beheld Mayahuel, the beautiful, and he fell in love. So instead of hunting down Tzintzimitl, he and Mayahuel fled together from the sky."

"Now Tzintzimitl was very angry at losing her granddaughter, and she pursued the couple. Quetzalcoatl and Mayahuel ran and hid from her, but Tzintzimitl sent out her light-destroying dark stars to seek them, and eventually the stars found the lovers. Quetzalcoatl fought with Tzintzimitl, but the dark stars killed Mayahuel. Quetzalcoatl eventually banished the evil one, and light returned to the earth. But Quetzalcoatl was very sad and mourned the beautiful Mayahuel. The gods saw his sorrow, and on her gravesite, they caused the agave plant to grow. From the agave plant Quetzalcoatl made a sweet nectar, the Blood of Mayahuel, and with this, he soothed his sorrow."

"So you see, Tzintzimitl is an Avatar of the sky. Coyotl is an Avatar of the earth. The power of the sky is destroying Coyotl, and he can be saved only through power of the earth. He must be in contact with the earth to receive its healing. But there is more work now to do," Rose concluded, and she asked Kaylee and Fred to help place various objects in a wide circle, enclosing them and the fire pit. Rose quickly kindled a small fire with fatwood sticks. On the fire, she placed bundles of herbs, which caught and began issuing a thick and fragrant white smoke. Rose wafted the smoke over Chaco's body with a fan made of brown and white feathers, chanting in a language Kaylee did not recognize.

The singing went on for a long time, and Kaylee found herself drifting off despite her anxiety for Chaco and the dawn chill. When Rose stopped chanting (causing Kaylee to rouse herself from a dream of swimming in the Arctic), she picked up the bottle of amber liquid and uncorked it. She lifted Chaco's head, putting the bottle to his lips. As she removed it, a rivulet of fluid ran from the corner of his mouth, and Kaylee smelled the sharpness of alcohol and something sweet, almost flowery.

Rose put Chaco's head gently down on the stones again, and watched him. Minutes passed, but there was no change. Chaco lay like a broken toy on the stones, not even shivering from the cold. Then Rose repeated the process, this time succeeding in getting more of the liquid down his throat. Still nothing. Rose applied the amber liquid a third time. The women and Fred silently watched Chaco's face, the flickering of firelight and shadow over the contours of his cheek and brow the only movement to be seen. Kaylee opened her mouth to ask Rose what she was going to do next, when suddenly, Chaco's eyes flew open and he gasped. Then he curled up, choking, as Rose bent over him.

Kaylee and Fred pressed as close as they could to Chaco without getting in Rose's way. Again, Kaylee smelled that peculiar fragrance with its sharp, alcohol undertone. She was certain she had smelled it before, but could not bring to mind what it was. Finally, Chaco stopped coughing and wiped his streaming eyes. He looked up at the women leaning over him and smiled tenderly. He reached out his arms, folded Kaylee into his embrace, and kissed her passionately.

"That might be the tequila talking," observed Rose dryly. "The Blood of Mayahuel. He's had a fair amount of it."

CHAPTER 19

Sierra awoke again to impenetrable darkness. This time, it was clear she was not in a soft and comfortable bed, but lying on a hard, cold floor, and she was gagged with some sort of soft cloth. She lay on one side, her ankles bound, and her wrists tied together behind her back. Her head ached abominably, and when she strained against the ropes, testing them, pain stabbed through her skull and she saw colored starbursts behind her eyelids. These were pretty, but she was not in the proper frame of mind to appreciate them. She was cold, in pain, and she desperately needed to go to the bathroom.

The adventure novels don't go into mundane things like needing to pee, she thought glumly, and wondered how long she could hold out before the dam burst. Despite the pain, she tried the ropes again. Apparently whoever had tied them had known what they were doing, so all she accomplished was to chafe her wrists and cause more painful, pretty lights to dance around inside her head.

About the time she had counted to ten thousand in an effort to distract herself from her full bladder, she heard a key grate in a lock. A door swung open, and a light went on overhead.

Sierra's attention was focused on the person at the door, not her surroundings. Where she was didn't matter; what counted were the newcomer's intentions toward her. As her eyes adjusted to the light, she recognized Theresa, the diminutive maid summoned by Chris Jumlin to the breakfast table. So she was probably still in Jumlin's house.

"MMMpffff!" Sierra said, looking pleadingly at Theresa. Surely, the woman was here to help. Theresa came to Sierra's side and looked coldly down at her.

"You probably need to go to the bathroom," she said. "I'll let you up, but don't even think about trying to escape." Sierra saw that Theresa held a pistol in her right hand. It was pointed at the ground, not at her, but there was no question that Theresa was not interested in helping Sierra to escape.

Keeping the pistol ready to hand, Theresa untied Sierra's arms. Then she picked the pistol up again and pointed it directly at Sierra. She waved the pistol at Sierra's ankles. "Untie your feet." Sierra leaned over, head spinning, and picked at the tough knots with numb fingers. She finally managed to free her feet, and Theresa grasped one of Sierra's elbows and pulled. "Get up," she said, and Sierra somehow got her legs under her and stood up, head swimming.

Theresa stood behind her. "OK. Put your hands together in front of you." Sierra obediently did so, and Theresa tied her wrists again with swift, efficient motions. She said, "Now walk slowly to the door."

Sierra did so. There was a short hallway outside the door, and directly across was a bathroom. The whole setup was a stark contrast to Jumlin's elegant rooms with their Persian carpets. This was clearly a basement. There were windows at either end of the hallway, with sunlight streaming down through the grimy glass. The hallway floor was concrete, none too clean, and there were old cardboard boxes, a mop and a broom, and miscellaneous odds and ends stacked along the walls. The bathroom consisted of a rusty old toilet, a metal sink, and a cracked mirror.

Theresa pushed Sierra roughly from behind as she was getting her bearings. "Stand in front of the toilet," she ordered. Sierra stood facing the toilet, and Theresa said impatiently, "Not like that, stupid. Turn around." Sierra did, wondering how she was going to get out of her jeans when Theresa jerked down the zipper of Sierra's jeans and yanked everything down to the floor. She stood there watching as Sierra relieved herself.

As Sierra was still gagged, she couldn't ask how she was going to take care of the cleanup, but Theresa made it clear that she wasn't going to have the opportunity.

"Get up," Theresa said, and pulled at Sierra's arms. She then pulled up Sierra's jeans, zipped them roughly, and led Sierra back to her original location, Sierra was too alarmed to worry about the nastiness of not being able to clean up. As she stepped into the room she had just left, she took it in for the first time.

It was not the stone hall of her visions, but it bore a strong resemblance to it. It had originally been just a large basement. Houses built in California prior to World War II sometimes had basements, but after the war, the builders who scrambled to put up cheap subdivisions to house post-WWII families had dispensed with the trouble and cost of building basements. Jumlin's house had been built long before World War II, and the basement was roomy. In this large room, there was none of the usual detritus of broken chairs, boxes, trunks, and other things that families tucked away in basements, thinking to mend, or use again, or save for some future need.

The room was almost empty. There were murals painted on the walls, murals that Sierra recognized with a lurch at the pit of her stomach. There were the paintings of bloody sacrifice, of captives bleeding to death with a thousand cuts to their bodies, of hearts held triumphantly over their owners' torn corpses. Over and over, there was the same bizarre figure presiding, so abstractly rendered with yellow and black lines that it was barely discernible as anthropoid. Sierra thought it represented Necocyaotl, the Obsidian Mirror. She had looked up images of Necocyaotl on Google, and the painted figure here had an ominous similarity, a black band painted across the face, one foot drawn to represent an obsidian mirror, while the other was drawn as a deer's hoof. A single bulb hanging from the ceiling illuminated the space, but blackened sconces fixed to the wall showed that the room could be lit by torches—perhaps to create a less prosaic atmosphere than the bald glare of the single bulb.

With horror, she recognized the stone table at one end of the room. A black stone knife lay on the altar, which was discolored with brown stains. Behind it stood another rendering of that fierce, abstract figure, and in its hands it held a roughly rounded, black shape that shone unevenly in the light of the bulb. It was, Sierra realized, a tiny version of the great, black obsidian mirror of her visions. She twisted around to face Theresa, trying to communicate a plea for help through her eyes alone.

Theresa paid no attention. "Down on the floor," she ordered, waving the pistol, and watched as Sierra awkwardly kneeled, then flopped awkwardly on to one side, unable to brace herself. Theresa competently tied Sierra's ankles together again and then freed Sierra's hands, retying them at her back. The servant stood, slipping the pistol into the pocket of her apron.

"It's not as if I don't have enough to do," she said in a resentful tone, glaring at Sierra. "Now I have to babysit *you*. Well, you'll be gone soon enough, I guess." With that grim pronouncement, she turned off the light and closed and locked the door, leaving Sierra alone in the dark again.

It's funny how small things make such a huge difference when you're reduced to having no options, Sierra thought. Just the relief from her distended bladder made all the difference, in spite of her still-throbbing head and the general discomfort of lying bound hand and foot on a hard and chilly floor. Now at least she could think.

Although what good thinking did, she wasn't sure. Her bonds were as immovable as before, she quickly discovered. She was helpless, no one knew where she was, and she was evidently in the hands of Necocyaotl's followers. She had hoped for some empathy from Theresa, but if the woman felt any sympathy for Sierra's plight, she was adept at concealing it. And there seemed to be only one possible outcome of the situation, if the evidence of the murals, the altar and the stone knife was anything to go by.

Now would be a good time to use her alleged power. She closed her eyes and remembered the leaping flames under Quetzalcoatl's warm touch. She focused on the flames, hoping to breathe real life into them, but they flickered and faded like real flames, leaving her in the hopeless dark of her captivity.

Remarkably energized by this thought, Sierra tried to inch her way across the floor to the altar. Maybe she could somehow knock the knife to the floor, and use it to saw through her bonds. Inch by painful inch, Sierra scraped her way across the rough concrete. A particularly energetic movement brought her head sharply into contact with the altar. More pretty lights ensued.

Once her head had cleared, she braced her shoulder against the stone, and managed to get up onto her knees. Her body felt as though she had been slowly passed over a cheese grater. Again, she leveraged herself against the stone, and climbed awkwardly to her feet. This placed a nearly intolerable strain on her joints as it painfully increased the pressure of the ropes, which bit into her flesh.

Sierra leaned over the altar, cringing at the thought of touching those grim brown stains, and swept her torso across its surface. She quickly encountered the knife, but it seemed reluctant to move across the uneven stone, stubbornly twisting aside. Grunting with the effort, Sierra tried again and again. Finally, the knife dropped to the floor, and she heard it land. Land, and shatter into what sounded like a thousand pieces.

Swearing unintelligibly behind her gag, Sierra carefully lowered herself to the floor once more. She leaned against the side of the altar. Her hands, bound tightly behind her, had only limited scope of movement, but she swept her fingers across the floor, searching for a shard of the knife. There were many small, sharp pieces that her fingertips encountered—far too small to use for her purpose, but she felt several sharp stings as some of the razor-thin slivers bit into her skin.

Finally, her questing fingers found a piece that was large enough to pick up. Squirming back against the stone altar, she tried to maneuver the edge into a position to saw at the ropes, using the side of the altar to stabilize her hands. At last, shoulders cramping, she felt the edge of the shard bite into the rope. She worked slowly and carefully, afraid that more vigorous movement would make her lose her grip on the shard.

Just as she felt the rope's strands parting, she heard the key grate in the lock again. Quickly, she rolled to the ground, hands behind her still wrapped in a few fibers of rope, hoping that Theresa wouldn't see what she had been doing.

The overhead light snapped on. Chris Jumlin, looking stylish and cool, stood in the door. In a split second, he was by her side. As she twisted away, freeing her hands, he gripped her throat and forced her back against the floor.

"Well, well," he said, "Looks like you've been a busy girl."

CHAPTER 20

"Where are we?"

Kaylee rolled over. Another odd dream. So many odd dreams…

"Hey. I asked where are we?" said Chaco.

Kaylee opened eyes that felt sandy and sore. She knuckled them and peered up at Chaco, who was looming over her.

Kaylee sat up. She had fallen into exhausted sleep after Chaco finally freed her from his grasp and slipped into blissful unconsciousness. She had been perfectly happy to sleep on the carpet under borrowed blankets, leaving Chaco snoring on the couch and breathing tequila vapors into the early morning air. Now she was stiff and groggy, and she hurt in odd places. Her left cheek, which had rested on the carpet, felt chafed. She sat up.

"We're at Rose's house. Do you remember anything that happened?"

Chaco stopped looming and sat on the couch, looking confused. "No. I guess I don't. What happened? Who is Rose?"

Light streamed in through Rose's glass wall. It was still a bit foggy, but the mid-morning sun poured through the redwood trees in glowing shafts, highlighting the moisture that still clung to the trees' flat, dark-green leaves, making them glitter. Kaylee located Fred by the bubbly snores coming from under a jacket that Rose had loaned him for the night.

"I'll tell you all about it," she said, "But I hope we can get some coffee first. Why don't you wrap that blanket around yourself? You look kind of cold." She got to her feet and went to the kitchen while Chaco was taking her advice. Rose might be a traditional woman in many ways, but her coffee maker was up-to-the-minute, and she had thoughtfully filled it and set the timer the night before. The carafe was full of fresh, hot brew. Kaylee found two mugs and filled them, gratefully breathing in coffee-scented steam. She and Chaco removed themselves to the table on the other side of the room from the sleeping Fred.

Chaco took a generous mouthful of coffee and swallowed. "So what happened, Kaylee?"

Kaylee explained about Tzintzimitl and finding Chaco in that strange, frightening condition. She told the entire story, right up to his embrace after briefly regaining consciousness. He looked down into his coffee mug with a small smile on his lips.

"So you don't remember that?" Kaylee asked.

"No," admitted Chaco. "What a shame." He looked up at her with clear eyes and grinned. Kaylee, after a slight stab of annoyance, grinned back.

"So, do you have a hangover?" she finally inquired.

"Avatars don't get hangovers," he responded. "Why would I have a hangover?"

"Because Rose poured half a bottle of tequila down you last night."

Chaco nodded without surprise. "Just the thing. Good that she happened along." He shuddered and clutched his mug. "I truly am deeply grateful. I can't even think about what I might have become if it hadn't been for her. And you. And Fred." He smiled his devastating wide grin at Kaylee, but his eyes were serious.

"I don't think she just 'happened along,' Chaco," she told him, and then a realization struck her anew like a bucket of ice water in the face. "Oh, no. I almost forgot." She put her face in her hands.

"What? What is it?"

"Tzintzimitl stole the silver pieces that Sierra made from Quetzalcoatl's feathers," Kaylee groaned. "I was so worried about you that I forgot all about it. But they're gone. You were lying on the floor of the garage—you must have been trying to stop her when she attacked you."

"That doesn't make any sense," Chaco said, raising his eyebrows in surprise. "Tzintzimitl *can't* have taken the feathers."

"What do you mean? The feathers are gone, I can tell you that. The drawer where Sierra put them was yanked out of the workbench and lying on the floor, empty."

"That may be so," Chaco said slowly. "But Tzintzimitl isn't capable of even touching them. They're imbued with the essence of Quetzalcoatl. That's as deadly to Tzintzimitl as her dark stars are to me. If she had touched them, you'd have found us *both* lying on the floor."

Kaylee stared at him, thoughts reeling. "Then who took them?"

Chaco shook his head. "I have no idea. I don't remember a thing. From my perspective, one moment I was cooking chicken molé and the next moment, I woke up here."

"Well, they are gone, no matter who took them," said Kaylee.

"That's very, very bad news," he said.

"Yes, I know…"

"No, it's worse than you think," he said, shaking his head. His brow was furrowed, and for the first time, Kaylee saw real fear in his eyes.

"Why? I mean, I know Sierra was trying to get the feathers to Simmons, and that was supposed to release Simmons from Necocyaotl's influence. That's a real setback…"

Chaco put his hands to his head. "No, it's worse than that," he said, almost moaning. "Quetzalcoatl's feathers are incredibly powerful. That power can be used for good, as we were trying to do. Or they can be used for evil."

Kaylee stared at him. "But Quetzalcoatl is good, isn't he? How can his feathers be used for evil?"

"Think about it, Kaylee. You can use a kitchen knife to make a great dinner that nurtures your body, delights the palate, and feeds your family and friends. Or you can stab someone to death with it. The knife is the same knife. It's the intention of the user that makes the difference between good and evil," Chaco explained.

"Oh," Kaylee said in a small voice. A long silence followed, in which neither of them could think of a thing to say.

"Well, maybe Sierra has a theory," replied Chaco, looking around. "Where *is* Sierra, by the way?"

Kaylee realized that she had not, in fact, told Chaco the entire story. She groaned again. "She's in jail."

"What!" exclaimed Chaco, slamming his mug down on the tabletop and spilling his coffee.

"Who's in jail?" Rose had come silently into the room while they were talking. She got a mug from the kitchen, sat at the table, and poured herself some coffee. She was wearing sweatpants and a T-shirt that had a picture of a grizzly bear on it and the legend, "Bear With Me."

Kaylee explained Sierra's role in the story and that the police had arrested Sierra as the women prepared to drive Chaco to the park in downtown San Jose. Rose listened quietly, asking a few questions. She never seemed horrified, dismayed, or disbelieving. Finally, Rose stood up.

"You seem to have gotten yourself into a heck of a situation, Kaylee," said Rose. "But even heroes and Avatars have to eat." *Heroes?* thought Kaylee. *Is that what I am? I haven't done anything heroic at all.*

"Wait a moment," Chaco said, rising. Rose turned. He put his hands out to the shaman. "Thank you, Wise One," he said, humbly. He took her hands and bowed over them, speaking a few words in another language. Rose stood quietly until he straightened up.

"It was my honor to serve you, Coyotl," she said.

"And I will serve you, Wise One, whenever you need me," he responded. She smiled at him, then turned and went into her little kitchen and began rummaging in the refrigerator, humming tunelessly. "Eggs and sausage all right with you?" she called. "I have some whole wheat bread, too."

"Eggs and sausage and toast?" piped Fred, climbing into a seat at the table. "That's my favorite!"

"Everything's your favorite," said Kaylee glumly, her mind still on the lost silver feathers and Sierra's arrest. "Yes, thank you, Rose. It's very kind of you to fix breakfast for us."

"No problem," returned Rose, who was scrambling eggs in a huge, black cast-iron pan.

Rose finally bore plates of scrambled eggs, sausage, and toast to the table, and everyone dug in. After a bit, Kaylee sat back and looked around the table. There was Chaco, black hair falling into his beautiful face. Fred, gray-green and blobby, stuffing eggs into his mouth. Rose, as still and deep as an alpine lake. *As good a group of people—and creatures and Avatar—as I will ever know,* she thought.

"Rose, thank you so much for everything," she said. "I'll wash the dishes, and then we'd better get home. We need to find those feathers and try to get Sierra out of jail. I don't know why they arrested her. She's never done anything even slightly illegal, I'm sure."

Rose nodded. "You're welcome," she said. She handed Kaylee a card that read: "Rose Ramirez, Native American Shaman," with a telephone number, email address, and web site. "Call me," Rose said. "Coyotl's people are my people." She smiled and took Kaylee's hand. "Will you accept a blessing?"

Kaylee had never felt more in need of a blessing. She nodded her head. Rose held her free hand up, palm toward Kaylee, and intoned a few words in a language Kaylee took to be an Indian dialect. "That means, 'May you walk in beauty. May you walk upon the hummingbird way,'" explained Rose.

With no idea of what that meant but feeling better somehow, Kaylee washed the breakfast dishes. Fred volunteered to dry, proud of his new skills. Soon they were back in Sierra's car, Chaco and Fred in the back. They drove carefully down the gravel drive, Rose waving to them from her front door.

"OK, everybody," said Kaylee. "Now that Chaco is safe and sound, let's talk about how to get Sierra out of jail. And how to find the feathers." There was a rather prolonged and thoughtful silence. Finally, Kaylee spoke again.

"Let's try to approach this logically," she said. "Who knew about the feathers? Who else would have known where to look for them?"

"Aiden," said Chaco promptly.

"Okay," said Kaylee. "Who's Aiden?"

Chaco explained about meeting Aiden at the campground and his later appearance at Sierra's house. "So you see, he must've been the one who wrecked our campsite, and he was in Sierra's workshop with her for a long time. He might have seen the feathers while he was in there," Chaco concluded with a growl. "Tzintzimitl couldn't have touched them, so she must have brought Aiden with her to help."

"Oh," said Fred, sucking meditatively on his paw. "But Aiden wasn't with Tzintzimitl. The other man was."

"*WHAT* other man?" Kaylee demanded. The cast of characters was growing exponentially. She pulled the car off the mountain road as far as she could, jammed the transmission into "Park," and turned around to glare at Fred. Chaco was also glaring at Fred, who shrank down against the seat. Chaco pulled the little mannegishi's paw away from his mouth and narrowed his eyes dangerously.

"Why didn't you say anything before?" Chaco snarled. "You idiot!" Kaylee had never before seen Chaco so upset.

Fred quailed. "I...I...I duh, didn't think," he quavered. "Everything happened so fast, and I...I...I ran away," he finished miserably. Hot tears splashed down his face.

"Stop crying!" snapped Kaylee brusquely. "Tell us what happened again. *All* of it," she said, in a menacing tone of voice. "Don't leave anything out this time."

"The doorbell rang. Chaco went to answer it. There was a woman and a man on the doorstep who spoke to him, and he let them in. I don't know why, because I recognized Tzintzimitl right away. I mean, I didn't know she was Tzintzimitl, exactly, but I knew she was bad. Really bad, Chaco, why did you..."

"I don't remember," Chaco snapped. "Get on with it." Kaylee couldn't help thinking there was something feral about Chaco.

He had the beauty and grace of a wild animal, and an animal's unpredictable otherness. All encased (part time, anyway) in the lithe body of an athlete. Scary, but intriguing.

"So I disappeared and ran away," said Fred.

"And?" asked Kaylee.

"And then I came back, and Chaco was unconscious, and you were talking about taking him to a doctor or something. You know the rest."

"But what about the *man*?" Kaylee demanded. Chaco looked as though he were about to reach over and throttle Fred if they didn't get some sense out of him. She wasn't entirely sure she would mind.

"I don't know. I hardly noticed him. He was just a man. Not an Avatar. Not a spirit. Just a man!" squealed Fred.

"It wasn't Clancy, was it?" asked Kaylee, the hair on the back of her neck suddenly bristling.

"No. I saw Clancy when he came to Sierra's house that day, so I would recognize him. I didn't know this man."

"Well, what'd he *look* like?" asked Kaylee.

"He was sort of medium height. Medium brown hair. Wearing those funny clothes—you know those stiff, dull-colored clothes with the bits of cloth around the neck?"

"A suit?" asked Kaylee.

Fred nodded. "A gray suit."

That could be anyone, thought Kaylee with frustration. "You can't remember anything else about him? Nothing that stands out?"

Fred shook his head. "No. I would tell you if there was anything else. He was just ordinary. Really shiny shoes, though."

Kaylee put the car in gear and pulled out on the road without another word. The disapproving silence in the car was as palpable as smog, broken only by the sound of Fred sucking nervously on his digits. Before long, she heard a muffled whack from the back seat and the sucking noise stopped.

The unhappy silence stretched out for miles, as Kaylee drove back to Sierra's house. She was still very tired from last night's adventure and discouraged by Fred's latest, unhelpful revelation. In the rear-view mirror she could see that Chaco continued glowering at Fred, who slumped—small, green, and dejected—in a corner of the back seat. She turned on the news on the radio.

"President Harmon today announced that he is seeking to lower the standards on the levels of heavy metals that would be allowed in the nation's waterways," fluted the female announcer. She was followed by Harmon's rich baritone. "America has always depended on industry for its commercial and military strength," intoned the president. "And industry has been unfairly penalized in its endeavors by arbitrary restrictions that are simply not founded on scientific evidence. My science advisors assure me that raising the levels of permissible lead, mercury, and other metals in our waterways by this tiny amount will have no adverse effect on fish, wildlife, or human water supplies..." Kaylee punched the off button savagely.

After what seemed like hours, but was probably only a little more than an hour, she pulled up outside Sierra's house. Wearily, she climbed out and walked to the front door without checking on the rest of the party. The door was locked, but she knew where Sierra kept her spare key and retrieved it. Once inside, she went upstairs. Chaco and Fred remained in the front hall, peering up at her. "Listen, I'm going to get some sleep. I can't even think straight."

Chaco nodded and slouched into the living room, trailed by Fred. Kaylee crawled, exhausted, into Sierra's bed, and closed her eyes. Sleep overcame her almost immediately.

CHAPTER 21

Sierra was standing in a cathedral, a green cathedral. Fluted columns towered up until they were lost in the misty reaches above. Shafts of white light spilled down from invisible, high windows, illuminating the interior. Instead of candles or incense, she smelled…green, growing things.

It wasn't a cathedral. It was a redwood forest, and the great columns were actually the trunks of vast trees, wider in circumference and taller than any of the coastal redwoods she knew. This was an old-growth stand of trees, ancient beings that were half a century old when Jesus was born. Sierra had read about the ecosystems that evolved in the canopies of such forests; frogs and salamanders dove and swam in pools of fog-borne water high above the ground, never dreaming that another world existed far below. Tanbark oaks and huckleberries sprouted hundreds of feet above the forest floor, rooted in the interlocking tangle of branches, duff, and debris of the tree canopy.

As she stood in one of the shafts of light that managed to penetrate the canopy, a hummingbird appeared before her face, its wings a buzzing blur. A cap of bright, iridescent ruby covered its head and throat like a balaclava, while its back was jewel-green. As it hovered in front of her face, smaller than a mouse, she could hear its high-pitched chirp, "Tzip! Tzip!" As she watched, entranced, it said "Aiden!" and buzzed off into the gloom between the tree trunks.

"What?" she called after it, but the bird was gone. *"Aiden?" What was that supposed to mean?* She walked in the direction taken by the tiny bird but could not see it. Her footsteps were silent, muffled by the soft, red-brown duff that forms from redwood bark. As she ventured farther and farther, the trunks seemed to flow into one another and the canopy grew denser overhead, shutting out the light. Fallen branches and tangled brush began to impede her path, forcing her to walk around or clamber over these barriers.

She came to an immense and seemingly endless deadfall of broken branches, tangled and impenetrable. Vines and brush wove between the old wood, thrusting green leaves and tendrils out to seek the light. Stubbornly, Sierra began to climb this mountain of dead and living plant material. She slipped again and again on the treacherous footing and began to bleed from many scratches as sharp twigs stabbed at her.

And then the rotting branches gave way beneath, and she fell. And fell. And fell.

• • •

Sierra opened her eyes, sweating and breathing hard. She expected to see the familiar surroundings of her bedroom, the usual comforting envelopment of reality after a nasty nightmare. But she was not in her bedroom. The surroundings were familiar, but not in any way comforting; she was back in the stone hall of her nightmares, facing the great slab of obsidian and the cold stone altar before it.

A figure stepped forward out of the shadows. The figure was reflected, distorted and wavering, in the torchlight gleaming from the obsidian's surface. She bit back a scream; its face was inhuman, blocky and cruel. A black band was painted across its yellow face, framing glittering eyes. Then she realized that the face was actually a mask, a mask that echoed the faces of the painted warriors and gods that thronged the walls. A robe of black material covered the rest of the figure, but its bare, quite human hands clasped the obsidian knife between them, the wicked, transparent point aimed at her heart.

"You've stolen my sacrifice!" said a familiar voice, but it was not the masked figure that spoke. It was the same voice that had spoken in all her visions of this place, and it seemed to come from every direction at once.

Then the figure turned to the altar, pointing the dagger away from her and toward the prone shape that now appeared on the altar's rough surface. Sierra saw that it was Aiden, bound and bleeding. His eyes, puffy with bruises, were closed, and his mouth was cut and bloody. He was naked and defenseless. The ropes that bound his ankles and the bonds that forced his arms cruelly behind him were studded with thorns that sliced into his flesh, blood trickling onto the stone beneath.

"What are you talking about?" shrieked Sierra, her suspicions of Aiden forgotten in her rush of terror and pity for his suffering. "What sacrifice?"

"I told you to bring me the one to be sacrificed. Coyotl. My enemy's lap dog. He was in my hands. But you defied me, and he escaped. There *must* be blood shed for me, and now you must be the one to do it." The black-clad figure turned and held the knife out to her. The hands were slimy with dark blood, as was the knife. She shrank away from it, shaking her head.

"No! I won't do it. No!"

"You can't escape me," said the voice. "You may be protected, but eventually, you'll come to me willingly. And then...then I will debase and violate you in ways you can't imagine. You will be so degraded that you will willingly allow me to rape your mind even as I use your body. Further, you will beg me to do more and more, even to the point of death. For all your suffering, you will plead with me for just another moment of pain, of shame. At the end, when it seems you cannot continue to live, I will sustain you—so that I can extract another iota of agony from your spent body and your ravaged spirit."

Sierra clapped her hands over her ears and closed her eyes. Then she thought of Aiden, helpless and bleeding on the stone altar. She opened her eyes, took a deep breath, and rushed at the masked figure, heedless of the knife.

It was cold, cold, cold. She could see nothing. She couldn't breathe. It was black, and she was sightless and suffocating, her consciousness dying away like a candle flame in a bell jar. She couldn't breathe…

. . .

Cold water shocked her awake, gasping. This time, she really was awake, but not in the familiar surroundings of her bedroom. Nor was she lying in Chris Jumlin's elegant guest bed. She was lying on the stone altar in Jumlin's basement. Despite being caught by Jumlin and bound hand and foot yet another time (this time with duct tape, the rope being shredded by the obsidian shard), she had somehow fallen into exhausted sleep in the dark once he had left her.

"Wake up," said Jumlin's smooth voice. A movement behind the altar made Sierra strain her head over her shoulder to see who was there. Theresa made another sweeping motion along the floor, and Sierra heard the glassy clatter of the knife shards being swept into a dustpan. Theresa glanced up at Sierra's anxious face and scowled as if Sierra had broken the knife expressly to annoy her.

"Well, you bought yourself some time," Jumlin said. "But I don't think you're going to enjoy the time you have left. It will take time to make another sacrificial knife. A day or two, perhaps. But Lord Tezcatlipoca is impatient for his offering, so no longer than two days, I assure you." He reached down and roughly tore the thick duct tape from Sierra's mouth. The ripping away of the tape was just one pain among many, and she winced only slightly.

"Where are the feathers?" he demanded, as Sierra gingerly licked her burning lips. She stared up at him.

"I don't know," she croaked. Her throat felt dry as hot sand. "They were gone when I got home. You should know—it had to be one of your people that stole them. Or one of your—things."

Without any change in expression, Jumlin reached down and hit Sierra across the face. "Don't fuck with me, woman. Tell me where the feathers are." His voice remained steady and cold, with no sign of emotion.

Tears sprang to Sierra's eyes from the blow, but she refused to let them fall. "I don't know!" she snarled. "You can hit me all day and you still won't find out, because I DON'T KNOW!"

Jumlin raised his hand as though to strike her again, then he let his arm drop to his side. "Someone's playing a double game. It better not be you," he stated flatly. "Dying isn't the worst thing that can happen to you, you know. Theresa, finish up and get out of here." He turned and left the room.

Once the door closed behind him, Sierra looked at Theresa. "Please," Sierra croaked, "Could I please have some water?" Theresa looked at her with open hostility.

"Later. If I remember," was all Theresa said, as she turned out the light and locked the door. Sierra heard her footsteps in the corridor outside, retreating, then the sound of shoes on stairs, going up. Sierra was alone in the dark. Again.

"Dying isn't the worst thing that can happen to you." Jumlin's parting words played over and over in her mind. Sierra recognized the moment he had said it that he was right. There were many more hideous things a person could be made to endure, after which death would be a blessing and a balm. The thought made her quail inside; it made her guts liquefy and her head spin, and she struggled to focus her mind on the question of escape.

It was laughable, really. She'd been clobbered over the head and probably had a concussion, and now she was wrapped up in silver duct tape like a spider's hors d'oeuvre. Her best chance of escape seemed to be the hope that someone would arrive to rescue her, and she calculated the odds of that happening at roughly zero to none, as no one knew where she was. Except for her captors, of course.

But Jumlin had not gagged her again. Her skin burned and itched where the adhesive had torn away, but her mouth was unimpeded. For a mad moment, she thought of chewing through the duct tape, but that hope died before it was born. Her wrists were tied behind her back, and she would have to be more limber than a Chinese acrobat to reach her ankles with her mouth.

Frustrated and weary, Sierra lay in the dark, her mind skittering about in search of a solution. In the profound darkness, her brain conjured up sparks and flashes of colored light, as though straining to provide something for her eyes to do in the absence of real light. She closed her eyes, but the colored lights did not go away. When she saw a glow through her closed lids, she thought it was another hallucination. But the glow did not diminish, flash or spark, and Sierra opened her eyes.

A woman stood next to the altar, looking at Sierra. She was of medium height, with long, black hair falling to her feet. She wore several heavy necklaces of turquoise, shell, and red coral. Her clothing was white, filmy, and indistinct, as though spider webs had been woven into a long tunic. Her face was serene and she wore a small, kind smile upon her lips, but her eyes—her eyes were completely inhuman. They were large, round, and black, and seemed to be compound, like the eyes of a bee. Lidless, they glittered darkly in the strange light surrounding the woman. She moved soundlessly closer to the altar on white buckskin boots, heavily ornamented with turquoise and silver. Sierra cringed, wondering what this apparition meant to do to her, bound and helpless upon the altar.

The woman stopped next to the altar and spread her hands, palms parallel to one another. As she moved her hands apart, webs formed between them, perfectly formed like a new web at dawn, when the spider has just finished the night's painstaking work.

The woman intoned, "As I break these bonds, so shall your bonds be broken." She flung her hands wide, breaking the webs, and Sierra felt the constriction of the thick tape around her wrists and ankles snap. She winced at the stab and prickle of blood rushing back into fluid-starved tissues. She sat up cautiously, rubbing her wrists. The woman's eyes were terrifying, but she had freed Sierra, so perhaps she was not an enemy. Sierra's ability to trust had been dealt several bad blows lately.

"Thank you," Sierra whispered, her mouth dry. "Thank you." And then, "Who are you?"

The woman smiled tenderly at her, and her compound eyes glittered. "I am Kóhk'ang Wuhti," she replied. Seeing Sierra's uncomprehending look, she added, "I have many names. In your tongue, I am Spider Grandmother."

Sierra saw that her long tunic was moving. Its filmy tendrils swayed with every tiny movement of the woman's body. Then Sierra saw, scattered among the shining threads, tiny spiders of every color, shining like jewels, constantly spinning new threads.

"Why did you help me?" Sierra asked. She knew she should make a run for it, knew she had no time to linger, but she needed to know. Was this—creature? Avatar?—friend or foe?

"You spared my children, so I spare you," was the reply, accompanied by another sweet smile. "If you wish to repay me, protect my children."

"Your children?" Sierra wondered out loud, and then she remembered the little spiders in her workshop, and the ugly black monster she had discovered in the drawer of Jumlin's guest bathroom. She made a quick resolution to never squash a spider again, no matter how huge or repulsive, then swung her legs over the edge of the stone and stood. Her body protested at its recent mistreatment, but she ignored it.

"Do you know Chris Jumlin, Spider Grandmother?" Sierra asked.

"I know Jumlin," was the answer. "If you do not wish to die, you must leave. I would not usually interfere with that one's hunting; he will be very angry and very hungry when he finds you are gone."

"Hungry?" asked Sierra, her skin prickling. "Do you mean that...?"

"My meaning is that you must leave now," Spider Grandmother said firmly. "Follow the Hummingbird Way, Sierra." She held up a hand as though in blessing.

Sierra didn't need to be told again. By the light of the shining woman, she made her way to the door. Though she had heard Theresa lock the door when she left, it was now unlocked. But as she put her hand to the doorknob, she heard feet stomping down the cellar steps. Heart pounding, she shrank back.

"What do I do?" she whispered to Spider Grandmother, who still stood by the altar. The Avatar stood unmoving for a fleeting moment, then she moved toward the door, motioning Sierra to step aside. Her silver-white robe floated around her in shredded veils.

. . .

When Theresa unlocked the door, she was vaguely surprised to find that she had instead locked it. Impatiently, she turned the key again and shoved the door open.

As she turned on the light, Theresa found herself enveloped in a mass of something white and sticky. She batted at it, but it just clung more tightly, gluing her eyes shut, filling her nostrils, stifling her mouth.

A voice hissed at her just as Theresa saw the hundreds of tiny spiders gathering around her eyes and mouth. "This is for all the cans of poison. This is for the newspapers. This is for the crushing of your shoes," the voice whispered in her ear, and Theresa's vision went dark.

CHAPTER 22

Kaylee woke to the sound of banging on the front door. She was still dressed, so she rolled out of bed and staggered downstairs. There was no sign of Chaco or Fred, so she opened the door. She had expected it to be Sierra, but instead it was Clancy, looking disheveled, his hair standing up in clumps. Kaylee knew that, if anything, she looked worse in her rumpled, slept-in clothes and hair that must be standing out like a dark dandelion puff.

As she stood in the doorway, blinking at him in surprise, Clancy pushed past her. "Where's Sierra?" he demanded, head swiveling around alertly. Kaylee shut the door and trailed after him.

"She's not here," said Kaylee. "I think she's—well, the police arrested her last night, so I think she's in jail. We—I had a very late night. I was planning to go down there and see about bailing her out this morning."

Clancy looked at her for the first time. "Don't I know you?" he asked, eyebrows knit in concentration.

"Not exactly. I work at Black Diamond, so you've probably seen me around. I'm Kaylee Shore. I work in Marketing, like Sierra used to."

"Oh." Clancy walked into the kitchen and peered around as though Sierra might be hiding in there. "Are you a friend of Sierra's? Her roommate?" He pulled out a chair from the kitchen table and sat down heavily.

"Yes. Friend, not roommate. I was just, um, staying here until Sierra got back. Taking care of her...dog. Why were you looking for her? Is there a problem? I mean other than her being in jail? But you couldn't have known about that," said Kaylee, looking around for the coffeemaker. She spotted it and began rummaging in the cupboard for coffee.

"Well, that's the problem," Clancy said. "Sierra's *not* in jail."

Kaylee ceased rummaging, a package of paper coffee filters in her hand. "What? How do you know? That's not possible. I was there when they arrested her. She *must* be in jail. Unless someone bailed her out. Maybe she called a lawyer."

Clancy ran his fingers through his already-chaotic hair. "No. I listened to my voice mail messages early this morning. Sierra left a message explaining where she was, and asking me to get her a lawyer. I rousted my lawyer friend Sam out of bed and took him down to the jail, but when I got there, they didn't know what I was talking about. I asked to see the records, and there *weren't* any records. That is, there was no record of her arrest, no record of anyone posting bail. No booking, no sign-out. Nothing. The cops just shook their heads and said I was mistaken." He looked at Kaylee bleakly. "I was really hoping that somehow she'd gotten home and was safely in bed by now."

Kaylee resumed making coffee, her full lips pursed in thought. Finally she asked, "What do you think happened? I *saw* the cops arrest her. They put her in a squad car and drove away. How could there be no record of that?"

"I have no idea," replied Clancy. "Prisoners don't just disappear from the county jail. Records don't just vanish. Cops don't forget someone they've booked into jail just a few hours previously. It's as though she stepped through a door into another universe or something. I'm worried, Kaylee. I don't have any idea what's going on, and I'm worried."

Kaylee pushed the start button on the coffeemaker. She put her hands on the back of a kitchen chair to keep them from shaking and leaned forward, looking into Clancy's eyes. "Clancy, I'm *terrified.* I know a bit more than you do about this, and there's something terribly, horribly wrong. I am certain that Sierra's life is in danger."

He stared at her. "What do you mean?" In reply, she called out, "Chaco, please come in here. Not as Coyotl, please."

Clancy looked dazed. "Chaco? Sierra's 'friend'? What does..."

Chaco strolled into the kitchen. He looked rested and fresh, as though last night's events had never occurred. His odd eyes were clear amber and his skin glowed with health. He looked at Clancy and said, "Clancy Forrester, I presume?"

Clancy narrowed his eyes, but before he could speak, Kaylee cut in.

"Chaco, I'm afraid Sierra's in big trouble. She disappeared from the jail last night, after leaving a message on Clancy's phone. I think we need his help right now, but he can't help us if he doesn't understand. Could you please help him to understand what's going on here?"

"Wait just a minute," Clancy began, but he broke off with a strangled gurgle as Chaco transformed. His lithe body flowed and shifted like a handful of melting crayons as a large coyote took shape at Kaylee's feet. Within seconds, Coyotl stood on the tiles, bracing four slender legs and shaking out his fur. A long, red tongue slid over his furry chops, and he sat, staring at Clancy with bright eyes.

Clancy froze in his seat. He had gone pale, and beads of sweat stood on his forehead. He rubbed his eyes. He looked at Chaco again. He put his head in his hands, raked his fingers through his hair again, and took another glance. Chaco sat patiently, panting a bit. Then he twitched and began to scratch behind one pricked ear with a vigorous hind paw, wearing a rather vacuous expression. Clancy watched this, mesmerized and unspeaking.

Kaylee waited for Clancy's questions, but the man said nothing. Finally, she asked, "Are you ready to hear about it now, or do you need more time?"

Clancy glanced up at her, face ashen. "More time," he said, swallowing hard. His voice was barely audible. Kaylee tried to imagine the roil of emotions, questions, dismay, disbelief, and perhaps terror behind the pale mask of his face. She found a bottle of brandy in the cupboard, poured a generous shot into a mug, and filled the rest with steaming coffee. She set this down on the table next to Clancy.

"It's a bit early, but you look like you could use some rein-forcement," she said. He picked it up, still staring at Chaco (who was now nibbling with sharp teeth between his paw pads) and took a hearty gulp. Instantly, he sprayed coffee into his lap and began coughing.

"Hot!" he managed to gasp, and then, "What the hell did you put in this?" as Kaylee mopped him up with a dishtowel. Chaco morphed back into a human to help with the cleanup. By the time they finished and Clancy wiped the tears of pain from his eyes, he seemed to have recovered from his shock. He took another cautious sip from his mug, which had cooled off during the commotion, and eyed Chaco, now sitting across the table from Clancy with his own (brandy-less) mug of coffee.

"I don't even know where to begin asking questions," Clancy said, his face having regained its normal, healthy color. "I don't know the right questions to ask."

"You got that right," said Kaylee grimly, and began to tell the story from the beginning. Mid-narrative, Fred wandered into the kitchen, looking for breakfast. When he saw Clancy, his orange eyes whirled in agitation and he popped into nothingness. Clancy yelped, "Whatthehell?" and shot up from his chair like a bottle rocket. As he stood staring around for the small monster he had glimpsed, Chaco said, "It's all right, Fred. Clancy's in on the whole story, just about."

Fred reappeared and climbed into the chair with the tele-phone book on the seat, raising him to table height. He popped a digit into his mouth and sat on his fat bottom, staring solemnly at Clancy. "Clancy," said Chaco, "This is Fred. Fred, Clancy." Fred held out a rather damp paw, and Clancy shook it gingerly.

"I don't mean to be rude," Clancy said tentatively after a few moments of silence, "But just what *are* you, Fred? I don't believe I've ever seen anything—anyone—quite like you before."

"Mannegishi," Fred replied. "Mostly, you don't see us. That's kind of the point." Unenlightened, Clancy began to ask another question, but Kaylee interrupted.

"Sorry, Clancy. We can go into Fred's background later. Sierra is in danger, and you need to understand the situation here." She picked up the story again and drove relentlessly to the end. Clancy listened quietly.

"So we came home early this morning, and then you showed up," she concluded with relief. "Now you know everything. Any questions? I mean, questions that I might know the answer to?"

Clancy smiled ruefully at her. "So this is what Sierra was trying to tell me," he said. "No wonder it sounded fishy. I could never have imagined anything like this. Never in a million years." He eyed Fred and Chaco.

"Does anyone have a clue as to where Sierra went, or why?" he asked the little group.

Chaco leaned forward, elbows on the table. "It's obvious that she's been taken by Necocyaotl's servants. Otherwise there would be records of her arrest or release. Is there any way a human could eliminate police records?" he asked Clancy, who shook his head.

"Not right under the cops' noses," he said. "It can be done, but it's not easy. Besides, the police didn't even remember her being there. So you think whoever bailed her out was not...human? That he—it—somehow erased all the records, and the cops' memories?"

"That's what it sounds like," said Chaco, looking unhappy. "So now what do we do?"

"I was hoping *you* might have some ideas," returned Clancy. "You're the Avatar here. Don't you have, um, magical powers, or something?" He looked at Chaco hopefully, but Chaco was shaking his dark head.

"I have certain...abilities," Chaco said. "But I'm not omniscient. I don't know where she is. I don't know who took her, but whoever—or whatever—means to do her harm. That I do know. Otherwise, Sierra would have come home."

"That's right," Kaylee chimed in. "Sierra was frantic about

Chaco. She would never have stayed away on her own account, not knowing if he were alive or dead. Someone—something—must have taken her."

The four of them looked at one another in silence. Chaco finally broke it. "All I can think of is to ask Quetzalcoatl for help," he said slowly. "He is far more powerful than I am. He may know, or perhaps he can intervene. I can't think of anything else to do."

Kaylee looked up, hope brightening her face. "How do we call him?" she asked eagerly. Chaco sighed, looking uneasy.

"I don't know," he admitted. "I can perform one of the old ceremonies. I don't think you'll like it much, though." He explained quickly what was needed. Clancy looked revolted, Kaylee looked resigned, and Fred volunteered for requisition duty.

"Well, we'd best get started," Kaylee said firmly. "Whether we like it or not. What choice do we have?"

Some time later, a taxi drew up outside Sierra's house. A rather bedraggled figure got out, and as the taxi waited at the curb, walked up the front steps and opened the door.

The group huddled in the kitchen looked up as the figure appeared in the doorway.

"What *are* you doing with that chicken?" demanded Sierra.

CHAPTER 23

Sierra found herself surrounded and nearly smothered to death by her friends. Kaylee was weeping openly, Chaco was grinning ear to ear, and Fred was soaking her knees with tears—at least, Sierra hoped it was tears. Clancy hovered anxiously outside the melée, waiting for an opening. The chicken, released from Chaco's grip, fluttered around the kitchen, squawking and decorating the floor with black feathers and splotches of white chicken poop. Clancy finally saw his chance, swooped in and hugged Sierra until she squeaked.

When the excitement died down a bit, Sierra said, "There's a taxi outside, waiting to get paid. Would someone please take care of that for me? I left my purse when I got away."

Kaylee grabbed her own purse from the hall table and ran outside while the others clamored for information and Sierra peppered them back with her own questions.

"Where have you been…"

"Chaco, you're all right! I was afraid…"

"What happened? Kaylee said that…"

"We thought that Necocyaotl…"

Sierra sat down at the table and looked around. "Would someone please do something about that chicken? I can't hear myself think with the racket, and it's making a mess. Thanks, Chaco. What were you doing with a chicken in here? It looked like you were going to sacrifice it, or something—but that couldn't be right."

Chaco, now gripping the chicken firmly, looked sheepish. "We were," he admitted.

"But that's awful!" Sierra exclaimed. She felt, all too keenly, the horror of the impending sacrificial victim. "How could you do that, Chaco? Kaylee, were you going to let him kill this poor, innocent bird? Why?"

Kaylee mopped her streaming face. "Because we thought you were in danger. We didn't know where you were, and Chaco thought maybe Quetzalcoatl could help find you. But he didn't know how to call Quetzalcoatl, so we were going to perform one of the old ceremonies. The chicken was the best alternative we could think of."

Sierra didn't ask what the chicken was an alternative to; she knew very well. "Give me that chicken," she said to Chaco, who handed it over with alacrity. Sierra cradled the agitated bird in her arms while it pecked at her hands, grumbling loudly in Chicken about its poor treatment. "Ouch! Chaco, there's a cat carrier in the garage. Would you please get that for me?" Chaco obligingly retrieved the carrier, and the chicken was sequestered inside.

The chicken was provided with water and some birdseed Sierra kept for the wild birds in her tiny garden, and everyone gathered in the living room to catch up. Sierra's story made Chaco sit up alertly.

"Jumlin? Are you sure that was the name he used?"

"Yes, Chris Jumlin. He said he was a lawyer."

Chaco smiled grimly. "Lawyer. That's funny. Don't they sometimes call lawyers sharks?"

"Yes. Why? Do you know him?" asked Sierra.

"I know *of* him," said Chaco. "He's been around a long time. Millenia, in fact. But he's not one I would care to know personally. He's an anthropophage."

"Huh?" said Sierra.

"The Europeans called them vampires. But he isn't interested in blood by itself—he likes the whole thing."

"You mean he's a cannibal?" asked Sierra, her skin crawling to think she had spent so much time in Jumlin's presence.

Chaco shrugged. "He's not human, so it's not really cannibalism. You must have figured that out while you were there."

Sierra shook her head. "No. I actually thought he was really good-looking at first. But there's something about having a man truss you up like a turkey and come at you with a knife that really detracts from the guy's personal charm. And speaking of chickens," she looked at the cat carrier. "What are we going to do with this one?"

"Have it for dinner?" suggested Fred.

"No!" Sierra said indignantly. "It deserves to live!"

Clancy looked at her mildly. "You don't mind eating chicken from the grocery store. Why do you mind eating this one for dinner?"

"Because now I have a personal relationship with it," Sierra said, looking at the small peck-marks on her hands. "I'm not Jumlin. I don't consume people—or creatures—that I know personally."

Clancy gave her a look she found difficult to interpret. Was he laughing at her? He had not the faintest trace of a smile on his face. "Well, then," he said gravely, "We can't return the chicken to its former residence, because it certainly will be eaten. I suppose I'll have to build you a chicken coop in your little yard. But it's only one chicken; it won't take up much space."

"Thank you," said Sierra, surprised. "That would be great." She hoped the neighbors wouldn't mind. Or better still, wouldn't notice. She looked around at her friends, among whom she now counted Clancy.

"We have some planning to do," she said. "But first—I need a nice, hot shower."

CHAPTER 24

Damp and clean after her shower, Sierra decided the time had come to tell the others about her nightmares. As they all sat around her kitchen table, she detailed as much as she could remember. "I thought they were just bad dreams," she finished, "But I'm not so sure now. What do you think, Chaco?"

Chaco looked serious. "I don't know," he admitted. "They could be visions, sent by Necocyaotl. But I don't know how real they are."

"What do you mean by real?" Sierra asked. "I always wake up. I'm obviously not actually in that awful place."

"Hmmm. Well, Rose would tell you that your spirit can go places that your physical body can't. And when your spirit sickens, you sicken. So perhaps you really are in that stone hall. Just not your body," Chaco said gravely.

Sierra didn't like the sound of this. "So they *aren't* really nightmares, and they *can* really hurt me?"

"I think it's possible."

"What does the hummingbird have to do with Neco—the Bad Guy? When I followed the hummingbird, I fell into…that place."

Chaco shrugged expressively. "The hummingbird is a messenger of the gods. But perhaps you were diverted by Necocyaotl, and were unable to resist. I think maybe you should go see Rose. The Big Q said you had power, but you had to learn to use it. She might be able to help you with this."

Clancy looked impatient. "I don't think all this talk about dreams and gods is very helpful. Let's find Jumlin. I bet I can get some answers out of him." He flexed his fingers as though imagining how they might feel around Chris Jumlin's neck.

"No," Sierra said, holding up her hand. "I think Chaco is right. Maybe this shaman woman can help me." She turned to look at Clancy. "You don't know how horrible and nasty these dreams—or visions—are. It feels as though someone else is controlling me, or trying to control me. I have to struggle and struggle to break away and wake up. And then I'm afraid that the next time, I won't wake up. It feels as though something is sucking my soul away. I can't go on like this. Really, I can't." She tried not to sound as desperate as she felt, but Clancy reached across the table and covered her hands with his own.

"Okay, Sierra. If you think this woman can help, let's see what she can do." He turned to the rest of the party. "Does anyone know how to contact the, um, shaman?" The word "shaman" seemed to stick in his throat like a fish bone.

Kaylee fished around in her purse, emerging triumphantly with Rose's business card. "I have it right here!" She handed it to Sierra, who took it and studied it for a few minutes before heading to the telephone. From the kitchen, the others heard a murmured conversation. After a few minutes, Sierra returned.

"Rose will see me as soon as I can get there," she said, looking less than thrilled. "I understand it's quite a little trip up there to her cabin, so I'd better get going." She stood, and everyone else stood as well.

"Are you all going with me?" Sierra asked, smiling. "I think I can manage well enough on my own."

"No!" said Clancy and Chaco simultaneously. They glanced at each other, then Clancy said, "I don't think any of us should go anywhere alone at this point, Sierra. It's not a matter of not being able to manage. It's just that we don't really know what we're dealing with here, but we do know—beyond any doubt—that we're in danger. I'll go with Sierra. If the rest of you stay here and secure the house—that's about the best we can do right now."

Fred piped up, "You know how in the scary movie, everyone

in the haunted house breaks up and goes off by themselves? And the pretty girl takes a candle and walks up the cobwebby, creaky stairs alone? And you're going, 'No! No! Don't open that door!' And then something horrible jumps out and rips her to shreds? And you're going, 'I *knew* that was gonna happen'?" Fred looked around the circle of faces. "Well, it's like that. I think we should stick together."

Without another word, everyone gathered their things and prepared to depart as a group. As she knew the way, Kaylee drove Sierra's car, taking Sierra and Chaco. Clancy followed in his Jeep, with Fred (invisibly) sitting in the front passenger seat and asking to stop at every fast-food restaurant they passed. To divert him, Clancy finally asked, "Fred, how did you ever get to see any movies? Didn't you live in the forest or something?" He felt odd, addressing this question to the thin air, but Fred's chirpy voice replied, "I went into town a lot. I just climbed into cars, then hopped out when they stopped for food or something. I've seen lots of movies!"

"Oh? What are your favorites?" Clancy asked.

"I like the realistic ones. You know, slice-of-life stories."

"Like 'Dead Man Walking?' Or 'Vera Drake'?"

"Huh? No. I liked 'Lord of the Rings' best. Talk about realism." Clancy drove the rest of the way in thoughtful silence.

When they pulled up to Rose's cabin, she came to the door to meet them, wearing a long, blue skirt topped by a blue velvet blouse fastened with silver conchos. Her hair was swept back in a carved shell clip. When she saw the small crowd in her driveway, her dark eyebrows lifted like wings over her eyes.

"I don't usually deal with groups," she commented with a smile. She turned her penetrating gaze on Sierra. "I take it you are the one with the troubling visions?"

"Troubling?" said Sierra, bitterly. "That's one way to describe them." Rose merely nodded and stretched out her brown hands. Sierra put her hands in Rose's and the two women stood for a brief moment, looking into each other's eyes. Rose turned to the others.

"It's a hot day. Come in and have some water," she said, gesturing to the door. "But then I have to ask you to wait inside. I do my healing work outside. Once we get started, I need to ask you not to interrupt for anything. Anything short of Necocyaotl showing up, I mean," she added with a twinkle.

As they quenched their thirst with Rose's sweet well water, Rose went around her house as she had done before, gathering materials from woven baskets and wooden boxes. Satisfied at last, she and Sierra went together out to the patio area under the tall redwoods. The day was hot, but in the shade of the trees, it was pleasant enough. Sierra could smell the trees' resinous perfume and the dustiness of the rust-red, shredded duff that lay beneath them. She and Rose sat side by side in Rose's twiggy chairs. Sierra closed her eyes, letting the light and shadow play across her lids, and felt the nearest thing to peace that she had felt in a week. She hadn't exchanged two words with Rose, but the other woman's solid, grounded presence reassured her. Sitting here with Rose, Sierra felt safe, much safer than in her own house.

"Tell me about the visions," said Rose, and Sierra did. With every detail from each vision seared into her memory, she spent a long time just describing them, down to the minute details of the murals on the walls of the stone chamber. As she related these horrors, she relived the terror. Sweat started out on her pale face and her hands trembled. Rose listened quietly for the most part, occasionally breaking in to ask a question. By the time Sierra concluded with the tale of how Spider Grandmother came to her aid and freed her from Jumlin's grasp, her eyes were wide and shining.

"You have been blessed indeed," she breathed, looking into Sierra's eyes.

"Blessed?" Sierra snorted. "With what I've been through the past week, I hardly feel blessed!"

Rose shook her head. "I know it's hard to see it that way. But think of it! You are the *compadre* of Coyotl, the Trickster, and also friend to a mannegishi. Kóhk'ang Wuhti herself came to your side when you were threatened. You have even been in the presence of

Quetzalcoatl himself. These are ancient, powerful beings watching over you. Had they not been there, you would be dead by now."

Sierra was in no mood to think positively. "If I didn't have these ancient, powerful beings involved with me, I'd probably be living a normal life. I'd be writing press releases right now and getting a paycheck." When she phrased it that way, normalcy didn't sound so wonderful, but she hoped Rose would take her meaning.

"There's something else," Sierra said. Rose waited for her to go on. "When I met Quetzalcoatl, he said I had a power that I could use to defeat Necocyaotl. He touched my head, and I saw a vision of flames. Colored flames. But I haven't felt any special power—and I really could have used some lately!"

Rose began building a fire in the fire pit, talking to Sierra as she did so. "That kind of power is also a blessing, but doesn't come cheap," Rose said, laying small sticks in the pit, crossed at the corners like Lincoln logs. "But it's like any other strength. You have to develop it, exercise it and keep it strong." She squatted by the pit and touched the dry twigs with a match. They caught slowly, smoldering rather than burning, and Rose began adding herbs.

"And the nightmares? The visions?" Sierra asked. "Are they a blessing or a curse?"

"Oh, a curse, no doubt about that," said Rose, fanning her little fire with a brown feather fan. Fragrant smoke began to rise from the fire pit. It coiled in the air and drifted toward the chair where Sierra sat. "The Obsidian Mirror sends them to terrify you, to weaken your resolve. It sounds like he has nearly succeeded at times. But you were too strong for him."

"Strong?" queried Sierra, feeling relaxed now. The smoke reminded her of campfires built with incense cedar or balsam pine—some perfumed wood. It wasn't harsh and didn't sting her eyes as it weaved around her. "I didn't feel strong when I was having the visions. I felt weak and stupid. Scared."

"That's what he intended. But nonetheless, you were strong enough to break free of him," Rose replied. "After today, you will be stronger still. I'm going to teach you how to command those visions. How to take control and make the vision serve *you*, instead of Necocyaotl. Now, hush, listen, and do what I ask you."

Describing this experience later to her friends, Sierra could only liken it to a workout at the gym. She experienced visions, at first harmless, then more and more threatening. Rose instructed her, telling her to go within herself to find the strength to create her own counter-vision. It wasn't too hard in the beginning. Sierra saw a large bird swoop at her, claws outstretched, beak slashing at her eyes. Rose said, "Bring up your own bird and fight it!"

Sierra went inward, inward and down. She became aware of something formless, but real, deep inside. Suddenly, colored flames leaped up, glowing fiercely. She stretched out mental fingers and grasped some of the light, rolling it like burning clay between her palms, and willed it to be a fierce eagle. The eagle seemed to spring from her chest, and swooped at the attacking bird, which… shattered. As Sierra's eagle struck it, the bird shivered into a thousand tiny pieces that became mist and whirled away on the breeze from the eagle's great wings. The eagle screamed in triumph and disappeared.

"That was great, Sierra!" Rose enthused. "You've got a talent for this. Do you by any chance have Native American ancestry? Or someone in the family who had…let's say, psychic gifts?"

"Well, the family legend is that we had an ancestor named Suzy Long-Knife who was a Sioux. But if we had any psychics, they weren't telling," Sierra replied.

"Let's try another one," said Rose. Buoyed by her victory, Sierra was eager to take on another vision.

In the next session, Sierra seemed to be alone in a nighttime forest. The trees stood so close together that she couldn't see the moon, or even any stars. It was not a friendly or familiar wood, but a forest out of some grim fairytale, complete with ominous creaking and rustlings in the dark. In the distance, she heard a long, drawn-out howl. *Wolf*, she thought, and began drawing on the flames as she had when the bird attacked her. She had a cougar in mind, something that could take on a wolf and win.

But the thing that burst through the trees and surged toward her like a runaway locomotive was no wolf. It was as large as a pony, with thickly muscled legs that ended in clawed feet. It gnashed yellow, twisted tushes that clashed like sword blades, and its red, piggy eyes glowed with an insane look of hatred. Sierra didn't have time to think about what it might be; she flung the flames at the creature with no conscious intention other than to escape its oncoming rush. An inchoate globe of light erupted from her body and engulfed the charging horror...and it disappeared like a dandelion puff blown by the wind, dissolving into wispy bits that floated away into the dark.

"What *was* that thing?" gasped Sierra as she emerged from the vision, drenched in sweat.

"It was fear. Just fear," replied Rose. "It came from your own psyche, not from me."

Sierra considered this. "But I didn't make up the visions that Neco-whatever sent me," she protested. "I swear, I didn't know anything about obsidian mirrors, or Mayan sacrifices, or Aztec gods. None of it. That didn't come from me."

"No," Rose agreed, "the form of the visions didn't come from you. But fear is archetypal. The fear of darkness, the fear of being eaten, the fear of being helpless—these are universal. The Obsidian Mirror guided the shape your fears took, but those fears were there inside you all along. All he had to do was call them up. Now you know that you can banish fear, as well. Let's try something different this time, shall we?"

Sierra, shaken by the last encounter, was not as eager, but agreed. "This time," explained Rose, "take charge of the vision. No matter how it appears to you, remember that you have the pure power inside of you to make it your own. If you can, turn it back on me."

Sierra nodded her agreement and sank back in her chair. She closed her eyes, apprehension making her tense. Suddenly, she found herself in that cold stone hall, sconced torches flickering on either side. Just as she had seen it before, the huge, black stone stood at the far end with the stone altar before it. On the altar rested the obsidian knife, gleaming wickedly down its flaked edges. All along the walls, Sierra could see the scenes of death and torture that had so revolted her each time.

Then she heard the voice she had been dreading. "Sierra. You can't keep running from me. I am everywhere. My servants even now are closing in on you and your *friends*." The last word was pronounced with scorn and sarcasm. "See how long they'll stay with you when my servants come. They'll dry up and blow away, like worms in the sun."

Sierra searched inside her for the light. She couldn't find it. A thrill of panic ran down her spine, and her knees felt ready to collapse.

"There's the altar. See what's in store for those who defy me." She was grasped as though by invisible hands, and rushed down the hall, stumbling and off balance. The unseen force dragged her to the altar and released her. On the altar she saw Clancy, sprawling and lifeless. His chest gaped open, and blood pooled on the rough rock floor below. His eyes were open and empty, his mouth gaped.

"He died screaming," the voice said. "Screaming and whimpering. A worm. Will you die the same way? I have plans for you. I know how to make a death count for something. I'll wring everything from you until there's nothing left but pain, pain, pain."

The voice continued on in this vein, but Sierra stopped listening. She felt frozen, stiff, unable to move. Where was the light? Rose had said to take charge of the vision, but she couldn't find the light. How could this upwelling of filth come from Rose? It wasn't possible; she didn't believe it. Somehow, Necocyaotl had interfered, caught her in a vulnerable state, interposed his own hellish dream, and she had nothing with which to fight it.

Again, Sierra drove her consciousness inward, seeking for even a glimmer of the power she had wielded before. Then it came to her; she *was* the flame, the light. She didn't have to conjure it up; she was made of light, it imbued her every cell, her very soul. With this realization came a fierceness of which she hadn't known she was capable. She was a warrior, fearsome in her own right. The darkness and evil in this forsaken temple could never stand against her. She felt as though every finger were a weapon, her breath a stream of cleansing fire. She directed the fire to the altar, and to her amazement, it burned and crumpled like tissue thrown on a bonfire, blackening into dust before her eyes and blowing away.

Then she turned on the great sheet of obsidian, directing her power against it. It glowed red, slumped, then poured like lava across the floor. It didn't burn her feet, but ran around her as though there were an invisible barrier protecting her. She turned her attention to the hideous paintings, and they flaked away from the walls and evaporated, the blocky figures of chieftains and their miserable, tortured captives curling together as they turned to ash. The walls heated as she scoured them clean, then began to crack and crumble like so much stale bread. She heard a faint howling as she worked, but it dimmed and faded as the temple fell to dust around her, and she found herself sitting again in the dappled shade of Rose's patio, panting as though she had just run a marathon. Rose was bent almost double in her chair, hands to her face, retching. Sierra sprang from her seat and rushed to Rose's side.

"Rose! Are you okay?" Sierra asked. Had *she* done this to the shaman?

Rose straightened, passing a hand across her face, which was a shade paler than before. She took several deep breaths, and her color began to return. Finally, she beamed up at Sierra, and extended her arms for an embrace. "You did it!" she cried. "You did it, you did it! I knew you could. How do you feel?"

"Whipped," Sierra confessed. "But never better. Never better, Rose." She embraced Rose in turn. "Thank you so, so much, Rose. But was that vision really from you? Or did Neco—the Obsidian Mirror—did he somehow send it? It seemed just like the visions he sent."

"It actually came from you, Sierra," returned Rose. "Remember, I told you he was just working on the primeval terrors that everyone has, buried somewhere deep. He uses your own power against you. All I had to do was tap into that. Although, it was one of the hardest things I ever had to do," she added ruefully. "It isn't easy for me to deliberately cultivate such evil thoughts. But you fought back with such power, Sierra! Such strength!"

Sierra sobered somewhat. "I'm sorry it was hard on you. But I am so grateful, Rose, thank you." She had another thought. "But, when I actually confront him again, won't it be different? Will I still be able to control what happens?"

"I'm not telling you it will be *easy*," said Rose. "I am telling you that you can do it." She held Sierra's eyes steadily, with conviction. "You can do it!"

CHAPTER 25

Nearly a week later, Sierra arrived back at her house, drained and weary. After her initial triumph over the visions, Rose had schooled her again and again, throwing ever-more-difficult scenarios at her. Sierra hadn't always done well, but day after day, she felt more secure in her strength. *It's kind of like riding a bicycle*, she mused. *It seems impossible at first. Then you fall down a lot. And one day, you just…ride.* Then she climbed into bed and slept for fourteen hours.

Sierra deferred her telling of the events at Rose's until everyone was able to regroup at her house. It was late afternoon and though it was hot, they had sealed the doors and windows, and Chaco burned a bundle of sage, wafting the smoke through each room and murmuring prayers. They gathered in the living room over cups of tea, and Sierra told them how she had learned to conquer the visions—or at least, conquer the visions that Rose had engendered. Then she reminded them of the missing silver feathers and the new questions posed by the sudden appearance of Chris Jumlin on the scene.

"Jumlin doesn't know where the feathers are," said Sierra. "He was angry with me because I couldn't tell him what happened to them. I have to get the feathers back! We've lost so much time." She didn't regret the time spent with Rose, but she had no idea how to begin tracking down the feathers. Then she fixed on the word "tracking."

"Chaco, in your coyote form, do you think you could *smell* the man who came here with Tzintzimitl?"

Chaco frowned, considering. "It would be better if the trace were fresher. But, yes. I can do that." Without another word, he shifted in that unnerving canid metamorphosis. As soon as the transformation was complete, he dashed out the door and down the hall into the kitchen. The door into the garage blocked him, but Sierra and Kaylee, close behind him, opened it. Clancy and Fred followed close behind.

They watched in silence as Chaco cast about the garage floor, nose quivering. Then he went back into the house and stood by the front door, waiting. Sierra opened the door and the coyote ran down the front steps, onto the sidewalk—and came to a halt at the street. His thick, brushy tail drooped, and his ears went flat back against his skull. He looked at the three humans standing in the doorway and shook his head in a miniscule gesture, then padded back into the house. By the time Clancy and the women made it back through the door in his wake, he was in human form again, looking dejected.

"Car," he said. "He left in a car. The trail ends at the street. I should have thought of that." The two women groaned.

"Well, good try, Chaco," said Sierra, trying to be positive. This earned her a cynical look from Chaco.

Kaylee sighed. "Well, I'd better go fetch some things from the office and get some work done, or I'll lose my job." She kissed Sierra. "I'll be back later. Let me know if you think of anything."

"Wait a moment," said Clancy. "I don't think you should go by yourself. It's too dangerous. We've seen what they're capable of."

"Maybe I should go with you," suggested Chaco. Kaylee looked at him for a long beat, warm brown eyes locked on amber.

"Sure," she said. "Come on." And then they were gone. Sierra stood uncertainly at the front door for a few minutes, but Clancy gently pulled her away and shut and locked the door. He began a perimeter check, testing doors and windows to see if they were secure. Sierra wondered what good locked doors would be against the supernatural, but recognized that Clancy was, in his own way, whistling in the dark.

Fred began to ask questions such as, "Are you cooking tonight? 'Cause Chaco's not here to make dinner. What do you suppose we'll have for dinner?"

Sierra busied herself in the kitchen, managing to produce pasta with marinara sauce and salad. Fred tucked in with relish, but Sierra had little appetite. She toyed with the spaghetti strands disconsolately, thinking about the lost feathers and the difficulty of reaching Jenna Simmons. She felt utterly unprepared and vulnerable. Jumlin was still at large, the feathers were still missing. She had no job and no prospect of getting one yet. Aiden was a possible enemy—at best, there was something fishy about him. She had no idea what to do next. Gloom settled over her like a fog bank, clammy and impenetrable.

I could just quit, she thought suddenly. It was tempting. After all, she wasn't getting paid to do this, and she needed time to find another job. Then she thought about encountering the old man in his cave, the powerful presence of the ancient being who had called on her. She wasn't frightened that he would take revenge if she quit, but she was frightened of...disappointing him. And the stakes were so high—Simmons' unhindered campaign would continue to damage the wild things Sierra loved.

She realized that she was stabbing her fork fiercely and repeatedly into the mound of pasta and sauce on her plate, making an unappetizing mess.

"What's going on?" Clancy asked. His appetite seemed as hearty as Fred's, and he had cleaned his plate.

"Nothing," Sierra said. "Everything." Tipping her unwanted food into the garbage, she poured herself a glass of wine and drifted to the living room. She turned on the television before flopping moodily into an armchair. The news was on.

"...In other news, Dolores Perdoo, the chairwoman of the Senate Committee on the Environment and Public Works, has announced that research has been commissioned on the threat of a new ice age. Here is Ms. Perdoo." A new voice began to speak.

"A new report released today by the Senate Committee on the Environment and Public Works indicates that instead of global warming, we may be facing an era of global cooling, much like that seen during mankind's earliest years, ten thousand years ago. Experts say that reducing greenhouse gases may indeed speed up the threat of a new ice age..."

Sierra lunged for the remote, switching to a BBC special, which she watched for an hour or so. Clancy watched for a few minutes at a time, rising and prowling the small house repeatedly. Although at first Sierra was rather touched by his vigilance, she found it irritating after a while and wished he would just sit still. She was about to say something about taking it easy when the doorbell rang, followed by frantic pounding. Clancy moved cautiously to the door, hand on his holster, and called, "Who is it?"

"It's us—Kaylee and Chaco!" came Kaylee's contralto voice. Clancy opened the door, and Kaylee and Chaco tumbled in.

"Sierra! Chaco says he's been at BDSC!" Kaylee called.

"Chaco says that *Chaco's* been at BDSC?" Sierra asked, confused.

"No! Chaco says the man who took the feathers has been at BDSC. He smelled him!"

Chaco nodded, looking slightly smug.

"You smelled him?" Sierra asked skeptically. "At BDSC? While you were in human form?"

Chaco looked as sheepish as a person who is also a coyote can look. "Well, we thought it would be better if Kaylee put me on a bit of rope and walked in after hours as though I were her dog."

"If I got caught at night with someone who didn't work there, it'd be my job for sure," Kaylee put in. "Anyway, Chaco smelled him as soon as we got into the building. Everywhere! I bet he works at BDSC."

Sierra said, "Next question—how do we find this guy? You can't take Chaco in there during the day. I mean, casually dropping by in the evening with your dog to pick up your stuff is one thing, but they'll object to having him there during working hours."

"Right," Kaylee said eagerly. "We talked about it on the way back. I'll go into work like I always do, and you and Chaco hang around in the parking lot. When Chaco sniffs him out, you call me on your cell and give me a description. I'll get down there as fast as I can, and find out who he is. He has to have a badge to get in, and the badge will have his name on it."

Sierra considered this scheme. Hanging around in the parking lot seemed dubious; too many people at BDSC knew her. She tried to think of ways of appearing innocent while lurking on private property with a coyote in tow.

"Well, I suppose I might be inconspicuous if I wore running gear, put my hair in a cap and wore dark glasses. I could pretend to be running with my dog," she said.

Chaco rolled his eyes. "Oh, great," he said. "I get to trot around after you for hours while you circle the parking lot? It gets hot this time of year!"

"Got a better idea, smart guy? I'll bring water."

"Yeah, *you* just try running around in a fur coat," muttered Chaco. "What do you think, Clancy?"

Clancy sat for a minute, thinking. Finally, he said, "I suppose it could work. I'll be close by, in case things go wrong."

They discussed it for a while, but no better plan emerged, so it was decided. They made up a short list of necessities for the venture, and Chaco and Clancy volunteered to venture out to the All-Hours Bargain Bonanza to see if they could locate a dog leash and other supplies. Chaco and Kaylee parted after a passionate clinch in the front hall. Kaylee wandered back into the living room with her hair disheveled and a moony smile on her face.

Sierra looked at her severely. "I hope you know what you're getting into," she said, feeling absurdly like someone's mother. "Chaco's not just another guy, you know. He's not even human. Strictly speaking."

Kaylee sat on the couch, still with a dreamy expression on her face, and patted her hair into place. Her hazel eyes sparkled, and her tawny cheeks were flushed. Sierra groaned inwardly. It's hard to be around people with crushes—unless you happened to be one of them. *Any minute now, they'll be calling each other ghastly little pet names. "Woofie," maybe, and "Pumpkin"? Gack.*

"Oh, don't worry about me, Sierra," said Kaylee. "I don't think I'm looking for the same things in a man that you are."

"Really?" asked Sierra, a bit stung. "What do you think I want?"

"Oh, moonlight and roses, and eventually babies," said Kaylee frankly. "Nothing wrong with that, but it isn't what *I* want."

"You know he won't stick around forever," Sierra told her friend. "He's a wanderer. And he won't be faithful, either."

"But he'll be a *whole* lot of fun while it lasts," said Kaylee. "Those eyes! That gorgeous mouth! His…"

"Yes, all right," interrupted Sierra hastily. "I've checked out his inventory, too. You're right. If that's what you want, I'll shut up."

"Good," Kaylee said, but she said it sweetly, and smiled.

Far too early the next morning, Sierra dressed in her running clothes, grabbed a baseball cap and stuffed her dark hair under it. She added dark glasses, and examined herself critically in the mirror. She could be any random runner, she decided. Kaylee and Clancy had spent the night in Sierra's increasingly crowded home (for safety in numbers, Clancy had said), and everyone met for breakfast and went over the day's plans over toast and coffee. Sierra and Chaco would arrive just after: six o'clock and take up their pretense of runner-with-dog.

Sierra made sure there was plenty of water in the car. Chaco was right about the heat. It was now five-thirty in the morning, and though still on the cool side, the day promised to be warm. Chaco morphed into his fur and hopped into the car. Sierra clipped the new leather leash to his beaded collar and added a water bowl, and they drove away.

"Can we stop and get coffee?" pleaded Chaco, long pink tongue hanging between his toothy jaws. "I'm no good in the morning without it."

"C'mon, Chaco. How would that look? You slurping coffee out of a cardboard cup? Someone will turn me in for abusing an animal."

"Oh, all right," grumbled Chaco, and stuck his head out of the window for all the world like a Labrador retriever, ears fluttering in the breeze. Within ten minutes, they pulled into the BDSC parking lot. Like many Silicon Valley companies, the parking lot was huge, open, and unguarded. Trees had been planted to provide shade, and the building had tasteful landscaping around the exterior, punctuated here and there with fountains. Open patios were dotted with picnic tables for the employees to use for lunch, or just to work outdoors—something the Mediterranean climate of Northern California permitted for much of the year. The air was still cool and clear, and the nearby hills rose up, gold against a clean, blue sky.

Sierra parked near the main entrance and began her stretching exercises. Chaco sat on his haunches and kept his nose in the air, scanning for scent. They saw Kaylee drive up, park and walk in, with no acknowledgement on either side.

"OK, Chaco, let's go." Sierra grasped the end of the leash and began her warm-up stride, easy, not too fast. She didn't plan to accelerate to the next level, as she had no way of knowing how long they would be running around. She didn't want either of them to get too tired or overheated.

Chaco and Sierra trotted around the parking lot that surrounded all four sides of the building. There were entrances on three sides, and shipping and receiving docks in the rear. On the way, Sierra saw several BDSC employees she knew, but she kept her head down. No one paid the slightest attention to her. Intent on beginning the workday, they walked straight ahead with their computer cases, some seemingly talking to themselves as they chatted over their Bluetooth devices. *It used to be when someone did that, they'd lock him up,* she thought. *Now it just means you're a busy professional at work.*

As they went around for the third time, it was beginning to get warm, and Chaco was panting slightly. "Not to worry, Chaco," she said softly. "We'll stop for water at the car this time." As they rounded the corner of the building, Chaco came to an abrupt halt. Sierra, running ahead, came to the end of his leash, and nearly tripped. "What…?" she started to say, then saw he had his eyes fixed intently on a figure approaching the front door of the building. Chaco's black nose worked furiously.

"That's him!" she heard Chaco whisper.

"That's the guy who took the feathers?" she asked incredulously. "Are you absolutely sure?"

Chaco looked at her with his feral eyes and gave the smallest of nods.

"But that's Jack Clapper!" Sierra exclaimed.

CHAPTER 26

Heart pounding from more than just a few laps around the building, Sierra pulled her cell phone from her shorts pocket and dialed Kaylee, who answered promptly.

"Kaylee, Chaco found him!" she hissed into the phone.

"I'll be right down. What'd he look like?"

"You don't need to identify him. I know who it is—Jack Clapper."

"Who? You mean the PR agency guy? The one you used to work for?"

"Yes!" Sierra said. "Chaco says Jack is the one. He's positive."

"Wow," said Kaylee. "What does *that* mean?"

"I don't know. Listen. I'm going to find his car," she hesitated, glancing at Chaco. "I mean *we're* going to find his car. Maybe he hid the feathers there. Or maybe we can find out where he's staying."

Kaylee seemed alarmed by this scheme. "Wait a sec, Sierra. That could be dangerous. That's not what we planned…"

"I know. What choice do I have? I'll call you." Sierra broke the connection. "C'mon, Chaco. Let's get some water. Then do you think you can find Jack's car?"

Chaco looked at her, affronted. "I already *know* which car is his," he whispered. "I'm not nose-blind, you know."

"I never took you for nose-blind, whatever that is," she said, rummaging in her car for the water. She took the bowl from the back seat, set it on the asphalt and poured water in it for Chaco. While he lapped it up, she drank deeply from the rest of the bottle. Then she looked around carefully, assessing the likelihood of being observed by employees on their way into work.

"Where is Jack's car?" she asked Chaco softly. Chaco looked up at her, drops of water caught in his whiskers. He jerked his head to the right, and began to walk in that direction.

Sierra hastily caught up the end of the leash and followed him. Chaco stopped by a black Boxster, low-slung and gleaming in the bright sunlight.

"It's a convertible," said Sierra. "I could cut through the top if I had a knife. But I don't."

"Not a problem," muttered Chaco. Screened by cars on every side, he reared up on his hind legs and bared sharp fangs. Within seconds, he had slashed a hole in the tough fabric near the passenger side door. Sierra regarded the sheared gap with respect. It ran through her mind that it was better to be Chaco's friend than his enemy. She reached in through the hole, and stretching, was able to reach the door release. To her intense relief, no alarm sounded. She opened the passenger door, and was inside in a flash, opening the glove compartment. Registration. A bottle of aspirin. And oddly, gloves. But no silver feathers.

She found a compartment between the seats and opened it, but it was full of CDs. *The trunk!* she thought, and looked for a release on the driver's side. She couldn't see it, so she unlocked the driver's door and walked around to climb in. Chaco was anxiously scanning the lot to see if anyone was taking an interest, but the only people around were in the distance, walking purposefully toward the front entrance and paying them no attention.

"Found it!" Sierra crowed, and popped open the trunk. She hopped out of the driver's seat, leaving the door open, and went to the back of the car. The trunk lid revealed a small, carpet-lined space that was completely empty, with not so much as a fleck of lint to mar its pristine black interior. Frustrated, she climbed back in and scanned the interior of the car for more storage, but saw no more compartments. She leaned back against the leather seat and sighed.

"Nothing. Nothing, nothing, nothing, and more nothing!" she said between her teeth. Then she noticed that Chaco was standing at the front of the little car. He was mouthing something, but she couldn't make out what.

"Come closer," she said. "I can't hear you."

Impatiently, he trotted to the open driver's side door. "Front!" he muttered between his teeth, keeping his head low.

"Look, I know you don't want anyone to notice you talking. That's very intelligent, but I have no idea what you mean," she replied.

"Front! There's a trunk in the front!" Quickly, he shoved his head into the passenger compartment and flipped a lever with his black nose. To Sierra's astonishment, the hood popped open.

"Where the heck did they put the engine?" she demanded, but followed Chaco to peer into the opening now revealed. It, too, was empty, but Chaco stiffened.

"Aiden's been in this trunk," he whispered urgently.

"Aiden? There's barely room for a suitcase," Sierra protested. "Aiden's a big man. He'd never fit."

"There's room for him if he were dead," Chaco returned *sotto voce*. "And there's blood."

Sierra peered into the space. It was, like the trunk, carpeted in black. She could see nothing. "Are you sure?" she asked Chaco, dubiously. He looked at her, and although his canine face had its limitations when it came to expressiveness, she could tell he was annoyed.

"Of course I'm sure," he hissed quietly. "And it's Aiden's blood. There's no doubt about it."

Despite the growing warmth of the day, Sierra felt cold. Aiden wouldn't fit into this cramped compartment…unless he was dead. Or if whoever had crammed him in wasn't much worried about his survival. And his blood remained to show that he *had* fit into this small space. She had to do something. He might yet still be alive, though the blood proved he was wounded.

"Back to my car," she whispered to Chaco, and then she closed the storage compartment and doors and retreated to her own car. They sat inside her car for a few minutes in silence. Chaco, who had been panting, changed back into his human form and immediately seemed more comfortable. Sierra's mind was churning with horror and anxiety. There seemed to be no good choices. If she called the police, they would certainly question her means of coming by her information. They would find the blood, but they would also see her as a probable suspect. Yet Aiden might be lying hurt and bleeding somewhere. Or—she shuddered—dead. She had to do something to try to help Aiden, assuming he was alive. And if he were dead, help bring his murderer to justice. Finally Sierra pulled out her cell phone.

"What are you doing?" inquired Chaco.

"Calling Clancy. We need his help. Clancy? Listen, there's some seriously bad news down here…"

Five minutes later, still sitting in the car, they saw Kaylee and Clancy walk out of the building. Kaylee spotted Sierra's Ford and began walking toward the car, Clancy striding beside her. Clancy was in his uniform, talking on his two-way radio, flashlight and other paraphernalia clipped to his wide belt. She thought he had a holstered gun as well. He was scanning the parking lot, on the alert, as always.

Clancy said into his radio, "Roger that. On the scene, and it's under control. Cancel the call to the police. Ten-four." He holstered his radio and said, "We nearly blew it there. Surveillance video caught you going through a car, and if I hadn't been there, the cops would've been here by now."

Kaylee came up to Sierra's car window. "I was hanging around Clancy's office, waiting for your call," she said. "I think his staff thinks I have a thing for him. So, what's up?"

"Let's walk off the premises," Clancy said. "We're going to be conspicuous, standing here and talking. Remember, we're being watched now."

They walked out of the parking lot and went a few yards down the street. Satisfied they were out of view of the surveillance cameras, Clancy stopped and faced the others. "So what's going down?" he asked.

"We broke into a car," Chaco began.

"So you're *that* kind of coyote, are you?" said Clancy.

Chaco ignored this. He went on, "And we found blood, human blood."

On hearing the words, "human blood," Clancy seemed to shrug on his cop persona like a coat. "Human blood. How do you know?"

Chaco looked exasperated. He tapped his long, chiseled nose. "My sense of smell as a coyote is at least a hundred times keener than any human's," he replied. "Not only do I know it's human, I know *which* human."

Clancy grew still at this. "Whose blood is it?"

"His name is Aiden," Sierra answered. "Um, I actually don't know what his last name is. But he's either in trouble or dead. We've got to find him!"

Clancy seemed reluctant to move. "So how do you know this Aiden?" he asked.

"Look, does it matter?" Sierra snapped. A man is wounded, he was transported in a car trunk the size of a shoebox, and he may be dead. What are we going to do about it?"

Clancy sighed and looked at Sierra. "Right. Just trying to understand the situation. So where's the blood?"

Sierra led the way to Clapper's car, leaving Kaylee and Chaco standing on the sidewalk. Clancy noted the slashed fabric of the convertible top, but didn't say anything. Sierra reached in and popped the hood open. Clancy peered into the front compartment, shining a flashlight carefully around the interior.

"I don't see anything...wait!" He scrutinized a spot on the floor of the compartment. He touched it with a gingerly forefinger. "It's dried, whatever it is," he reported, scrubbing his finger on his trousers. He straightened up. "Whose car is this?"

"His name is Jack Clapper. He runs a public relations agency in New York. Kaylee says he's been working for Black Diamond since I was fired. I used to work for him."

"You know him pretty well, then?" Clancy's green eyes caught the light as he asked.

"I know him well enough to not like him. He was involved in some pretty sleazy stuff, in my opinion. I never thought he was a murderer, though."

Clancy's expression softened, the cop receding for a moment. "OK, Sierra," he said. "First thing, I'm going to call the police…" He broke off as Sierra began to protest. "Hang on! Hear me out. I'm going to call the cops and tell them I got an anonymous report of blood in a car parked here in BDSC's lot. They'll come out here and do their testing. They'll find the blood if your furry friend here is correct. When they find the blood, they'll take Clapper into custody and search his house. Or wherever he's living. Did you find the feathers?"

"No. Aiden is dead or in terrible danger. Let's work on that, and I'll worry about the feathers later."

"Go home, Sierra," said Clancy. "I'll wipe down the car—you probably left prints all over it. Then I'll call the police."

Sierra realized with a sharp pang that indeed, she *had* left prints all over the Boxster. She'd never make a successful criminal at this rate, she decided. Leaving Clancy working on the Boxster, Sierra walked back to Kaylee and Chaco.

"Gotta run," Kaylee said. "I have a ton of work waiting." She locked lips with Chaco, and they clung together. He gave her rounded hip a gentle squeeze, and released her. Kaylee looked like a Persian cat that has just discovered an open can of tuna.

CHAPTER 27

Sierra, Chaco, and Fred sat and talked in Sierra's tiny patio garden. Red bricks made a more-or-less even footing for a round, glass-topped table with an umbrella and four chairs. The formerly sacrificial chicken was pecking around in the grass for bugs and clucking contentedly, black feathers shining in the sun. Sierra had planted climbing roses and star jasmine next to the redwood fence, and as these were now in full bloom, they were bustling with bees and hummingbirds.

Chaco and Sierra sat on two of the chairs while Fred lay in the sun on the bricks, tummy exposed to the sun and basking like a cat. Sierra had noticed that with more exposure to sunlight, Fred was now a darker shade of green. Where he had been the gray-green of lichen, he was now mossier in appearance. *Not a look that just anyone can carry off,* she thought, *but it looks good on Fred.*

"Mmmm," said Chaco, turning his face to the sun. His chin was covered with dark stubble, which only contrived to make him look ruggedly handsome instead of startlingly beautiful. "Things are in play, you know," he said obscurely.

"No, I don't know," responded Sierra.

"All I mean to say is, we don't even know all the elements that might be in play around this situation. We might just be one of many checkers on the board, as it were. Also, now we have Clancy involved. That could make a difference."

Sierra brooded on this for a while, thoughts straying from the situation at hand into more personal territory. She wasn't sure how she felt about Clancy. She barely knew him. Certainly, he had that rangy look that she was drawn to. She liked his eyes, jade green under black brows, and she liked his warm smile and sense of humor—when he chose to display it. But he was not a naturally trustful man, and he had a sense of distance around him. She wondered whether or not that distance could ever be bridged. She'd been in too many failed relationships with too many emotionally unavailable men to want to go down that road again. Then she felt guilty for dwelling on her emotional life instead of worrying about Aiden's desperate plight.

Chaco interrupted her thoughts by saying, "I mean, Sierra, that he could make a difference in contacting Jenna Simmons and getting the feathers in contact with her. He works at the company, and he's in a position of trust. Right?"

Sierra blushed. "Yeah. That's what I thought you meant. I mean, yes, I thought of that before. I mean, before, he, I…"

"Uh-huh," said Chaco, cutting short her flustered speech. "Anyway, I bet Clancy could arrange it if he wanted to."

Sierra was about to respond to this statement when suddenly, a tiny hummingbird detached itself from the busy crowd at the jasmine and buzzed over to the table. It hovered directly in front of Sierra's face, glittering like a brooch set with rubies and emeralds. She could hear its high-pitched "Tzip! Tzip!" And then she distinctly heard it say, "Aiden!"

"Chaco! Did you hear that?" she exclaimed.

Chaco was leaning forward, staring at the bird, which still hovered near Sierra's face. "Yes! It said 'Aiden!' The hummingbird way, Rose said. The hummingbird is a messenger between the spirit world and the physical world. Maybe you should follow it."

Sierra shrank back. "Oh, no. Not after what happened in my dream, or vision, or whatever it was. The dream hummingbird said 'Aiden!' and I followed it, all right. Right into Neco-whatever's nasty hangout." The hummingbird flew toward the patio gate, which let out onto a sidewalk leading to the street. Sierra stayed firmly put. The bird zipped back and began to hover, sounding its urgent "Tzip!"

"Did you really *follow* the hummingbird in your dream?"

asked Chaco. "Could you see it the whole time? Did it lead you right to Necocyaotl?"

Sierra tried to remember. "No," she said finally. "It disappeared. I just walked in the general direction it took. But I never actually saw it again."

"I think we should follow it," said Fred, who had been watching with interest. His eyes reflected the sunlight in a blaze of orange.

"So do I," Chaco said. "The hummingbird has never been a servant of the dark. I believe you can trust it. And Rose has shown you how to manage the visions."

"Oh, all right," said Sierra. "Fred, not you, though. You'd create traffic accidents everywhere we went. And get in the way."

"Then I'll disappear," said Fred, doing so. Sierra couldn't see any way of preventing him from accompanying them, so she shrugged and got up from the table.

The hummingbird zipped toward the gate again, and this time, Sierra, Chaco and the unseen Fred followed. It buzzed over the gate, hovered until they opened it, then flew down the street.

Following a hummingbird proved to be a difficult and exhausting endeavor. For one thing, it was incredibly fast. It could cover several yards in the time it took Sierra and Chaco to go a few feet. And Fred was not a fast mover. They had to wait for him several times after hearing his plaintive wails behind them. Each time, the hummingbird buzzed back, hovering impatiently for the little group to get going again.

The bird could sail effortlessly over barriers such as fences or busy streets that the others required more time to negotiate. And then there was the problem of tripping over Fred. He had an uncanny knack of getting underfoot, and as neither Chaco nor Sierra could detect where Fred was, this happened a number of times—each time resulting in a squeal of indignation and pain from the mannegishi, and on more than one occasion drawing curious stares from passersby, as Chaco and Sierra staggered drunkenly where no obstacle could be seen.

They quickly left the residential part of Sunnyvale and started through the industrial area of town. The streets were lined with tilt-up office buildings, anonymously similar, block after block. Contractors had constructed these buildings in the nineteen-seventies by pouring the cement walls in forms on the ground, then literally tilting the now-solid walls up from the forms. They quickly and cheaply fulfilled the booming demand for office space in a burgeoning Silicon Valley, but no one would ever have been able to distinguish one office building from another if it hadn't been for the street numbers.

They passed from office buildings to a district of warehouses with huge shipping docks in front, and finally came to a personal storage facility. The sign in front read, "U*Storall." The driveway had a gate across it, but the pedestrian gate was unlocked and open. The hummingbird flew over the chain link fence topped with razor wire surrounding the facility and waited within, "tzipping" urgently. Sierra and Chaco (and, presumably, Fred) went through the pedestrian gate, and the bird flew off between rows of storage units, each with a locked and numbered garage-style door. The facility was like a tiny city, with "streets" running in a grid between the buildings. The bird flew down several of these, turning corners as it went. It stopped, hovering, in front of Unit #121, trilling, "Tzip! Tzip!" and then again, "Aiden!"

Sierra and Chaco came to a halt. "Is it telling us that Aiden is in that storage unit?" asked Sierra doubtfully. Suddenly the bird flew straight up, hung suspended for a moment against the blue sky, and sped away.

"Great," said Sierra, staring up at the blank and birdless sky. "Now what?" She looked down. A coyote was sniffing urgently at the door of Unit #121.

"He's in there," Chaco said.

"Can you tell if he's alive?" asked Sierra anxiously.

"No," said Chaco, then at her gasp of dismay, "I mean, no, I can't tell. Fred, where are you?"

"Here," said the mannegishi, popping into view.

"Okay, do any of us know how to pick locks?" asked Chaco.

"No," chorused Fred and Sierra.

"What do you mean, you don't know how to pick locks, Fred?" asked Chaco. "You steal food out of locked cars at Indian Grinding Rock—you could get in here, too."

Well, sure," responded Fred, looking offended. "But I don't know how to pick locks. That's what you asked—do I know how to pick locks. No, I don't." He directed an orange glare at Chaco.

"Just DO IT!" Chaco snarled, his lowered voice in no way obscuring his menacing tone. The padlock immediately clattered to the pavement, accompanied by a smug look from Fred.

"We'd better call Clancy," Chaco said. "Even if he's alive, Aiden's not going to be in good shape. Clancy will handle the police a lot better than we could. And we're probably going to need an ambulance. If we're lucky."

Sierra pulled out her cell phone. When Clancy answered, she explained that she and the others had found Aiden, but they weren't sure what state he was in. She asked Clancy to come to the storage facility as quickly as possible.

"He's on his way," she reported, snapping the phone shut. Then she saw that Chaco was on the alert, ears pricked to listen. Straining to hear what he was hearing, she heard footsteps. Someone was walking past one of the adjacent rows of units. The walker was out of sight for the moment, but the footsteps were coming closer. If the person turned the corner, he or she would be able to see their little group.

"Someone's coming!" she whispered. Chaco was on his four feet, quivering with tension. Sierra assessed the situation. Fred had popped out of sight, so only Sierra and her "dog" could be observed if the walker came down their way.

"Chaco," she hissed, "Sit down and look...more doggy." Chaco sat, looking unhappy. She assumed what she thought was a casual position, leaning against the wall and consulting her wrist-watch as though she were waiting for another person to arrive.

A man in a gray suit turned the corner and stopped. He

reached into his pocket, drawing something out, and said, "Sierra Carter. How nice to see you again."

Before Sierra even looked at him, she knew the voice: Jack Clapper. Her heart pumped wildly, fueled by an adrenalin rush. And when she looked up at him, she saw he was holding an ugly-looking handgun, pointed straight at her. Her mouth went completely dry, and to her disgust, she realized her knees were trembling. She stood, speechless, as Clapper walked toward her, looking relaxed and confident.

Not a tall man, Clapper nonetheless radiated a sense of power. He was well-muscled, evident even beneath the pearl-gray silk business suit he wore, and looked tough and strong. It was the same sense of toughness and strength conveyed by even the smallest of scorpions. His gray eyes under heavy brows were unreadable, and his thin lips were drawn back in smile that had all the affability of an annoyed rattlesnake.

"You've certainly been a busy little bitch today, Sierra," he said in a relaxed, almost easy, tone of voice. "Good thing I saw you down in the parking lot, searching through my car. I sure didn't expect to see you *here*, though." He looked down at the open padlock lying on the concrete.

"Well, well. You managed to get the lock open. I didn't know that your skill set included picking locks. Open the door."

Sierra fumbled with the heavy overhead door. Finally the door slid up on its runners, revealing a jumble of boxes just visible in the gloom of the small space beyond.

"There's a light switch on the right side. Turn it on."

Inside the storage room, it was dark and very hot. She searched for the switch and turned on the light. Before she had a chance to take in the interior of the storage unit, he waved her in with the gun. Chaco followed, just like a dog, with no indication he understood what was happening. Clapper stepped inside as well, and said, "Close the door, Sierra, like a good girl. And no screaming. I'd just as soon shoot you, so don't give me the excuse."

Dumbly, Sierra closed the door, shutting herself off from

the world of sunlight, blue sky, and freedom outside. She looked around anxiously for Aiden. All she could see were boxes. And there was a large trunk, the kind that was once commonly used for long journeys by train or ship. There were dark splotches on the cement floor. In the feeble yellow light emitted by a single bulb hanging from the ceiling, Sierra couldn't tell if the splotches were blood or something less sinister, like oil.

Clapper kept the gun trained on her. "What tipped you off, Sierra? I'd like to know why you decided to ransack my Boxster. I'd also like to know how you ended up here, of all places."

Sierra found her voice. Licking her dry lips, she said, "You wouldn't believe me if I told you, Clapper."

He gestured at her menacingly with the gun. "Try me. You'd be surprised what I would believe. Does the name Tezcatlipoca mean anything to you?"

Sierra gaped at him. She struggled to remember where she had heard that word before. Then she heard Chaco give a low growl by her side. He rose to his feet. His lips were drawn back in a snarl and his fangs were bared. Clapper noticed, but did not shift his gun from Sierra.

"I see your friend there knows the name," he said with a nasty smile. "You can't kill me, Coyotl. Lord Tezcatlipoca shields me from your sort. But your girlfriend here can die. She can die very easily, so stay where you are."

He knows what Chaco is! her brain screamed. And then the name Tezcatlipoca suddenly registered. Quetzalcoatl's brother, the evil brother. The one Chaco and Fred always call Necocyaotl. (Despite the desperate situation, Sierra felt a fleeting moment of pride at having finally remembered the name.) The Obsidian Mirror. Another mental gear turned. And Clapper works for him. Sierra's knees turned to water, and she sat down abruptly on a box.

"No sudden moves!" snarled Clapper. "Unless you want to get shot. You know," he went on in a conversational way, "I never did like you, Carter. Always with the disapproving look when I padded the invoices a tiny bit. You didn't like the clients I took on.

Said that special-interest group from Syria was a terrorist organization. Thought the chemical company in Stanislaus County was a polluter and dumped toxins illegally. Such a priss. I'm glad I fired you." Shifting gears, he went on, "I went to a lot of trouble to get BDSC's business."

"Why, so you could get me fired again?" asked Sierra bitterly.

Clapper smiled again. "Well, that was an added pleasure. I remember all too well how you nosed around the agency, looking for dirt. Simmons and I have a little project going, and we didn't need you sticking your nose into things that don't concern you. But here you are, anyway, peeking and prying. It seems like I just can't keep you away from me. Now, you're going to tell me why you broke into my car, and how you ended up here."

Sierra was saved from replying to this by a faint groan. Chaco's ears swiveled toward the large trunk. Clapper swore. "Damn it! I was sure he was dead. Now I'm going to have to do it all over again." Keeping the gun trained on Sierra, he strode over to the trunk and opened it. From her seat on the box, Sierra could not see what was in the trunk. She shuddered, wondering how badly Aiden was hurt.

Clapper switched the gun to his left hand, allowing him to reach into the trunk with his right. *Was he going to strangle Aiden?* Sierra wondered with horror. Abruptly, he jerked his hand away, screamed and began batting the air near his expensively trousered leg. As Clapper slapped at his leg, he fumbled, and the gun spun away across the floor. Chaco was on him in a flash, sinking his fangs into Clapper's other leg as Sierra dived for the gun. She grabbed it with both hands and rolled across the floor to avoid the scrimmage between Clapper and Chaco.

She saw with amazement that although Chaco's bite apparently had not wounded Clapper, the man's other leg was bleeding profusely from a ragged gash in the calf. His trousers were torn, and blood poured down his leg and onto the concrete floor. She aimed the gun at Clapper and said, "OK, Chaco. I've got the gun. You can let him go now." As Chaco backed away, still snarling and with fur bristling, Fred appeared next to Clapper's bleeding leg. He opened his tiny, pursed mouth wide, and a set of wicked, snaggled, needlelike teeth emerged and sank into Clapper's other calf. The man gave another piercing scream and struck at the mannegishi. Fred whipped out of the way easily as another stream of blood began to stain the floor.

"Fred! That's enough. Though I thank you from the bottom of my heart. You're a *good* mannegishi," Sierra said. Fred backed away from the whimpering Clapper and sat upright, looking pleased. Chaco morphed into human form. He hurried over to the open trunk and looked in. A sharp intake of breath told Sierra that the news was not good.

"He's in really bad shape, Sierra," Chaco reported. "He's alive, but barely. We have to get him to a hospital, fast."

"What *IS* that thing?" moaned Clapper, vainly trying to staunch the flow of blood from his calves with his hands.

"Use your Hermès tie, why don't you?" suggested Sierra. "That's Fred. And that's all you need to know about him. Now shut up. We're busy."

"Aiden's all tied up in duct tape," said Chaco. "I think we ought to get the tape off him and get him out of this trunk. I'm going to need some help here."

Sierra pulled out her cell phone and dialed 911, reporting that a man was in a serious medical condition, and no, she didn't know what had happened to him. She gave the particulars of their location and hung up. "They'll be here in a few minutes," she said. "I can't help you *and* keep this weasel covered. Can you tie Clapper up, Chaco? I'll bet there's more duct tape around here somewhere."

Hastily, Chaco began opening boxes. Looking into the third box he pried open, he gave a triumphant shout. "Sierra! The feathers! They're in here." He turned to her, three silver feathers shining on his brown palm. She pocketed them under Clapper's baleful glare. Then a thought occurred to her.

"If you touched these feathers, they would have freed you

from Necocyaotl's influence. How did you get the feathers without coming under Quetzalcoatl's influence?"

Clapper favored her with a scornfully curled lip. "You've heard of gloves?" he asked. Sierra didn't bother to reply, but she was troubled by a further thought: if a pair of gloves could circumvent Quetzalcoatl's power, did she really have any chance of getting the feathers into contact with Jenna Simmons? This tiny question swiftly burgeoned into full-blown doubt.

"If you know about the feathers, I suppose Simmons knows about them, too?" she asked, working hard to keep her voice under control.

Clapper looked back at her with disgust. "Of course she knows, you little idiot. Lord Tezcatlipoca has eyes everywhere. He told us days ago, and sent Tzintzimitl and me to retrieve them. Our master has a use for them."

"Oh, really?" returned Sierra. "What might that be?" But Clapper just smirked at her.

Chaco found a roll of duct tape in the box and began to unwind it. The thick tape came away with difficulty, and Chaco struggled with it as he approached Clapper. Suddenly, the man lunged at Chaco and grabbed him, holding the Avatar in front as a shield between himself and the gun Sierra was holding. He had Chaco's right arm bent behind his back in a painful hold.

"Don't even think about it, Coyotl," said Clapper. "You can't hurt me. But I *can* hurt you." Indeed, as Chaco struggled against the hold Clapper had on his arm, he appeared to grow weaker. Sierra watched in horror as Chaco began to droop in the man's arms.

"Shoot, Sierra," panted Chaco. "Bullets can't harm me."

"Better not," warned Clapper. "I have protections that weaken him. Shoot me, and you kill Coyotl." He kicked out at Fred, who nimbly skipped away. "Stay away from me, you little horror," snarled Clapper. "I'll break his arm if you move." Fred crept to Sierra's feet, eyes whirling wildly in distress.

Sierra stood, wavering, then dropped the hand holding the pistol. "Sierra!" cried Chaco. "Shoot! Please!" But she could not bring herself to do it. In her mind's eye, she saw his lifeless body, as it had been after the attack of Tzintzimitl, but this time, with his red blood leaking his life away on the dirty floor of the storage unit.

"Good girl, Carter," approved Clapper. "Now stay right where you are. Slide the gun over to me. Carefully—we wouldn't want any accidents to happen, now, would we?" Sierra placed the gun gently on the floor and gave it a push. It spun around as it slid across the floor, ending up at Clapper's feet. He gave a sharp tug upward on Chaco's arm and a simultaneous shove. There was an audible crunch, and Chaco screamed as he sprawled on the floor. Clapper bent swiftly, picked up the gun and sprinted for the door. He had it open partway, ducked, and was under it in an instant.

As Clapper's halting steps receded in the distance, Sierra knelt by Chaco, who was rolling in agony, cradling his arm. He had tears of pain in his eyes. "Go see to Aiden," he hissed between clenched teeth. "I'll be all right, but he's dying."

Sierra looked into the trunk for the first time. Aiden was bound in a cramped, fetal position. He was unconscious, his face a swollen mass of dark bruises. His arms had been bound in a prayerful position in front of him, and his hands were purple and swollen as well. Several of his fingers were obviously broken. Sierra could not tell if he was breathing, but the earlier faint groan proved that he still lived.

Quickly, with trembling fingers, Sierra began searching for the ends of the tape and ripping it off him, starting with the piece taped cruelly over his mouth. Beneath the tape, Aiden's lips were split, bleeding where the tape had re-opened earlier wounds. The tough tape came away reluctantly, and she was fearful of causing Aiden pain or additional injury. If only she had a pair of scissors! Then she remembered Fred's astonishing dental equipment. "Fred!" she called. "Help me with this." Carefully, they gradually tipped the trunk over on its side, and Fred helped her move Aiden out onto the floor, inch by painful inch.

"Do you think you can bite through this stuff without hurting Aiden?" Sierra asked. Fred came to Aiden's side and began gnawing delicately on the tape. It parted like tissue paper beneath his razor-like fangs. Sierra pulled the tape away as it was severed. Once free of their bindings, Aiden's arms and legs sagged into more natural positions and his color, she thought, improved slightly under the bruises.

As they pulled the last of the tape away, the partially open door was abruptly yanked up from the outside and bright daylight blinded them. Sierra squinted her eyes against the light and cringed, thinking that Jack Clapper had returned to kill them all. Silhouetted against the light was a man's tall figure.

CHAPTER 28

Clancy surveyed the little group inside the storage unit. "Have you called an ambulance?" he asked when he saw the unconscious Aiden. Sierra nodded.

"Just a couple of minutes ago," she replied.

Clancy noted the blood pooled on the floor. He glanced sharply at Sierra, and finding her intact, scanned Chaco, who was lying on the floor, cradling his right arm with his left.

"Are you hurt?" he asked, as he moved closer to inspect Chaco. "Is that your blood?"

"That's Clapper's blood," said Sierra. "Clapper was about to murder Aiden, and Fred bit him. Oh, and Chaco bit him, too. That's where the blood came from." Fred blushed a deep shade of viridian and modestly lowered his eyes.

"What a handy guy to have around," Clancy said, kneeling next to Aiden and feeling for his pulse, fingers at the corner of Aiden's jaw. "Pulse weak, but still there," he said. "He looks to be in pretty bad shape, though." He rose from his knees and turned his attentions to Chaco.

"What happened, Chaco?"

"I think Clapper dislocated my shoulder," said Chaco between gritted teeth. "I don't think I ever hurt so much before. Avatars don't get hurt much," he added glumly. "I'm not used to pain."

"OK. Let's get you on your feet. I saw this work once. Maybe it'll work again," said Clancy, holding out a hand. Chaco looked up at him apprehensively.

"Do you know how to relocate a dislocated shoulder?" he asked dubiously. "It always looks so painful when they do it on TV."

"Nope," said Clancy. "But I promise not to hurt you. Grab a hand." Chaco used his good left hand to grasp Clancy's hand, and got to his feet. He was still eyeing Clancy nervously.

"Bend over at the waist. Ninety degrees," said Clancy. "Let your arms dangle." Chaco followed suit.

"Hurts," he said in a muffled voice, his dark hair falling into his face.

Sierra could see the unnatural hump of Chaco's dislocated right shoulder and it made her slightly queasy. Suddenly, the lumpiness slid away.

"It's back in!" Chaco exclaimed. He stood slowly upright and carefully moved his arm. "Thank you, Clancy. Where'd you learn how to do that?"

"Long story and not enough time. You need to get lost. The ambulance will be here soon, and this is obviously a police matter. It's going to be hard to explain all this, so you'd better be gone."

"But what about you? Won't the police want to know what *you're* doing here?" asked Sierra.

"Easier for me than for you or Chaco. I doubt that Chaco has any legal identification, for one thing. Birth certificate? Driver's license?" Chaco shook his head. "Thought not. And the blood on the floor—they're going to be really curious about that. Anyway, the police already know about Clapper's car, and the blood in it. They know I was looking for him. I'll just say I followed him here, walked in after he got the door open, and found Aiden like this, but no Clapper."

"Do you think they'll buy it?" asked Sierra, dubiously.

"Well, they know me. They might not like it, but they won't grill me about it. Not right now. Anyway," he added, "You'd better skedaddle. I hear a siren."

And Sierra heard it, too, distant at the moment, but quickly getting closer. Fred winked out of existence and Chaco became a coyote again. They walked rapidly back the way they had come, peering cautiously around the final corner at the front entrance. They were too late—the ambulance was driving down the street toward the front gate, sirens blasting and lights flashing. Behind them came a police cruiser, also in full alarm mode.

Sierra shrank back around the corner. "Now what?" she groaned. Chaco had taken in the situation as well. "Follow me!" he said and began loping awkwardly back down the alleyway, favoring his right front leg. Sierra ran after him, lagging far behind on her two human feet. Fred would never be able to keep up, she thought, and stopped. She could hear Fred, panting and wheezing some yards behind her, and the slap of his stubby, six-toed (or fingered?) paws on the asphalt.

"Fred! Where are you?" she whispered, holding out her arms at Fred-level. Fred materialized a mere few feet from Sierra, and a nanosecond later, she felt as though she had been hit with a bag of wet cement as he leaped into her arms. Grunting, she straightened and looked for Chaco, arms full of Fred. Chaco was nowhere to be seen.

Sierra began running, slower now that she was burdened with thirty pounds of mannegishi. She ducked down one alleyway and then another, hoping to avoid being seen. Finally she came to the end of one of the alleys, terminating at the chain link fence that surrounded the facility. A space ran between the blank rear walls of the storage units and the fence. On the other side of the fence was a vacant lot, thick with tall weeds drying in the late spring heat.

Chaco suddenly appeared out of the weeds on the other side of the fence. "Down this way," he whispered, running along the fence to the right. Sierra followed him and soon saw the shallow trough he had dug under the fence.

"I can't get under there," she said. "Fred, you go first." Clods of dirt displaced as the mannegishi slid under the chain-link fence and scuttled into the weeds. He might as well have disappeared; his gray-green skin blended invisibly into the weedy background. Then Chaco began digging frantically to enlarge the opening. But his right foreleg was obviously painful, hampering his efforts. Sierra started pulling at the bottom of the fence, trying to bend it up to make more room. She could hear voices coming from the maze of alleyways that ran through the facility, and they seemed to be getting closer. She tugged desperately at the wire, decided it was now or never, and fell to her stomach. She used her elbows to drag herself forward under the points of the fence wire, never noticing as pebbles scraped her skin. Then, halfway through, one of the wire points caught her jeans belt loop, holding her fast.

"Chaco! Help!" she hissed at him, hearing the voices growing louder. Chaco's teeth sheared through the tough denim, releasing her. She squirmed the rest of the way under the fence and rolled into the tall weeds just as two police officers, a man and a woman, emerged from the mouth of an alleyway. Their voices were clear, though Sierra couldn't hear every word. The police looked up and down the narrow space between the walls and the fence.

"...ask me, maybe they're in on it," said the woman's voice.

"Naw," said the man. "They were in the back office, smoking weed. Didn't you smell it?"

"...a cold," said the woman. "Hey! Look at that."

"What? It's just a stray dog."

Chaco slunk into the weeds and lay carefully down beside Sierra. Though his sides shuddered with his panting, he was completely silent.

"I could've sworn it was a coyote," the woman said.

"What if it was? C'mon, we're wasting time. We've got the rest of this dump to search." The two turned back down the alleyway and their voices receded. Sierra waited for several moments, then rose and began to run across the vacant lot. She nearly fell flat on her face when her jeans fell down around her knees. Chaco's teeth had sliced through not just the belt loop, but the waistband of her jeans. She hauled them north, and kept going with what dignity she could muster. When she reached the sidewalk, she began sauntering nonchalantly down the sidewalk, away from the storage facility. Chaco ran out of the weeds to follow her, now in human form.

"Why are you poking along like that?" he whispered urgently. "We've got to get away from here!"

"We're just an innocent couple out for a walk," Sierra responded. "No one's going to notice us. Unless we run. Then everyone will notice us. Just take it slow and easy."

"You don't think anybody will notice that you're holding up your jeans with both hands as you walk?" Chaco put his left arm around Sierra's waist and grabbed her waistband. "There. That's a little more natural looking. You can let go, now."

Sierra walked alongside Chaco, feeling as though they had entered a four-legged version of a three-legged race. They walked down the street and took the first intersection. In a couple of blocks, they were back in the district of tilt-up office buildings. They walked several more blocks, without any clear idea of where they were going, but heading back in the general direction of Sierra's house. No one else was out walking in this part of town.

A car drove down the street behind them, and abruptly, Chaco's arm tightened around her waist with an iron grip. He pulled her close, leaned down and kissed her deeply. Sierra brought her hand up to his chest, intending to deliver a mighty shove and maybe follow that up with a resounding slap across his beautiful face, but he grasped her hand and held it tight against his chest.

"Shut up. Don't move. Cops," he murmured between her lips.

Sierra began to respond with more enthusiasm than she would have thought possible a mere second before. She heard two car doors open, and after a moment, an impatient-sounding throat clearing.

"Excuse me, sorry to interrupt..."

Chaco released Sierra from his embrace, but managed to hold on to her waistband. He looked around with a surprised expression and said, "Oh, hi. We didn't see you, officer. Wassup?"

A police cruiser was parked near them, both doors open. A somewhat red-faced police officer was standing on the sidewalk, both hands at his belt. His partner was standing on the other side of the cruiser as though using it as a shield.

The red-faced cop said, "Have you been out walking long?"

Chaco cast his eyes upward, considering. "Yes, well, about fifteen or twenty minutes. Or so."

"Have you seen anything unusual?"

Chaco contrived to look innocently puzzled. His eyes grew wide and his brow furrowed. Sierra hoped he wasn't going to overdo it. "Like what, officer?"

"Just unusual. Seen anybody running, or doing anything strange?"

"Nope," said Chaco cheerfully. "It's been pretty dull. Oh, not you, baby," he said solicitously to Sierra. "You're the most exciting thing around."

The red-faced cop rolled his eyes to the heavens as though asking the gods to spare him. "OK, fine. Thanks." He wiped his face and shook his head at his partner. They climbed back into their cruiser and drove away.

"That was very quick thinking," Sierra said, adding, "Baby." Chaco just grinned.

"You know," he said, "You can still take me up on my offer. That was a very nice kiss. Mmmmm!"

Sierra eyed him coldly. "I thought you and Kaylee had a thing going," she said.

"Well, we're more like *planning* on having a thing going. It's been kind of busy lately," responded Chaco cheerfully. "But Kaylee's...not the jealous type."

"Well, I am!" she retorted.

They continued their elaborately casual stroll, Chaco's arm still around her waist doing suspender duty. It was a warm day, and Chaco's proximity created more body heat than was strictly comfortable. Both were hot and sticky, but they arrived at Sierra's house with no further incidents.

After several glasses of cold water all around, Sierra applied an ice pack to Chaco's shoulder. "Do Avatars take ibuprofen?" she asked him.

"I don't know," he replied. "I've never needed it before. But I'll have some now." She gave him some tablets, handed him the ice pack, and jerry-rigged a sling from one of her scarves.

Then they sat at Sierra's kitchen table, talking about what had happened. "What about Kaylee?" Chaco asked suddenly.

"What do you mean?" Sierra said.

"If Clapper saw us in the parking lot, messing with his car, he must have seen Kaylee with us," Chaco said. "She's in danger, too. Where is she?"

"She went back to work," Sierra said. She called Kaylee's work number, but got voice mail. Worried, she tried Kaylee's home phone and got the answering machine. Now with cold chills running up and down her spine, she called Kaylee's cell phone, and to her vast relief, Kaylee answered. Quickly, she filled Kaylee in on the afternoon's events.

"And Kaylee, he must have seen you and Clancy down in the parking lot with us. So that means that you're both in danger as long as he's on the loose," she concluded.

"Okay. I'll be careful," Kaylee replied, sounding completely unworried. "What about Clancy?"

"Clancy knows about him, and anyway, he's got a gun. I think you ought to come over here and stay with us. I hate to think of you being all alone right now. Here," she handed the phone to Chaco. "Get her to come over here."

Chaco took the phone and went into the living room, where they could hear his coaxing tones, but not the words. Before long, he was back in the kitchen. "She's on the way over," he said, looking quietly satisfied with himself. "And while we're thinking about it, let's make sure everything is locked up." He went from door to door and from window to window, checking. "Locked up tighter than Fort Knox," he reported, just as the doorbell rang.

Sierra, feeling increasingly unsettled by the notion of a murderous Jack Clapper at large, peered cautiously through the peephole in the door. Clancy stood on her doorstep, looking solid, strong, and reassuringly calm. She unlocked the door and stepped forward with both arms out. As she had not yet changed out of her Chaco-modified jeans, they dropped around her knees.

"I don't think I've ever before seen a woman this glad to see me," said Clancy, his eyes appreciatively traveling down her exposed thighs.

Her cheeks flamed as she winched her jeans up and held out a single arm, holding the waistband firmly with her other hand. He put both of his arms around her.

"You're just full of surprises, aren't you?" he said against her hair, and she realized he was laughing. She was too relieved to mind.

"Boy, am I glad to see you," she sighed, feeling momentarily safe within the enclosure of his arms. He held her for a few moments, then released her.

"I'm glad to see you, too," he said. "There were cops all over the place, once they saw Aiden. They called in reinforcements. I was worried that they'd pick you up as suspicious characters on the way back." They stepped inside and went to the kitchen where Chaco was waiting.

"Well, some cops did stop us," Sierra said. "But they just wanted to know if we'd seen anything strange. Then they left." *No need to go into Chaco's little ploy*, she thought, giving Chaco a stern glance and hoping he would take the hint. "How is Aiden? Will he be all right?"

"He's in intensive care at El Camino Hospital," said Clancy. "Concussion, some broken bones, maybe internal injuries. The worst of it is actually severe dehydration. But with luck he'll be fine. Tell me how you met him, Sierra."

Sierra explained their camping expedition to Indian Grinding Rock, meeting Fred, the vandalizing of her camp, and Aiden's subsequent surprise visit.

"Then he asked me what it was like working for Jack Clapper," she concluded. "I never mentioned Clapper to him by name, so that seemed suspicious to me. I threw him out."

Clancy nodded at this. "Turns out, meeting him probably

wasn't a coincidence," he said. "Aiden is actually Agent Aiden Sullivan, of the FBI." He looked at their thunderstruck faces.

"FBI!" Sierra exclaimed. "Why would the FBI be bothering with me?"

"Not you," Clancy corrected. "Clapper. Apparently Aiden was investigating him. He contrived meeting you to ask questions about Clapper. Do you happen to know why the FBI might be taking an interest?"

"I always thought he was sleazy," Sierra replied. "I thought he took on clients who weren't on the up-and-up. And I know he padded the bills."

"What kind of clients?"

"Well, one of them was a Syrian special-interest group. I thought they might be connected to terrorists, maybe a front that funneled money to fund terrorist activities. And there was a chemical company that I thought was dumping toxic waste..."

"And you knew about this?" demanded Clancy, eyes narrowed. "Why didn't you report it to the police?"

"No! All I had were suspicions. I had no documentation, no proof at all. What would your friends the police do with a bunch of unfounded allegations?"

"Nothing," admitted Clancy, softening. "You're right. Sorry."

"Hmph," Sierra said. She was a bit stung by Clancy's manner and wasn't eager to forgive. "Anyway, I guess I wasn't too subtle about not liking what Clapper was doing, because he fired me, and then he moved to New York and that was the last I heard from him. Until Black Diamond hired his firm and booted me out."

The doorbell rang again. "That's Kaylee," said Sierra quickly, and rose to answer the door. But Clancy waved her away.

"I'll get it," he said. He drew his handgun and went to the door, looking through the peephole. Then he relaxed, sheathed his gun, and opened the door to Kaylee. Sierra was happy to see that Kaylee had brought a sleeping bag. When she insisted that her friend come to stay, she hadn't considered that her sleeping arrangements were all taken—including the sofas.

The kitchen table could no longer accommodate everyone, so they repaired to the living room. Clancy was still asking questions, and Sierra was having trouble remembering what she had told him and what she hadn't. She finally started over from the beginning, trying not to leave anything out.

"...so I was making a necklace from the silver feathers. When the feathers come into contact with her skin, that's supposed to liberate her soul—or something—from Necocyaotl."

Clancy asked to see the feathers and she dug them out of her jeans pocket and placed them in his hand. He looked down at them, shining softly on his palm.

"I don't feel any different," he said, dubiously.

"Well, that's a *good* thing," Sierra said. "It means that you aren't influenced by Necocyaotl."

"Well, I guess you'd better get to work. I think I might be able to help you with getting the feathers to Simmons," Clancy said, standing up and handing the silver feathers back to Sierra.

She looked up at him hopelessly. "Thanks, but I don't think it's going to do any good at this point," she said.

"Why not?"

"For a start, don't you think that Clapper will tell Simmons that I have the feathers back? I don't think she's going to let anyone walk up to her and drape a necklace around her neck. As a matter of fact, I haven't got the faintest idea of *what* to do at this point. It seems like the whole plan is pretty much blown."

Clancy sat down again, and Sierra saw the realization dawning on every face. Chaco buried his dark head in his hands. Kaylee groaned and did likewise. There were several long moments of silence.

Finally, Chaco spoke. "Well, I guess we'll just have to come up with another plan, then. Let's start laying out some new ideas." He looked hopefully around the room.

There was a prolonged bout of silence as the evening shadows crowded around Sierra's little house. Finally, Kaylee spoke.

"Where's Fred?" she asked, looking around the room.

CHAPTER 29

For a moment they all looked blankly at one other.

"Fred?" called Kaylee. "Fred, are you here?" There was no response. Sierra ran upstairs, calling the mannegishi. Chaco, morphing quickly, began pacing through the house, black nose quivering, while Kaylee and Clancy searched the garage and the small yard. Finally, they all reassembled in the living room shaking their heads and looking worried.

"When was the last time you remember being with Fred?" Clancy asked Sierra and Chaco.

Sierra said, "I was carrying him at the storage facility. He scrambled under the fence before me. Chaco had to make the hole bigger for me, but it was plenty big enough for Fred."

"Did you talk to him at all on the way back?" asked Clancy.

"I don't remember. Do you remember talking to Fred, Chaco?"

"Nope. I just assumed he was with us, and what with the cops and everything, I didn't really think about him until just now," Chaco responded.

"Where do you suppose he is?" fretted Sierra. "Maybe he got lost on the way home. Or maybe something happened to him!" He had been so brave and helpful to them in dealing with Clapper. How could she have forgotten about him?

"Well, there's really no point in looking for him," said Clancy, reasonably. "Fred is invisible when he wants to be. Maybe he just feels like being invisible right now."

Kaylee shook her head. "That doesn't sound like Fred at all," she observed. "If he were here, he'd be wanting food. We'd have heard from him by now."

"You're right," admitted Sierra, with another pang of guilt. She imagined Fred wandering the hot streets, famished and thirsty.

Chaco said, "Fred's a big mannegishi. He can take care of himself. He's been doing it for millennia. And don't forget those teeth. He'll show up when he's ready." He scooted a little closer to Kaylee on the sofa and leaned forward. "We ought to be making plans, not worrying about Fred."

"That's right," said Clancy. "We need to figure out what to do next, now that Plan A is apparently a no-go."

A long and gloomy silence followed as they pondered the situation. Finally, Sierra retrieved pads of paper and pens from her desk, which she passed out to everyone.

"Let's brainstorm," she suggested. "All ideas are welcome. There are no bad ideas. Let's just get them down on paper."

They sat for several more minutes, pens poised and brows furrowed. No one wrote anything, although Kaylee began listlessly doodling. The silence was so complete that Sierra could hear the ticking of her kitchen clock, even from the living room. Every tick seemed to underscore the fact that no one appeared to have any useful ideas. Or even any wild and crazy ideas.

Finally, Clancy set his pen down and looked around. "Okay," he said. "Let's just reset and start over from the top. Jenna Simmons, our esteemed leader"—here he glanced at Sierra and Kaylee—"... is a servant of, um, Necocoyote."

Chaco sighed gustily. "Necocyaotl."

"Of Necocyaotl, right. Necocyaotl is trying to get humanity to destroy itself, apparently because he just enjoys that kind of thing." He glanced at Chaco. "Right so far?" Chaco nodded.

"Okay. Jenna is using Necocyaotl's obsidian, imbued with his evil essence, to make products that are incorporated in electronic devices everywhere, all around the world. These products emit some sort of, um, field? Radiation? Aura?..."

"Magic," said Chaco, and Clancy looked as though he had bitten into a chocolate, only to find a worm at the center.

"Magic, then," he said, letting the word drop from his lips

with distaste. "Some sort of magic that enraptures people, causes them to—what? Ignore the consequences of what they're doing?" He looked at Chaco again. Sierra and Kaylee said nothing, but Sierra nodded.

"That sums it up, I guess," responded Chaco. "We call it *looking into the obsidian mirror*. They see only themselves, and care only about their own short-term gratification. They don't see or don't care about the consequences to other beings or to the earth."

"Right. So that explains why people do stupid stuff like dumping toxins or storing radioactive materials in caves, where it can leak into groundwater supplies," Clancy said. "What I don't understand is why some people still do smart things, or unselfish things, like banning chlorofluorocarbons or developing alternative fuels. You can't tell me these people don't have cell phones or microwaves."

"I don't know," said Chaco serenely. "Why do some people get colds all the time, and other people don't? Maybe some people have a sort of psychic immune system."

Clancy pondered this briefly. "It would be worth finding out why," he said, finally. "But I don't think it enters into our current problem. So Quetzalcoatl, Necocyaotl's good twin, calls on Sierra to stop Jenna Simmons. He gives her several, um, *magical* feathers that will exorcise the influence of the evil twin if they come into contact with Jenna's skin.

"Now we come to the part I don't understand—I mean, *one* of the parts I don't understand. This other evil avatar, Zin-Zin—the one that is presumably in cahoots with Necocyaotl—comes to the house with Jack Clapper, Sierra's old boss, and Clapper steals the feathers. Clapper is working with Simmons and is part of the gang. We know he attacked Aiden Sullivan and tried his best to kill him. So far, it makes a weird kind of sense.

"But someone else was also looking for the feathers: Chris Jumlin. Jumlin is one of the bad guys. He eats people, he tried to sacrifice Sierra, and apparently he is also a worshipper of Necocyaotl. But Jumlin didn't know that Clapper had stolen the feathers—he thought Sierra still had them. If Jumlin's part of the

Necocyaotl gang, why didn't he know? Why was he looking for the feathers, and what was he going to do with them if he found them? How does Jumlin fit in with the rest of what's going on?"

There was silence for a few minutes. "Maybe he *isn't* in with the rest of them," Sierra suggested. "Maybe he's not one of the inner circle." Another period of silence greeted this speculation. Then Sierra shook her head. "I still don't get it," she said. "Jumlin worships Necocyaotl. He called him 'Lord Tezcatlipoca.' He has his creepy dungeon set up with an altar to him. He was going to sacrifice me to Necocyaotl. How could he not be in with the rest of them?"

After several minutes, Clancy sighed and said, "Well, maybe we should set Jumlin aside for the moment and concentrate on the main crew. The problem at hand is how to get the feathers into contact with Simmons, now that the, ah, bad guys understand our strategy. Alternatively, how do we accomplish the same thing without using the feathers?"

"I wish we could communicate with Quetzalcoatl," Sierra said, with an edge of irritation in her voice. "It would be a lot easier to know how to do this if we had some good advice. Or better still, some *help*." She turned to Chaco. "Short of sacrificing Henrietta there, how do you get in touch with him?"

Chaco looked confused, "Henrietta?"

"Yes, the chicken," Sierra explained. "Sacrificing a chicken is not going to happen. So how do you normally communicate with him?"

Chaco continued to look confused. "I don't," he said simply.

"What do you mean?" Sierra queried on a rising note. "How do you tell him what's going on?" Everyone looked inquisitively at Chaco, who began to exchange his confused expression for an embarrassed one.

"It doesn't work like that," he muttered, looking at his feet as though he had never seen anything so interesting before. "You mortals always think it's all...*organized*, or something. Like a business. But it's not like that at all. Q has his interests, I have mine.

Sometimes we work together, and sometimes not. When he doesn't want to be found, nobody can find him. Not even me." He looked at Sierra, as though willing her to understand.

Sierra looked at him in disbelief. "You mean that you don't have any way to communicate with Quetzalcoatl?" Chaco shook his dark head. "What kind of a way is that to run a world?" she demanded angrily. "I was counting on Q to help us out if we got into trouble. Now you're saying he doesn't want to be found? He's leaving us high and dry? He started this mess, and now he's just gone *fishing*?" her voice reached a pitch of outrage so high that it almost came out as a squeak.

For the first time, the look that Chaco gave her was cold. Although to the eye, he was still an impossibly beautiful young man, his presence now filled the room. The waning light outside faded completely, and the room became dark. Chaco seemed to grow, taking on a persona that was remote, ancient, and powerful, and his eyes burned like molten gold in the dark room. There was no trace of the amiable youth that Sierra knew. Kaylee, seated beside Chaco, shrank away, though her eyes never left his face. The others were equally mesmerized, sitting utterly still with startled and wary faces. Sierra heard a roaring in her ears, and her awareness seemed to narrow down to the twin suns of Chaco's eyes.

As though from a great distance, she heard a voice. It was as loud as the roaring of the wind in a great storm and yet also as quiet as the tunneling of worms through leaf mold. "The Plumed Serpent did not lay waste to this planet. His work is his work, and not for you to know. My work is my work, and not for you to know. Your people, and your people alone, have given themselves to the Obsidian Mirror. It is for your people to set it right again. Do it or don't do it. But do not wag your little finger at the Old Ones and lay your blame at *our* door."

The silence that followed was the stillness of the desert, where there are no trees to sough in the wind, in the remote arroyos where the cars and airplanes and other devices of man's making never intrude. The room gradually returned to the everyday twilight of impending night. Chaco slumped on the sofa and sighed—a small sound in the stillness.

"Please don't make me do that again," he said wearily. He lifted his eyes, no longer burning suns, but merely the warm, friendly amber they had always been. "That really takes it out of me." He moved closer to Kaylee and put an arm around her shoulders. She eyed him with eyes so wide that the whites showed all around her pupils, but did not move away.

After a respectful few minutes had passed, Sierra said quietly, "Chaco, you're right that people have done the damage. But Necocyaotl isn't human. How can we go up against something so powerful, with so many agents working for him? We are only human, after all."

"That's right," Clancy chimed in. "How can he—or you—expect us to combat magic? We have nothing that we can use in return. Except for the feathers, and I don't know how we can use them, now."

"But that is what you must do, nonetheless," Chaco said. "It's just the way the world works. It's the way that magic works, too. You broke it, you fix it."

"I didn't break it!" said Kaylee. "Neither did Sierra, or Clancy. Why do we get the job of saving the world?" She looked at Chaco rebelliously.

"No, you didn't break it," Chaco said. "You're missing the point. And you and Clancy aren't the ones who have to do it. Quetzalcoatl chose Sierra. Q gave her his feathers, and maybe more besides. You're only here because you *want* to be here."

"And I'm the only one who doesn't have any choice in the matter? Is that it?" snapped Sierra. The awe that accompanied Chaco's transformation into something—other—had waned slightly, though she would not forget the experience.

Chaco turned his eyes to hers. "You *always* have a choice," he said. "You just have to decide if you're willing to take the consequences."

Sierra buried her head in her hands. "I don't know!" she cried.

"I mean, no, I don't want to see Necocyaotl win. But I don't...
know...what...to...do!"

Clancy stood, apparently intending to go to Sierra to comfort
her, but just as he straightened up, the doorbell rang. He tensed
like a nervous cat. His hand went to his holster. "I'll get it," he
said grimly, and went to the front door. The others heard a brief
murmur, then the door shut, and they heard the sound of Clancy
locking the deadbolt. He came back into the living room, carrying
a small package, which he handed to Sierra.

Sierra held the package on her lap. She couldn't remember
ordering anything lately, and the address was unfamiliar. "Where
is Lee Vining, California?" she asked.

"Eastern Sierras," responded Clancy. "East of Yosemite, on
Mono Lake. High desert. I've camped out there. Lee Vining is just
a wide spot in the road, really."

"What could this be?" Sierra wondered aloud, tearing off the
clear plastic tape that sealed the box. She opened the flaps and
pulled out something flat and white, wrapped in bubble wrap,
which she peeled away. She picked up the contents, and drew out
a single sheet of paper and read it. Gasping, she dropped the white
object, which fell to the floor and broke in half as the sheet of
paper floated onto the floor.

"Fred!" Sierra rasped, fighting back tears. "They've got Fred!"

CHAPTER 30

"What?" exclaimed Chaco. "How is that possible?" He leaned down to pick up the two pieces of the object Sierra had dropped. As he slid the pieces together, everyone crowded around to see. It was a rounded pancake made of plaster of Paris. Kaylee remembered making something like it in grade school as a Mother's Day gift, imprinted with the shape of her six-year-old hand. Embedded in the center was the impression of a small, six-fingered paw, similar to a salamander's foot, with rounded ends to the digits. It was unmistakably a cast of one of Fred's paws.

"What does the note say?" asked Clancy quietly. Sierra mutely handed him the paper.

"'We've got your little green friend,'" he read. "'If you don't do exactly as we say, the next package will contain his actual paw. Then each of his paws, one by one. Then bits of the rest of him, one bit at a time. So don't screw around with us. Sierra Carter is to come ALONE to the location on the map.'" Clancy turned the paper over. There was a map printed on the reverse side. He flipped the paper again. "'...to the location on the map. You will receive further instructions there. Be there by noon tomorrow, WITH THE FEATHERS, or you'll get another special delivery.'"

"Is it signed?" asked Kaylee. Clancy shook his head.

"No, there's just this little drawing." He held up the paper for them to see. At the bottom of the printed note, there was a small drawing:

K.D. KEENAN

Chaco craned forward to take a closer look. "That's Necocyaotl's sign," he said softly. "It's actually the glyph that means 'Two Reed,' which was used for the spring sacrifice to Necocyaotl."

Sierra viewed the small glyph with distaste. The blocky, stylized shape reminded her of the bloody murals lining the walls of Necocyaotl's stone temple. "Well," she said, "I guess I'd better get going. Noon tomorrow? Can I make it, Clancy?"

In a decisive tone of voice, Clancy said, "You can't go there alone, Sierra. These people are thugs. Murderers. You can't go. It's too dangerous."

Sierra stared at him. Of all the people—and beings—in the room, she knew best exactly how dangerous it was. She knew Jack Clapper. She knew Jenna Simmons. And she had encountered some of Necocyaotl's other friends, as well. Something shifted inside her, as though the tumblers of a lock were shifting open. She straightened in her seat.

"Didn't you hear what Chaco said? Quetzalcoatl called me. He asked *me* for help. He believes that I can do it. And Fred is in danger!" She felt her throat close with emotion and stopped to recover herself. No tears, not now. Things had gone too far. "I don't think for a moment that I'm equipped for this, but I have to go," she concluded quietly.

The arguments that followed lasted until Sierra, firmly and with finality, cut them off, pointing out that she didn't have much time to drive out to Mono Lake, and that being late might cost Fred his life—and would certainly cost him a paw. After that, the little group put their heads together and did some serious planning.

• • •

It was a long drive, especially at night. The road through the Sierras, bisecting Yosemite National Park and bypassing Yosemite Valley altogether, was pitch dark on a moonless night. Sierra could see only looming darkness on either side, relieved by moments of terror when deer flashed into the headlights as they sprang into

246

the road. Sierra drove cautiously, peering intently ahead. She kept the radio on to keep herself awake and as a substitute for company in the car. She missed having someone in the car to talk to, and resorted to singing along to the music on the radio. And she tried not to give way to her fears about Fred.

Eventually, she hit the long grade down into the Mono basin. She could see no lights as she descended, but as the grade began to level out, lights began to appear by the side of the road, which eventually ended as it intersected Route 120. The sign informed her that a left turn would take her into Lee Vining, where the package had been posted, while a right turn would take her to Mammoth Lakes. Dawn hadn't yet broken, and she couldn't see the lake or anything much beyond the glare of her headlights. She consulted a map briefly. The rendezvous site was south, in the direction of Mammoth, but she needed to pull off the road and get some sleep. She would never be able to recognize the landmarks given in the note as long as it was dark. She turned south on 120 and soon encountered a sign for the Mono Lake Tufa State Reserve. Sierra had never been to Mono Lake before, but like most Californians, she was aware of the weird stone accretions called tufa that grew out of Mono's salty, alkaline waters.

As she drove cautiously down the dark road, she began to look for a place to pull off and nap. There were no lights and no sign of people around, but she knew that if a ranger or sheriff discovered her, she would be an unwelcome guest outside designated camping areas in the state park. She hadn't seen a sign for camping since leaving Yosemite. *Well, they'll have to find me first*, she thought, pulling off the park road onto a gravel track. The one-lane track was thickly lined with tall brush, and she drove slowly until she was sure she could not be seen from either the main road or the park access road, at least not in this inky blackness.

Sierra shut the engine off, killing the lights, and gasped as the stars flooded the indigo sky with trembling diamonds. She locked the doors and cracked the windows to let in the crisp, dry air of the high desert, redolent with resins from the bushes crowding to either side of the car. She put her seat back and stargazed as she listened to the cooling engine ping and tick, then knew nothing more until the rising sun streamed through the windshield and woke her.

Sierra sat up and began to stretch, but froze mid-extension. She was on a low rise overlooking Mono Lake. With nothing to impede her view, she could see the entire lake where it lay in its rocky basin. Two islands, one white and one dark, floated mid-lake like great birds on the intense blue waters, just touched with pink from the early sun. Flocks of birds, spinning like bits of torn white paper in the wind, wheeled and called above the still waters, and she could see many more of them resting on the water's surface. The brush surrounding her car was crowded with bright gold flowers, the air spicy with their fragrance. The air was still cool, but the day promised to be warm.

Sierra backed the car carefully down the gravel track and took the park road down to the tufa viewing area. After availing herself of the park restrooms, she breakfasted on an apple and a couple of granola bars, washed down with water from her canteen that she devoutly wished were coffee. She dearly wanted to go see the tufa formations—she could see some of them from the parking lot—but she was taking no chance of missing the noon deadline. She wanted to give herself a margin of time to allow for getting lost in unfamiliar territory.

Sierra turned her car on to Route 120 and headed south. But there were no roadside cafes to be seen. There was little of anything to be seen. Now and again, roads came in from the side, with signs pointing to unknown destinations. She consulted her map several times, anxious that she might have missed the turnoff. Route 120 turned into 395, and still she drove. She bypassed the turnoff to Mammoth Lakes and kept driving. The terrain here was very different than the open, rocky Mono Lake basin. She was in pine forest now, at a much higher elevation. Her stomach growled, having completed digestion of her meager breakfast, and she wished again for a cup of steaming, hot coffee.

Finally, she thought she saw the turnoff. It was an unmarked gravel road, running into the pine trees to the left. She slowed and pulled off the highway. Dust plumed up around her car as it idled, and Sierra consulted the map again. The mileage was right. There was a tall tree to the left of the track that had been scorched by lightening, with a massive granite boulder at its foot, all according to the directions. This had to be the right place. Slowly, she pulled into the one-lane track and began easing over the ruts and rocks in the way.

The track gradually became bumpier and narrower, and she could feel rocks grating on the undercarriage of her car. Finally, the track petered out in a clearing just small enough to turn the car around. Sierra considered this for a moment and decided it would be a good idea to turn the car so that its nose pointed toward the way out. She might need the few extra moments if things got nasty. And things were bound to get nasty, she reflected grimly.

Sierra exited the car and shouldered her backpack. She locked the car, wondering when—and if—she would see it again.

She stood for a moment in the small clearing, listening. She could hear her car's engine ticking, the wind sighing through the pine needles overhead, and birds chirping. The occasional whoosh of a car on the road was audible, but there were no other sounds, and she could see no other living thing, barring the green growing things all around her. The dust from her drive down the track was settling, and its dry, piney scent coated her nostrils. Nothing but the winds and the birds moved, but her senses were all on edge, the hair on her arms bristling as though there were an electrical storm. She began to follow the trail deeper into the woods.

As she walked, her uneasiness grew. She felt as though there were unfriendly eyes fastened on her back, and she was grateful for the pack, which felt like a barrier between her and an attack from the rear. She slipped her hand into the pocket of her jeans, her fingers closing over the hardness of the silver feathers, warmed from her body heat. She hadn't made them into a necklace yet, having had little free time. Given recent events, she hadn't seen the point of doing so, either.

She walked farther into the woods, scanning her surroundings for the landmarks mentioned in the directions. There was the stump of a huge tree, felled a hundred or more years ago. There was a waterfall on her right, pouring down from still-melting snows higher in the mountains. Once or twice she froze like a startled rabbit, thinking she had heard soft footsteps behind her. But each time, there was nothing to be seen. Finally, when she estimated she was about halfway to her destination, she stopped and sat on a large chunk of granite. She listened intently for a few seconds, hearing nothing untoward, and took her canteen out. She was sweating heavily—not the honest sweat of exertion, but the cold, roiling sweat of fear. She thought about the ghastly heads that had first attacked her and about Mahaha. She knew there were more fearsome things than these at the bidding of Necocyaotl, and the sense of being alone and vulnerable, with nothing but the feathers' dubious protection between her and some monster, was exacting a heavy toll. Sierra swallowed thirstily, glad now that she had water and not coffee.

She never heard the step behind her, and she never felt the blow that felled her to the pine-needle-strewn forest floor.

CHAPTER 31

"Is it safe?" whispered Kaylee to Mama Labadie. They were crouched in the shelter of the trees surrounding Jumlin's estate. The mambo had just finished muttering something under her breath, scattering salt and a reddish dust around the gathered group. Each member of the little group responded according to his or her nature. Chaco stood calmly watching. Clancy stood impassive, his face betraying nothing but an occasional flicker of discomfort or embarrassment. Rose gazed with interest, her hand grasping a doeskin bag hanging from a thong about her neck, while Kaylee clutched at her stone vévé, fingers slick with anxious perspiration.

"Done," whispered Mama Labadie. The whites of her eyes flashed in the light from a nearby street lamp as Rose moved forward and began murmuring. She reached into the doeskin bag and began sprinkling cornmeal as she chanted almost inaudibly under her breath. The group waited in silence until the chanting ceased. Chaco suddenly bristled, scenting the air.

"Wait here!" he growled, melting into his coyote shape like a candle in a house fire, then darting into the darkness.

The little group waited in silence, sometimes tensing as a car passed along the street, hoping that the headlights wouldn't catch them loitering by the walls of a gated Atherton estate. When a police cruiser turned into the road and began driving leisurely by them, everyone seemed to stop breathing, and eyes were closed to prevent their reflecting in the car's headlights. When it disappeared down the street without slowing, everyone finally relaxed and began to breathe again. This was obviously not the kind of neighborhood where small, huddled groups of people could go unremarked. There were no sidewalks and few streetlamps. Long stretches of hedging or stone walls, uninterrupted by anything except automatic driveway gates, marked the outlines of palatial estates. There was no one else on foot—only an occasional long, sleek car swooshing by to indicate the presence of other people.

As they stood under the moonless sky, Chaco slid back out of the bushes and once again became a man. He was slightly out of breath and his brow was furrowed with worry.

"He's gone," Chaco reported. "The house is empty." They looked at him blankly.

"Maybe he's just out for the night," suggested Kaylee. "Maybe he'll be back later."

Chaco shook his head. "No, I mean the house is empty," he repeated. "No furniture, no servant, nothing. The basement is just as Sierra described it, though—the murals on the walls, anyway. There's no altar, no obsidian mirror. Jumlin's packed and gone. I'm sorry, Mama Labadie, Rose. I thought we would need some additional help here. But it looks like we wasted your time."

The two women began to speak, but Clancy cut in, "What about Sierra?" His voice was sharp-edged. "She's out there with no protection, alone, and we don't know where any of these characters are. They may all be after her—we know for sure some of them are. I'm going after her. *Now!*" He turned on his heel and began striding away, sticks and gravel crunching under his feet.

"Wait," called Rose in her soft voice. Clancy hesitated, then turned back toward them. "You're right, Clancy," Rose said. "But we need to stick together. We don't want to be like those people in the horror movies who split up and get picked off, one by one." Clancy's mouth twitched, but he didn't actually smile. "We still don't know what role this Jumlin creature is playing, but we do know where Sierra was heading. I suggest we head out there, too, but we can't just blunder around. Let's take the time to plan this out—we can't put Sierra in more danger than she is already."

Clancy stood still as a statue for a few moments, then nodded.

"Okay. Let's head back to Sierra's house to talk—if we stay here, someone's going to decide we're up to no good and call the police."

Back at Sierra's house, the group was restless and had difficulty settling down to confer. Clancy finally barked at them and they obediently sat in the living room. Silence prevailed. Each looked at the others, hoping someone else had a brilliant idea. The silence grew oppressive, the ticking of Sierra's kitchen clock louder. Finally, all eyes turned to Chaco, who had been sitting quite still with his strange eyes closed and a strained expression on his lean face.

Chaco opened his eyes and looked around at their expectant faces. "Why are you all looking at me?" he inquired peevishly.

"Possibly because you're the only god present in the room?" Clancy suggested nastily. "The only one who has supernatural powers at his beck and call. The only one who can find Quetzalcoatl—and we could really use his help right now. If he can be bothered."

Chaco shot Clancy a look of irritated frustration. "I'm not exactly a god, any more than you're a exactly a cop!" Chaco and Clancy glowered at each other.

"Okay, let's not get our panties in a bunch," interjected a rich, low voice. Mama Labadie looked from Chaco to Clancy. "If someone wanted to explain one or two things to me, I might be more helpful." No trace of her odd accent remained in her voice. She was wearing a smartly cut black jacket over tailored trousers, and looked nothing like the exotic figure that had danced over Sierra's prone body. The only trace of the voodoo priestess that remained was her jewelry, large beads of green and red stones carved with symbols. The chunky beads looked as *au courant* as the rest of her outfit.

Kaylee looked contrite. "I'm sorry, Mama—should I call you that? Or by the other name? The one you use at work?"

"Mama Labadie is just fine, girl. Get on with it—when you called me out tonight you didn't give me a lot of data. All you said was come quick, 'cause you and your friends needed protection.

Other than that, I know squat." She sat back, her full lips compressed, thin eyebrows arched, waiting for answers.

Rose nodded. "I could use more information as well," she said quietly. "If Coyotl is involved, it must be a great cause, but unless Mama Labadie and I understand what we're dealing with here, we'll be useless to you—and to Sierra."

"They got Fred," Kaylee choked on a sob, and her words tumbled over one another like pebbles in a stream as the story came rushing out. Chaco and Clancy filled in details, and Mama Labadie and Rose asked questions until the entire tale was told. Finally, words were spent, and Chaco gave Mama Labadie and Rose the two halves of the plaster imprint of Fred's little paw.

After examining this for a minute, Mama Labadie looked up. "You say these semiconductors are everywhere? Cell phones, TVs, microwave ovens—all over the world?"

"Yes," responded Chaco. "That's how they were able to spread this evil so easily. But it seems that some are immune to it, and some are not. We don't know why."

"Hmmm," she said and fell silent, turning the piece of plaster over and over in her long-fingered hands, not seeming to see it.

"I presume," said Rose in her soft voice, "That you have tried to call Quetzalcoatl?"

They all nodded unhappily. Chaco hung his head, seeming to feel it was more his fault than the others'. "Yes," he replied drearily. "We even went back to the statue in the park, but—nothing."

"Well, I suggest we ask for some guidance from Quetzalcoatl. Maybe he will come—maybe not—but it can't hurt. Then I suggest we figure out how to find Sierra and provide some backup for her without getting her killed." Rose removed the doeskin bag from her neck and began removing objects from its depths. As Rose sang, waving sweet smoke from her sage bundle over their heads, Kaylee and Chaco joined in and Clancy fidgeted, but Mama Labadie just turned the broken piece of plaster over and over in her hands, staring at nothing.

• • •

Sierra opened her eyes and winced. Her head was throbbing, her mouth was dry, and she was tied up like a fly in a spider's web. *Not again!* she thought, testing her bonds, *Shit! Shit! Shit!* The ropes that bound her were tight enough to be painful, and she had lost feeling in her fingers and toes. She was lying on something cold and hard; she fervently hoped it was not a stone altar. There seemed to be something wrong with her eyes; light was flickering crazily, sending stabs of pain through her skull. She shut them again.

She must have lost consciousness again. When next she opened her eyes, the light was still flickering, but the pain in her head had subsided a bit. She could hear voices. Depressingly familiar voices. She shut her eyes and didn't move, listening intently, straining to hear the words.

"…and brought them here," said a smooth, tenor voice. "And a blood sacrifice as well."

"What makes you think you can just barge in here and take over?" asked Jack Clapper, clearly both annoyed and aggressive. Sierra's skin crawled. Two of the most frightening men she had ever met. And one wasn't even a man.

Sierra opened her lids a crack. The resulting scene was nearly enough to make her pass out again. She was lying on the floor of the stone hall she had seen in her visions—but this was no vision. Loose rocks poked into her back and she could feel the pounding of the blood in her cramped limbs. She was freezing. Her body was sending her sensory information from every quarter—largely painful sensory information—in a way that made it clear this was no dream. At one end of the hall—the loathsome altar, placed in front of an impossibly large, sheer slab of gleaming black stone. An obsidian mirror. Its midnight facets shone and flashed in the light from torches placed in sconces down each side of the hall. And, crawling across the walls' surfaces, the brightly painted scenes of torture, sacrifice, suffering, and death. Sierra felt her gorge rise and swallowed repeatedly to make the urge subside. She wanted to call no attention to herself at that moment. Or ever, for that matter.

The voices continued. Jumlin said coldly, "I do my Lord's bidding, as I have always done. I have the feathers. I have the woman. That's more than either of you were able to achieve."

Clapper's response was immediate. "*You?* You're just an errand boy. Jenna and I have done the hard work here, and you've done nothing but get in the way. Now get the hell out of here. We have work to do."

A woman's voice now, one that Sierra knew well: Jenna's rich contralto. "Now, Jack, we're all on the same side here. I know we haven't exactly been friends with Jumlin in the past, but maybe we need to reconsider. We are all servants of the Obsidian Mirror, after all. Where are the feathers, Jumlin?"

Sierra couldn't quite see what Jumlin was doing, but soon he approached the altar and laid something on its surface. Sierra could see he was wearing black gloves. They shone dully, as though made of fine leather. Something clinked, metal against stone. *The silver feathers.*

Light footsteps. Jenna approached the altar and stared down. "Pretty," she said. "They don't look dangerous."

"Neither do Black Diamond semiconductors," said Clapper. "But they are, all the same."

Jenna turned to face Jumlin. Her rosebud mouth smiled, but her flat blue eyes were as cold and empty as ever. "Let's join forces," she said, in an inviting tone, her voice warm. "We have everything to gain by not continuing this quarrel. We could use another good brain on our side—don't you think, Jack?" she said, smiling at Jumlin and not looking at Clapper. There was a brief pause, then Clapper said, "Sure. Yeah. Let's bury the hatchet, so to speak. Let's bury it in that little green freak and the bitch over there, specifically." He turned and aimed a feral grin at Sierra. She let her barely parted lids close completely so as not to betray she was awake and listening.

"I'm sure that would be for the best," said Jumlin smoothly.

"Two blood sacrifices for Lord Tezcatlipoca. And my strength and powers joined to yours. Our Lord will reward us for this."

Sierra glanced around the hall, wondering where Fred was. Apart from the altar and the obsidian slab, there was nothing in the hall but the people. But there, in the dark corner beyond the altar—what was that? A cage? A box? She couldn't see it well enough. Was Fred crammed into that little thing? *Poor Fred,* she thought. *He must be terrified.* Then, *Poor me. I AM terrified.*

"Yes," said Jenna. "He will. We should prepare for the sacrifice. Jack, get that little beast out of his cage, please." Sierra noticed that as she made this request, she made a very slight gesture with her hand, positioning it low and between the two of them. Jack glanced down at it. He looked up at her again.

"You do it," he said rudely. "I've still got the stitches from that little monster's teeth."

Jenna sighed impatiently and turned to Jumlin. "May I borrow your gloves, please," she asked sweetly. "Jack never had much of a backbone, you know."

Jumlin eyed her and said, "I'll do it." Jenna brightened. "Yes, please, if you wouldn't mind," she said. "It's got quite a nasty set of teeth, as Jack certainly knows. What a gentleman you are."

Jumlin walked over to the cage or box on the floor. He bent down, apparently trying to see in. He straightened. "There's nothing in there," he said suspiciously.

"Yes, there is," Jenna said patiently. "There's a kind of trick to making him visible—he's a mannegishi, you know. They can disappear at will. But I know how to handle him. First, we need something to poke him with..." she looked around. "Where did that knife go? Do you see it, Jack?"

Jumlin walked back to where the others stood in front of the altar, stripping off his leather gloves. He held them out to Jenna. "Here," he said. "You do it if you know how."

Jenna took the gloves and pulled them onto her own slender hands. She flexed them, and held them out admiringly. "Very nice!" she exclaimed—and swifter than a striking cobra, snatched the silver feathers from the altar and pressed them to Jumlin's face.

Sierra watched in helpless revulsion as Jumlin's scream of agony echoed through the stone hall, making the flames of the torches shiver and dance. He struck out blindly at Jenna, who slid deftly out of his way, still clutching the feathers. His smooth, tanned cheek began to smoke, then sizzle, then burst into flame, and in a matter of seconds, Sierra could see the bones of his skull. The flames burst out anew from his chest—the ribs standing out in blackened profile against the red light of the flames—and traveled down the length of his body as though Jumlin's torso were a Fourth of July sparkler. His bones glowed and collapsed, then he vaporized in a gout of flames and smoke. The most ghastly aspect of it was his scream, which reverberated through the cave, dying only after Jumlin's body had completely disappeared and leaving nothing behind but a faintly glowing pile of greasy ash. Jenna and Clapper stood side by side, staring down at the ashes on the floor. As they gazed, the red-orange glow winked out entirely.

"Well," Jenna said. "I guess that settles that." She set the silver feathers on the altar and turned her cold eyes on Sierra.

CHAPTER 32

Clancy drove the entire way, silent and grim. Kaylee sat next to him in the front passenger seat, while Rose, Mama Labadie, and Chaco sat in the back. At first, Kaylee tried to relieve her growing anxiety with conversation, but Clancy responded with nothing more encouraging than grunts or the occasional "uh-huh," so she gave up and tried to nap. This effort was rendered futile by Rose and Chaco, who passed the time with songs and chants, which Kaylee thought were probably in some Native American language. After an hour of this, she was ready to request "A Hundred Bottles of Beer on the Wall," but they finally stopped. After several minutes, small snores issued from the back seat and Kaylee finally dropped off. Throughout the journey, Mama Labadie sat bolt upright, alert and silent.

Kaylee woke up when the SUV came to a halt, gravel scrunching under its tires. She rubbed her eyes blearily. It still looked like morning, as the sun hadn't yet cleared the tall pines around them.

"Where are we?" she yawned, as the others stirred in the back seat.

"We're down the highway a little way from the turnoff where they told Sierra to go," responded Clancy. He opened the door and swung out of his seat without apparent stiffness. Kaylee dug her fingers into her hair, realizing that it must be standing out around her head like a black dandelion puff. She peered into the rear-view mirror, shuddered, and gave it up as a bad job. She joined Clancy outside the car as the others tumbled out and stretched.

"Okay," Clancy said, checking his holster and glancing alertly around. "You know the drill. Rose, Mama Labadie and Kaylee, stay here with the car. Chaco, come with me."

"Wait a minute," Kaylee said, having just realized some of the more feminist implications of the plan. "Why do the men go off and do the rescuing and the women stay behind in the fort? Don't you think we might be helpful? There's strength in numbers, you know. And there's more estrogen than testosterone here."

"Do you have a gun and know how to use it?" inquired Clancy. Kaylee shook her head.

"Can you change into a coyote and sneak around in the underbrush without being noticed?"

Kaylee just glared at him, hands on hips. Clancy gave her a half-smile and shrugged. "I'd switch with you if it made any sense," he commented. "C'mon, Chaco." Chaco made as though to kiss Kaylee, but she turned her head, annoyed. Chaco shrugged and grinned before morphing into a coyote and sliding soundlessly into the brush, vanishing almost before she realized it. Clancy, less soundlessly, began to walk along the highway. Within minutes, he was hidden by a turn in the road.

Kaylee looked at her companions. "Well, the brave knights have charged off, and the maidens are twiddling their fingers back at the castle," she remarked sourly. Rose smiled her slow, warm smile.

"We can contribute, too," she said.

"How?" Kaylee asked. "If someone—or something—found us here, we'd be sitting ducks. And if Clancy and Chaco—or Sierra—are in trouble, we'd never know, sitting here like vestal virgins."

"We can cast protective spells for them all," responded Rose. "And for ourselves." She looked thoughtfully down the road in the direction Clancy had taken. "I remember hearing about those... heads. And Mahaha. I don't care to sit here unprotected, do you?"

Kaylee clutched her pendant. "No, I don't," she said, firmly. "Mama Labadie, we should call on the loa for their help." She looked at her hands in frustration. "I don't have anything with me," she said. "No offerings, or anything."

"Doesn't matter," said Rose. "There's water in the car. I have some corn meal. And there's a few apples."

"We also have Fig Newtons," commented Mama Labadie. This was her first comment since leaving the Bay Area. "Fig Newtons, they work better than cornmeal. Not so good as rum, though," she added thoughtfully.

So the women, each in her own tradition, performed ceremonies side by side, calling on the unseen for assistance. At the end, as they were standing in a circle of cornmeal, salt and crumbled Fig Newtons, scattering droplets of water on the roadside gravel, a sheriff's car pulled up. There were two uniformed officers in the front seat. The passenger-side officer, who proved to be a woman, rolled down the window and leaned out.

"Are you ladies in trouble here?" she inquired. She was wearing dark aviator shades that completely hid her eyes, giving her a slightly sinister look. Her partner, a man, had one hand on the steering wheel and the other hand at his hip. Rose recovered her composure first.

"No, officer," she replied with a luminous smile. "Just enjoying the fine weather and looking for a hiking trail."

"That's good," returned the woman. "Glad you're not broken down, or something. If you want to hike, you should drive back to Route 203 and drive to the trail that goes to the Devil's Postpile. That's worth seeing, and it's a pretty hike, too."

"Great!" said Rose. "We'll do that. Thanks, officer!" She waved gaily as the car pulled away from the verge and sped down the highway. She and Kaylee watched the car's taillights disappear around the corner. Dust drifted quietly around them, sparkling in the sun as the pine trees soughed in the breeze.

"Hmph," said Mama Labadie, squinting her eyes against the bright sunlight. "I think that's the first time a cop ever passed up the opportunity to give me a run-around. What we did must be working."

"Maybe," Rose said. "Or maybe we just seem like nice ladies out for a hike."

Kaylee surveyed the protective Fig Newton circle. "Maybe. And maybe we should also get off the road. I feel exposed here."

Rose nodded. "Okay. Let's walk into the trees a ways. Far enough so that passing cars won't see us, anyway." The women took small packs with water, apples, and snacks from the car.

As she was making these few preparations, Kaylee suddenly felt...wrong. Her head snapped up. She listened, but could hear nothing. Absolutely nothing—no wind, no birds, no cars. Minutes earlier, the comparative silence of the lightly traveled highway through the woods had seemed peaceful. This frozen stillness seemed utterly wrong, as did a sudden chill. Though the sun shone as brightly as before, the light seemed devoid of brilliance or warmth. Rose, too, was suddenly alert, turning her dark head this way and that. Mama Labadie stood as still as a statue, eyes wide.

"Something's wrong!" hissed Kaylee.

Rose nodded. "I know," she said, looking anxious.

Mama Labadie rummaged through her pack. She took out a colorful bundle decorated with feathers and tied with bright yarns. She held this object in her hands, muttering something as she scanned her surroundings. Rose had her doeskin pouch clasped in one hand, the other hand outstretched, hand cocked back with the palm outward as though pushing away something invisible. Kaylee clutched her vévé. Without speaking, the three moved to stand back to back.

A sudden wind came up, blowing an icy breath that made the trees sway alarmingly, though still no sound could be heard. It felt to the women as though their ears were stuffed with cotton. And down the deserted highway, something dark could be seen, coiling like smoke, or like a snake, with none of the insubstantiality of the one or the substance of the other. And it was moving toward the women—fast.

Kaylee could feel the other women's backs against hers. Rose was trembling. Kaylee wondered if she were trembling as well, but couldn't tell. Mama Labadie's body was still, but her muscles were tensed, braced for whatever was coming.

"Don't move from this place," Mama Labadie whispered to the others. "We're stronger together." Kaylee and Rose nodded, but didn't speak.

The dark, coiling thing moved closer. Kaylee thought now that it looked like a great snake, and suddenly wondered if this were Quetzalcoatl. But surely not—wasn't Q a beneficent being? Surely he wouldn't bring this watery-kneed sense of mortal dread? The roiling mass was dark, but not black all through. There were slowly turning streams of many deep colors, continually shifting and changing. The thing was hypnotic, fascinating, almost beautiful. It moved closer, closer, closer—and abruptly stopped. It hung for several moments, far too near for comfort, but several yards distant from the waiting women. It didn't seem to want to approach any closer. The women turned their bodies to face it but remained standing in tight formation, drawing strength from one another.

Suddenly, the amorphous, turning mass was gone, and a man stood there. He was every bit as beautiful as Chaco—even more so. His face was that of an Aztec prince, with high cheekbones, an arched nose that flattened at the nostrils, and wide, sensual lips. His eyes, large and almond-shaped, were as black and glittering as obsidian, showing no whites. Kaylee took a firmer grip on her vévé and leaned hard against Rose, who returned the pressure.

The creature—whatever it was, it was clearly and aggressively male—wore a tall, spiked crown of feathers. Heavy gold and jade jewelry hung from his neck and banded his arms and legs. Gold pierced his lips, earlobes, and cheeks. He wore nothing else on a body that looked—Kaylee thought dazedly—like one of those kitschy paintings on black velvet: all bronzed flesh and rippling muscles. She forced herself to stare at his face.

The man smiled tenderly at the women, showing white, even teeth. "Don't be afraid," he said. They said nothing.

"I have so much to offer you," he said. "Can't we have a few friendly words?" He stretched his muscular arms out, palms open. The ornaments fastened around his biceps swayed dreamily, back and forth, back and forth. Kaylee followed their motion as though hypnotized. She could feel the bodies of the other women swaying in time.

Then it seemed to Kaylee that she was flying above herself and looking down. She could see her little figure, crowded tightly against Rose and Mama Labadie, just for an instant, and then she was flying above the pine trees. She could see the forest beneath her, sloping down into the Mono basin and the lake itself, with its two islands floating like water birds in an expanse of blue.

Then she seemed to fly through time and space, alighting suddenly in a lush forest, a tropical forest utterly different from the dry pines where she had begun her journey. She could smell this forest, its fecund rankness, and the perfume of a thousand flowers. The heat and moisture settled around her like a familiar blanket. She was home. This is where she belonged, the place where she reigned as queen. She realized that she was nearly naked, but this didn't concern her; she was the queen. Her arms dripped with ornately wrought gold bracelets, and a heavy headdress pressed down her hair. The insignia of royalty, she knew.

This is yours by right! said a voice in her head. You are the queen here. And only I can give you back your heritage. Only I, my love. Let me love you, Kaylee. Let me bring you to your rightful place. Kaylee shivered, recalling the Aztec prince, his beauty and his power. But her shiver brought an answering shiver at her side, and abruptly, she was standing again in the pines, pressed against the other two women.

Kaylee clutched her talisman and stepped away from the others. Rose cried out. Kaylee took a few steps toward the beautiful figure and stopped, arms held straight out, her palms facing him.

"Rose." She spoke calmly. "Mama Labadie. You, too." The others joined her, hands also positioned as though to push the apparition away.

"I command you to go," Kaylee said, for all the world like the queen she had so briefly been. "In the name of Damballah-Wedo, in the name of Ézilee, in the name of Papa Legba, go and come no more."

"In the name of the Manitou, in the name of Quetzalcoatl, in the name of Kóhk'ang Wuhti, go and come no more," said Rose, and her voice was as strong and steady as Kaylee's.

Then Mama Labadie's deep voice joined in. "In the name of Ogu Bodagris, in the name of Aida-Wedo, go and come no more."

The princely figure stood still. His hands clenched and unclenched, and he seemed on the point of rushing toward them. Then he laughed. It was not a pleasant chuckle; in fact, it sounded more like an avalanche.

"I should crush you now," he said, and the flesh seemed to melt away from his handsome face, showing the bones of the skull, dripping with corruption—horribly, his eyeballs still rested in their bony sockets, alive with malice. In each upraised fist, he squeezed a human heart, dripping blood that streaked down his arms, down his torso, down his legs to the ground. Where each rivulet of blood touched the ground, it smoked and hissed, and a figure sprang up like an animated stone statue, blocky and stylized. Soon, the area around the skull-crowned apparition was alive with these smaller figures, their stony eyes fixed on the women. They began to move forward in unison, each squat figure crunching pine needles under its heavy feet.

The three women turned as one and bounded into the woods, running like deer that had blundered into a convention of wolves.

An hour later, the sheriff's department cruiser came back along the highway, slowing and stopping by the deserted Jeep. The woman got out and checked the doors and looked around. Everything appeared peaceful and undisturbed, so she climbed back into the car.

"Guess they decided to hike right here," her partner remarked. "Too bad. They'd've had a much better hike back at the Devil's Postpile."

"Yeah," said the woman, fastening her seat belt. "I hope they don't go too far in. This area is riddled with sinkholes and rotten limestone. I should've told them that." She sighed, taking another look at the car. "I guess we better radio the Forest Service and let them know there's some idiots hiking off-trail again."

"Okay," said her partner. "Where do you want to get lunch?" The car drove off down the highway, and all was quiet again.

CHAPTER 33

Clancy quickly found the turnoff with the lightning-blasted tree and the boulder. He unfastened his pistol in its holster and released the safety. He turned down the track, noting that a vehicle had recently passed that way. The bushes and small wildflowers by the side of the track were coated with dust. Clancy couldn't hear Chaco shadowing him through the trees and brush, but he knew the coyote was nearby. He began to walk, as quietly as he could manage, scanning the woods around him as he went.

When he came upon Sierra's car, Clancy hung back for several minutes, listening and looking. Nothing stirred. He glimpsed Chaco for an instant, ahead of him on the dwindling track, before the coyote slipped noiselessly back into the undergrowth. By the time he got to the rock where Sierra had rested for a while, Chaco was there, nose to the ground, tail stiff and body tense. Chaco looked up as Clancy approached.

"She was here," Chaco growled low, ears laid back against his skull. "And she's been hurt."

"What? How do you know?" demanded Clancy.

"There's the smell of blood," replied the coyote. "Not a lot of it," he said quickly, as Clancy turned pale beneath his tan. "But there's definitely a smell of her blood here. And her spoor stops here. And Jumlin was here too." He snorted. "The stink of him is everywhere. And fresh, too."

Clancy felt a frozen fist close around his heart. Jumlin. The monster that would have sacrificed Sierra like a chicken. The anthropophage. The cannibal. His stomach clenched.

"Where now?" he asked Chaco. "Where did he take her?"

Chaco set off down the track, now diminished to little more than a deer trail wandering through the trees. Clancy followed, as quickly and quietly as he was able, but he was no match for Chaco's four paws, and the coyote sped out of sight.

Clancy tried to keep his mind on the task at hand, but it was no easy feat. He pushed away nightmare visions of Sierra's body, slit open like a gutted fish, bleeding on a stone altar. He tried not to think about the horrors the others had witnessed. Such things would only sap his will and suck away his courage. He hiked stolidly ahead, alert for any sound or motion. Every nerve was raw, and he started at the sudden winging of a bird from branch to branch, or the shrill scolding of a squirrel.

When Chaco suddenly reappeared on the path, Clancy's heart scrabbled against his chest wall like a small animal trying to escape.

Chaco said in a low voice, "There's a cave. Around the big pile of boulders there, to the right. No, you can't see it—the opening has been enlarged, but it's hidden in the rocks."

Clancy couldn't see an opening, but he was sure Chaco knew what he was talking about. He unholstered his pistol.

"What do you think you're doing?" hissed Chaco. "You think you can kill Jumlin with a *gun*?"

"I don't know," Clancy replied. "But I'm pretty sure I can kill Clapper or Simmons with it, if I have to. Have you been inside yet?"

Chaco shook his head. "No," he whispered. "But they're in there. All of them."

"Sierra? Fred?"

"Sierra, definitely, but I'm not sure about Fred. Also Jumlin, Simmons, and Clapper."

Clancy almost couldn't ask the next question. "Is she alive?"

"Can't tell." Chaco said.

Clancy tamped down his frustration. Patience had always been the key to his work, and he needed it now more than ever. "Let's go," he said, moving cautiously around the rocks until he could see the cave opening.

The entrance wasn't huge, but clearly someone had worked

to enlarge it. There were piles of rock and dirt to either side that hadn't arrived there by natural processes. There was a sizeable heap of dead brush to one side, and drag marks showed that the debris had been used to disguise the cave opening, and had recently been pulled away to allow entry. The opening was low enough to require stooping, but Clancy was relieved to see he wouldn't be forced to crawl—this would put him at a disadvantage, though it wouldn't inconvenience Chaco in his current form. Chill air wafted from the dark opening, along with a faint odor of corruption that made Clancy's hackles rise. Glancing at Chaco, he saw the coyote's hair standing on end as well, and his ears were laid back tight against his head.

"I'm going in first," Chaco said, and this made sense to Clancy. Chaco could move more swiftly and silently than he could, and Chaco could see better than he could in the dark. The coyote vanished into the cave like a shadow among shadows, and Clancy stepped in close behind.

• • •

Rose, Mama Labadie, and Kaylee pelted through the trees, slipping and sliding in places, but never faltering. Rocks and tree roots might reach to trip them, but when one woman tripped, another grabbed a hand or arm and yanked hard. They were too terrified to stop and look behind to see if the dragon's-teeth army of stone figures and the skull-faced apparition were still in pursuit.

Eventually, a particularly sneaky tree root caught Kaylee's fleeing foot and down she went before anyone could grab her. She bellyflopped, knocking the wind out of herself.

"Are you okay?" panted Rose, her sides heaving and sweat pouring down her face. She knelt next to Kaylee, who, struggling for air, couldn't speak. All Kaylee could do was writhe in the dust and gasp like a landed fish.

Mama Labadie knelt, wrapped her arms around Kaylee and propped her up, staring wildly back at the way they had come.

Now that the crashing and pounding of their flight had died away, the forest was silent. Not the silence that had descended just before they saw the apparition—this was the natural and everyday silence of a forest well away from the insistent cacophony of human civilization.

The women huddled on the ground, shaking, streaked with sweat and dirt. Once she was breathing again, Kaylee became aware that she had torn her jeans and her knee was seeping blood through a ragged hole in the denim. She noted this objectively, and flexed her leg to see if any more serious damage had been done. She winced. Sore, but nothing she couldn't live with.

"Where did they go?" Rose whispered. Mama Labadie shook her head.

"I have no idea, but let's not wait around for them," she responded. "Do you think we should try to go back to the car?"

The idea found no favor with any of them. After a bit, they also realized they didn't know how to get back to the car, even if they had wanted to return. They were, Kaylee realized with a nasty, sinking feeling, quite lost. She mentioned this aloud.

"Lost?" Rose exclaimed. "I am *never* lost." She squinted up at the sun, which was nearly overhead. "See? The sun is nearly right above us. It's almost noon. That means," she hesitated. "That means that, um, the car is in that direction." She pointed into the woods in what seemed to Kaylee to be the opposite direction from which they had run.

"No," Kaylee argued, "we were running from *that* direction before I tripped." She pointed in the opposite direction.

"Couldn't be," said Rose. "We ran east from the road, and you're pointing east."

"Do you have a compass?" asked Mama Labadie.

"I don't need a compass. I know these things," said Rose.

"I suppose you're going to claim that you have Indian wilderness skills. Well, if that's the case, all you have to do is follow our tracks back to the road," suggested Kaylee.

"No need to get snotty," said Rose. She stood up and brushed dust from her clothes. "And as it happens, yes, I do have Indian wilderness skills, as you put it." She began to move around their resting place in a gradually widening spiral. After a few minutes of this, she abruptly stopped and came back to the other two. Her cheeks were rather pink beneath their coating of grime, Kaylee noted.

"Um, we didn't leave any tracks," Rose said.

"Huh? How could that be?"

"Well, the ground is covered with pine needles. Remember how slippery it was? We made a huge mess right there, where you slipped, but everywhere else, it just looks like, um, pine needles. No tracks."

"Aren't Indians supposed to notice all the little landmarks as they travel through the wilderness and all that?" asked Mama Labadie.

"I don't know about you," said Rose with dignity, "but I was running like hell, and I didn't notice a damn thing."

"Fair enough," Kaylee admitted. "Neither did I!"

Eventually, they just picked a direction and started walking, still alert for sounds of pursuit or strange phenomena. Kaylee had dropped her pack in their flight, but Rose and Mama Labadie both had theirs, and they shared the water sparingly. It was hot, even in the shade of the pines, and though they didn't voice their fears, all were worrying about having too little water to keep all three going for any length of time.

The sun had reached a position indicating three o'clock in the afternoon, according to Rose, when they came to a shallow hollow among the trees. Rough, gray rocks poked up from the pine needles around the edge of the hollow, and trees crowded closely on either side. However, the way was clear straight through the hollow and up the other side, so the three women scrambled down, creating a cloud of dust that added to the crust already coating their skin.

Kaylee was just thinking about how thirsty she was, when with a sliding rattle like pebbles pouring down the hollow of the world's largest rainmaker, all three women slid into the hollow and disappeared as though the earth had swallowed them. The only evidence of their presence left behind was a cloud of dust that roiled up through the tree boughs like golden smoke.

• • •

Clancy stooped and entered the cave entrance behind Chaco. He paused inside for a moment, letting his eyes adjust. Chaco noticed this and paused as well, his black nose working, ears pricked.

They were in a narrow defile in the limestone rock. Daylight from the entrance prevented Clancy from seeing very far ahead, but it seemed quite shallow, ending only a few yards in front of them.

He pitched his whisper low. "Chaco, are you sure they're in here? It looks like it ends just ahead of us."

In reply, Chaco, moved forward. As Clancy watched, he passed behind a jutting stone that had appeared to be the back of the cave. Realizing that he couldn't see the turn of the passage, Clancy followed, trying to keep his boots from scraping against the loose stones on the floor of the cave. To his ears, he sounded like an elephant taking a stroll.

"Could you be a little quieter?" Chaco hissed. "You sound like an elephant." Clancy began to walk as softly as he could, placing each foot with painstaking care.

The cave passage turned several more times, always sloping down. By now Clancy was in complete darkness, trusting to Chaco to warn him if a hazard lay ahead. He moved blindly and with great caution, worrying that he might crack his head against the roof of the cave. He had been in caves where rocks hung well below the cave roof, posing just such a hazard—but at the time, he had been in well-traveled and well-lit tourist attractions. The memory of jutting stalactites and sudden drop-offs into hundreds of feet of nothingness forced him to move with agonizing slowness.

Finally, he felt, rather than heard, Chaco's return to his side. Then, a soft whisper, "Just around the next bend. You'll see some light. Keep to the left—the left, got that? If you go to the right, they'll never find you."

Great, thought Clancy. *This just gets better.* He put out his hand to touch the left side of the passage, which seemed to grow wider here. His right hand could no longer touch the other side. He inched along, still striving for silence. Chaco moved forward just in front of him; Clancy could feel the brush of the coyote's tail against his knees. As Chaco had said, he began to see a faint glow ahead that grew brighter with each step. Now he could see Chaco, his fur picked out in the growing light.

Then he could see a much larger space ahead, lit with wavering light. After the complete blackness of the cave, it seemed as bright as day, though the light flickered as though from a fire. Again, he stood still for a few moments to let his eyes adjust. He was standing in a niche just to the left of the widening hall. To the right of the opening was impenetrable blackness; Clancy wondered if there was a precipice hidden in that engulfing darkness. He stood just outside the reach of the light, peering onto a large cavern, or hall. First, he saw the torches in their sconces, then the painted murals. *This is the stone hall of Sierra's nightmares,* he thought. *It's real, then.* He felt ashamed; he had never really believed they were anything more than disturbing dreams. He hung back, trying to see more, letting the darkness of the cave conceal him.

If this was a nightmare, it was his nightmare, too. There was the stone altar, fronting a vast, black sheet of stone. *An obsidian mirror,* Clancy thought, incredulously. Two indistinct figures were bending over something on the floor. They were talking, quarreling, it seemed to Clancy from the tone. He tried to catch the words.

"...that you let it escape. It was in there the last time I had anything to do with it!" said a female voice. That was Jenna; he'd know that knife-edged tone of displeasure anywhere. He had himself been its target from time to time.

"Shut up, Jenna," said to the other, and he recognized Clapper. Where the hell was Jumlin? Behind him, in the dark? The thought made him turn and scan the blackness behind him, but nothing stirred. Chaco crowded at his feet, quivering, tense, but silent.

The two figures tugged at the thing on the ground, which let out a whimper of pain. *Sierra! At least she's alive.*

"Just cut the ropes, Clapper," Jenna said. "It's taking too long. That thing is on the loose, and I don't want to have to deal with it, too." She seized something from the altar and held it out to Clapper. Clancy saw the torchlight glittering darkly off its surface.

"You're the one wearing gloves," responded Clapper unpleasantly. "*You* do it."

Without another word, Simmons bent to the bundle on the floor and began sawing at it, which almost made Clancy burst from his concealment outside the hall, until he realized Simmons was cutting the ropes that bound Sierra. She finished the job and pulled Sierra roughly to her feet. Sierra staggered, off balance. Simmons quickly grabbed one arm and Clapper the other, and they forced her toward the altar. Simmons was holding something to Sierra's throat, and Clancy could now see it was a gleaming black stone knife. He had seen flaked obsidian weapons before, and handled them; he knew they could be sharper than razors.

The trio staggered toward the altar, Sierra obviously making herself a dead weight as much as possible. She aimed a feeble kick at Simmons, but the woman easily avoided it.

"Take your best shot, Carter," Simmons said, and laughed. Sierra took a deep breath and—at last—found within herself a core of surging flame.

It was at that moment the roof caved in.

CHAPTER 34

It started as a deep groaning, as though the cavern itself were moaning in pain. As the groaning echoed in the vast hall, a few stones dropped from the ceiling, clattering on the floor, and everyone looked up, including Chaco and Clancy. A few moments of silence followed, then with a roar, a round hole opened, releasing an avalanche of stones, dirt, and debris quite close to the altar, but missing both it and the people standing so close to it.

Dust billowed up, and as fine grit and debris continued to pour from above, Chaco and Clancy darted forward. The air was so thick with dust that they couldn't see Sierra or the other two, and Chaco's sensitive nose was useless. The torches were extinguished, adding to the murk.

Finally, Clancy saw Sierra. Dribbles of pine needles and dirt were still falling from the hole, but now daylight was pouring down from the world above, lighting the dust-laden interior of the cavern with clouds of gold. Sierra was choking and coughing, but she had an arm firmly wrapped around another figure, which proved to be Simmons. The wicked obsidian blade was now in Sierra's hand, held high against Simmons' throat. Sierra's dark hair was ashy with dust, and blood ran down the side of her head.

"Are you okay?" gasped Clancy. His mouth felt as though he had been licking sand, and his nostrils burned. As Sierra nodded, he began searching for Clapper, who was nowhere to be seen.

"We need to get out of here," Chaco said. He had shifted to human shape, apparently to remove his mouth and nose as far as possible from the choking dust filling the cavern. "It's dangerous. Let's go!"

Simmons made a convulsive jerk away from Sierra, with the result that the edge of the stone blade scored a shallow wound on the side of her throat. She hissed like a scalded cat.

"Hey!" snapped Sierra, resettling her grip on Simmons—and on the knife. "Don't jerk around like that. Where's Clapper? We can't just leave him here."

"He's dead," snarled Simmons. "Get me out of here!"

"Where's Jumlin?" asked Clancy. "We know he's in here."

Simmons shook her head. "Dead. Get me out of here!"

Sierra looked uncertainly at Clancy. "We don't know that he's dead," she began, but then all eyes were drawn to movement under the mound of pebbles, rocks, dirt, and pine needles on the floor. Rising up from the mound was a monstrous shape, almost wider than it was tall, with many limbs that it was using to crawl away from the rubble.

Sierra drew her breath in sharply, and Clancy went for his gun. It was gone, lost in the shock of the collapse and the confused scramble to get to Sierra. Chaco's lips drew back from his square, most uncoyote-like teeth, and he growled. Jenna Simmons merely stared, the glassy blade at her throat.

The figure, thickly coated with dirt and detritus, lurched towards the little tableau by the altar—and abruptly resolved itself into three dirt-encrusted people, each supporting the other.

"Sierra," croaked Kaylee. "Is that you?"

• • •

The cave entrance was smoking with dust, as though a fire raged within. The little group staggered out into the sweet, clean air of the forest. Clancy had taken charge of Simmons, tying her with the ropes that had been used to bind Sierra. Once Jenna was secured, Sierra had flung the obsidian knife against the wall of the cave as hard as she could, and it had shattered into a thousand glittering black shards. They had made another cursory search for Clapper, but it was clear the cave was slowly continuing to collapse, and they were forced to leave.

Not one of the little band of survivors was unscathed. Sierra's head was bleeding from Jumlin's attack, and she was dehydrated. Rose, Mama Labadie, and Kaylee were scraped, cut, and bruised from their fall, and Rose's ankle was extremely swollen, black and blue. Chaco and Clancy had been well away from the initial collapse and were relatively untouched, though both were still coughing and wheezing. The wound on Jenna's neck had bled freely, through the cut was superficial, and she coughed spasmodically between bouts of profanity and threats that involved everything from the vengeance of Tezcatlipoca to United States senators who would be displeased by their treatment of her.

Clancy handed Simmons over to Chaco for safekeeping—Chaco grinning wolfishly—and turned to fold Sierra in his arms. They rested against each other for several long minutes. *If only we could stop coughing, this would be so romantic*, thought Sierra. Then Clancy reluctantly released her and stepped back.

"I hope you have water in your car," he said between parched lips. She nodded. "We'd better get back there." Water, packs, gun, and everything else had been lost in the collapse.

"But what about Fred?" asked Sierra, eyes suddenly wide with horror. "They had Fred in there, too!" She started back toward the cave entrance, but Clancy blocked her.

"You can't go back in," he said gently. "It's too dangerous."

"But…"

Chaco spoke up. "He's right, Sierra. We can't go back."

Sierra looked at the dark mouth of the cave, still billowing smoke, and tears dug channels through the dirt on her cheeks. She put her filthy hands over her eyes and stood in silence for a long beat.

Mama Labadie examined Rose's swollen ankle.

"Clancy, I think Rose may have a broken ankle. Can you help me?"

Rose gratefully accepted the support, and they began to make their way back down the path, Chaco and Jenna Simmons in front, Rose hobbling between Clancy, and Mama Labadie, Sierra, and Kaylee bringing up the rear.

"How did you get that knife away from Jenna?" asked Clancy, panting as they made their slow and painful way along.

"I looked at Jenna's face when the roof began to fall in. She was so surprised that she wasn't paying attention to anything else. I grabbed her wrist and twisted it, and she dropped the knife on the altar. Then all hell broke loose, but I went for the knife because," Sierra paused. "Because my life depended on it," she finished simply.

CHAPTER 35

Before reaching the road, the little band paused to discuss their next move while they were still screened by the trees and undergrowth. Everyone sat wearily on the soft pine needles except for Chaco, who stood alertly by Jenna's side, never taking his fierce eyes from her drooping form.

"We need to get Rose to a doctor," said Clancy. "Does anyone else need medical attention?" He ignored Jenna, who pointed at the shallow cut on her neck. No one else said anything.

"All right. We're going to have to split up, I'm afraid," Clancy continued. "Someone needs to take Rose to a doctor. The rest of us have business with Ms. Simmons here." He glanced briefly at Jenna, who glared at him defiantly.

"What about Fred?" Sierra asked. "We can't just abandon him."

Clancy sighed. "I understand how you feel, Sierra. I think we all feel terrible about Fred. But we don't know where he is. Remember, he spent hundreds of years right here..."

"Thousands," Chaco put in, without taking his eyes from Jenna.

"...thousands of years here in the Sierra Nevada. He's probably OK, but if he isn't, I personally don't see any way to help him. We've just got to hope he'll find his way back to us. Right?"

Sierra swallowed hard, feeling as though she had a stone in her throat, and nodded, unable to speak. She felt she ought to be triumphant. She had bested Jenna Simmons. Jack Clapper was probably dead in the cave-in. But then, Fred might also be among the casualties, and she could only feel grief for the tubby little creature. She had come to rely on his presence and companionship—and while often annoying, Fred had also been loving and loyal. No, triumphant was the last thing she felt.

"Listen Sierra," said Jenna suddenly. "You won this round. I admit it. Just let me go and we'll call it even, OK? You can't get away with kidnapping me, you know. If I disappear, Black Diamond will call in the cops, the FBI, the whole enchilada. I don't know what you think you can accomplish by doing this. Just let me go, and I promise I won't come after you. You can even have your job back at BDSC. And you can keep your job," she looked at Clancy. "We'll just call it quits and agree to a truce."

Sierra stared at the woman in disbelief. "You've got to be kidding," she said. Clancy opened his mouth to speak, but Jenna preempted him.

"You're going to get nailed for this, you know. Disgruntled employee. Head of security disappears the same time I do. Don't you think you're going to be in the crosshairs when they realize I'm gone? They're going to be all over you like flies on shit within forty-eight hours." She allowed herself a small, contemptuous smile.

"So if we agree to let you go, everything will be back to where it was before you fired me, is that the idea?" asked Sierra. Jenna nodded, smiling more broadly. "How are you going to explain Mr. Clapper's disappearance? And, while we're on the subject of repulsive creatures, what happened to Chris Jumlin?" Even speaking Jumlin's name made her skin crawl.

Jenna shrugged. "Jumlin's not a problem anymore," she responded. "He got in the way." Her tone was cold, dismissive. "As for Clapper, well, he's just gone back to his agency in New York. There will probably be a terrible plane crash. His remains were never found. So sad."

"You'd crash a plane with hundreds of innocent people on board just to cover your tracks?" Clancy demanded, disgusted. "Don't you have any conscience at all?"

Jenna returned his horrified gaze with an icy stare. "No, I gave up being weak when I joined Tezcatlipoca. And I have never regretted it. Now, what about my offer?"

Sierra shook her head. "I'd have to be crazy. I'll take my chances with the police, the FBI, whatever, before throwing in with your bunch." Turning away from the disheveled, bleeding Jenna, she asked Clancy, "That being said, what the hell are we going to do with her?"

"We need some place private to talk to her," he replied. "Chaco, any suggestions?"

"Yep. There's a lot of territory east of here with no one and nothing in it. All the privacy you could possibly want," Chaco said, baring his white teeth at Jenna in a wolfish smile. She glared back. "As a matter of fact, I know just the place. Go back to Mono the way we came. Then turn right on 167. When we get past the Nevada border, there's lots of little sidetracks that go off into arroyos and there's nobody around. We'll need to take our own food and water, though. And firewood."

Clancy considered this for a few minutes. "That OK with you, Sierra?"

"I guess so. I have what's left of my camping gear in my car. And I brought a lot of water and food because I didn't know what might happen out here. But what about Rose?" *Food, yes. Water, yes. But no coffee*, she remembered.

Rose spoke up. "I do think my ankle is broken," she said in her calm voice. "Anyway, we've got seven people here," she turned a suddenly steely gaze on Jenna, "if you count this one as human. That's a lot of people to be running around the desert without anyone noticing, no matter how desolate it is. I'd just get in the way."

"Right you are," said Kaylee. "If I can borrow Sierra's car, I can get Rose to a doctor, and then home. The Jeep is big enough for the rest of you. Clancy, did you bring camping gear?"

"Yes. I brought a couple of sleeping bags, a tent and some other things. We're not going to be out there for days, just over-night. That ought to be plenty of time to do what we need." He ignored Jenna's scowl. "Mama Labadie, are you going with Rose and Kaylee, or with us?"

"Oh, I am coming with you, most certainly. Wouldn't miss it," said Mama Labadie.

"Okay. Let's get going, then. Ms. Simmons, where's your car?" Clancy asked.

"Why?"

"Because I want to know, that's why," Clancy returned, a dangerous glint in his eye.

"It's hidden. You won't find it, and neither will the cops," Simmons said stubbornly.

"Okay! That's good to know," said Clancy, and clambered to his feet. Dust clouds arose from his clothes as he stretched. The others rose as well. Jenna's hands and arms were tied, so Chaco lifted her to her feet with a businesslike tug.

When they arrived at the cars, they laid Jenna on the floor of the back seat. "That's going to be uncomfortable for you," said Chaco cheerfully. "Sierra and Mama Labadie will have to rest their feet on you, too. But we can't have you popping up and yelling for help when we drive through Lee Vining, can we?" Jenna gave him a look of pure loathing as she was bundled into the car. After Sierra's equipment was transferred from her car to Clancy's, Rose and Kaylee said an emotional goodbye to the others.

"I'm sorry, Sierra," said Kaylee. "I feel like I should go with you, but Rose really needs to see a doctor. She may be a healer, but a broken bone is a broken bone. Anyway—you know how I am about camping. But I'll be worried about you the whole time until I see you again." She looked at Sierra with worry in her warm brown eyes.

Sierra hugged her friend. "Not to worry," she reassured Kaylee. "Rose is right—there's too many of us. We'll be fine."

Kaylee handed over Sierra's backpack, which had been stowed in the trunk of her car. "You sure packed for every contingency," she observed. "This thing is heavy!"

Sierra took the backpack. It did seem heavy, but then, she had packed a lot of food and water. "Thanks," Sierra said. "Be safe. We don't know what else might be out there. Please be careful."

As Kaylee opened the Ford's door, she said, "Sister, after what I've seen, you don't need to warn me. Careful does not begin to describe what I will be." She blew a kiss at Sierra and shut the door.

As Kaylee drove away with Rose in the passenger seat, Sierra stowed her backpack in the rear of the Jeep. She turned to Clancy. "So what exactly are we going to do with Jenna out in the desert?" Clancy looked grim.

"That's what we're going to find out," he said.

CHAPTER 36

Kaylee drove behind Sierra's car until they came to Lee Vining. At the highway turnoff just before town, Kaylee pulled off the road. She and Rose waved at the others as they went by. Clancy's Jeep headed through the little town—which took perhaps five minutes—and then they were in open country again.

Four or five miles out of Lee Vining, Chaco spoke up. "Take a right here," he directed, and Clancy pulled onto Route 167. The road stretched ahead, straight for as far as they could see, rising up the other side of the great stone basin.

For part of the way, Mono Lake was easily viewed to their right. Sierra gazed out across its blue waters, speckled with flocks of white birds, thinking that if it were not a saltwater lake, it would be refreshing to take a swim. She felt grimy and sticky, as though she had been two weeks backpacking without washing. Jenna squirmed under her feet. Everyone had considerately taken their boots off before resting their feet on the woman, but it must still be hot and uncomfortable.

"Do you need water?" asked Sierra, feeling slightly guilty. She had been pulling freely from her water bottle, but Jenna was tied up and must be thirsty.

"Fuck you," growled the president and CEO of Black Diamond Semiconductor.

"Language!" said Chaco primly.

They began to ascend as they neared the rim of the rocky bowl. The landscape was desolate; only low scrub grew in this dry wasteland. They began to see the low hills that began at the Nevada state line. There was very little traffic out here. A car or a long-haul semi might appear and pass them every now and again, but Sierra began to feel they were a very long way from civilization. Even Lee Vining began to seem like a major metropolis.

They passed the state line, marked by a modest blue-and-white sign that read, "WELCOME TO NEVADA THE SILVER STATE." Not far from this delineation, Chaco instructed Clancy to pull into a dry wash to the right.

"I know this is a Jeep," said Clancy, "but is this really drivable?"

"Yep," said Chaco. "For as far as we need to go, anyway. See where it curves around into that little canyon up there? That's where we're going to set up. We don't want to run into backpackers or campers. And we sure don't want anyone to see our campfire. This is nowhere. No sights, no hiking trails, no campsites. Just pray it doesn't rain—not that it's at all likely."

"Flash floods?" Sierra inquired.

"Uh-huh. That's what formed this wash, not a seasonal creek."

Clancy carefully guided the Jeep up the rock-strewn wash, causing Jenna to emit a nasty miasma of curses as she suffered every jolt. They entered a steep-walled canyon, well hidden from the road below. After they had progressed a hundred yards into the canyon, a huge boulder blocked their path. The boulder was wedged as tightly into the canyon's rocky walls as a cork in a bottle of wine.

"This is it," Chaco said, as he hopped out of the car. Sierra and Mama Labadie unfolded themselves from the back seat and helped Jenna to her feet. Jenna did not reject the proffered water this time and drank thirstily. They sat her, still bound, in the shade of the canyon wall under Mama Labadie's vigilant eye while they unpacked the car and set up camp. These preparations complete, Sierra turned her attention to food. It had been a long day, and she had long since digested the morning's apple and granola bars. She felt fatigue creep over her as she hefted her backpack. It had also been a long time since she had slept. She opened the backpack, screamed, and leaped backwards, dropping the pack to the rock-tumbled floor of the wash. Fred crawled out of the pack and stared at her with his bright orange eyes, woefully rubbing his rear end.

"Sierra," he said in a reproachful tone of voice. "I thought you'd be *glad* to see me."

• • •

Once the tears of relief and the hugging and celebration were over, it was discovered that Fred had made room for himself in the backpack through the simple expedient of eating all the food Sierra had packed and jettisoning the water to make room for his ample self. Despite their tremendous relief at seeing Fred again, they might have been seriously annoyed with him for this, but Clancy produced adequate supplies from his own gear.

"How did they catch you?" Sierra asked Fred. "When Chaco and I left the storage facility, you were invisible. How did they find you?"

Fred turned a deeper shade of green and looked at the ground.

"Chocolate," he muttered.

"Chocolate? What do you mean?" Clancy queried.

"Um, well, Chaco and Sierra were doing fine, so I was just sort of looking around, you know, and, um…"

"Mannegishi!" snapped Mama Labadie.

"Yes?" Fred said, looking at her inquiringly.

"Get on with it!"

"…so I was kinda near Sierra's house, when I smelled, you know, chocolate. It was in this really fancy box, and it was the kind of chocolates that have that pretty colored foil on it?" He looked hopefully at the group, apparently expecting sympathy and understanding. Chaco nudged him rudely, and Fred continued.

"So it was sitting in the back seat of this car, and there was no one around and the door was wide open, so what else could I do?" He looked at them hopefully, twiddling his digits.

"So you climbed in the car to get the chocolate, and then what happened?" Sierra prompted.

"It was a trap!" Fred looked so indignant at this that Sierra couldn't help laughing. She laughed until tears streamed from her eyes. Clancy handed her a handkerchief *He must be the only man left in America who carries a handkerchief,* she thought. And she continued to snort helplessly as Fred's orange eyes rolled and his mouth pursed up.

When Sierra's helpless laughter subsided, Fred said severely, "It wasn't funny, you know."

"Right, I know," said Sierra, who stifled further giggles with moderate success. "So how did you get out of that cage thing they had you in?"

"Actually, it was a pet carrier," explained Fred seriously, and Sierra didn't snort. Not out loud. "It actually was pretty easy. If you push up against the plastic hard enough, right where the wire cage front goes through those little holes? You can pop it out. I guess they hadn't counted on *that,*" he concluded, with an air of smug accomplishment.

"Why did you let them carry you all the way up here? Why didn't you just disappear and slip away when they opened the car door somewhere?" Clancy asked.

"Well, I disappeared as soon as they grabbed me," said Fred. "They had these heavy gloves on, and there were two of them, so I couldn't get away. Then they shoved me in the carrier. Jack Clapper put chains all over the carrier. It took me a while to figure out the locks on the chains, but eventually I did, and…"

"Figure out the locks?" Clancy asked, one eyebrow raised. "You mean you picked the locks from *inside* the carrier?"

Fred aimed both his eyes at Clancy. "Well, no, I didn't pick the locks. I figured them out, so they opened."

"Huh?"

"Mannegishis do that," Chaco said, apparently thinking he had explained everything.

"Do what?" asked Clancy plaintively.

"They get in and out of places. It's one of their gifts. Don't ask. It won't make any more sense if he tries to explain it," sighed Chaco.

"So I figured out the locks and opened the cage. They were so busy arguing with the other guy that they never noticed. Of course, I stayed invisible the whole time," Fred said.

"Very clever, Fred," said Sierra, who had kept a grave face throughout this explanation. Fred blushed a little greener and gave her a grateful look. "Now, what happened to Jack Clapper? Do you know?"

Fred shook his head. "I was creeping around the side of the altar. I wanted to get close enough to bite one of them. But the roof fell in before I got close enough, and then I didn't see anything. I just ran out as fast as I could, before the whole thing came down. I ran right back to the car and opened it…"

"Because that's what mannegishis do," supplied Chaco.

"…and climbed in and found your backpack, and ate the food, and went to sleep," Fred concluded. "And then you found me, Sierra." Fred beamed fondly at her.

Then they settled down to deal with Jenna. It was early evening and still quite light, but they lit a fire for warmth. The high desert night promised to be chilly.

Jenna, propped against the great boulder, was predictably uncooperative. She refused to answer questions about Black Diamond, Necocyaotl, or the semiconductor material imbued with Necocyaotl's essence.

The general gist of her response was, "Take me back, let me go, and I might ask Tezcatlipoca to let you live." She relieved the tedium of this theme with threats about what Tezcatlipoca would do to them if they didn't cooperate.

As the night fell and stars began to glitter in a deep indigo sky untouched by light pollution, they began to droop. No one had had much sleep, apart from Fred, who was fresh and jaunty. He watched the interrogation with interest, and finally spoke.

"What are we trying to do here, anyway?" he asked, his eyes reflecting the firelight with an orange glare.

Clancy breathed a tired sigh. "We're trying to get Ms. Simmons here to tell us how to prevent Black Diamond's semiconductors from doing any more damage. We need to stop production of any more of them, and if we can, we have to figure out how to disable the rest of them—the ones that are already out there." His voice dragged, as though he had little faith that any of this was possible.

"I bet I can get it out of her," snarled Chaco and before anyone could say or do anything, he shifted. The coyote crouched in front of the bound woman, black lips drawn back from his sharp, white fangs. He snapped suddenly at her face, coming so close that Sierra was sure he had slashed Jenna's cheek. Jenna closed her eyes, and jerked frantically away from the coyote's hot breath, but said nothing. She was pale and sweating, despite the increasing chill.

"No, Chaco!" Sierra said sharply. "That's coming down to her level. We need to use our heads, but right now, I can barely think. I need some sleep—we all do, but…"

"So," Fred interrupted. "All we need to do is to get Ms. Simmons to see our point of view, right? If she really understands why we want to stop what she is doing, it should be easy, right?" He sat on his fat bottom, looking expectantly at the little group like a first-grade teacher explaining to students how to raise their hands to ask a question.

Clancy visibly restrained himself from rolling his eyes, Chaco snarled, still in coyote form, and Sierra felt a deep, cold discouragement settle on her heart with such leaden weight that she couldn't respond. *He's like a little kid*, she thought. *He just doesn't understand.*

Mama Labadie leaned forward. She was seated cross-legged on a picnic blanket from Sierra's stash. "OK, Mannegishi, yes, you got it right. That's all we need to do—get this woman to come over to our side. Got any suggestions?" Although the words were challenging, her tone was mild—even inquisitive.

"Yup," said Fred, inserting one green digit into his slit of a mouth and sucking meditatively. Silence followed. Everyone's attention was on Fred, including Jenna's. She was smirking slightly, one eyebrow raised. A minute passed. Fred continued to enjoy his digit.

"Well?" said Chaco, shifting back to man and moving quickly

as though to snatch Fred up in his strong hands and shake him, but Mama Labadie interceded.

"C'mon, Fred, What have you got? How do we bring her over to our side?" she asked.

Fred removed his digit from his mouth. He flickered slightly, making everyone dizzy, and held out his other paw—the less-sticky one. Cupped within his six digits were three objects that gleamed orange and yellow in the light of the campfire.

"What are those things?" asked Mama Labadie. Sierra drew in a long, shaky breath.

"They're the feathers of Quetzalcoatl," she said, just before Jenna began to scream.

CHAPTER 37

Jenna's earsplitting shrieks echoed off the canyon walls, magnifying the effect. It sounded as though several women were being cut to ribbons with a dull knife. The little band sat frozen where they were, staring at Jenna, who was clearly in a state of hysterical panic. She was screaming words aloud, though nobody could understand them.

Mama Labadie was the first to recover her composure. She arose gracefully from her picnic blanket, walked calmly over to Jenna, and administered a stinging slap to the other woman's cheek. This brought the shrieking to an abrupt halt, though Jenna continued to babble. Now she could be understood, her panic lending painful urgency to every word.

"Don't let him do that to me," she pleaded over and over. "Don't let him! Please! Please!" None of them had ever seen her in a state of extreme emotion before; Sierra was sure she had never seen Jenna express a genuine emotion in all the time she had worked at BDSC.

"Don't let him do what?" asked Mama Labadie, looming over the seated woman. "You better start making sense, woman."

"Don't let him near me with those things! You have no idea what they can do. You just don't know."

"I do," said Sierra, shuddering. She would never forget the effect the silvered feathers had on Jumlin. She could still see Jumlin's ghastly skull with its knowing eyes before it crumbled into a rain of ashes. She told the rest of the group the details of Jumlin's grisly end. There was a prolonged silence as each of them pondered the implications.

"We can't do that," said Sierra finally. "I can't do that to another creature, not even Jenna."

"Even though she tried to kill you?" asked Clancy.

Sierra nodded. "Even though."

"Then let me do it," said Mama Labadie, her eyes glittering as she surveyed the quivering woman huddled against the boulder. "Wouldn't bother me." Jenna shrank away. Her eyes were wide with terror.

Chaco spoke up. "Sierra, do you remember what Q told you that day? In his cave?"

Sierra searched her mind. Quetzalcoatl had said a lot of things. "What do you mean?"

Chaco's voice dropped an octave. The voice that issued from his lips was not his voice. It was the voice of Quetzalcoatl, with a timbre as deep and ancient as the cave where Sierra had first heard it. "Necocyaotl cannot inhabit the soul of any creature who has contact with me or my essence. Take some of my feathers. If you find a way to bring them into contact with her skin, my brother's influence will vanish. He will never be able to touch her again."

"There," said Chaco in his normal pleasant tenor. "He told you to touch Jenna's skin with the feathers. Necocyaotl's influence over her will be broken. Q also said he wasn't asking you to kill anyone. You remember that, don't you?"

Sierra sat silent, recollecting. Yes, he had said he wasn't asking her to kill. Yes, he had asked her to touch Jenna's skin with his feathers. But always before her mind's eye was the hideous extinction of the being that called himself Chris Jumlin, his fiery disintegration into nothingness.

"Yes," she replied doubtfully. "But then why did Jumlin die so horribly? Did Q…did Quetzalcoatl lie to me about the feathers? About not killing Jenna?"

Clancy came to sit beside her. He put an arm around her shoulders, and his warmth drove the desert cold from her body. She nestled into the crook of his arm, comforted but not reassured.

"Well, why did Jumlin die?" Clancy asked. "Chaco? Fred? Do you know? Mama Labadie, do you know anything about this?"

Mama Labadie stepped away from the cowering Jenna and reseated herself on the picnic blanket. The firelight limned her features with gold as she spoke. "No. I have no knowledge of this. I could ask the loa, though."

"He wasn't human." This calm statement came from Fred. Heads swiveled to look at him. A pause ensued as they waited impatiently for more. Fred appeared to think he had concluded his remarks, and looked calmly around the group.

Chaco broke the silence. "Fred!" he snapped.

Fred, startled, stuck his entire paw in his mouth. "Whuh?"

"What do you mean, he wasn't human? What's that got to do with it?"

Fred's paw emerged from his mouth. "Oh, that. Well, Jumlin was one of the A'tahsaia. That's what the Zuni called them. Cannibalistic evil spirits. He could assume the appearance of a human being, but he was no more human than Tzintzimitl." He sucked thoughtfully on a toe, then popped it out again. "Or me. Or Chaco. But Jenna is human—or she was until Necocyaotl got hold of her."

Chaco put in, "So Q's feathers destroyed a purely evil being, but Jenna, being human, isn't purely evil. Or, rather, probably not." He looked dubiously at Jenna. She was still obviously terrified, eyes moving from one speaker to the next. Chaco's generous mouth turned down at the corners. "I don't think you have a choice, Sierra."

"Me?" Sierra cried. "Why me? Mama Labadie volunteered here, not me!" Mama Labadie nodded, with a another meaningful dark glance at Jenna.

"But Q called *you*," Chaco pointed out. He sat cross-legged on the sand of the wash, soft, dark hair falling into his eyes. The firelight reflected in shades of amber and gold in his eyes. "You are the one he chose to be his instrument. I don't think anyone else can step up to this, Sierra."

Sierra struggled with herself in the waiting silence. She was conscious of their eyes on her—especially Jenna's eyes, wide with fear, the whites showing around her irises like a spooked horse. Despite the dangers Sierra had faced because of Jenna and her crew, Sierra found she could still feel pity. She imagined holding the cold silver feathers against Jenna's smooth cheek—only to see that soft cheek shrivel away from the bone like burning paper. She looked inward, trying to find a clear path between her fear and her pity. She knew if Jenna died as Jumlin had, she would never forgive herself, even though Jenna stood against everything Sierra loved and believed in. Was there no middle way?

None of her friends offered a word. The fire crackled and popped in the silence, throwing giant, wavering black shadows against the rock walls of the little arroyo. Sierra remembered the weathered, brown face of the great Avatar she had encountered. Did she believe him? Or was Quetzalcoatl, like so many others she had met recently, lying to her to achieve their own aims? She felt Clancy breathing quietly close beside her. She looked at Fred, who was now playing absently with his toes and humming to himself. She gazed at Chaco, who returned her look with a calm face and level eyes where the reflected flames of the fire danced. She saw that Mama Labadie was steadily watching Jenna, her face impassive. She shivered, and not because of the cold night air.

Sierra rose to her feet and held out her hand to Fred. "Give me the feathers, Fred." The mannegishi laid the silver objects in Sierra's palm. The feathers were rather damp, and she wiped them hastily on her shirttail. She walked over to Jenna, who began to tremble, but did not start screaming again. Jenna's wide eyes began to leak tears, turning the thick dust on her face to tiny rivulets of mud.

"Don't do this Sierra, please! I'm sorry! I'm truly sorry!" Jenna begged. "You don't have to do this—I'll stop the production. I know how to disable all the Black Diamond Semiconductors in the world, and I'll do it. I promise!"

Sierra stepped closer, the feathers in her hand. "Yes," she said, placing the feathers against Jenna's shrinking face, "you will."

At first, there was nothing. Sierra almost drew her hand away out of nerves and a sense of anticlimax. Then Jenna's eyes rolled back in her head, and she slumped to one side, mouth agape. She lay on the sand, unmoving, for several minutes. Sierra, still holding the feathers, stared down at her as the others rose to their feet and looked down. Then Jenna began to twitch and shake.

"She's convulsing," Clancy said, kneeling by the fallen woman. Quickly, he removed his leather belt and began to insert the strap in Jenna's mouth. "She could bite her tongue off in this condition," he muttered. But Jenna's mouth began to stretch open, a grotesque muscular rictus, and he pulled back, belt in hand.

"Get back!" ordered Mama Labadie. She spread her long arms wide and urged everyone away from the woman writhing on the ground.

"But she's ill," Sierra protested. "She could hurt herself." Sierra leaned forward, still on her knees next to Jenna, but Chaco and Mama Labadie grabbed both her arms and pulled her up and away.

"What are you doing?" Clancy asked. Then his eyes widened. He pointed at Jenna. "Oh my God. Look." They looked.

Black vapor boiled out of Jenna's wide-stretched mouth. It roiled in the air like a living creature, extending dark tendrils toward Sierra. Sierra's hair prickled across her scalp, and she shrank away from the restless, questing fingers of smoke. The shapeless mass began to twist, coiling itself into the shape of a giant serpent. But this was no Quetzalcoatl. Its flat, evil head was swollen with poison sacs on either side, and its fangs dripped black ooze. It drew back as though to strike, and Clancy fumbled for the missing pistol on his belt. Abruptly, Sierra stepped in between the others and the coiling terror issuing from Jenna's body.

"Sierra! No!" yelled Clancy. He put out a hand to stop her, but she evaded him and strode toward the snake, right hand extended, the feathers gripped in her fingers.

"Go away. Now. Leave this place, leave this woman, leave us forever. Go away," Sierra said in a firm, even voice. The semblance of a snake drew back, hesitated—and struck directly at Sierra's face. But before it could connect, it began to fly apart on the desert breeze like sodden paper, whirling into the night and disappearing. Within seconds, nothing was there but the now-still form of Jenna lying on the sand, mouth slackly open and froth on her lips.

Clancy recovered first. "Nice job," he commented to Sierra as he moved toward Jenna. "Looks like Rose's training came in useful." He knelt next to Jenna and examined her, taking her pulse and peeling her eyelids back. "Someone got a flashlight?" he called. Fred produced a flashlight from nowhere and trotted over with it. Clancy switched it on and peered into one eye and then the other. He sat back on her heels.

"Unconscious," Clancy announced. "But she ought to be okay. Let's wash her off a bit and cover her up."

Chaco and Clancy untied Jenna and laid her down on a blanket, covering her with another. Sierra sponged the dust and tears from Jenna's face, grateful that there was a face left to wash.

"I suppose someone should keep an eye on her while the others sleep," she said. "All of us have been going ninety miles an hour for a very long time. Fred, can you take the first watch? That means no sneaking off and getting into trouble! Sit right here and watch her, and if she wakes up—yell for the rest of us. Don't let her get up. Can you do that?"

Fred plopped himself down by Jenna's head. "Yes," he said solemnly. He fixed his traffic-reflector eyes intently on Jenna. The rest lay down close by, some wrapped in blankets, some in sleeping bags provided by Clancy. Chaco declined the offer of a blanket, morphed into a coyote, scrabbled the rocks and sand for a few minutes, turned around three times and curled up on the ground, nose hidden in his brushy tail. Clancy and Sierra lay side by side on an open sleeping bag, covered with a wool blanket. He put his arms around her.

Sierra sighed and tried to relax, but her thoughts were whirling madly. She couldn't stop thinking about the moment she had faced the snaky monster coiling from Jenna's mouth. She was astounded that she had faced this horror and not been afraid—stepped toward it with perfect confidence that she could confront something so unnatural, so evil and so strong, and defeat it. Because Sierra was certain this had been no mere vision. The snake had been real—not a real snake, but a genuine manifestation of evil, alive with malice and brimming with poisonous power. It should have been able to annihilate her on the spot, but she had prevailed—easily. She was certain it had partly been due to Rose's careful training, but now she also knew there was more to it. She had felt the leaping flame of power within, and she had shaped it as easily to her purpose as she shaped the silver clay she used in her jewelry. Did the power come from Quetzalcoatl? Or did it arise from within herself? Sierra didn't know, but her mind ran round and round the possibilities and it was a long time before her tired brain sank into exhausted sleep.

CHAPTER 38

Sierra woke early the next morning, as soon as the sun's rays found the bottom of the dry arroyo. She sat up and stretched as Clancy turned over, murmuring sleepily. Then she stopped, realizing that Fred and Jenna were seated side by side, talking. Sierra rubbed the sleep from her eyes and listened.

"...and then, I don't know, it all seems like a bad dream," Jenna said. Her arrogance and confidence had dropped away like a discarded costume. She looked tired, drawn, and horribly sad. Fred nodded solemnly, but didn't speak.

"I don't even know what I was thinking," continued the woman, shaking her head. "At the time, it all seemed so right. So perfectly logical. Why shouldn't Tezcat...Necocyaotl spoil the world, so long as I got what I wanted? Now it seems so appalling, but I can't really remember how I was feeling or what I was thinking. I did some...truly terrible things, Fred. Terrible things." She put her face into her hands, her body hunched. Fred patted her head with a six-fingered paw. He seemed at a loss for what to say to her, but finally came up with "There, there."

Sierra nudged Clancy, who was snoring. He spluttered, rolled onto his back and blinked blearily at her. "What?" he asked. She pointed to the woman and the mannegishi, absorbed in their discussion. Clancy snorted and came fully awake.

"Fred!" roared Clancy. "You were supposed to wake us up!"

Fred, startled, disappeared. Jenna's head snapped up and she stared at Clancy as the rest of the camp roused, unwilling, to the day's realities.

"Fred?" growled Clancy, "Show yourself, you little, green …mannegishi."

Fred popped back into sight, looking apologetic. "Sorry, Clancy," he said. "Jenna and I were just talking. She was telling me what it was like, being a servant of Necocyaotl. She wasn't trying to get away or anything." He blinked his large eyes several times. Because Fred never blinked his eyes in synchronization, this had the effect of an uncontrolled tic. Sierra had to look away before her own eyes crossed in sympathy.

Clancy's roar had thoroughly roused the rest of the group. The others began moving groggily about, some preparing what food they had, others stowing gear away. Fred continued to sit with Jenna, talking. Breakfast consisted of granola bars, fruit, and water and took little time to consume. Gradually, people began to coalesce around Jenna and Fred. Sierra was desperately craving coffee, but they had to settle a number of issues before they could return to civilization (defined as a place she could get a nice, hot, steaming cup of java).

Clancy settled himself in the group around Jenna. He sat with his long legs bent, with his arms wrapped around his knees. His dark hair shone and his jade-green eyes sparkled in the morning light. He looked as comfortable as Sierra felt—achy, grimy, and tousled. Somewhere in the nearby scrub, she heard a quail calling to its covey. The sound echoed off the rocks.

Jenna looked around at her captors. Her face had changed, Sierra thought. It wasn't just that her makeup had long since been either worn or washed off. Jenna's face had always been perfectly composed, closed and guarded—at least until her terror of the night before. Her eyes, which had never warmed even when she was at her friendliest and most engaging, had changed as well, Sierra realized. Yesterday, they had been an impenetrable flat china blue, and unreadable. Today, her eyes were a deep, crystalline blue flecked with green, a ring of gold around the pupils. It utterly transformed her face. What had once been a perfectly composed mask now looked like a woman experiencing deep emotions, a face in turmoil.

"I am sorry," Jenna said humbly, "I am so sorry for what I've done. I can't blame anyone—not even Tezca...Necocyaotl for what I've done. I went to him willingly, and he took my soul in exchange for...well, in exchange for what I wanted. I don't even recognize the woman I became. It's as though I were sleepwalking. I felt nothing. And now, I feel..." she paused and took a painfully ragged breath. "...and now I feel everything, all at once." She put her face into her hands.

After a bit, Mama Labadie said coldly, "So?"

Jenna lifted her face to Mama Labadie's cool gaze but said nothing. She looked confused.

"So, what are you gonna do about it?" asked the mambo.

Jenna began to speak, but Clancy interrupted. "Specifically, what are we going to do about all those Black Diamond semiconductors out there?" he asked.

Jenna told them.

"Really?" asked Sierra. "It's that easy?"

• • •

They arrived back at Sierra's house, exhausted. Sierra thought of all the things she needed to do—touch base with Kaylee and Rose. Laundry. Call her father. Figure out what she was going to do with the rest of her life. It seemed a bit overwhelming. She was too tired to think.

She moved on leaden feet to unpack the car. While Clancy and Chaco helped, Fred went off purposefully to the kitchen. Once the car was emptied, Chaco called Kaylee. "Rose is fine," he reported later. "She's got a cast on, but it's a walking cast. Kaylee picked up some groceries for her and drove her home. I'm going over to see Kaylee for a while." He flashed them a rather wolfish smile and left. Sierra wondered how he was going to get to Kaylee's house, but gave it up. Chaco would probably trot over on four feet, swift as a desert dust devil.

Sierra slumped onto the couch in the living room. She longed for a shower, but was too tired for the moment to climb the stairs. She needed time to process the things she had done, the things that had happened to her. Events seemed to overtake her, one after another, not giving her any time to think or consider. Clancy looked at her long face. He sat next to her on the couch, draping a comforting arm around her shoulders. He kissed the top of her head.

"What's the matter?" he asked.

"Everything," she groaned. "No, nothing. After what we've been through, it's kind of a letdown, I guess. And our problems aren't exactly over."

He considered this. "You're right about that." He crossed his lanky legs and let her lean against him. "But you did great, you really did. There's no reason to think you won't keep on doing great."

"I need to find a job," she said.

"So do I," he replied cheerfully. "You don't think I could go back to work for BDSC after this, do you? Like nothing ever happened?"

Sierra hadn't thought about this. "What will you do?"

"Oh, I don't think I'll have much trouble," he said. "I have a buddy who's head of security over at Mammoth Memories. He's been after me to come work for him. It's a bit of a step down, but Mammoth is a much larger company. There's room to grow."

Sierra was impressed by Clancy's resilience. Maybe she should take the same attitude, instead of bemoaning her situation.

"That's great," she said. "I'll start calling around on Monday. I'm just too, I don't know, worn out right now."

"As much as I'd love to stay and exercise my masculine wiles on you, I have to go," said Clancy, kissing her and rising to his feet. "Get some sleep. I'll call you tomorrow."

Sierra stayed on the couch. She heard him go out the front door. She heard his Jeep start and drive away. Then the house was silent, except for munching sounds issuing from the kitchen. She was too tired to eat. Finally, she stood up, yawning.

"Fred," she called. "I'm going to bed." She received a muffled

"'Kay," in reply and went upstairs. She dropped her clothes on the floor, showered quickly, shrugged on a nightgown and collapsed into bed. A heavy sleep descended on her almost immediately, and the world and all her problems dissipated like morning fog.

• • •

She awoke abruptly, someone's stifling hand across her mouth. She could barely breathe, much less scream. After the first terror of awakening with an unknown person in her room, she hoped it was Clancy, back to exercise some masculine wiles. But no such luck.

"Please don't scream, Sierra," begged an all-too-familiar voice. *Shit! Jack Clapper. He's supposed to be dead!* "Please. Just let me talk to you."

She nodded, and Clapper cautiously removed his hand from her face. She sat up. The room was dark, but there was enough light through the curtains from the street lamps outside to see him. She moved to turn on her bedside lamp, but he grabbed her hand.

"Don't do that," he ordered. She stopped. He found her chair and pulled it close to the bed. "Just listen to me. I need your help."

Sierra stared at him in disbelief. This was the man who had made her life miserable, gotten her fired—not once, but twice—called her horrible names, and was only too eager to sacrifice her life to his master. What on earth made him think she would do anything to help him? Yet she didn't dare upset him; she was uncomfortably aware of the extremes to which he could resort. *Where the hell was Fred, anyway?* The green glow of the numerals on her clock radio caught her eye in the gloom. It was three-thirty in the morning.

"Listen, Sierra, I know you don't like me, but I'm really not such a bad guy," Clapper went on. "I never would've done any of that stuff, but Jenna…well, you know Jenna." He waited as though expecting a response from Sierra. None came. He went on, "I need to know what happened to Jenna. Is she still alive?"

Sierra couldn't see much by the light coming through the

curtains, but she could see that Clapper was in bad shape. He was filthy, and his clothing was torn and stained. All his elegance, his sheen, had vanished. He looked wild-eyed and desperate. Blood had dried on the side of his face, looking like black tar in the dim light. He glared at her fiercely, as though willing her to speak. She couldn't. Fear sat like a frozen stone in her throat.

"I…need…to…know…where…Jenna is!" he ground out. She shook her head wordlessly. He glared at her and then tried again.

"C'mon, Sierra! We had our differences, but this is too important. You know," his voice suddenly became friendly, confiding. "I can get your job back at BDSC. Or—better idea!—come to work for me. You're fantastic at your job. I was stupid to fire you. Really. Always regretted it. Come and work for me in New York. I'll make you vice president. You can work on any clients you want to, and I'll give you a free hand. Just please tell me about Jenna. Please—I need to know." He smiled at her with monumental insincerity, and she shrank away from him as far as she could, hoping that Chaco or even Fred would realize what was happening to her and come in. *Chaco is probably staying all night at Kaylee's,* she thought, letting that shred of hope blow away. *Fred is probably sound asleep.*

Clapper's arm snaked out suddenly and dealt her a stinging slap across the face. Sierra cried out, raising her arms too late to protect herself. He yanked a snub-nosed pistol from his belt and leveled it at her.

"If I fail Tezcatlipoca, all the demons of hell will rip my guts out and eat them while I watch. You *will* tell me what happened to Jenna or I will blow your brains out." This time, there was no doubt of his sincerity.

"She…she's alive," Sierra whispered.

CHAPTER 39

She told him as little as she dared. Jenna was alive, and they had let her go. As soon as he heard this, Clapper's face twisted angrily.

"There's only one reason you would have let her go," he hissed. "She's betrayed Tezcatlipoca. How did that happen?" He jabbed the pistol in her face again, so abruptly that she thought he was going to strike her with it. "How?"

As fearful as she was of Clapper, Sierra was unwilling to tell him about the recovery of the silver feathers. They were an ace in the hole, and she might need them. She wished devoutly they were in her hands right now, but they were in her backpack downstairs and might as well be on Mars.

"We performed a cleansing ceremony," she extemporized. "Mama Labadie called on, on…Madame Ézilee, and she appeared and purified Jenna of Necocyaotl's influence."

Clapper drew back. "What?" He shook his head. "I don't know what you're talking about. What the hell are you saying?" He looked both baffled and frustrated, but mostly he looked dangerous.

"Long story," said Sierra. "We had a kind of priestess with us, she practices Vodún…"

"Voodoo? Are you saying *Voodoo*?" He was looking angry now as well.

"No. Yes. OK, Voodoo. And this priestess exorcised Necocyaotl's spirit or whatever from Jenna's body. No, really," she cried, as Clapper tensed, seeming to grip the pistol even more tightly. "So she's not working for Necocyaotl anymore. And we let her go."

Clapper appeared to be thinking about what she had told him.

He looked frustrated and uncertain, but his aim never moved from dead center on Sierra's forehead. Finally, he asked, "Did she say what she was going to do? Or where she was going next?"

"No," Sierra lied, praying that her attempt at a poker face would succeed.

Jack Clapper appeared to make up his mind. Keeping the pistol trained on her, he yanked her elbow upward. "Get up," he ordered. You're coming with me."

"What? No. Why do you want me? I can't help you." *Here we go again,* thought Sierra, resisting the pull of his arm. Clapper only jerked harder.

"You can't help me, that's for sure," Clapper said grimly. "But you can *hurt* me, you and your friends. If I leave you here, before I know it, they'll be all over me, and I don't need any more hassles." He dragged her toward the door of her bedroom.

"Can I at least get dressed?" Sierra asked. It was one thing to face danger fully clad, and quite another to brave the unknown wearing nothing but a thin, white cotton nightie.

"Forget it. I need to find Jenna. I don't have time to worry about your modesty. Don't worry—*that's* the last thing on my mind," he said, poking her painfully in the ribs with the barrel of his pistol. "Now, get downstairs and out the back—quietly. I don't want to hear *anything* from you, understand?"

Sierra nodded without speaking but pointed to a pair of flip-flops next to the bed and cocked an eyebrow. He nodded impatiently and she slipped them on as quickly as she could before walking out the door, her arm in Clapper's tight grasp. They made their way silently downstairs.

"Can I get my backpack?" whispered Sierra. Jack Clapper's only response was to push her into the darkened kitchen—Sierra could see the wreckage in the wake of Fred's late-night snacking—and through the sliding glass door into the small yard. The glass door had not been locked, making it plain how Clapper had entered the house so easily. *I'm gonna kill that mannegishi,* fumed Sierra. *If I ever get the chance.* Then they were in the street. Clapper waved

Sierra into the driver's seat of a nondescript sedan with his pistol. She supposed that his Boxster was still a guest of the Sunnyvale Police Department. She slid in without buckling the seatbelt, with the vague thought of finding an opportune moment to throw herself out of the car. Clapper seated himself on the passenger side and passed her the keys, carefully keeping the pistol aimed at her. She turned the keys in the ignition, which set off an annoying chime.

"Put your seatbelt on," said Clapper impatiently. *It's almost funny,* she thought. *The villain asks me to fasten my seatbelt.* Obediently, she fastened the belt.

"Where are we going?" she asked, and was startled when he responded, "Black Diamond."

"What are we going to do at BDSC?"

"*We* aren't going to do anything. *I* have some business to take care of. Drive. Carefully. Don't do anything the cops might notice. Don't even think about trying something."

Sierra nodded. At this point, she had no intention of "trying something." Clapper was wound up, thrumming with anxiety like a high-tension electrical wire, and she didn't think it would take much for him to decide Sierra dead was less trouble than Sierra alive. He may already have made that decision and was just taking her to a less-obvious place to do the deed. The thought turned her guts to ice, and she tried to focus on the second-by-second mechanics of driving. *Turn left here. Twenty-five-mile-an-hour zone, slow down. Turn right. Stop at the light. Accelerate slowly.*

The streets were deserted, and it wasn't long before Sierra pulled the sedan into BDSC's parking lot.

"Park in back, by the employee entrance," Clapper instructed. In the light of the sodium lamps illuminating the parking lot, Sierra could see that under the dirt, blood and grime, Clapper was pale. Sweat trickled down his face, though the night was cool. She parked by the employee entrance. He gestured for her to hand over the keys, which she did. Pocketing the keys, he slid out of the car, and waved the pistol at her to do the same. She exited the car and joined him at the door, where he handed her his employee badge.

"Open it," he said. "And keep your damn mouth shut. Don't make a sound, Sierra, or I'll kill you."

Sierra passed the card over the reader, and the door clicked. She pushed it open, feeling the muzzle of the pistol against her back, pressing painfully against her spine. The building lights had dimmed in the hallways and were turned off in most of the offices. She looked at him, not knowing where he intended to go. "Elevator," he whispered. She set off quietly down the carpeted hallway.

Banks of elevators were located in the center of the building. Most of them went from the basement to the tenth floor. One, which only a few individuals could access, went from the ground floor to the eleventh floor, where Jenna had a private office, conference rooms, an executive dining room, and labs. To her surprise, Clapper urged her over to this elevator.

"My badge works," he mouthed. She passed the badge over the reader, and the elevator doors parted with a whisper. She stepped in, Clapper close behind her. She managed to notice that the interior of this elevator was more like the elevator in a posh hotel than the utilitarian décor of the one she had taken to her office every day. The space was paneled with cherry wood. Overhead, rosy lights were set into the ceiling, and there were gleaming brass rails around three sides.

There was no conversation on the way up. When the door sighed open, Clapper stood quite still for a few moments, cautiously checking the corridor. It was deserted. Then he stepped out onto the plush carpeting, making no sound, and waved Sierra out, too. Obviously familiar with his surroundings, he motioned for her to go to the right. Sierra obediently turned and walked stiffly in front of him, always aware of the gun jammed against her spine.

A few feet down the corridor, Clapper said softly, "Stop," and she did. They were in front of a sleek, heavy steel door. The sign on it read, "Computer Lab." There was no window in the door, but light leaked out around the edges, visible in the dimmed light of the corridor. In the stillness of the empty offices, Sierra heard movement inside. Someone was in the lab. Clapper seemed to expect this. He grabbed Sierra's arm again and held up his badge to the reader. The door lock clicked open. Clapper quickly flung the door wide and pushed Sierra into the room ahead of him.

Sierra, taken by surprise, stumbled. She recovered, only to find Clapper leveling his pistol at the frozen tableau in front of them. Jenna and Clancy were seated in front of a large flat-screen monitor. On the screen, there was a complex rendering that looked to Sierra much like the drawings she had seen used to depict the Internet: glowing gold, green, red, and blue lines arcing across a Decatur map of the world.

"Don't move," Clapper warned, dropping Sierra's arm. "Put up your hands." Jenna and Clancy slowly raised their arms, eyes fixed on the pistol in Clapper's hand. "Step away from the computer," Clapper ordered. Jenna and Clancy obeyed, arms still high. Jenna looked exhausted and frightened. Clancy looked unreadable.

"Are you OK, Sierra?" Clancy asked. She looked back at him, uncertain what to think. *What was Clancy doing here? Why was he working with Jenna? Had Jenna's redemption from Necocyaotl been genuine, or...?* She nodded without speaking just as Clapper said, "Shut up. No talking." He gestured with the pistol toward the computer screen. "Sit down at the computer, bitch."

Sierra walked over to the computer and took the chair Jenna had been using. She looked at the screen. Some of the glowing lines were shifting as she watched, others were stationary. It was clear that the diagram represented a network or part of a network, but why was it moving? What was that red, flashing button in the lower right of the monitor? It read, "Disabling." Next to it was a blue button that read, "Cancel Operation."

Clapper pointed his pistol at Sierra. "Don't move, you two," he warned Jenna and Clancy, "or I'll shoot her. Then I'll shoot you. Sierra, move the cursor over that blue button and click it. Now!" he barked.

Sierra put her hand on the mouse and moved the cursor rapidly. She stopped and clicked—the red button. The glowing lines on the screen began to flicker and die, one by one, like candles snuffed out by the wind. Clapper shrieked wordlessly, and the last thing Sierra heard was the deafening report of a pistol going off at close range.

In the next few moments, what happened was so disorienting that Sierra would have thought she was hallucinating, had not Jenna and Clancy confirmed her experiences.

She had squeezed her eyes tightly shut in a futile anticipation of the bullet's impact. When no impact came, she cautiously opened them. Jack Clapper lay sprawled on the floor, a scarlet pool spreading out from his head. Clancy lunged forward, his pistol still in his hand, to check the man's body. Just as Clancy reached the still form, black smoke appeared to coil up from the dead man's open mouth, just like the nightmare serpent had coiled from Jenna's mouth that night in the desert.

Clancy lurched abruptly back and away from Clapper's corpse. He, Jenna, and Sierra froze as the oily black smoke coalesced into a wavering form. Though it shuddered in even the smallest of air currents, it was not hard to see that the form was Jack Clapper, identifiable through his aggressive stance, heavy brows and slash of a mouth. The form wavered several moments like a candle flame, then seemed to grow stronger, more defined and substantial. It slowly turned its head toward Sierra and crouched, as if preparing to spring at her. Its mouth gaped opened in a soundless snarl.

Sierra gathered her inner powers. She had proved stronger than Jenna's snake, but she had no idea how she compared to this apparition. She breathed deeply, slowly, as Rose had taught her, feeling energy gather at her core.

Suddenly, as though a door had opened between this world and another, dark figures appeared, also seemingly composed of black smoke. They didn't look like anything familiar to Sierra—tangled snarls of tentacles lined with sabers was the closest she could come to a description. The Clapper shade flickered away, clearly alarmed, but before it could move far the dark beasts were upon it. There was no blood, no noise, but it was horrible to watch. The tentacled horrors consumed the Clapper thing as it struggled, then Clapper's corpse, everything flying about like torn rags in a wind. Then they swelled like ghastly blowfish to enormous proportions—and disappeared as though erased by some great hand.

• • •

Someone was talking, but Sierra couldn't hear very well. Her ears felt stuffed full of cotton, but there was also an insistent clamor that prevented her from hearing what the voice was saying. She cordially wished the voice would go away, but it wouldn't.

Then there were hands. Hands tried to pull her, unlock her from her nice, safe fetal position on the floor. *No,* she decided, *it's better here. I should stay here, where it's safe.* But the hands wouldn't stop pulling at her. Annoyed, Sierra opened her eyes and saw two pairs of feet. One pair, size thirteen or so, was clad in dusty hiking boots. The other pair, rather daintier, was clad in stylish leather pumps. Sierra uncurled herself and looked up. Clancy and Jenna peered down at her. Clancy looked worried and held out his hand to her. Jenna looked relieved.

Clancy helped Sierra to her feet. "Are you okay?" he asked, steadying her with one hand at her elbow.

"Yes. Sort of," she replied uncertainly. She looked around the lab but saw no sign of the man who had broken into her house and forced her here at gunpoint. No body, no blood. The lab looked as though nothing more violent than spilled coffee had ever happened there.

Jenna handed her a paper cup of water, which Sierra drank, shakily. Jenna's deep blue eyes looked at her with concern. *That has got to be a first,* thought Sierra.

"Would someone please fill me in?" she asked, sipping carefully.

"Let's go back to the beginning," said Jenna. Remember what I told you out there in the desert? About nullifying the effects of the Black Diamond silicon?"

Sierra nodded.

"Well, I hurried over here right after you dropped me off at my house," Jenna continued. "Okay, I did stop to take a shower. But right after, I came over here to take care of it, just like I told you. I thought I had access to every part of the IT system. But," Jenna turned to Clancy. "it turned out that I didn't have full access anymore."

Clancy picked up the story. "After you told me what was going on, Sierra, I used my priority access to change some things around. I thought maybe there was something funny going on with the books or maybe there was something fishy about the sales and shipping records, and I wanted to be able to monitor network activity. In the process, I locked Jenna out of her secret project—completely unaware I was doing so."

"Jenna called me when she discovered the changes, and I came down to help her," Clancy continued. "We were about to disable the—oh, let's call it the 'N Factor'—when you and Clapper came through the door."

"The N Factor? You mean the essence of Necocyaotl?" asked Sierra. Her ears were still ringing and she had trouble making out what they were saying.

"Yep. When we saw Clapper, we thought it was all over," Clancy said. "But you did the right thing, Sierra. Even though I'm sure you thought Clapper would shoot you—and us—you disabled the N Factor yourself."

Why yes, Sierra thought. I did believe he would kill us all. Does that make me a jerk or a hero? Or both?

"Erm, so what *did* happen to Clapper?" she asked. Her brain could not make sense of what she'd seen. Jenna responded. Her voice was the rich contralto it had always been, but with a hint of quaver behind her calm tones.

"They came for him," she said. Her hands twisted together. "He failed Tezca…Necocyaotl, so he paid the price."

Confused, Sierra nodded. "But he was already dead."

"Yes," Jenna replied. "Necocyaotl wouldn't be satisfied with the death of his body. He assured the death of his soul. Complete annihilation, you see."

Sierra did see, noticing that both Jenna and Clancy were quite pale. She probably looked just like them. She remembered Jack saying, "If I fail Tezcatlipoca, all the demons of hell will rip my guts out and eat them while I watch." *Oh.* She swallowed hard.

"I thought you lost your gun in the cave-in?" she said to Clancy.

"I have more than one pistol—I picked it up when I got back to my house." Clancy sighed deeply. His broad shoulders slumped.

"If you hadn't shot Clapper, I'd have been the one on the floor," Sierra said to him. "Thank you. Thank you."

Clancy stood up, tugging her gently to her feet. "Let's go home now." He started for the door, Sierra's hand in his. Jenna's voice stopped them both.

"Thank you," she said, in a small voice that had little resemblance to her everyday authoritative tones. "Thank you for bringing me back, for making me human again. For saving me from," she shuddered, "…those things, whatever they were. I have a lot to answer for. And I will answer for it, I promise." She looked at them with pleading in her eyes. Eyes that had depth and feeling, and the feeling showing in their depths was shame.

Clancy just nodded, but Sierra said, "Yes. You do have a lot to answer for, and I think you know how to make good on that, don't you?"

Jenna nodded decisively. "Good night, then. Goodbye." The ringing in Sierra's ears suddenly stopped. She heard something in Jenna's voice, and alarms went off in her brain. She halted and gently disengaged her hand from Clancy's. She walked back to where the other woman was sitting.

"Jenna, you can't do that," said Sierra. She sat down next to Jenna in the chair Clancy had vacated. Jenna looked at her with eyes that were still shocked, pupils huge.

"I think it's probably best," responded the other woman. "I don't want to live with the guilt for the rest of my life. I don't think I can do it."

"I think you have to, if you really want to make amends. You have power, influence, and money. You can use those things to reverse some of the damage you've done. You can change people's minds by speaking up, even lawmakers. You can help those already working to make the world a cleaner place. You can fund research. There's a million things you can do to help repair the damage. But if you die, all the good that you might be able to accomplish dies with you," said Sierra. She gave Jenna another piercing look and stood up. "I believe you'll do the right thing, Jenna."

Sierra took Clancy's hand again and walked to the door. She turned as she went through and said, "See you soon, Jenna. I'm expecting great things."

As the heavy door swung shut behind them with a soft whoosh and thunk, Clancy said, "Were you telling her not to kill herself? Did I get that right?" Sierra nodded. Clancy looked alarmed. "Maybe we shouldn't leave her alone right now." He hesitated, looking back. Sierra tugged at his hand.

"She'll be okay."

Clancy looked at her. "How do you know?"

Sierra continued toward the elevators. "Because Jenna Simmons has never yet given up on something she's committed to, that's why. Anyway," Sierra stepped into the open elevator, "she's not the suicidal type. She feels pretty bad, but she'll channel all that emotion into action, just like she's always done."

The elevator descended in silence. As the doors slid open, Clancy said, "How did you know she was thinking of killing herself?"

Sierra looked at him, surprised. "It was kind of obvious, I thought. Something in her voice. You didn't hear it?"

Clancy looked up and down the dim corridor on the first floor before stepping out, hand at his holster. "Nope. Didn't have a clue. Good thing you noticed, though. That would have been a disaster. And I would have felt like a complete jerk, leaving her alone."

Sierra just nodded. It had been as clear to her as if Jenna had said, "Goodbye. I'm going to kill myself tonight." She wondered if this kind of insight was part of her new...powers? Gifts?

They left the building without encountering any security guards. Sierra wondered if Clancy or Jenna had anything to do with that, but she was too tired to ask. As they stepped into the night, the cool air hit Sierra's skin and she suddenly remembered she was wearing nothing but a thin nightie and flip-flops. She wrapped her arms around herself and shivered. Clancy smiled at her. "Cold?"

he asked. He slid a long, warm arm around her shoulders as they walked to his Jeep.

Back at Sierra's house, all was dark and quiet. They went in through the open glass door into her messy kitchen.

"No time to wash up?" Clancy inquired.

"Fred," she responded, and he nodded. It explained everything, including the trail of something sticky that led from the refrigerator to the table and then to the sink. And the many empty containers discarded on the floor and counters.

"Just where was Fred while Clapper was abducting you? More to the point, where was Chaco?" Clancy asked.

"I don't know where Fred was. Asleep, probably, after snorking all that food. Chaco went to Kaylee's."

Clancy shook his head as he turned on a light. "Mannegishis," he said disgustedly, shaking his head and surveying the wreckage. Then his eyes went to Sierra, and he began to smile, a wide, white smile. Laugh lines crinkled the corners of his eyes.

"What?" she asked, not seeing anything particularly amusing in the situation.

"What a fetching outfit," he replied, eyes running appreciatively over her. "The only improvement you could make is to take it off."

Sierra met his eyes directly. She could feel a warm flush spreading up her body to her face. She smiled a slow, warm smile, and narrowed her eyes at him. She stepped out of her flip-flops, whipped her nightgown off with one smooth motion and flung it at Clancy before pelting out of the kitchen and up the stairs, laughing.

"Catch me if you can!" she called over her shoulder, dark hair flying. Clancy, needing no further invitation, followed as fast as his long legs could take him and pursued her into her bedroom, whooping. The bed whumped under their combined weight—and the laughter and whooping were abruptly cut off by high-pitched squeals of indignation.

The door was flung back. Fred sailed through the air, landing on his fat bottom. The door slammed shut, followed by the ferocious click of a lock. Giggling and muffled noises resumed from the other side of the door.

Fred picked himself up and rubbed his bottom. "People!" he muttered to himself, beginning a slow descent of the stairs. "I wonder if there's anything left to eat?"

EPILOGUE

It was August, and there had been many changes since the awful night at Black Diamond. Chaco had gone to live with Kaylee, but was a frequent visitor to Sierra's townhouse. He seemed quite devoted to Kaylee, Sierra observed. Once she asked him, "I thought Coyotl was, um, footloose and fancy-free by nature? Always moving on? A woman in every port and all that?"

Chaco had looked a bit baffled. "Kaylee's the one who's footloose and fancy-free," he had growled. "I find that...fascinating. So I need to keep an eye on her, or I'm afraid she'll be on to the next guy." So far, Sierra saw no sign that Kaylee's passion for Chaco had waned; they always seemed to be wrapped around each other. It had become a bit boring for everyone else, of course.

After Fred's over-indulgence in champagne to celebrate their success in nullifying the N Factor, he had sworn off alcohol. (He had been quite pink with the pain and nausea of a hangover the day after.) Fred had begged to stay with Sierra, showing no desire to return to his home in the mountains. With some misgivings, she had agreed. He was good company, in his way. Although his subject matter tended to be largely food-oriented.

"You know, I think you've earned your name," Sierra had told him.

"Fred?" Fred had asked, puzzled.

"No, the other one. The one that means 'High-Backed Wolf,'" she told him. "You were very brave to defend Chaco and me against Clapper at the storage facility. And you were resourceful and brave when you escaped from the pet carrier. But you were *brilliant* when you took those feathers and gave them back to us!" Fred had flushed a becoming emerald hue at her praise.

Jenna Simmons had made many changes, as well. She seemed determined, not only to undo the damage she had done, but to push forward several groundbreaking "green" agendas of her own. She had funded several organizations that were working to clean up the environment, conserve resources and protect endangered species. She was becoming known for her advocacy of "green" business practices and considered an innovator in that field.

Rose's ankle had mended well. She and Mama Labadie had become fast friends and were exploring each other's spiritual healing practices. They were discussing a business partnership, but Kaylee had advised them against it on the grounds that it would be too confusing for potential customers. "They won't know whether to pay you in eagle feathers or chickens," Kaylee had said.

• • •

Sierra and Clancy sat on one of Sierra's old camping blankets on the beach at Half Moon Bay, a small community on the Northern California coast near Silicon Valley. It was the tail end of a glorious day in August. The usual summer weather on the coast was damp and cold with fog, but this day had been clear and warm. The sun had just gone down behind the blue swells of the ocean, leaving a mercurochrome-colored sky behind. The wind was brisk, and Sierra and Clancy had donned light jackets as the evening cooled.

Sierra sipped wine from her plastic glass. "I still wonder sometimes. What if Jack had killed us? Sometimes I think I was stupid to disobey him—it was a terrible risk. And then I think, well, he was going to kill us all, anyway. Most likely." She sighed and wriggled her toes in the sand. "Do you ever feel guilty about shooting him?"

Clancy thought for a moment, considering. "No," he said at last. "If I hadn't shot him, he would have killed you. And then Jenna and me. But I wouldn't wish what happened to him afterwards on anyone—not even Jack Clapper." He shuddered, and the cool wind had nothing to do with it.

"Mmmm. Yeah," Sierra responded. "Although, to be completely honest, it solved a lot of problems. I mean, how would we explain shooting the head of a New York PR agency?"

Clancy sipped his wine thoughtfully. "He was already wanted by the police for abducting Aiden and trying to kill him. I don't think it would have been too hard to explain, really. I guess I would've been happier if I'd taken him alive, but that wasn't an option." He stretched out on the sand and rested on his elbow. "As it played out, the police think he's still a fugitive. And speaking of Agent Sullivan, he's fine. Out of the hospital and on sick leave to recuperate."

"Did you see him?" Sierra asked.

"Yeah. He asked if you could come to see him in the hospital, but I told him that you and I are...you know."

"Really? That you and I are what?"

"You and I are going to be married," said Clancy firmly.

Sierra sat upright, sand flying. "Maybe you should have asked me first!" she exclaimed. "I haven't said yes. Because you never asked!"

As a full moon began to rise in the ultramarine sky, it paved a road of glittering silver across the waves. The breakers hissed in, spume flying seaward in the wind, like the manes of spirit horses. Clancy reached into a nearby bag. He extracted a bouquet of red roses tied in ribbon, and gave it to Sierra, who was glaring at him indignantly. Her expression softened as she accepted the roses. Clancy climbed to his knees and struck a pose.

"Sierra Carter, will you marry me?" he asked. "Make jewelry-designing your job. I'll help you get started. I hear that two can live as cheaply as one. I don't believe it, but I'm willing to give it a try." He was smiling, but his face was open and vulnerable, his voice tender. *Where did that feeling of distance go? Where's that tough cop?* Sierra wondered. *Where is all the loneliness I used to feel?*

She laid the roses on her lap. She looked up at him with eyes full of warm laughter and said, "Moonlight and roses. How perfect." And kissed him. Then, "No ring? Isn't a ring part of the tradition?"

"You think I have the courage to purchase a ring for a *jewelry designer?*" Clancy said, laughing. "I thought you'd prefer to design the rings yourself."

"Too true," Sierra agreed, and kissed him again.

"Now," she said, quite a while later. "There's something I need to tell you about Fred…" But before she could tell him that the mannegishi was now a permanent fixture in her life, Sierra caught a movement in her peripheral vision. Something floated down from the indigo sky, dancing on the salt breeze. Sierra stopped speaking and pulled Clancy into another ardent embrace as the sparkling blue and green feather came to rest on her old blanket. Without breaking her clinch with Clancy, Sierra discretely edged the feather off the blanket with her bare foot and pushed it deep into the soft sand. It could wait.

GLOSSARY AND PRONUNCIATION GUIDE

Note on pronunciation: The terminal "tl" in meso-American languages is a single consonant pronounced somewhat like the "tl" in "Bentley" without the "y" sound. It is produced by pressing the tongue against the roof of the mouth and forcing air over the middle of the tongue to both sides. This produces a soft click unlike any sound used in English. Modern Mexican Spanish tends to drop the "tl" sound, resulting in a glottal stop.

Coyotl: [koy-OH-tl] Coyotl, or coyote, is a Native American folk-hero to many different tribes across the Americas. Like his African counterpart, Anansi the spider, he is a trickster and a fool whose sly schemes often turn out quite differently than he intends—but often with better results. He is generally portrayed as a friend to the people, bringing fire to mankind, for example.

Damballah-Wedo: [dahm-bah-lah-WAY-dö] The Vodún sky god and the creator of all life. His vévé, or symbol, includes two serpents.

Ézilee: [EY-zih-lee] The Vodún personification of love and sensuality. In some ways, she is the equivalent of the Greek goddess of love, Aphrodite.

Hounfour: [HUM-for] Vodún temple.

Loa: [lwa] Loa is both a singular and plural noun referring to members of the pantheon of Vodún spirits or gods that reign over human life. They range from Damballah-Wedo, the father-creator serpent god, to minor spirits such as Congo, whose major characteristic is that he likes a cocktail now and then. Many of the loa are benevolent; some are evil. Baron Samedi—most often portrayed in movies about Voodoo because his skull face and black top hat are so evocatively gruesome—is actually more akin to Coyotl the Trickster of Native American lore and not an evil loa at all.

Mahaha: [Ma-HA-ha] Inuit ice demon. It catches people and tickles them to death with its long, clawed fingers, laughing all the while.

Mambo: [MAHM-bö] Female priestess of Vodún.

Mannegishi: [MAN-eh-GË-shë] Wikipedia says, "The Mannegishi...are a race of trickster people in Cree folklore, similar in nature to the Memegwesi of the Ojibwa. They are described as semi-humanoid, being sexdactylous humans with very thin and lanky arms and legs and big heads minus a nose. According to one Cree schema of the mythology, there are two humanoid races, one being the familiar human species and the other being the 'little people', i.e., Mannegishi." Being small, mischievous, and tricky creatures, Mannegishi are also similar to the Menehune of Hawaiian folklore.

Necocyaotl: [neck-cö-kya-OH-tl]: Quetzalcoatl's evil twin brother. He has many names, including Tezcatlipoca. While Necocyaotl is portrayed in *The Obsidian Mirror* as purely evil, like most gods in the pre-Columbian meso-American pantheon, he was a mixed bag. Necocyaotl was associated with the night, hurricanes, enmity, discord, sorcery, temptation, and war—but he was also associated with the north, the earth, obsidian, rulership, divination, jaguars, and beauty. He and Quetzalcoatl both feature in several creation myths. Perhaps because Necocyaotl is the opposing twin brother of Quetzalcoatl (who was a culture hero), he assumed a darker reputation than his brother. He had many names in addition to Tezcatlipoca (Obsidian Mirror or Smoking Mirror) and Necocyaotl (Enemy of Both Sides), including: Titlacauan (We

Are His Slaves), Ipalnemoani (He by Whom We Live), and Yohualli Èecatl (Night Wind).

Quetzalcoatl: [Kets-al-kö-AH-tl] Quetzalcoatl was often portrayed as a giant, feathered snake. He was one of the most powerful gods in the Aztec pantheon, the creator, and associated with fertility. Over time, Quetzalcoatl was adopted by other meso-American groups. His identity became combined with other gods, perhaps leading to the development of his equal and opposite, Tezcatlipoca, the Obsidian Mirror.

Shegoi: [shuh-GOY] Also known as larrea, shegoi is a brushy, flowering plant in the caltrops family. It was used medicinally for a number of ailments by Native Americans and is still sold as an herbal remedy for a number of disorders.

Tezcatlapoca: [tez-cat-lah-POCK-ah] See Necocyaotl.

Ti Bon Ange: [të-bahn-ahnj] In Haitian creole, "little guardian angel." In Vodún, the belief is that every person's soul is composed of a "gros bon ange" (big guardian angel) and a ti bon ange. The ti bon ange can leave the body during sleep and other events and can be damaged or stolen.

Tzintzimitl: [tsin-tsi-MË-tl] Female deities associated with the stars. While they were the protectors of women and reproduction, they could be destructive and cruel at times.

Vévé: [vay-vay] In Vodún, a symbol that represents one of the loa.

Vodún: [vö-DOON] A religion practiced by the descendants of African slaves (and others, in modern times), based partly on several indigenous African religions and partly on Catholicism imposed on the slaves by their colonial masters. It is a complex, genuine religion and belief system focused on healing, and should not be confused with Voodoo, which is a Hollywood invention.

K.D. KEENAN has worked in the high technology industries since 1978 as a writer, content creator and public relations expert. She founded her own PR agency in 1986 that was named one of Silicon Valley's Top 25 PR agencies for 10 years running by the Silicon Valley Business Journal. She currently works as a freelance content developer and social media expert.

Keenan has always been a voracious reader. Having worked through her grandparents' extensive library of Victorian children's literature, she began reading fantasy and science fiction at the age of nine—a move that curbed her tendency to write with a mid-nineteenth-century flair that was greatly under-appreciated by her English teachers.

Keenan began writing *The Obsidian Mirror* because she had just finished reading another sword-and-sorcery fantasy set in an archetypal European pre-Industrial Age society where the heroes wore cloaks and the world was populated by elves, trolls and assorted other Euro-trash. Having hit a downturn in her freelance work at the time, she decided to write a fantasy based on New World prototypes. (Her interest in Native American folklore began with her mother, an archeologist specializing in Southwestern Indian civilizations.) To her surprise, Keenan actually finished the novel, although it took seven years due to the fact that writing all day for a living and writing all night for fun is a bit tiring.

Keenan and her husband of forty-five years have two grown children and two grandchildren. She is currently writing *Lords of the Night*, the third and final book in the trilogy that begins with *The Obsidian Mirror*. *Fire in the Ocean*, the second novel in the trilogy, is scheduled for debut in February 2018.

CPSIA information can be obtained
at www.ICGtesting.com
Printed in the USA
BVOW09s0052190218
508412BV00004B/142/P